SHEILA ROBERTS

The Cottage on Juniper Ridge

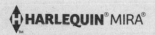

Recycling programs
for this product may
not exist in your area.

ISBN-13: 978-0-7783-1454-7

THE COTTAGE ON JUNIPER RIDGE

Copyright © 2014 by Sheila Rabe

For questions and comments about the quality of this book, please contact us at CustomerService@Harlequin.com.

Printed in U.S.A.

Dear Reader,

I think this book has been bubbling at the back of my mind for some time. A few years ago my husband and I moved from the house we'd been in for eighteen years, and I was shocked to see how much stuff we'd accumulated! After so many runs to Goodwill that I lost count and packing enough boxes to fill a stadium, I was so done with stuff. I could drive by a garage sale and not even be tempted! Of course, that didn't last long. Pretty soon I was, once more, braking for garage sales. Then we lost my husband's parents and were up to our eyeballs in stuff again. What to do with it all? Where to put it? Let me tell you, it wasn't easy. And keeping the pile of things to a reasonable level is still an ongoing process, but I think I'm getting it down to a system.

And that wasn't the only thing I was dealing with. I was trying to simplify my life. Between trying to keep up with work, family responsibilities, house, garden, church and friends, I was on overload. When we first moved to our little lake house, I'd envisioned myself puttering in the garden, growing my own fruit and veggies, sitting on the patio and enjoying the view, sipping cocktails with the neighbors. Ha! Who had time for that? I needed to simplify my life!

I suspect I'm not the only one who's been faced with this. I've talked to a lot of women stuck in that same cramped boat. It's easy to get overcommitted and overloaded. It sort of sneaks up on us one bargain at a time, one "Sure, I can do that" commitment at a time. Next thing we know, life is complicated.

The women in Icicle Falls have realized this and they're going to do something about it. But they've got some challenges ahead. I hope you'll enjoy their journey. And if it resonates with you, well, I always love hearing from my readers. Find me on Facebook or visit me at my website, www.sheilasplace.com.

Happy reading!

Sheila

For my buddy Liz

The Cottage on Juniper Ridge

Chapter One

Sometimes we get so used to the status quo that we forget we can change it.
—Muriel Sterling, author of *Simplicity*

Jen Heath hurried along the downtown Seattle side-walk, hunched against a freezing rain, her holiday to-do list dogging her every step, breathing down her neck. The trees that lined the street twinkled with white lights, and store windows boasted displays of Santas, presents and happy elves. A steel drum band had set up in the Westlake Mall and was playing "Jingle Bells." *Bah, humbug,* she thought grumpily as she strode past them.

Anyone peering inside her head would think she hated the holidays. She didn't. She loved them. What she didn't love was being so darned busy.

How had she gotten stuck in charge of planning the office Christmas party? Oh, yeah, Patty Unger, her supervisor, had volunteered her. *Thanks, Patty.* Not that Jen minded planning a party. But having to plan one this year wasn't fun. It was just one more thing to add to a very long to-do list.

In addition to her full-time job as office slave at

Emerald City Promotions, she sold Soft Glow Candles on the party plan—all so she could whittle down what she owed on her credit cards, keep up her car payments and make the mortgage on her First Hill condo, which she could barely afford. The car she'd needed, but the condo? What had she been thinking when she bought it? Oh, yeah. She hadn't been thinking. She'd taken one look at the granite countertops, the hardwood floors and the view of the Seattle skyline, and condo lust had come over her like a fever. By the time the fever broke she was a homeowner. (Thanks to the bank and her parents.) And her credit cards were maxed out. (Because, of course, she had to furnish the new condo.) Now she was a stressed homeowner.

Who was never home. She had three candle parties booked this week and two more on the weekend. The following weekend she had another candle party on Saturday, and then on Sunday a cookie exchange at her sister's, followed by the church choir concert. Oh, she'd be home later that evening, right along with the eighteen other people she'd invited to her place for the postconcert party. (This was the symptom of yet another fever—new-owner pride. She'd been dying to show off the condo, and hosting a party had seemed like the perfect way.) The day before, she'd gone to see the gingerbread house display at the Sheraton Hotel with her mother, her sister and her niece, Jordan. She'd been pooped, but when she tried to wiggle out of going, Toni had reminded her that this was a tradition, and anyway, she needed to spend time with her family. Guilt, the gift that kept on giving. After that, she'd visited her grandma, who was complaining that she'd almost forgotten what her granddaughter looked like.

It seemed everyone in her family was giving guilt for Christmas this year.

Tonight she absolutely had to do laundry. But what she really wanted was to flop on the couch and watch *It's a Wonderful Life*. None of her friends understood what she saw in that old movie, but she'd been watching it with her family every Christmas since she was a kid. Well, except for the past couple of years. Between having her marriage fall apart and getting a divorce, she'd been too busy for a wonderful life.

Those days were over now. No more fights about money. No more fights about how she mismanaged her time or how impetuous and irresponsible she was. No more fights about...well, you name it.

When they were first married, Serge had loved her spontaneity, her joie de vivre. After a year he developed a vision problem and saw only her flaws. They fought about everything from money to the amount of time she spent with her friends. "I don't know what we're doing together." Serge had finally stormed one night, throwing up his hands.

Neither did she. So Serge had moved out and moved on. She'd run into him at the Last Supper Club six months after the divorce was final, when she was trying to enjoy a night out with the girls. He'd been with a skinny tattoo queen sporting maroon hair and ear gauges. And he'd complained about how impulsive *Jen* was?

She'd wanted to hit him and his new woman, too. Instead, she'd buried herself in the crowd and danced until her feet and her heart were numb. Good riddance, she'd told herself, but later that night she'd cried herself to sleep.

Now it had been a year since the big D and she was *so* over him and so moving on.

Now she was in charge of her own destiny, her own life, and that was fine with her.

Except so far this new life wasn't exactly playing out as she'd envisioned. When a girl hardly had time to wash her bra, she was in trouble. When was she supposed to squeeze in things like dating? And if she didn't even have time to date, well, what was that going to do to her sex life?

She scowled. Many of her friends were now having babies and she'd love to have one of her own. She sure didn't see a bassinet on her horizon, though. At thirty-two, were her eggs giving up all hope of ever meeting a sperm?

Well, girls, I don't know what to tell you. You'll just have to hang in there because right now I don't have time to find a new man. There was a depressing thought.

Jen caught her bus on Marion Street. It was crowded as usual with tired workers, students, street people and shoppers carrying bags crammed with merchandise. Standing room only. That made her grumpier.

Oh, heck, everything made her grumpy these days. Maybe it was living in the city, crammed in with so many other people. What would it be like to have a cute little house in a small town or a cottage in a mountain meadow? What would it be like to hark back to a simpler time, a simpler lifestyle?

She thought of the book her sister had given her for her birthday the month before—*Simplicity*. She'd been trying to read a little of it every night before she went to bed, but she couldn't seem to get past page one. She'd wake up halfway through the night with the book on her face.

She'd managed to get through the blurb on the back of the book, though, and it sounded impressive. The author insisted that anyone, no matter how busy, could simplify her life. It was a matter of prioritizing and letting your days slow down and fall into a natural rhythm in sync with nature.

What would her life be like if she lived it at a slower pace? What if she took a few minutes to sit by her condo window and watch the snow fall (not that much snow ever fell in Seattle), instead of running around like a gerbil on a wheel, dashing from event to event, working at a feverish pace so she could live the good life? When it came right down to it, *was* her life that good? She was racing through it so fast, she had no time to savor any of it. It would be nice to learn how to bake bread, grow a garden, knit. Date! Heck, it would be nice to have time to breathe.

The bus lurched to a stop and a fortysomething woman got on, balancing a huge armful of purchases, shopping bags dangling from her fingers. She squeezed in between Jen and an older man in an overcoat that smelled of damp wool. The newcomer smelled like perfume overload and Jen sneezed.

"Bless you," said an older woman who was occupying a seat behind where Jen stood.

"Thank you," Jen murmured.

The newcomer grabbed for a hand rail and bumped Jen with one of her bags. That, plus the sudden forward motion of the bus, nearly sent Jen toppling into the lap of the older woman. "Sorry," she muttered.

Meanwhile, Suzy Shopper was still wrestling with

her bags. One got away and landed on Jen's foot, nearly crushing her toes and making her yelp. What did she have in there, weights?

"Oh, I'm so sorry," the woman said, picking it up and whacking Jen with another bag in the process. "My daughter's Christmas present."

Jen's eyes were watering. Was her foot broken? She caught her breath and managed a polite smile. "Looks like you got a lot done." Which was more than she could say. She hadn't started her shopping yet.

"This is the last of it," the woman said. "I found these dumbbells on sale at Penney's."

"Dumbbells." Jen nodded. "You had weights in that bag."

The woman blushed. "Mmm-hmm."

May the next toes you drop them on be yours.

The bus driver called Jen's street and she hobbled toward the back exit, trying to make her way through the crowd. "S'cuse me, s'cuse me. Sorry."

One passenger was too engrossed in what was on her ereader to even know she was on a bus. She stood in the path of the exit like a boulder in a red coat. An inconsiderate boulder.

"Excuse me," Jen said, trying to slip past. The boulder didn't budge.

The bus doors heaved open.

Jen tried again. "Excuse me," she said a little louder. Still nothing. She said it a third time and gave the boulder a nudge. It was just a nudge, really.

The red boulder lost her balance and grabbed for the nearest source of stability—a tall, skinny woman in sweats and a Santa hat bearing a pink bakery box. The tall, skinny woman lost her hold on the box and down it went, spilling cupcakes with green frosting everywhere. She gasped and the woman next to her, who now had green frosting skidding down her sleeve, let out a groan.

A nearby man wearing a dirty peacoat and a scruffy beard picked up a cupcake that had landed on the floor, frosting side first, and began to eat it.

All three women glared at Jen. The skinny one with the Santa hat bent to pick up her ruined goods. "You should watch what you're doing."

"Sorry," Jen said. Willing the bus doors not to close, she fumbled in her purse and pulled out her wallet. "Let me pay you for those." The minute she opened her wallet and found nothing there she remembered that she'd impulsively put her last three dollars in a Salvation Army bucket the day before. "I guess I don't have any cash on me."

The skinny woman scowled at her.

"If you're gonna get off the bus, get off," the driver called. "We have other stops to make."

"I'm really sorry," Jen said again. "Um, merry Christmas," she added as she hobbled down the steps onto the curb.

Neither woman wished her a merry Christmas in return. In fact, the skinny one wished her something about as far from it as a girl could get. The doors shut and the bus lumbered off, shooting up a rooster tail of icy water and splashing her.

Bah, humbug.

It was the first week of December, and at Stacy Thomas's house the stockings were hung by the chimney with care. They were lucky to find *any* place to hang because the mantel was already packed with greens and ribbons and candles, as well as brass letters spelling *Peace*.

And that was only the beginning of the holiday decorations. There was no room on the coffee table for coffee cups, due to the presence of Stacy's nativity set, and her lighted Victorian village took up every inch of space on the buffet in the dining room. She still had to unpack the box with all the other candles, the candy dishes and the gingerbread man cookie jar, as well as the one with her holiday centerpiece. Then there was the bag with the Christmas quilt, the tub with all the wall hangings and the box containing her collection of Santa figurines. And then there were the two storage boxes of ornaments waiting to go on the tree....

"This is the last of it," her husband, Dean, said as he set down the long box containing their artificial tree. "Thank God." He wiped his damp brow and looked around him. "Do we really need all of this?"

"Of course we do!"

Stacy surveyed the pile of boxes in front of her. How was she going to get everything put up before her book club arrived? She wished they'd gotten the decorating done the day before. But the day before had been consumed with putting up all the outside lights and the yard art. It had been an exhausting team effort, and by the time she'd finished helping Dean she'd been too tired to even think about the inside of the house.

Tree trimming wasn't quite as much fun as it had been when the kids were living at home. In fact, none of the decorating was. And taking everything down after the holidays was *really* not fun. But Ethan and

Autumn would be back home in Icicle Falls for Christmas. They'd expect holiday razzle-dazzle.

"One of these days I'm going to keel over with a heart attack after lugging all this stuff around," Dean grumbled.

"Oh, you're much too strong for that," Stacy assured him as he started to unpack the fake fir. "Really, Deano, I don't know why you're complaining. All you have to do is help me trim the tree and set up the train around it."

"Don't forget hauling down all these boxes."

"The exercise is good for you," she informed him, looking pointedly at his growing belly.

He tried unsuccessfully to suck it in. "I'm not *that* fat."

That was exactly the same thing she told herself every time she looked in the mirror, but her hips had definitely spread. And at forty-six, those gray hairs were popping up among the blond ones like dandelions in a neglected yard. If not for Rory at Sleeping Lady Salon, she'd be in big trouble.

"We could both stand to lose a few pounds." She sighed. "We should go on a diet."

"Well, let's not start now," Dean said in horror. "It's Christmas cookie season. And speaking of food, I'm hungry. Were we planning to fit dinner in somewhere between now and your book club?"

Dinner. She'd been so busy decorating she'd forgotten about that minor detail. "Let's order a pizza from Italian Alps."

"Good idea," he said, pulling his cell phone out of his pants pocket.

"Make it quick, Deano. We need to get this tree

done." The thought of how lovely it would be with the little electric train running around it and presents spilling everywhere made her smile.

He shook his head. "With all the ornaments you've collected, that should take a millennium. I'm married to the pack rat of Icicle Falls," he muttered as he searched for the number in his phone.

"Ha-ha," she said irritably.

He came and put an arm around her. "I'm sorry, hon, but really, look at all the stuff you've collected. And you keep adding more. Pretty soon there isn't going to be room in the house for us."

"I don't have that many Christmas decorations," she protested.

"You're kidding, right? And it's not just Christmas stuff. Have you seen the attic lately?"

"Some of the things up there belong to the kids. And you." Well, okay, most of them were things she'd acquired. She hurried on before he could point that out. "Anyway, when you've been married for twenty-five years you're bound to end up with a lot."

"Stace, you could load up a landfill with all the stuff you've got. My God, between the closet full of presents—"

"We have to have presents for the kids, and for Ethan's new girlfriend. Anyway, I bought everything on sale," Stacy said righteously.

"The material in Autumn's old room."

"I'm a quilter. I have to buy fabric."

"The dishes. How many sets do you need, anyway?"

"One for every day, good china for special occasions. And we use those Christmas dishes every year."

"And shoes."

"A woman can never have too many shoes."

"And purses."

"A purse is an important accessory."

"Clothes. You know there's barely room in the closet for my clothes. And I don't have that many. And don't tell me I can put them in Ethan's old room. I opened that closet the other day and a shopping bag full of bubble bath fell on me."

That bubble bath had been a steal. Honestly, sometimes her husband had no idea how much money she saved him. "Maybe it was a cosmic hint to clean up your act, Mr. Scrooge," Stacy said. "Anyway, it isn't all for me. Most of that bubble bath is for Christmas presents."

"How many people have you added to your Christmas list? You've got enough bubble bath to clean everyone in Icicle Falls. And their dogs." He flopped on the couch, put in his call to Italian Alps and ordered a large pizza supreme.

"There. Feel better?" she taunted.

"I'd feel better if I could take all this junk to the dump."

She opened the box with her collection of Santa figurines and took one out. "Someone's being very naughty," she told the ceramic Santa. "I think you need to bring him a lump of coal for Christmas."

"Good. Something I can burn and get rid of," he retorted.

Okay, enough was enough. "You know, you're ruining my holiday spirit here. I'm trying to make our house look nice and you're being a Grinch."

He patted the couch cushion. "Come here and give your Grinch a kiss."

"Will it help?"

He smiled, and she joined him on the couch for a kiss and another hug. "I'm sorry," he said. "I'll try to un-Grinch myself. I love you," he added, and kissed her again.

"And I love you, too." But his attitude stank.

Besides, he didn't have a clue about how important holiday decorating was. Or decorating in general. Those pretty things set the mood for fun. They were the backdrop for surprises and family togetherness. Without them it would be like watching a play take place on a barren stage. And that crack about the dishes? Come on. Using those Christmas dishes was part of what made everything so festive.

She glanced at the herd of boxes scattered around her living room. Okay, there was a lot of festivity here. *Was* she a pack rat?

Chapter Two

The first step toward positive change is acknowl edging the need for that change.
— Muriel Sterling, author of *Simplicity*

By seven-thirty the Thomas residence looked like Christmas central. Most of the decorations were up and the rest had been stuffed in their daughter's old bedroom, squeezed in with the piles of material and the quilt in progress. Dean was now ensconced in the TV room, grading tests for his eighth-grade English class, and Stacy was ready for her book club to arrive.

She set her artichoke dip and crackers on the dining room table next to the plate of brownies and the punch bowl full of eggnog, then stepped back to admire her handiwork. The table looked lovely if she did say so herself. Her centerpiece was simple—an elegant Fitz and Floyd pitcher shaped like Saint Nicholas and filled with red carnations she'd purchased at Lupine Floral and surrounded with holly taken from the bush in their backyard. Very festive, she thought with a smile. Every woman should own something by Fitz and Floyd.

The doorbell rang and she hurried to welcome the first arrival. There on the porch stood Cass Wilkes,

bearing her signature contribution, a plate of gingerbread boys and girls. She and Stacy were close in age
and, as with Stacy, Father Time and Mother Nature
were conspiring to put extra pounds on Cass's hips.
Of course, owning a bakery probably contributed to
the problem.

"You seem tired," Stacy observed, stepping aside
to let her in.

"Tired doesn't begin to describe it," Cass said, handing over the plate. "Every year I say I'm not going to
be so busy, but every year I get busier. I'm up to my
ears in orders for gingerbread houses. Both Amber and
Willie want to have Christmas parties, which they expect me to bake for." She shook her head. "I've got to
get those two more at home in the kitchen. Dani was
always my right-hand woman and I'm afraid I let it
slide with the other two."

Cass's oldest daughter, Dani, had worked in the bakery with her for years. But when Dani married she'd
moved away. It looked as if Cass was still trying to
pick up the slack, both at work and at home. A business to run, two teenagers and a dog—no wonder she
was tired.

"Speaking of Dani, how's she doing?" Stacy asked.

Cass's face lit up. "Great. She loves culinary school.
And she and Mike are coming home for Christmas."
Cass sighed. "I hope I can manage to get my Christ-
mas shopping done before they get here."

"At least you don't have a wedding to plan this year."

"No, but my ex and his family had such a good time
last year they're all coming up for Christmas again."

"Tell me they're not staying with you." Cass had
wound up turning her house into a B and B for her ex-

husband and his new wife when they came to town for her daughter's wedding. Somehow, before she knew it, all her former in-laws had descended on her. They wound up having so much fun, they'd decided to stay on and celebrate the holiday at her place. Apparently they were making that a tradition now. Poor Cass.

"No," Cass said. "This year I was smart enough to book ahead. They're all staying at Icicle Creek Lodge. But the whole mob's going to be at my place for Christmas Eve and Christmas Day."

She was still talking when Charlene Albach (Charley to her friends) arrived. Tall and slender in her stylish jeans and boots, her red wool coat and black beret, she could've been in a shoot for a winter edition of some magazine.

"Hey, gang," she said, and gave Stacy a bottle of wine. She studied Cass a moment. "You look more tired every time I see you."

"Nothing a week in the Caribbean wouldn't fix," Cass joked. "You look great as always. Love must agree with you."

Stacy hoped so. She hadn't known Charley before Juliet Gerard started the book club. She did know that Charley had endured a rough couple of years. Her skunk of a husband had left her for another woman, then returned last Christmas, asking her to try again. Stacy wasn't sure what had happened. All she knew was that things hadn't worked out, and he beat feet back to Seattle. On top of that her restaurant had burned down and she'd had to rebuild. But now the restaurant was better than ever. So was Charley's love life.

Juliet came in right behind Charley.

"Speaking of tired," Cass said to Juliet as the women

moved into the living room. "You look like you could use a month's sleep."

Hardly surprising considering that Juliet had an eleven-month-old and was working part-time at Mountain Escape Books.

"Jon has a cold. We were up half the night." Juliet walked into the living room and fell onto the couch. "Somebody should have warned me how much work babies are."

Stacy and Cass exchanged smiles, two maternal warriors who had survived the early years. "I'd like to say it gets easier," Cass said, "but my mama told me never to lie."

"Where's everyone else?" Juliet asked, glancing around.

"Cecily's sick," Stacy said. "And Chita called a few minutes ago to say she's running late."

"What about Dot?"

Dot was the senior member of the group. She was a chain-smoker with a smart mouth and everyone loved her. The fact that they forced themselves to eat the smoke-infested cookies she brought to their monthly meetings was proof of it.

"Dot's dropping out."

"Dropping out?" Cass echoed. "First Chelsea and now Dot."

Juliet let out a sigh. "I can see why Chelsea gave up. She's exhausted. And…" She paused, building anticipation.

Chelsea had been in the book club since the beginning and the members had been there for support when her clueless husband was driving her nuts. He'd finally figured out how to be both a good husband and a good father. So, with him helping so much at home, there could only be one reason Chelsea was too tired for book club.

"She's pregnant," Stacy guessed.

Juliet confirmed it.

"With two kids under the age of three, I don't blame her," Cass said. "But what's Dot's excuse?"

"She said she's got too much on her plate."

Cass rolled her eyes. "Oh, brother. What's that got to do with anything?"

Dot was an inspiration to them all. In her sixties, she could run circles around almost everyone in the group. She owned Breakfast Haus, the town's favorite breakfast restaurant, and was a member of the Chamber of Commerce. In addition to that, she led an active social life.

"I think it has more to do with the books we read," Juliet said. "They're not racy enough for her."

Cass shook her head. "That's our Dot. She probably wore her last husband out."

"She's had more than one?" asked Charley, who was still a relative newcomer to Icicle Falls.

"The first one…well, no one knows exactly what happened to him," Cass replied.

Over the years Stacy had heard rumors but they'd seemed too fantastical to believe. Even though Dot was a tough old girl, it was hard to picture her bumping off her first husband.

"When I was a kid I remember Hildy Johnson telling my mom that she did him in," Juliet said. "Hildy said she shot him but got off because it was self-defense."

"I heard she poisoned him," Cass said.

"Now, why didn't I think of doing that?" Charley joked.

"Good thing you didn't. You'd have been in jail instead of divorced and then you wouldn't have met Mr. Wonderful," Cass told her.

Dan Masters, who owned Masters Construction, had been the man in charge of rebuilding Charley's restaurant after it burned down, but in the past year he'd been a major factor in the rebuilding of her life, as well. These days he hung out at the restaurant every night, and they were often seen at a corner table, sharing a piece of wild huckleberry pie. Most nights, after the restaurant was closed, his truck could be found parked in front of her house.

"True." Charley casually pulled a black leather glove off her left hand and wiggled her fingers. A fat diamond winked.

"Whoa, check this out," Cass said, moving to the couch where Charley had settled in order to get a better look. "That's some sparkler." She hugged Charley. "You deserve every karat. But, you little stinker, why didn't you call me the minute it happened?"

"Because I knew you wouldn't be awake at midnight last night."

"I'm so happy for you," Cass said. "When's the wedding?"

"We're thinking Valentine's Day."

"Wow, that doesn't give you much time," Stacy said.

"Tell me about it. But, hey, if Cass can throw together a great wedding in record time so can we."

"I wouldn't wish that madness on anyone," Cass said. "I almost had a nervous breakdown."

"We're just going to have a small, simple wedding."

Cass snorted. "That's what Dani said."

The doorbell rang and Stacy opened it to let in Chita Arness, their newest member. Chita was a thirty-something single mom who looked like Jennifer Lopez. Why she hadn't remarried was a mystery to Stacy. Chita claimed that between work and her two children she didn't have time to date but Stacy wasn't buying it. A woman could always find time for love.

"Sorry I'm late." Chita handed over a plate with a cake on it that made Stacy's mouth water. "My *tres leches* cake," she said.

Brownies, gingerbread and cake—Stacy's hips were going to explode. But she'd die with a smile on her face.

In addition to the cake, Chita brought two books—the Robyn Carr holiday tale they were discussing and what was probably her suggestion for their January selection, since it was her turn to choose.

She apologized again to the others as she entered the living room. "I had to pick up Hidalgo from the vet's. And then, after dinner, Anna needed help with her math."

Juliet shuddered. "Math. Eeew. When Jon reaches the point where he needs help I'm having him call his uncle Jonathan."

"I wish we had an uncle to call," Chita said, and sank into Stacy's new armchair (Thanksgiving sale, forty percent off). She heaved a giant sigh. "I'm so tired. And I still have so much to do before Christmas. Enrico and his friends got into the cookies I just made and ate almost all of them. Now I have to bake some more before my sister's cookie exchange on Saturday. Which I don't want to go to."

"Why?" Juliet asked.

"Because I don't have time to party," Chita replied. She ran a hand through her long, dark hair. "All I want to do this weekend is crawl into bed and stay there."

"Bed and a good book," Juliet said with a sigh.

"I wouldn't be able to stay awake to read," Chita said. "Even though I loved this month's book. By the way, what gossip did I miss?"

"Oh, not much," Charley said, waving her left hand around.

"Look at you!" Chita exclaimed. She grabbed Charley's hand. "Oooh, that is some diamond."

"He's some man." Charley smiled and proceeded to fill Chita in on the wedding details.

"Ah, I love weddings," Chita said dreamily.

"Maybe there's one in your future," Stacy suggested.

"No time for a wedding. No time for a man," Chita said firmly.

"You really need to rethink your priorities," Charley teased as the women moved to the dining room table.

"Oooh, your homemade brownies," Cass said. "These are the best."

Stacy smiled, dismissing the compliment. She was no professional like Cass and she knew Cass was just being nice. Still, she was gratified by the praise. She liked to bake.

She also liked to entertain. She'd been happy to take over hosting the book club after Juliet had her baby. With the kids gone, the house seemed so empty. Homes should be filled with people and laughter.

And life should be filled with meaning and purpose. Stacy had to admit that when their daughter, the baby of the family, moved to Seattle to attend the University of Washington in the fall, she'd lost her sense of purpose. Empty-nest syndrome—she never thought she'd experience it. She'd always kept busy with her home, her quilting and her volunteer activities.

She still had the volunteer work. She was on the Friends of the Library committee and was in charge of the monthly book sales. Between that and her quilting and church activities, she had enough to do. And yet she didn't.

"This is a new chapter in your life," Dean kept saying. "Now's your chance to finally get out and explore your options." He was right, of course, but she still found herself in a quagmire of indecision. Should she go back to school and finally finish her degree? After twenty years? Maybe not. She'd been more into boys and parties than studying when she was in college. She wasn't sure she was college material.

She could get a job doing…something. Everyone worked these days. She'd worked in retail when she and Dean were first married and had enjoyed it, but now that she was older, going to work for someone didn't sound all that appealing. The idea of starting her own business intrigued her but she had no idea what kind of business to start. What skills did she have other than baking and finding bargains on sale? And quilting. She supposed she could sell her quilts.

Except who would buy them? Most of the people she knew already had one of her quilts. Anyway, there were many women out there who turned out better work than she did. Her cousin Helen Ross could quilt circles around her.

"Everything looks so great," Juliet said. "With all these pretty things, your house should be in a magazine," she told Stacy.

Ha! Take that, Deano. "Tell that to my husband," Stacy said.

"He doesn't like your decorations?" Charley asked.

"He thinks we have too much stuff. But I don't think I have too much," Stacy added quickly before anyone could agree with Dean.

"I love looking at all of this," Cass said, "but I wouldn't want to be in your shoes putting it away in January." She returned to the living room, sat down on the couch and searched in vain for a place to fit her cup of eggnog among the host of ceramic animals and people visiting the Holy Family. She ended up holding it and Stacy found herself wondering if she should've set out fewer camels.

"Sometimes our things can own us," Chita said, making Stacy frown.

"That's true. And pretty darned profound," Cass told her.

If you asked Stacy, it sounded like something you'd hear on Dr. Phil.

"I didn't think it up," Chita said. "I read it." She put her cup on the carpet, and then, balancing her plate on her lap, reached for the book she'd brought in. "I'd like us to read this for the new year."

She passed it to Cass, who held it at arm's length and squinted at the title. *"Simplicity?"*

"It's not a novel," Chita said.

"Oh." Cass was obviously disappointed and handed it to Juliet.

"We just got this in at the bookstore," Juliet explained. "It's Muriel Sterling's new book."

"I love her books," Charley said.

"This one is all about simplifying your life," Chita

told them. "She talks about discovering what's important and learning to shed what isn't."

Was this some kind of decluttering, purge-your-
closets book? Stacy felt herself squirming.

"You mean having fewer things?" Juliet asked.

"Having less, period. Less stuff to deal with, less
stress, less craziness in your life. I'm only halfway
through it but there are some really good ideas in here."

"Well, it's your pick." Stacy knew her tone of voice
probably betrayed that she was less than thrilled with
the selection.

"I think it'll be worthwhile," Chita said. "I mean,
we're always talking about how busy we are." She shot
a look at Juliet. "And how tired."

"This will only help me if it comes with a bottle of
vitamins and a live-in nanny," Juliet quipped. "But I'd
love to read it."

"And if it's by Muriel we know it's going to be worth
reading," Cass added.

Chita smiled. "I think this book could change our
lives."

Change. Stacy wasn't fond of it…unless it was good
and it was happening to her. And she wasn't sure there
was going to be anything all that good for her in this
particular book.

"I think it's a great pick for the new year," Juliet
said.

"Sounds great to me," Charley said.

"Me, too," said Cass.

"Me, too," said Chita.

"Anyone want more eggnog?" Stacy asked.

Chapter Three

Life should be a joy, not a burden.
        —Muriel Sterling, author of *Simplicity*

Jen was rushing down the street, late for lunch with her sister, when her cell phone rang. It was her friend Ariel.

"Hey, a bunch of us are going to try that new restaurant in Belltown Friday night. Want to come?"

A night out with the girls would have been a welcome change but… "I can't. I have—"

"A candle party," Ariel finished with her. "All you do is work. Nobody sees you anymore."

"I know." Boy, did she.

"I'm not sure why I bothered to call," Ariel complained.

She was one of the few who did keep in touch. Most of Jen's other so-called friends had given up. "I'm glad you did."

Ariel gave a snort of disgust. "You're in deep shit with Caroline for missing most of her bachelorette party."

"I know, but I had—"

"A candle party. There's more to life than work.

And you'd better realize that before you don't have any friends left."

"Oh, that's nice," Jen said. "Glad to see you're so supportive." And understanding. Not. She couldn't help it if she had bills to pay and a failed starter marriage to recover from. And family obligations.

"You wanna talk supportive? Who got you through your divorce?" Ariel demanded. "Who hosted your first candle party?"

Actually, her sister had. She'd been there for Jen when she was going through her divorce, too, but this wasn't the time to point that out. Anyway, she wasn't the total scum girlfriend Ariel was making her out to be. "Yeah? Well, who's always been your designated driver whenever you wanted to go out dancing and get drunk?"

"Saint Jen, who I guess is now too good for her old friends."

"I'm just busy!"

"If you're too busy for your friends, you're too busy," Ariel snapped, and ended the call.

Jen stared at her phone in disbelief. What was that? Had Ariel just dumped her over the phone?

The clock on her phone screen told her she didn't have time to stand around trying to figure it out.

Late. It seemed as if she was constantly running to something, constantly trying to catch up with her own life. But, like a dog chasing its tail, she never seemed to. She picked up her pace.

"So you finally got here," her older sister, Toni Carlyon, greeted her as Jen approached their table at the Pink Door in Seattle's Post Alley.

"I'm lucky I could get away at all." Jen took in the

antipasto platter sitting on the table. "Aw, you ordered my prosciutto." She hugged Toni, then settled in her chair and snagged a slice of meat.

"Of course," Toni said. "I always watch out for you, baby sister."

Watching out for and bossing around were synonymous in her sister's mind, but Jen let it slide. Bossiness was unavoidable when your sister was five years older than you. This lunch was a command performance, and Jen suspected she'd be getting a sisterly lecture along with the meal Toni had offered to buy her.

She could feel her sister's eyes on her as she gave the waitress her order.

"You look like death on a stick," Toni said once the waitress was gone. "Mom's right. You *are* going too hard."

Jen opened her mouth to say, "I am not." Instead, she said, "I hate my life," and burst into tears.

Toni set her glass of wine in front of Jen. "Drink this."

"I have to go back to work," Jen protested.

"Drink it, anyway."

Jen managed to stem the tears enough to take a sip of wine.

"Jen-Jen, you've got to stop doing so much," Toni scolded. "Start saying no."

"I can't."

"Yes, you can. Think like that old Nike commercial and *just do it.*"

Easy for Toni to say. Yes, she was busy with her husband and her children, but when it came to work she could set her own hours. Toni wrote for women's magazines, focusing primarily on family issues. If she didn't feel like working she could take a day off, go to the gym, maintain her size-six bod, touch up her blond highlights.

Jen had given up on highlights. She hadn't been to the gym in months and she wouldn't be able to take a day off until…2043. "I can't," she wailed. Now diners at the other tables were staring at her. She gulped down some more wine.

"You take on too much, Jen-Jen," Toni said. "Tell your idiot supervisor to plan the rest of the office Christmas party without you."

Right. "You would never last in corporate America," Jen retorted.

"At the rate you're going you're not going to last, either," Toni said. "You don't have time for your friends anymore and you barely have time for your family. That's not you."

Toni had a point. "I don't know what to do," Jen confessed. "Every time I look at my calendar I want to run away from my life."

"Have you finished the book I gave you yet?" Toni asked.

"No. I keep falling asleep." Jen shook her head. "Pathetic. I used to love to read." Heck, she used to love to do all kinds of things. She used to love going out with the girls on the spur of the moment or catching a movie, walking around Green Lake with a friend on a sunny day. Or…breathing. She barely had time for that these days. "Sometimes I wish I could sell the condo and move to a small town somewhere and just start over. Maybe write a book." She'd always wanted to try her hand at writing…something. These days it seemed as if everyone was writing a book so it couldn't be *that* hard.

"I've heard life is slower in a small town," Toni said, "but I don't believe it. These days everybody's busy. But certain somebodies are busier than others. Too busy," she added, raising an eyebrow at Jen.

"If you think I want to be running around like a roadrunner on speed you're crazy," Jen informed her, "but I have to. I've got bills to pay." Obviously, her friends didn't get that.

"That's the American way," Toni said with a frown. "I wish I could help you out but my car's on its last legs and we found out yesterday that Jeffrey's going to need braces. It'll be a few months before our budget adjusts to the shock."

"I wouldn't dream of taking money from you, anyway. But if we had a rich uncle I'd have no qualms taking some from him." Jen sighed. "Working two jobs is getting old. You know, sometimes I wish I'd been born in a simpler time, when people weren't so busy."

"You can't go back. Sometimes I'd like to, though. I watched this old movie the other night about a family living during the Depression and I felt downright jealous."

"Of people living in the Depression?"

"Not of the money thing. It was all that family togetherness that got to me." Toni rolled her eyes. "Even when my family's together, we're not. Jeffrey's off in his room playing games on his computer, Jordan's always texting. Wayne's on his laptop, doing work. I hate it. Oh, and there's another expense. Jordan told me last night that she lost her cell phone."

There was a fate worse than death, if you asked Jen.

She couldn't *imagine* being without hers. "Part of me would just as soon not replace it."

Jen couldn't help smiling. "Mom would agree with that." Their mother had never been shy about expressing her opinion regarding kids and cell phones.

"Yeah, yeah. We didn't have cell phones when we were kids and we were fine. But it's a different world now." Toni reclaimed her wineglass and took a sip. "I'd never admit this to Mom, but sometimes I wonder if all our technology has really made our lives better." She fiddled with the stem of her glass. "Sometimes I worry that..." She paused and bit her lip. "My family is drifting apart."

"Of course it's not," Jen said, and shied away from the image of a very bored Jordan trailing them through the gingerbread house exhibit a couple of weeks before, texting her friends at every opportunity. When Jordan was little she'd loved going out with the big girls. Now that she was thirteen, not so much. But, Jen reminded herself, she hadn't been excited to hang out with the adults when she was that age, either.

"Oh, well," Toni said. "That's enough downer talk. Let's figure out what we're getting Mom for Christmas."

Talking about Christmas plans should have lifted Jen's spirits, but only served to sic her to-do list on her and make her edgy. She hurried through lunch, gave her sis a quick hug and then speed-walked back toward the Columbia Center building.

When she got halfway there, she stopped in midstride. What was she doing? *Why* was she running like a gerbil on a wheel? She didn't want to go back to work. She wasn't going to go back to work.

She whipped out her cell phone and called her supervisor. "Patty, I'll be at home for the rest of the day."

"Are you okay?" Patty asked, concern in her voice.

She was probably just concerned about whether Jen had found a caterer for the office party yet.

"I'm sick. It must've been something I had at lunch," Jen improvised. No lie, really. She'd had something at lunch that made her sick—a conversation about her life. She needed a break and she needed it right now.

"Okay, well, feel better soon," Patty said. "Let us know if you're not going to make it in tomorrow."

The only way Jen was going to feel better was if she got a new life. She went home, flipped on her faux fireplace and settled under a blanket on the couch with the book her sister had given her, starting with page one. Again.

When was the last time you enjoyed your life?

"My honeymoon," Jen muttered. No, wait. She'd enjoyed her life since then. She'd enjoyed it…the first week after she bought the condo, when she was spending money she didn't have to furnish the place. The fun had lasted until she saw the credit card bill.

If it's been a while, then chances are you're due for a change.

Well, there was an understatement. Jen read on, learning about the author's big life change, how she'd lost her second husband and had to start over. Left to figure out her finances and the rest of her life, Muriel

Sterling had sold her big house that she owed a fortune on and rented a friend's cottage.

> It wasn't easy letting go of that house. It rep-
> resented so much—the new life I'd begun with
> my second husband, security, happiness. But I
> quickly learned that two stories of wood and
> stone don't make a life. And owing money on
> that place certainly didn't make me secure. What
> I needed was freedom, not merely from debt but
> from the past and from my unrealistic expecta-
> tions. I needed to be free to start again.

Free to start again, huh? Jen read on.

> And so I ask you now, do you need to start over?
> The only way to do that is to get free.

Get free? She'd just bought this place. But did she own it or did it own her?

She shut the book and looked around her living room. Her couch was white leather and had a match-ing beaded chair. Her Beckworth coffee table, hand-crafted from exotic demolition hardwoods, was her pride and joy. It hadn't been cheap but she loved it. Her decorations were from Crate and Barrel. They hadn't been cheap, either, and she had the high credit card balance to prove it. She really liked this living room. She especially liked the fireplace. Her parents' house didn't have one and she'd always been taken with the romantic image of reading by a cozy fire on a cold day. And even though the fire going right now was electric, it was still pretty, and it gave her living room the perfect finishing touch. Except she rarely had a chance to enjoy it.

She really liked her bedroom, too, which she'd dolled up with a vintage brass bed, a pink comforter and a spectacular multicolored gypsy chandelier. It should have been a retreat, a place for sweet dreams, but often she tossed and turned on that vintage bed, thinking about everything she had to do.

The kitchen was another work of art and she enjoyed looking at its sleek granite countertops. But she hardly ever cooked in there.

She gazed out the window at the Seattle skyline. Buildings everywhere and gray skies.

"What am I doing here?" she asked herself.

Toni was up to her eyebrows in gift bags and wrapping paper when her sister called. "Hey, I was beginning to think you'd run away," Toni said. "I haven't heard from you since we had lunch."

"I've been busy."

"What a surprise."

"What are you doing this weekend?" Jen asked, ignoring her sarcasm.

"With ten days to go until Christmas? Shopping." Most of her shopping had been done by November, but she still had a few last-minute things to purchase.

"Want to go shopping in Icicle Falls?"

"What?"

"I want to check out Icicle Falls. We can go up Friday and spend the night. Come back late Saturday."

Toni wasn't spontaneous. She was a planner, and she had her weekend all planned. She was going to the gym on Friday, then out to dinner that night with her husband. Wayne was a programmer and sometimes it seemed he was married to his computer instead of her. But come Friday, they were going to have a romantic night out whether he wanted to or not. She'd already told him to program that into his computer. Then Saturday she'd finish up her shopping.

"I can't go until after Christmas."

"Come on. Please? My treat."

"You can't afford to treat."

"Okay, we can go halfsies, then we can both afford it."

Toni propped the phone between her shoulder and her ear and set to work, using a pair of scissors to curl the ribbon on the package she'd finished wrapping. "Why are you suddenly in such a tear to go to Icicle Falls?"

"Because I think I might want to move there."

Toni dropped the scissors. "What? What are you talking about? You just bought a condo!"

"I know. And now it's on the market. My Realtor is holding an open house this weekend."

All right. Spontaneous was one thing, but this was crazy. "You can't put your place up for sale just like that," Toni protested.

"Yes, I can," Jen said, her tone of voice deceptively sane.

"No. You can't. You don't have any equity built up. You won't make a cent."

"I don't need to make anything. I need to get free of my debt. Never mind the cheese, let me out of the trap."

Toni frowned. That didn't sound like something her sister would say. "What's this all about, anyway?" And then she remembered. The book. She groaned. "Oh, no. Don't tell me."

"Don't tell you what?"

"You read the book I gave you."

"Isn't that why you gave it to me? And yes, I did, and it made perfect sense."

"That was to help you prioritize your life, learn how to be less busy."

"That's exactly what I'm doing," Jen said. "I'm shedding all the things that have been complicating my life and holding me down."

"I didn't give you that book so you could go off half-cocked, sell your place and move to the mountains." She'd only wanted her little sister to learn to say no, to manage her time better. She should've known this would happen. This was such a Jen thing to do.

"I don't know if I'm going to move to the mountains yet. I'm taking this slowly, checking it out."

"Slowly? You read a book and two weeks later your place is up for sale!"

"Okay, fine. If you don't want to go…"

"Oh, no. You're not going up there without me," Toni said firmly. Who knew what her sister would do if left to her own devices? "I'll pick you up Friday at eleven, after I'm done at the gym." The romantic Friday night dinner with her husband would have to wait. Right now she had to keep her sister from simplifying her life with a new complication.

And so that Friday afternoon the sisters were on their way to the quaint Washington town of Icicle Falls. Nestled in the Cascades, it was the ideal place…to visit.

"Why up here in the mountains? Why Icicle Falls?" Toni demanded.

"That's where Muriel Sterling lives."

"Muriel Sterling?"

"You know, the woman who wrote *Simplicity*. I read it in her bio on the back of the book." Jen frowned. "Sometimes I wonder if you even read that book."

Of course she'd read it. That was why she'd given it to her sister. Now Toni wished she'd never heard of it.

"So, on a whim you decided you want to live there?"

"I've been looking it up on the internet," Jen said. "Did you know the town sponsors a yearly chocolate festival?"

"Well, there's a reason to move."

Jen matched her sarcasm with a grin. "I thought so."

"This is nuts," Toni said, frowning at her sister.

"Hey, watch the road."

"Don't worry. I can drive in the snow. And the Outback has all-wheel drive and snow tires. We're fine." She shook her head. "But listen to you. We're on the highway and the snow's hardly sticking and you're already nervous. You hate driving in this stuff, so you're moving to the mountains? That doesn't make sense."

"I hate driving in the snow in Seattle, which is all hills," Jen corrected.

"This, in case you didn't notice, isn't a hill. It's a mountain."

"It's a highway and you just assured me we're safe."

Toni sighed. "I can't believe I'm doing this." Aiding and abetting her sister in her insanity—what was she thinking? *I must be crazy, too.*

But once they hit the town she could understand why her sister had wanted to come here.

"Look how cute this is," Jen said, gazing out the

window at the Bavarian architecture of the shops as they drove down Center Street.

The downtown was cute, Toni had to admit, and especially with everything all decorated for the holidays. The old-fashioned streetlamps were bedecked with fat, red bows and greenery, the trees were strung with lights waiting to bloom come evening. The town was surrounded by glorious mountain peaks frosted with snow. So were the rooftops here in town. It all made Toni think of gingerbread houses.

"Let's check in and then come back and shop," Jen suggested.

That sounded fine to Toni and they drove to the Icicle Creek Lodge.

"Oh, my," Jen breathed as they pulled up in front of the rustic, old place.

It looked the way a mountain lodge should—large, rough-timbered and accented with stone. The sweeping lawn was thick with snow. A trio of children, probably staying there, was busy taking advantage of the white stuff and building a snowman. Inside, the lobby was done up to the nines for the holidays with greens and ribbon and little twinkle lights everywhere. And in the center of the lobby sat an old-fashioned sleigh, piled with presents. Somewhere, someone was roasting nuts and the aroma filled the place.

Toni could envision bringing her family up here for a holiday vacation. Jordan would love this.

Well, maybe. Jordan would have loved it a couple of years ago. These days she didn't enjoy doing much of anything with her family. Dad was mean, Mom didn't understand and Jeffrey was stupid and a pest. Sigh.

Their room was all charm—wood paneling, two

double beds with white down comforters, a view out the window that took Toni's breath away. It would be so easy to fall under the spell of this place.

Jen joined her at the window. "Gorgeous, isn't it?"

Oh, no. Jen couldn't afford to fall. "Great place to vacation," Toni said, hoping her sister would get the message.

"It might be a good place to live."

Living here would feel like stepping inside a storybook. But her sister had some real-life issues to deal with. "You have a place in Seattle you haven't sold."

Jen frowned. "You don't have to remind me."

"Yeah, I do." Someone had to keep Jen in line. Toni felt a sudden respect for Jiminy Cricket. Keeping someone out of trouble who was always bent on diving in nose-first was *not* a simple task. "I don't want to see you put the cart before the horse."

"I'm just looking. Remember? Come on, let's go check out some of the shops."

Jen had been right about the shops. The first one they walked into sold imported lace goods and teapots, and within ten minutes Toni had purchased a lace tablecloth for their grandmother. And a holiday table runner from Germany for herself.

That was only the beginning of the shopping spree. After that she went on to buy novelty hats for both her kids in the hat shop, several ornaments for the tree in a shop that specialized in all things Christmas and a box of chocolates from Sweet Dreams, the town's chocolate company.

Jen purchased some, too. "For later tonight," she said. She gave Toni's arm a sisterly hug. "Isn't this fun? Aren't you glad you came?"

"I am," Toni admitted. Who didn't enjoy girl time and shopping? And everyone here was so darned friendly. Even she was beginning to harbor dreams of moving to Icicle Falls, ogling the beautiful scenery and stuffing her face with chocolate. "But remember, I have to be back by six tomorrow evening," she told both her sister and herself. "Wayne and I have reservations for seven." She was still determined to get in that dinner with her husband. They were going to be romantic if it killed them.

"Hey," Jen said, stopping in front of Mountain Meadows Real Estate. She studied the pictures of homes for sale displayed on the window and her eager smile fell away. "Prices up here aren't cheap, are they?"

"Looks like real estate has held its value," Toni said. Another plus for residents of the town, but Jen couldn't afford those prices. "Of course, these are houses. Condos might be less." What was she saying?

"Good point. Let's go in and find out what's available," Jen said, starting for the door.

Toni held her back. "Come on, Jen-Jen, let's just have fun this weekend and leave it at that. You really shouldn't even be looking until your place is sold."

"It can't hurt to look," Jen insisted, and went in.

"Yeah, it could," Toni muttered, and followed her inside.

Once in the office, the woman on duty was happy to show Jen what they had in her price range...which wasn't much.

"None of those condos were as nice as what I have in Seattle," Jen said as they left the office.

"Then maybe you should stay put."

Jen frowned. "I really want to change my life."

"That's all well and good, but what would you live on if you moved up here? You work in Seattle. Remember?"

"I saw help-wanted signs in a couple of windows. I could find a job in town."

"Oh, yeah. You'd make a lot of money working in some shop," Toni scoffed.

"You don't need a lot of money to live simply," Jen told her. "That's what Muriel Sterling says."

"Muriel Sterling has never gone shopping with you."

Jen didn't answer. Instead, she pulled her cell phone from her coat pocket and began to surf the internet.

"Great," Toni muttered, "I feel like I'm back home with my daughter, being ignored. What are you doing now?"

"I just had a thought."

"What kind of thought?" What was Jen up to?

"Maybe I could rent something."

"You don't want to have nothing to show for your money but rent receipts," Toni protested.

"Not down the road. But for right now, it might be nice to rent. No responsibility. If there's a problem, the landlord fixes it."

Toni shook her head. "I think you're nuts."

Jen held her phone out. There on the screen was the picture of a cottage with wisteria climbing up the front porch railing and along the roof. "That's cute. And look at the price."

"For that price there must be something wrong with it."

"Well, I'm going to call and ask about it."

From a nice condo to a teensy house in the

mountains—her sister really had lost her marbles. "I wish I'd never given you that book," Toni said.

Jen ignored her. "Hi, I'm calling about your ad on Homelist. Is that house still for rent? Great. I'd like to see it. Tomorrow morning? Yes, I can do that. Ten? Perfect." Jen ended the call and smiled as if she'd accomplished something important. "We're all set. The owner will meet us there."

"Just remember. You're only looking," Toni cautioned.

"Of course," Jen agreed.

The next morning when they pulled up to the place, Jen quickly slid from looking down that slippery slope into lusting. "Oh, it's adorable!"

Yes, Toni had to concede, with its white shutters and little front porch it was darling. Camped out at the end of a long scenic road, it sat on a large lot surrounded by pine and various fir trees and came complete with a snow-capped roof. Some kind of tree, possibly a fruit tree, occupied a corner of the lot. But the place was tinier than Jen's condo.

"It's not very big," Toni pointed out.

"There's only me. I don't need a big place," Jen said, and climbed out of the SUV.

She's going to do something crazy, Toni thought. Was it too late to demand that Jen hand over her checkbook?

A big black truck drove up and parked in front of them and out of it stepped a six-foot hunk of dark-haired gorgeous. Toni forgot about getting her sister's checkbook. For a moment she even forgot she had a husband and a romantic dinner waiting for her in Seattle. By the time she remembered, Jen and the hunk had shaken hands and were halfway up the walk.

"Jen, wait," she called, and hurried after them. But she knew she was too late.

Chapter Four

Never be afraid to start again.
               —Muriel Sterling, author of *Simplicity*

Garrett Armstrong was the owner of this cottage. That meant he'd be Jen's landlord? She'd take it. No wedding ring on his left hand. She'd take him, too.

Don't be in a rush, she warned herself. She'd been there, done that. Serge had been a big, hormone-fueled mistake and she didn't need that kind of heartbreak again. One romantic misstep equaled a starter marriage, but two equaled no brains. She was going to be smart the next time around and pick a man who had his act together. No more falling for a pretty face.

But, oh, what a pretty face this guy had—dark eyes, square manly chin, big shoulders.

You're here for the house. Oh, yeah. That.

"Where are you from?" he asked as they walked up the little path to the cabin.

"Seattle."

"Where people have neighbors," Toni added, an oh-so-unsubtle reminder that Jen was a city girl.

"I'm sure there are neighbors here somewhere," Jen said.

"There are," Garrett assured her. "They're half a mile down the road."

"Well, that'll be handy if you want to borrow a cup of sugar," Toni said with a sneer.

"So I'll stock up on sugar." Jen sent her a look that said, "Shut up already."

She shut up, but scowled in disapproval.

"Anyway, this is only a few minutes from town," Jen mumbled.

"You're moving over here for…?" he asked.

A chance for my eggs to meet a nice sperm. "I'm simplifying my life," Jen said.

He nodded. "Always a good idea."

"Right now she's just looking around, getting ideas," put in Toni, and it was all Jen could do not to kick her.

Garrett the Gorgeous frowned.

Jen could hardly blame him. No doubt he had better things to do than waste his time with someone who wasn't really interested in renting his place. Was there someone in his life he was doing those better things with? Not that she was rushing into anything. She was just wondering. And wondering wasn't rushing.

"I'm definitely interested in renting up here," she said, sending her sister's mouth slipping even farther down at the corners. "Do you have cable? Wi-Fi?"

"Just got it," he said.

"That's great." Jen wanted to live simply, not primitively.

Then they went inside and she came to a complete, startled stop.

"Oh," Toni said faintly from behind her.

Oh, didn't begin to cover it. The cottage's inside definitely didn't match its cute exterior. It was one level and that consisted of a great room (well, sort of great) that included a kitchen, a dining area with a rickety wooden table and four equally rickety chairs and living room furniture that no self-respecting thrift store would accept. A tiny hallway scooted past the kitchen, probably leading to the bedrooms and bathroom. The place smelled musty and Jen wrinkled her nose.

Garrett must have noticed because he said, "It's been closed up for a while. All it needs is a good fire in the woodstove."

The woodstove was a bonus, she had to admit. Once she imported her furniture and hung some nice curtains at the windows, the living area would look totally different. She moved toward the kitchen, half the size of the one she had at the condo. The cabinets were old and battered, but they could have a second life if she painted them white.

Nothing would make those mustard-yellow Formica counters anything but disgusting, though. Jen pushed away the image of her spiffy granite counters in the condo. Instead, she pictured herself setting out freshly baked bread, making this kitchen homey with a mason jar full of wildflowers on the counter. There was enough room there to work. She could master the art of making pies, can fruit.

Speaking of fruit… "What kind of tree is that in the front yard?" she asked.

"Apple."

"Home-canned applesauce," she said dreamily.

He seemed impressed. "You know how to can?"

"I'm going to learn."

Toni was standing by the window now. "Is it my imagination or is the floor slanting over here?"

"The foundation settled," Garrett explained.

"I'll bet that's what they said about the leaning tower of Pisa," Toni muttered.

Jen started down the hall. "So, two bedrooms, right?"

"That's right," he said.

"One for me and one for guests. You and Wayne and the kids can come visit," she said to Toni, who was falling in behind them.

"It might get a little crowded with four of us in one bed."

"The sofa's a sleeper," said Jen's would-be landlord.

"Mmm," Toni responded diplomatically.

Jen knew what she was thinking. The ratty, old brown couch would have to be fumigated before she'd let her children sleep on it.

They stopped at the first bedroom, furnished with twin beds covered in ancient brown bedspreads with big orange flowers that must've been hanging out in there since the seventies. "I suppose this is the guest room," Toni said, her tone of voice speaking volumes.

"It's not bad," Jen insisted.

"The other bedroom is here," Garrett said, leading the way to the next room. He was beautiful to follow, broad-shouldered and tall with a stare-worthy butt.

He opened the door and Jen peeked into the room and got a pleasant surprise. Lace curtains hung at the windows. Yes, they needed washing, but they were pretty, nonetheless. There, in the middle of the room, sat a double bed with a carved headboard and a beautiful quilt, done in shades of pink. Matching oak nightstands flanked it. Against another wall stood an antique oak dresser complete with beveled mirror.

"This is so sweet," she said.

"The bedroom set was my grandmother's," Garrett told her.

"Did she make the quilt?"

"As a matter of fact, she did."

"Is she still alive?"

He shook his head. "No. But my other grandmother is. She lives here in Icicle Falls."

"It's important to be close to family." Toni gave Jen a meaningful look.

"This isn't that far from Seattle," Jen said.

"But it'll feel like it is if you get snowed in," Toni retorted.

"Most of us manage to get around okay in the snow," Garrett said.

Jen thought about how poorly she drove in the stuff. Only the year before she'd slid backward down Eleventh Avenue in Seattle's Queen Anne Hill neighborhood after a rare snowfall. She'd been afraid to venture out in her car ever since. But it was all level around here. Surely she could handle that. Anyway, they seemed to keep the roads clear.

"This is charming," she said, glancing around the room, which was paneled with cedar. Two pictures of flowers hung on the wall. Everything about the room said family and love. If she moved into this cottage, she was sure she'd be embraced by the warm memories haunting it. "In fact, this whole place has potential. I'll take it."

Her sister stared at her as if she'd lost her mind. "What she means," Toni began.

"Is that I'll take it," Jen said firmly, pulling out her checkbook.

He nodded. "I'll have to do a routine credit check."

"No problem. My credit's good," Jen told him.

"Which is more than I can say for your brain," Toni hissed as they preceded him out of the room. "What are you *thinking?*"

"That this place is perfect for living the simple life." Toni groaned.

"If you need time to decide…" Garrett said from behind them.

"Yes, she does," Toni said even as Jen said, "No, I don't." They glared at each other.

Jen wrote him a check for a deposit and gave him her contact information, and he said he'd be in touch.

Then there was nothing left to do but say goodbye and go back to the car. With her disapproving sister.

"You *have* lost your mind," Toni said the moment Garrett and his gorgeous behind were back inside his truck.

"That's probably what they told the Wright brothers when they invented the airplane. Or Walt Disney when he came up with the idea for Disneyland."

"You're not inventing anything. And this idea isn't practical. What if your condo doesn't sell?"

That was an unpleasant thought. Jen pushed it resolutely away. "Then I'll lose my deposit."

Toni's angry expression softened. "Jen-Jen, I'm not trying to rain on your parade. You've got to know that. I just don't want to see you jump from the frying pan into the fire. I worry about you."

That made Jen smile. Yes, her sister could be a bossy pain in the patootie. But she cared. Jen reached across the car and hugged Toni. "And I love you for it." She drew back so they were face-to-face. "I realize this seems crazy to you, but I've got a feeling that it's going to be good for me, that it's exactly what I need. Maybe I'm wrong but I'm willing to take a chance. I can't keep going on like I'm doing. I hate my life."

Toni sighed. "I know. I'm worried you're going to wind up hating it even more."

"If this doesn't work out, I can always move back to Seattle. And if it *does* work out, you can come up for the chocolate festival and stay with me," Jen added with a grin.

"After you get those beds fumigated," Toni said with a shudder.

The image of Jen Heath accompanied Garrett Armstrong as he drove to his mom's to pick up his son who'd been staying with Grammy while Garrett worked his shift at the fire station. With her strawberry-blond hair and those freckles, Jen was about the cutest thing he'd seen in a long time. A woman who wanted to do old-fashioned stuff like make applesauce? Man, he didn't know that kind of woman existed anymore.

His ex sure hadn't been interested in anything domestic. And she'd proved it by letting Garrett be the custodial parent while she settled for having their son every other weekend.

When he'd first met Ashley, he'd found her party-girl attitude exciting. She was a huge flirt and she'd dance anywhere at the drop of a hat—the dance floor of the Red Barn, tabletops, his lap. Oh, yeah, the sex had been incredible. She was blonde, beautiful and the hottest thing he'd ever handled and he'd just had to have her. He'd rushed to marry her before anyone else could steal her away.

His dad hadn't told him what to do since he turned eighteen, but his mother had been a different story. "That woman's going to break your heart," she'd cautioned. "Don't do it."

Of course he hadn't listened, because he'd figured that by twenty-six he knew everything. So he and Ashley had the big blowout wedding and a honeymoon in the Caribbean that ate up all his savings and then came home to settle down in Icicle Falls. Only one of them had settled down, though. Ashley never quite got the concept of home, sweet home. She'd much preferred to make herself at home at a restaurant or club. And she'd never let Garrett's work schedule keep her from going out. That was what girlfriends were for.

They hadn't planned on getting pregnant but once they were, she seemed to get into parenthood. She enjoyed the baby showers and all the preparation for the baby (probably because it involved spending money). But after she had Timmy, she quickly tired of staying home being a mom. She jumped from one crazy thing to another— redecorating the house (more spending), going out with her girlfriends, taking line dancing lessons at the Red Barn (and having an affair with her dance instructor). That roll in the hay had spelled the end as far as Garrett was concerned, and that had been fine with her. According to Ashley, he was a controlling stick-in-the-mud.

Garrett liked being stuck in the mud just fine. Anything was better than the emotional roller coaster he'd ridden with Ashley for the past few years. And because they had a son, he still had to deal with her. Whenever Timmy spent the weekend at her place, he came home a handful, testing boundaries and wondering why, when Grammy babysat him, he couldn't have pizza for breakfast.

And then there was the matter of money. Ashley seemed to think they were still married and she could hit him up anytime she needed a fresh infusion of cash.

He was already paying her a hefty support check every month as part of the divorce settlement so she could go to school and train for a career. As to what kind of career, she was still vague. Hardly surprising. Ashley seemed to be permanently stalled at the age of sixteen. He was willing to bet she cut more classes than she attended. And, of course, she wasn't working. Why work when you could get money from your stupid ex-husband?

She always needed extra money for something. The requests ranged from books to new pans. All of Icicle Falls knew about the pans, since she'd announced in the middle of Hearth and Home that he'd left her so broke she couldn't afford any. Right. He was the one who couldn't afford pans. He was using some his mother had given him. The others he'd purchased at the Kindness Cupboard, the town's thrift store.

Her latest ploy had been new clothes for Timmy. That one he wasn't about to let her get away with. He was the custodial parent and his mom bought Timmy's clothes. "I want to take him shopping," Ashley had whined. "But if you can't come up with a few bucks, I'm sure Timmy will understand. Daddy has other things to spend his money on than his son."

"Don't even try to pull that crap on me," he'd growled.

But she had. As usual, in the end, he'd caved.

He was done caving now. He had to stop letting

her use him as her own personal ATM. She was killing him.

It would help his bank account if he got this renter into the cottage his great-uncle had recently left him. It would also help if Ashley found some other sucker to marry. Surely there was someone in Icicle Falls stupid enough to do that. Maybe Billy Williams, whom she'd been seen with at the Red Barn. Except he wouldn't wish Ash on his worst enemy, let alone poor old Bill Will.

"I wish you'd never met that woman," his mother often complained.

Well, that made two of them. Between the money and the 2:00 a.m. calls when she was tipsy and "just wanted to talk," he was paying big-time for his hormone-induced insanity.

He'd learned his lesson, though. At thirty-two he was older and wiser. He was never getting involved with a flake again. His kid needed stability, and the next woman he picked was going to be someone stable, someone who had her act together.

Like Tilda Morrison. They'd gone out a couple of times and he liked her. She was buff and tough and she wouldn't take any shit from a kid who was misbehaving. She probably wouldn't take any shit from a misbehaving ex-wife, either. He enjoyed playing racquetball at Bruisers with her and he appreciated her no-nonsense approach to life.

But it wasn't Tilda he kept thinking about as he drove to his mom's. What was the story with Jen Heath?

Chapter Five

The to-dos on our list aren't always what we need to do.
                        —Muriel Sterling, author of *Simplicity*

Chita Arness only wanted one thing from Santa—some time to herself. She had no idea how she was going to simplify her life if she didn't even have a couple of hours to finish reading a book on simplifying it. She'd said as much to Cass when they ran into each other in Johnson's Drugs.

"I hear you," Cass had said. "Being a single parent isn't for sissies."

Especially being a single parent this time of year, Chita thought as she'd left the drugstore. Christmas was right around the corner, waiting to pounce on her. Her shopping wasn't done, the house was a mess and her washing machine was dying. Her work week at Sweet Dreams Chocolates was over, but the work at home was just beginning.

"When are we going to make *pasteles?*" Anna greeted her when she walked in the door.

"Oh, baby, give me time to get my coat off," she pleaded. She thanked Cass's daughter, Amber, who'd been her after-school babysitter for the past few months, and sent her on her way.

"We didn't make them last year and you promised we would this year," Anna persisted.

"Maybe *Abuelita* will make them with you." She always hated to ask her mother for favors, though. Not that her mother wasn't happy to come over from Yakima and spend a day helping out, but her assistance carried a price. Whenever Chita put out an SOS, Consuela Medina couldn't seem to stop herself from observing how much easier Chita's life would've been if only she'd married Danny Rodriguez instead of *that gringo*.

"Danny would never have broken your heart," her mother liked to say.

"Yeah, well, Danny's been on unemployment for the past eighteen months. I'd still be working just as hard," Chita liked to retort.

That usually ended the conversation.

Anyway, work was part of life. What Chita had to do was figure out how to balance it with the demands of two children and a dachshund who had a penchant for eating things he shouldn't, like bottle caps, crayons, Lego bricks and shoelaces (the reason for their last visit to the vet).

"I want *you* to make them with me," Anna said, bringing Chita back into the moment. "You never do anything with me."

Guilt and manipulation, a girl's best friend. Anna must have learned that from her grandmother. Consuela was an expert. *"You have to go to your sister's cookie exchange. She'll be hurt if you don't. Family is important."*

Chita thought of the pile of laundry, the cleaning that needed to be done, the shopping she had to finish and the packages she had to wrap before the big Christmas Eve celebration at her parents' house.

"You know, you're right," she said to her daughter. "We'll make them tomorrow."

The way Anna's face lit up put their Christmas tree to shame. And put her to shame, too. Having a clean house shouldn't be the most important thing in her life. At the age of ten, the days Anna would want to hang out with her were numbered.

Eight-year-old Enrico came racing into the front hall with Hidalgo chasing him, yapping at the top of his doggy lungs. "Can Bradley spend the night? His mom says it's okay."

What the heck? "Sure."

"Can we have tostadas?"

She'd planned on heating up leftovers. "Sure."

"And fried ice cream?"

Life was one big party when you were a kid. Sometimes Chita wished *she* was still a kid. "We'll see," she said.

Ten minutes later, she was making a run to the store for ice cream and cornflakes. And on the way home, she picked up Enrico's friend Bradley and Anna's BFF, Emma. What the heck? What was one more kid at this point?

She knew dinner was a success when Bradley announced, "I like coming here." Obviously, not everyone cared if a woman's house was clean. After they were done eating, she put the kids to work clearing the table while she cleaned up the stove. After that she could get started on the laundry.

Then she caught sight of her book selection sitting on the kitchen counter. Forget the laundry. She put on a Disney movie for the gang, got her blanket and stretched out on the couch to read, barely aware of the TV blasting.

Sometimes it's more important to get some rest than to get things done. I learned early on that when we go, go, go, we never give our bodies a chance to recharge. Schedule time in your life to relax and recharge and you'll find you have more energy and more enthusiasm for the things you need to...

Chita bolted awake when the book fell on her face. Come the new year, she was going to build in more time to keep her batteries charged...before they died for good.

Alma Tuttle opened her front door on Saturday afternoon and greeted Jen. "It's about time you arrived. Half my friends are already here."

"I'm so sorry," Jen said, lugging her case full of candles through the door. "Like I said when I called, I had a flat tire."

Alma clasped her hands in front of her. With her tacky Christmas sweater, her tightly permed white hair and her glasses, she looked a little like Mrs. Claus. But the minute the old bat opened her mouth she ruined that illusion. "You should plan for that."

Plan for flat tires? Was she serious? Jen shoved down her irritation. "I guess I should."

"Well, you're here now," Alma said irritably. "You'd better hurry and get set up."

This had been a mistake. Alma was the grandmother of the hostess at her last party, and she'd pretended she was booking a party to help her granddaughter earn the special candle set that could only be obtained when two guests booked a party, but Jen suspected she'd been motivated more by avarice than sacrifice.

"She's finally here," Alma announced, preceding Jen into the living room where three other senior ladies sat, holding plates filled with store-bought Christmas cookies.

Two of them looked as if they'd been sucking on the same lemon as Alma. The third woman, however, gave Jen a friendly smile. "I love candles," she said.

Well, that was encouraging. "We have some beautiful ones. And I'm selling all my Christmas stock for fifty percent off today," Jen told her as she started to unpack her case.

"It's almost Christmas," Alma said. "They should be seventy-five percent off."

What the heck? Profit was highly overrated. "Well, let me know if you see something you really like." All she wanted at this point was to get rid of these candles and this job.

And the financial burden of the condo. The stupid thing hadn't sold yet and she'd wanted to move the first Saturday in January. Now she was beginning to worry that she wouldn't get to move at all, which was really depressing because she was so ready to escape the hectic life she'd created in Seattle. She was so tired of working two jobs, especially these two.

Ever since the office Christmas party, going to work

had been far from fun. People were still grumbling over
the fact that there hadn't been enough food. (As if that
was her fault? She'd only had so much money to work
with.) Leon Eggers, her supervisor's boss, had made a
pass at her at that ill-fated party and she'd told him to
go soak his head in the punch bowl. After that, she'd
somehow found herself with more work in her in-box.
Nothing she could prove, but she knew.

And the candle parties…ugh. It seemed to be getting
increasingly harder to convince women they wanted
to make time to host a party. Yes, the candles were
shipped to them and they had to distribute them to
their friends. But so what? They got all kinds of free
merchandise as a reward. Of course, the more everyone bought, the more the hostess got. And the more
Jen made. Sadly, no one had purchased much at the
last party. Hopefully, the smiling woman at today's
event would buy a lot and encourage her friends to
do the same.

Now another woman had entered the room. "All
right," Alma said to Jen, "that's everyone."

Five women. Not exactly a huge group. But that
didn't mean anything, Jen told herself. All it took was
one or two women to go on a spending spree and Alma
could earn her holiday centerpiece. And Jen could earn
some money.

"Okay," Jen said in her perky candle-lady voice.
"Thank you all for coming today. I know you'll be
happy you did when you see the wonderful bargains I
have for you. Soft Glow candles are the finest on the
market, guaranteed to bring beauty and light to your
home. Today, just for hosting a Soft Glow party, Alma
will receive this lovely multipack of pillar candles as

a thank-you." She picked up the set of red candles and the women oohed and ahhed and nodded their heads. She had them now!

Jen went on with her spiel, talking up various candles, candleholders, centerpieces and hurricane lamps. "And, as I said earlier, all our holiday candles are fifty percent off today."

"Seventy-five percent," Alma reminded her.

"Seventy-five percent. So, feel free to come up and browse."

"Aren't we going to have a draw?" Alma asked.

She held a drawing for a free candle at every party. Between the flat tire and Alma's irritation, she'd forgotten all about it. Alma hadn't. "Let's do that right now," Jen said, pretending she'd been about to get to it.

One of the lemon-suckers won a set of taper candles. "You're sure these are dripless?" she asked Jen.

"Absolutely. I use those all the time."

The woman nodded, but still seemed unconvinced. "I bought some once that were supposed to be dripless. They ruined my silver candlesticks."

"These won't, I promise," Jen said.

"Well, I hope they don't." The woman's tone of voice promised big trouble for Jen if they did.

Now it was time to order. The women looked at the candles. They visited. They looked some more. They ate more cookies. Then the smiling lady announced she had to get going. She had her bridge club at two.

She took her leave and left her empty order form behind.

One of the lemon-suckers purchased a set of holiday votives. For seventy-five percent off. Big spender. "Would you like to host a party?" Jen asked.

"Heavens, no. I have all the candles I need."

At seventy-five percent off. Jen forced the smile to remain on her face. *That's sales,* she reminded herself. Sometimes you did well, sometimes you didn't. Anyway, the woman probably didn't have a lot of money.

"Well, dear," the broke lemon-sucker said to Alma, "I've got to go home and finish packing for my cruise."

The second lemon-sucker purchased a set of tea lights and called it quits. "I'd have bought more," she informed Jen, "but your candles are overpriced."

"They're very high quality," Jen said. Why was she bothering?

"Well," the woman huffed, "some of us are on a budget."

"I understand," Jen said. And that was why she was working two jobs and trying to sell her condo. Toni had been right. She shouldn't have made a snap decision, shouldn't have wasted money on a deposit on that cottage in Icicle Falls. *What* had she been thinking?

She'd been thinking of Garrett Armstrong. And home-canned goodies. And eating home-canned goodies with Garrett Armstrong. She'd been thinking of getting away and simplifying her life. Sadly, that was turning out not to be so simple.

"It was a lovely party, dear," the last of Alma's guests said to her, and slipped out the door without buying anything.

Alma turned to Jen. "Well, that was nice, wasn't it? What did I earn?"

"You earned this lovely multipack of pillar candles as a thank-you gift," Jen said.

Alma's smile drooped. "Is that all?"

"Well, you do have to have a certain amount in sales to earn—"

"I spent all day yesterday cleaning," Alma said miserably. "And I had to go to the store and get those cookies with my hip bothering me."

"How about I throw in the holiday centerpiece?" Jen offered.

Alma's smile perked right up.

Jen's drooped.

She packed up her candles, thanked Alma for hosting the party and thanked God she was done with candle parties for the season.

Make that forever. Alma Tuttle's nonparty was the last straw. She'd keep some of the candles for herself and sell the rest on eBay. Much as she loved the product, her heart wasn't in this anymore.

Her heart wasn't in Seattle anymore, either, even though it was a great city. What she wanted was life in a small town…a charming mountain town.

She loaded up her wares and drove back to the condo. Home, sweet home. She'd been so in love with this place when she first bought it, so intent on forgetting her unhappy starter marriage to Serge and carving out a new life for herself.

She'd gotten a new life. It just happened to stink.

There was no sense wasting what was left of a perfectly good Saturday afternoon moping. She'd find something simple to do, some small pleasure to give her life sweetness, the way Muriel Sterling recommended in her book. It was almost Christmas. She'd bake cookies. Gingerbread boys like the ones she'd enjoyed in that cute bakery in Icicle Falls. She could give them to Toni's kids for Christmas. A nice simple present…to go with the more expensive ones she'd bought with her overworked credit card.

She found a recipe online and got busy assembling butter, flour, eggs, sugar and spices. These were going to be delicious. Yes, there was nothing like spending a little time in the kitchen making old-fashioned goodies to lift a woman's spirits. Simple pleasures really were the best.

She was sliding a batch of cookies in the oven when her cell phone rang. Caller ID told her it was her Realtor, Hannah Yates. Hannah had shown the condo the other night, but Jen had given up hope when she didn't hear back that same evening. Maybe the person had decided to buy, after all.

Jen let the oven door slam shut, grabbed the phone and said a hopeful "Hello."

"Hi, Jen, it's Hannah."

"Yes?" Jen said eagerly.

"I just called to tell you that the woman I showed the condo to decided she'd rather have a house."

Jen's spirits took a nosedive and she sank onto her couch. "I thought she wanted to downsize."

"She changed her mind. It happens. But don't worry. I'll find you a buyer."

"Thanks," Jen said, trying to sound upbeat and appreciative. "I know you're trying to sell this place."

"Frankly, I can't understand why we haven't found a buyer. It's a great condo, and it's definitely priced to sell."

Because it isn't in the cards, Jen thought. The fact that the condo hadn't sold was a sign that she wasn't supposed to move. She was doomed to stay in her crappy life, working as an office drone and selling candles to the Alma Tuttles of the world.

She thanked Hannah, then hung up and slumped against the couch cushions. From her window she had a beautiful view of the Seattle skyline. This was really a lovely place. She hated it here!

She was still staring grumpily out the window when the phone rang again. This time it was her sister.

"How was the candle party?" Toni asked.

"A dud. Like my life."

"Well, that's upbeat."

"My Realtor just called. Still no bites."

"Maybe you're not meant to sell it," Toni suggested.

"Thanks," Jen said miserably.

"Maybe you're meant to rent it instead."

"Rent it?" Jen repeated. She hadn't thought of that.

"I shouldn't be doing this," her sister said. "I really hate to see you move. But at least if you rented and you didn't like it up there, you'd have someplace to come back to."

"Thanks for the vote of confidence," Jen muttered.

"Hey, it never hurts to have a plan B. Anyway, if you're interested in renting, I think I know someone who'd want your condo."

Jen bolted upright. "You do?"

"My neighbor. Her divorce became final and she's looking for a place where she can make a new start. She might even be open to renting with an option to buy if you decide you want to go that route. She works downtown, so your place would be perfect for her."

"Does she have a house to sell?" That would take time. Jen knew this now, from personal experience.

"No, she and her ex were renting."

"So, if she liked the condo she could move in right away."

"Probably," Toni agreed. "Should I give her your number?"

"Absolutely!" If the place didn't sell, she'd have someone who could make her payments. That would get her out from under just as well as a sale. Yes! This was a sign. She was meant to move.

The aroma of burning cookie wafted to where she sat and she remembered she was baking. She dashed to the kitchen, phone in hand and, propping the phone between her ear and shoulder, put on her oven mitt and opened the oven. A plume of smoke wafted out to greet her, stinging her eyes and making her cough. She pulled out the cookie sheet with her blackened ginger-bread boys. Eeew.

A moment later the smoke alarm went off.

"What's happening?" Toni asked.

"I burned my cookies. I've got to go."

"Okay. Try not to burn down the condo before you get it rented," Toni teased, and hung up.

Jen grabbed a towel and flapped it in the direction of the smoke detector, all the while scolding herself for forgetting to set the timer. Finally, the noise subsided. "Well, you guys are history," she informed the ruined cookies.

Maybe, if she was lucky, her life here would soon be history, too.

Chapter Six

Taking a hard look at the changes we need to make can be harder than actually making those changes.

—Muriel Sterling, author of *Simplicity*

Toni loved Christmas Eve. It was the one occasion when she could count on seeing her extended family. They all poured into her mother's house in West Seattle—grandparents, aunts and uncles, cousins, second cousins. Even Santa (her crazy uncle Dave) made an appearance, and everyone got to sit on his lap and receive a present.

"Do I have to have my picture taken with Santa this year?" Jordan demanded as Wayne parked their SUV in front of the house.

"Of course you do," Toni said. "We all do."

"Dumb," Jordan muttered.

"If you want a present you'll have to be dumb," Toni said.

"The present'll probably be dumb, too."

She hadn't complained about last year's present—the world's largest collection of lip gloss. And Toni knew for a fact that this year Aunt Jana had gotten Jordan an iTunes gift card. "If you're going to be a party pooper, then I'll sit on Santa's lap and take your present. I know what it is."

That worked. "I'll do it," her daughter said, but she managed to sound grudging all the same.

Toni hid her smile. It was never good to gloat when you won a victory over a child, especially one who was now officially a teenager.

"Me, too," said Jeffrey, who wasn't above a little humiliation if there was a present waiting at the end of it.

As always, her mother's house said Christmas, with icicle lights hanging from the roofline and a wreath on the door. Toni could hear raucous laughter and Christmas music even before they let themselves in.

They hung their coats in the hall closet and then went into the living room where Toni's uncle Dennis was saying, "No, I swear it's true."

That explained the laughter. Her uncle had told some preposterous story. At the sight of her and her family, he broke into a grin. "Well, look who's here." He demanded hugs from both kids, told Jordan she was getting way too pretty and then enveloped Toni in a big bear hug. Uncle Dennis was a large man and his hugs were almost suffocating, but, next to her father's, they were the best.

"Guess you got stuck with us again this year," he greeted her husband.

"Afraid so," Wayne said with a smile, shaking her uncle's hand.

"Hello, princess," her father greeted her. He kissed her forehead and took in her slacks, black sweater and jauntily draped red scarf. "You're looking lovely today."

"Thanks, Daddy," she said. Nice someone noticed. Wayne sure hadn't. He'd been too busy being one with his computer.

Okay, she told herself, *so what if Wayne didn't notice your outfit? Big deal. He's still a good man who works hard to provide for his family. The computer is not your competition.*

Although sometimes she felt as if it were. Even when he wasn't working, he was on it half the evening, surfing the web. He always had energy for the computer, but when his wife wanted to go out…

Oh, there she went again. It wasn't Wayne's fault he'd gotten sick the day they were supposed to have their romantic dinner. She'd come home from her Icicle Falls adventure to find he'd taken some cold medicine and gone to bed.

And fallen asleep with his arms around his iPad. Sheesh.

Stop it, she scolded herself. *It's Christmas. Don't be a bitch.*

She deposited her gifts under the tree and went to the kitchen to check in with her mother. Her aunt Karen, resplendent in a Christmas sweater with dancing polar bears, gave her a kiss in passing as she took the standing rib roast out to the dining table. Aunt Aggie, her favorite aunt, hugged her and popped an olive in her mouth, then followed Aunt Karen out, bearing a divided glass bowl filled with olives and pickles in one hand and a pitcher of milk in the other. Over at the sink, Jen was whipping cream for the night's big dessert—mint chocolate sundaes, with Christmas cookies—and called a cheery hello.

Toni felt a momentary twinge of guilt. She was usu-

ally the one helping in the kitchen. If they'd gotten out
of the house on time, she would've been, but Wayne
had found it necessary to work and was still sending emails long past four, when they would normally
have left.

"It's Christmas Eve," she'd reminded him—
repeatedly.

"I know," he'd said, "and most of us have to work
the day of Christmas Eve."

Okay, she'd thought, *but you'd better not be working on Christmas.*

She made the rounds, hugging everyone. "Sorry
I'm late."

"You're not late. You're right on time," her mother
assured her, offering her cheek for a kiss.

"What can I do?"

"I think we've got it all under control," Mom said.

But she *always* helped. She couldn't just do…
nothing.

As if reading her mind, her mother added, "How
about dishing up the mashed potatoes?" She pulled
the gravy pan off the burner. "Gravy's done. You can
dish that up, too. Then I'll take out the roasted vegetables and the seafood lasagna and we'll be good to go."

In a matter of minutes the food was on the table.
The revelers were summoned and everyone gathered
around and waited for her father to say grace.

"Well," he said, smiling at each of them, "here we
are, all together for another Christmas. Some of us
have faced challenges this past year."

Toni smiled encouragingly at her cousin Jimmy,
who'd lost his job three months earlier and was still
looking for employment. She glanced over at Aunt

Aggie, wearing what she called her half-and-half bra—
one half held a real breast, the other a prosthetic breast
form. Toni felt the prickle of tears as she took in the
smiling faces around the table. All these people were
so precious to her.

Her gaze drifted to where her children were sitting.
Her sweet babies. They were growing up so quickly.
They were...texting!

Well, one of them was.

"Let's pray," said Dad.

They all bowed their heads. Except the texting cul-
prit. And Toni, who was now shooting daggers at her
daughter.

"Dear God, we're so glad we can be together at this
wonderful time of year."

There was one "we" who wasn't exactly together
with everyone else. Toni stepped out of the circle and
began to move to where her daughter stood.

"Thank you for each one here," Dad continued.

*One of them may not be here much longer because
I'm going to throttle her.*

"And thank you for the joy of the season."

And for texting. Someone's joy was about to come
to an end. Toni slipped behind her daughter, reached
over Jordan's shoulder and snatched her cell phone.

Jordan gave a start. This was followed by a guilty
look over her shoulder, almost penitent, until she realized it was Mother the Enemy taking away her phone.
Then she scowled.

"Close your eyes," Toni hissed.

Jordan closed her eyes and clamped her lips into a
thin, angry line.

"May we always remember to be thankful for our blessings and thankful for one another."

Toni doubted her daughter was sending up prayers of thanks for her right now.

"In the name of our Lord, Amen," Dad concluded. "And in the words of Tiny Tim, God bless us, every one."

"Amen," everyone echoed.

"Amen," Toni said, and smiled sweetly at her pouting daughter.

"Can I have my phone back?" Jordan demanded.

"Yes, once you've remembered how to respect the people you're with."

Anyone seeing the expression on Jordan's face would have assumed she'd gotten horrible news that the Grinch had kidnapped Justin Bieber. "Mom!"

"Sorry, sweetie," Toni said sternly, "we're here to be with our family."

Jordan hurled herself into her chair and glared at her plate, and Toni returned to her seat at the table, her holiday spirit as good as smothered. Christmas was supposed to about togetherness. Even if children got sucked into their phones and their games during the rest of the year, this one day should be a time of interacting face-to-face with the people in their lives.

And, of course, her daughter would so want to interact with her now. Her mother, who was seated next to her at the end of the table, gave her arm a pat. Naturally Mom had seen. Heck, all sixteen people squeezed around the long table (plus the little ones at the kids' table) had seen that lovely mother-daughter moment.

Jen shot her a sympathetic look from across the table.

"This, too, shall pass," Mom whispered, and handed her the basket of French bread slices.

Jordan made a concentrated effort to enjoy her misery for the rest of the evening. She pouted through dinner and, later, refused to sit with Santa.

"That's okay, little girl. I know your mama told you never to talk to strangers," joked Santa, aka Uncle David.

"You're strange, all right," cracked Uncle Dennis.

Their comic interchange lightened the moment, and the party went on without Jordan, everyone playing Dirty Santa, a game that involved stealing presents back and forth, and singing Christmas carols while she sat in a corner like a miniature Scrooge in drag.

"What's wrong with Jordan?" Wayne asked as the family indulged in a raucous debate over whether or not angels could actually sing, as the old Christmas carol suggested.

"She's mad," Toni replied.

"I can see that. Why?"

"You didn't catch that little scene at dinner?"

"I saw her acting like a stinker."

"I took away her phone."

"Whoa. You cut off her lifeline."

"She was texting during grace."

Wayne frowned. "Oh."

"Yeah, oh. I think she can live without her phone for a few days."

"That'll be a merry Christmas," Wayne predicted.

Sure enough, as soon as they were out the door and going down the walk, the fun began as Jordan demanded the return of her phone.

"You can have it back after we're done with Christmas."

"What!"

"It won't hurt you to spend some face time with people."

"That's not fair!"

"Well, you know, it wasn't exactly fair to be texting while Grandpa was saying grace," Toni said. "In fact, it was downright rude."

"I was just finishing telling Sarah something."

"Good. And now you're finished telling her something until after our family Christmas tomorrow."

"I hate you," Jordan grumbled.

Ah, the power children had to hurt their parents with their careless anger. Not for the first time, Toni remembered every mean and snippy word she'd hurled at her own mother when she was a girl. *What goes around comes around,* she thought sadly.

"Yes, I know," she said to her daughter. "But I love you."

And maybe come Christmas morning, when Jordan found the American Eagle handbag she'd been drooling over, along with the clothes from Abercrombie & Fitch, she'd have dialed down the emotion from hate to strong dislike.

Meanwhile, next to Jordan, Jeffrey sat happily playing on his Gameboy.

"How come he gets to have his Gameboy?" Jordan asked petulantly.

"Because he wasn't playing during grace," Toni said.

"*And* I sat on Santa's lap," Jeffrey added.

"Of course you would," Jordan said scornfully. "You're just a kid."

Toni decided it would be useless to point out that the two older teens who'd been there hadn't had a problem posing with Santa in exchange for a goody. Even the grownups had all taken a turn, pulling on his fake beard or poking him in his pillow-stuffed tummy, and several of the women had posed kissing him on the cheek, including Toni.

It really had been a fun evening, enjoyed by everyone except one surly thirteen-year-old. Once Toni had decided to ignore both her daughter and her own irritation, she'd had a good time, too. She hoped she'd be able to enjoy Christmas Day, although she knew her daughter would do her level best to ensure she didn't.

Sure enough, Jordan woke on the grumpy side of the bed and stayed grumpy all through the morning's present-opening, as well as Christmas brunch. She was barely polite when they went to visit Wayne's family that afternoon.

"You know, if you keep up this bad attitude, you won't be getting your phone back until New Year's," Toni warned as they drove home.

"Well, it's not fair."

"We've already had this conversation. You need to think about how it makes the people who love you feel when you can't be bothered to look up from your cellular attachment and talk to them or even listen respectfully when they're saying grace. Maybe next time you want to tell Dad or me something important, we should just ignore you."

Jordan fell silent, and in the dark car, Toni couldn't

tell if she was seething or actually considering what her mother had said. Probably the former.

Once home, both her children vanished to their rooms, Jeffrey in his normal happy mood, Jordan subdued and serious.

"Do you think anything I said got through to her?" Toni asked Wayne.

"Oh, yeah. It's submerged somewhere in her brain and should surface in about ten years."

"Thanks."

He kissed her. "Hey, we still have to get through her learning to drive."

There was a scary thought. "And dating."

"Oh, God, I need a drink," Wayne said.

He helped himself to a beer, and then, just as she was about to suggest they put the fireplace to work and snuggle up and listen to some Christmas music, he pulled out his laptop. "Oh, no, not you, too," she groaned.

He looked at her, perplexed. "What?"

She shook her head and reached for the TV remote. "Never mind."

Whatever happened to the good old days when people spent time cuddled up with each other instead of their techno toys? *Hey, Santa, in the new year, do you think you could give me back my family?*

Christmas in the Thomas household had been perfect. Stacy had done everything possible to make sure the kids enjoyed their visit home—baking their favorite treats, putting her espresso maker to work making eggnog lattes for everyone each morning, playing

Christmas music, hauling out all their favorite holiday movies.

It had been late afternoon the day Autumn arrived and she'd taken in the lit tree and the glowing candles on the mantel with a happy smile. "It's so good to be home," she'd said, and hugged Stacy.

Ethan had been more interested in the aroma of melted chocolate wafting from the kitchen, but his girlfriend had been seriously impressed. "Gosh," she said, "everything's so…Christmassy."

"I told you, it looks like a department store in here," Ethan had said to her.

Stacy hadn't been so sure that was a compliment but she'd let it pass.

She'd found it harder to ignore his lack of enthusiasm for the Christmas surprise she'd set under the tree for him. His girlfriend had been delighted with her Target and Gap gift certificates, but Ethan had left his latte maker behind.

"I can just go to Starbucks," he'd informed Stacy when she saw he was leaving home without it. "Hang on to it, Mom."

Autumn had made the same request regarding the Victorian village starter kit Stacy had given her—a snow-frosted house and an old-fashioned church complete with stained-glass windows. Of course, Stacy had expected that. She'd known she'd end up storing the decorations until Autumn graduated from college and had her own place.

Still, graduation was only three and a half years away so the time to start was now. Stacy had gone out the day after Christmas and purchased more on sale to tuck away for next year. There was so much to get when you were building a village—houses, shops, trees, old-fashioned streetlamps, people, little gates and fountains and snowmen.

Stacy frowned as she looked at her own village. It was fun to put out but such a pain to put away. It was now New Year's Day, the day she always took down her decorations. Dean had promised to help her, but he'd gotten lured next door to watch a football game and, rather than wait for him, she decided she'd get started on this year's disappearing act on her own. By the time Dean got home, she'd have everything packed and ready for its return to the attic.

She went up there to fetch the boxes for her treasures. The sea of containers stretching across the floor made her sigh. This was going to take all day.

Oh, well. That was the price you paid when you had a lot of decorations. And a lot of decorations was the price you paid to set the scene for a happy family Christmas. When everything looked festive, everyone felt festive. She grabbed a couple of boxes and climbed back down the stairs. Why was it so much less fun putting things away than it was putting them up?

Several trips later, she was ready to begin stowing her treasures. She picked up a ceramic Santa. This little guy had sat on the dining room buffet when she was growing up, and her mother had given him to Stacy for her first Christmas with Dean. It was vintage, possibly valuable. She wrapped it in bubble wrap and stowed it carefully in the box.

She lifted a second Santa from the herd of Clauses. She and her mom and older sister had met in Seattle and hit the postholiday sales together three years back, and her sister had insisted on purchasing the little guy for her. She blinked back tears as she remembered her sister. Sue had died suddenly from an aneurysm ten years ago. This little guy got protected with two sheets of bubble wrap.

A third Santa was one Dean had bought for their tenth Christmas, back in the days when he didn't complain about all her "stuff." She had the accompanying note he'd written in her scrapbook. "I'll always be grateful to the old guy for bringing us together," he'd written, alluding to when they'd first met at a friend's Christmas party.

Yes, Christmas was special. And all these little mementos served to remind her of it. Obviously, they didn't serve the same purpose for her husband. Well, he was a man. There were some things men simply didn't get.

She worked for the next two hours, packing away both her decorations and her memories. By the time she was done, the living room looked positively naked. *It won't be once you get your other decorations back up,* she reminded herself. That in itself was a daunting job.

But not nearly as daunting as hauling these decorations back up to the attic. She wished Dean would come home. It would be nice to get this done.

So why wait? She wasn't helpless. She could take all this to the attic herself, and be spared listening to any complaining.

Stacy picked up the box containing the nativity set and went upstairs. She left it in the hallway under the trapdoor to the attic and returned to the family room for another load. Upstairs went the candles, then the tree decorations, followed by the long, heavy box containing the tree.

They were followed by many more boxes. Dean *had* been right. A person could drop dead lugging all of this around. Of course, she'd never admit that to him. He'd see it as some sort of capitulation and be ready to take everything away—to the dump.

Once all the boxes were stacked in the upstairs hall, the next step was to take her treasures to the attic. She pulled the chain to the trapdoor and let down the ladder. "You're almost done now," she told herself.

After lugging four cartons up to the attic, she realized she needed to work smarter, not harder. Rather than go all the way up the stairs and cross the attic to deposit each box separately, she'd be better off climbing the ladder and piling them nearby. Then, once they were all up there, she could arrange them as she wanted.

This plan worked really well until she decided to pile one box on top of another...while holding a plastic garbage bag filled with a stuffed Santa, his sleigh and reindeer. Somehow—who knew how these things happened?—she lost her balance. Santa went flying and she dropped the box. She missed her grab for the stairs and tumbled backward, tipping over the remaining pile of boxes as she went. She landed on the bag containing her Christmas quilt, giving herself a nice, soft landing. And she provided an equally soft landing for the boxes of decorations. One whacked her in the head and another landed on her middle. Both spilled their contents, surrounding her with Santas and candles. Ho, ho, ho.

Groaning, she clambered out from under the wreckage and assessed the damage. Other than a twinge in her back and a smarting head she was okay. And it looked as if the Santas had all survived. Except… Oh, no. There lay the newest member of the Claus family, decapitated.

It took some searching among the tissue paper and bubble wrap to find Santa's missing head, but she did. She packed up the others, carefully inspecting them to see that they were well wrapped, but set him aside. Dean would say, "It's broken. Why keep it?" But Dean didn't get that a treasure was still a treasure, even if it got broken. A little glue and Santa would be fine.

Back up the ladder she went, now taking one box at a time. For a millisecond she entertained the thought that maybe her husband was right and they didn't need quite so many decorations, that perhaps Muriel Sterling's book on simplifying one's life might actually make a valid point.

But only for a millisecond. Treasures equaled memories, and memories were priceless. And if it took some work storing hers, so what? One day her family would thank her for all the trouble she'd taken to surround them with pretty things.

And one day her son would actually want that latte maker.

Wouldn't he?

Chapter Seven

A new beginning is also a new adventure.
        —Muriel Sterling, author of *Simplicity*

Everything had worked out. Jen had been able to rent her condo in Seattle for enough to cover her mortgage and most of her rent. Now, the first weekend in January, she was moving into her charming mountain cottage with the help of her sister and family.

She'd nearly put dents in the steering wheel driving up the mountain in the snow, but once Wayne had gotten the chains on her tires she'd been able to relax a little. As they neared town, the roads weren't bad, and he had taken the chains off again. That had been enough to make Jen hyperventilate until Wayne pointed out that the roads had been cleared and they were now all level. This, she had to admit, was a nice improvement over Seattle, which was a city of hills.

Still, she breathed a sigh of relief when they made it to the cottage in one piece. Garrett Armstrong met them there with the key and offered to help unload. He was just as gorgeous as she remembered, and obviously kindhearted. It would be so easy to fall for this man.

"That's awfully nice of you," she told him.

"No problem," he said, shrugging off her praise.

Now Jeffrey had bounded out of his parents' SUV, which had been stuffed to the roof with boxes. "Can we go tubing?"

"Maybe after we're done unloading everything," his father told him.

As Jen was making introductions, Jeffrey picked up a handful of snow, made a snowball and hurled it at his sister, who was standing huddled inside her coat, waiting for her father to open the small trailer they'd been pulling.

It hit her in the chest and she snarled, "Cut it out, you butt."

Of course, being a boy, Jeffrey ignored her request and started forming another snowball. And that was enough to make Jordan forget she was now officially a sophisticated teen girl and start doing the same. "Come on, Aunt Jen, help me."

Well, why not?

"Okay, five-minute fight," Toni said, heading for the cottage with a box. "Then we're going to get the work done."

Jen was happy to join in and release the last of the tension from her scary trip up the mountain. She'd just stuffed a ton of snow down Jeffrey's back when she realized she was the only grown-up playing. Toni was inside the cottage, probably stowing things away in the kitchen cupboards where Jen would never find them, and Wayne, who'd tossed a few snowballs, was now pulling a box out of the trailer.

"Okay, I've got to go work now," she told the kids and herself.

"Aw, come on, Aunt Jen," Jeffrey pleaded.

"Sorry, guys," she said, and went to open the trunk of her car.

She stepped inside with her load in time to hear Toni asking Garrett, "You don't like snowball fights?"

"Not when there's work to be done."

She felt her cheeks heating. Way to make a good impression on a gorgeous man. Now she looked like a slacker. But she felt so much better. Just a few minutes of fun had reenergized her.

"Work is important," she said as she set a box of food on the counter, "but sometimes you need to take a break and get in touch with your inner child." The expression was kind of lame, she supposed, but as hard as she'd been working, she deserved a break.

Garrett said nothing to that, which made her feel mildly chastised. And that made her feel mildly irritated. This guy didn't know her. Was he making some sort of snap judgment about her? If so, he needed a life.

"I think the kids have had enough of a break," Toni said, and went outside to order the troops back to work.

"So, when was the last time you had a snowball fight?" she asked Garrett as he walked out the door.

He paused for a moment, then shook his head. "Can't remember."

"Me, neither," she said, but he was already on his way down the porch steps and obviously hadn't heard her.

Jen had asked Garrett to remove the ratty twin beds and the offensive living room furniture that had originally been in the cottage so she could use her own furniture. All that was left of the old stuff was the kitchen table, which she figured she could dress up with a cute tablecloth.

Now he and Wayne unloaded her white leather couch. Ah, couch, sweet couch. She had them put it down at an angle so she could sit on it and simultaneously gaze out the window and enjoy a fire in the woodstove. She smiled, pleased with how it looked. This cottage was going to be her little corner of heaven on earth.

Toni had packed food for the day, including hot cocoa mix, and she set about heating water while Jen put her perishables in the fridge.

Meanwhile, the guys had returned with more boxes. "It's starting to snow," Wayne announced. "Jen, you're going to have to learn to ski."

"With no job I can't afford to take that up," she said. She saw her landlord frowning, probably wondering why he was renting to a woman who was unemployed.

Sure enough. "I assumed you had a job lined up here."

"I'm going to find one," Jen assured him. "But if you're concerned about how I'm going to pay the rent…"

"The thought had crossed my mind."

"As I mentioned when you called, I've got my place in Seattle rented. That'll cover what I owe you."

Well, almost. Thanks to the Christmas money her parents had given her, she'd be fine for a while, but she'd have to get something part-time to make up the difference. Money also came in pretty handy if you wanted to eat. She was confident that wouldn't be a problem, though. As soon as she'd settled in, she'd call the shops where she'd seen those help-wanted signs.

He nodded, taking in what she'd told him. He still wasn't exactly smiling in approval.

"Don't worry. I'm not a deadbeat. I'll pay my rent," she said with a smile.

He just nodded and went outside to fetch more boxes.

Jen watched him go and frowned. "He thinks I'm a flake."

"Wait till he spends a little more time with you. Then he'll *know* you're a flake," Toni teased.

"There is nothing flaky about getting your priorities straight," Jen muttered. "Anyway, I've got enough money to tide me over for a little while." A very little while. Maybe she should've lined up a job before moving here.

The men were back in the cottage now. "This is the last of it," Wayne said.

Jeffrey came in behind them and dropped a bag of towels on the living room floor. "I'm hungry. When can we eat?"

"Right now," Jen replied. "We've got plenty of sandwiches," she told Garrett. "I hope you'll stay for something to eat."

"I've got to get going, but thanks for the offer," he said. "You've got my cell number. If you need anything, call."

"How about if I *want* something?" Jen teased. *Like you.*

He smiled but didn't look comfortable doing so. "You'll meet lots of people who can help you find what you want in Icicle Falls."

There must've been some clever remark she could use. Too bad she couldn't come up with one. Instead, she smiled. "Thanks again for helping."

"No problem." He shook hands with Wayne, waved farewell to Jen and Toni and then took off.

"That man is so gorgeous," Toni said as Garrett trotted down the steps.

Wayne turned and frowned at her. "Hey, do you mind not drooling over other men in front of your husband? That could give a man a complex."

Not that Wayne was lacking in the looks department. He was a little overweight, but he had a nice face, and blue eyes, which he'd passed on to both of his children.

Toni shot her sister a grin. "It pays to keep 'em on their toes," she joked.

But Jen knew she hadn't been joking about Garrett. He truly was an eyeful—in a good way.

After lunch the kids convinced their dad that they needed to do some serious tubing on Snow Hill, and they left the sisters on their own to set about putting the kitchen to rights. "You know," Toni said as they worked, "I thought you were nuts to move up here."

"I know you did." Garrett Armstrong seemed to be thinking the same thing.

"But I can see why you did. You're getting to completely reinvent yourself." Toni gestured to the snowy scene outside the cabin window. "And you've picked a beautiful place to do it. There's something about leaving the city behind. And I swear, my family's had more interaction in one day than we've had at home in the past six months." She glanced around with a half smile. "This place is a dump but there's something kind of retro and homey about it."

Yes, there was. "You know what we need now? We

need a fire in the woodstove. That'll make it really cozy," Jen decided.

"Great idea," her sister said.

Garrett had kindly left some wood and a small amount of kindling in a metal basket by the stove. Jen grabbed some of the newspapers they'd used for packing. She hadn't had a ton of experience making fires, other than one time at camp. Whenever their family went to the beach, her father had always been in charge of building the bonfire. But she'd watched. She remembered what to do. First you laid down paper and kindling to get the fire going. You set a match to that and then when you had a nice flame you put in a bigger piece of wood.

The stove door screeched in protest as she opened it.

"That obviously hasn't been used in a while," Toni said. "It is safe, isn't it?"

"Of course it is. Otherwise, it wouldn't be in here," Jen replied.

She crumpled the papers, added the kindling and then searched for matches, which she found in an old coffee can. "All right. Here we go," she said as she held the match to the paper. "Now it's going to be really cozy."

"Did you open the damper?"

"The damper?" Jen looked at the stove. Why was that smoke curling out from around the door?

"You have to open the damper," Toni said.

Jen examined the stove. The smoke began to come at her more aggressively. "Where is it?"

"Down below," Toni said, and rushed over. She pushed in a rod at the bottom of the stove.

But there was still so much smoke. "That can't be

right," Jen said. "You just told me you have to pull it out," she added, and pulled the rod back out.

"I said you have to *open* it. Get the door," Toni commanded, and pushed it in again.

"It's still smoky," Jen wailed as she threw open the front door. Her eyes were starting to sting.

"It's going to take a minute," Toni said, and coughed.

"That *can't* be right," Jen said again, and pulled the rod out once more. More smoke billowed up at her. In or out, the stupid thing didn't seem to be working. Coughing, she ran to the kitchen counter and got her cell phone, quickly dialing her new landlord. In spite of the open door the room was filling with smoke and now the smoke detector was going off.

"Hello?" he said.

"Garrett, I'm sorry to bother you but—"

"What's that noise? Is that the smoke detector?"

"Yes, I'm afraid we're having a little trouble—"

"I'll be right there," he said, and ended the call before she could finish.

Meanwhile, her sister had pushed the rod in again. "We had this same stove in the old house. I wish you'd listen to me."

"Well, you could've said that," Jen retorted, waving her arms at the cloud around her head.

"Get your towels," Toni commanded. "Let's try to fan some of this smoke out."

Jen pulled two towels from the bag and they set to work. "So much for my cozy fire," she groaned. "Now it's going to be freezing in here."

"Better cold than dying from smoke inhalation," Toni said.

A truck pulled up in front of the cabin, spewing

snow in all directions. Garrett Amstrong burst out of the cab and came flying up the stairs.

"What happened?" he asked, racing to the wood-stove.

"We couldn't figure out which way the damper opened," Jen explained.

He inspected it and stood up. "You've got it right now," he hollered over the smoke detector. "Got a broom?"

"A broom?" Jen repeated.

Toni dashed to the kitchen and seized the broom from the corner where Jen had propped it and handed it over. He began waving it in front of the smoke detector, which was hanging toward the top of the opposite wall. At last the thing settled down.

"That's great," Jen said. "Thank you."

"You'll want to open the back door," he said as he threw open the living-room window.

Jen nodded and hurried to the back of the cabin to open that door. What kind of idiot tried to turn herself into a smoked ham the first day in her new home? "I'm sorry," she said as she returned down the hall.

"It's okay," he said, but from the expression on his face she could tell he was wondering whether he'd rented to a total dingbat. "For future reference, always check the damper before you start a fire." He pointed to the rod. "Make sure this is in."

Jen nodded, refusing to look in her sister's direction. Toni wouldn't exactly gloat, but she'd have that I-told-you-so frown on her face.

"Don't burn anything waxy in there," he continued, "and don't burn cardboard. Don't use any liquid, like barbecue starter fluid."

"I won't," Jen promised. "This won't happen again."

"You'd be surprised how easily problems can happen," he said sternly. "Heating fires account for thirty-six percent of residential home fires in rural areas every year."

"Oh, my," Jen said weakly. "How do you know all that?"

"I'm a firefighter."

"Here?" she asked. *No, on the moon. Duh.*

He nodded. "Be careful. I'd hate to have to come out here with my fire truck."

Don't make me bring my fire truck. "I will," Jen said. She felt about ten years old. "Sorry we bothered you."

He gave the broom to Jen. "No bother," he said, but she wasn't sure he meant it.

"Thanks again," she said as he turned for the door.

"A firefighter," her sister said as he drove off. "That man just gets sexier and sexier."

Yes, he did.

The smoke eventually vanished, and by the time Wayne and the kids returned, the cottage was almost back to normal. Jeffrey sniffed as they walked in. "It stinks in here."

"Not half as bad as it did," Toni told him.

A scented candle, a proper fire crackling in the woodstove, along with popcorn, hot chocolate and a board game added up to a perfect family evening.

The snow was falling gently the next day when Toni and her family left and Jen treated herself to a walk in the woods. The air up here was so fresh. The snow was so beautiful. And it was so quiet, so peaceful. Oh, yes, she was going to love it here.

* * *

Jen was going to go crazy if she spent another day in this place. After four days stuck in her cozy cottage, she was ready to pull out her hair. It was just her and the trees. And the snow. The white stuff was everywhere—on the deck, on the ground, on her car. On the road. In the driveway.

What did it say about her that she wasn't adapting to this new life she'd been dying for only a few weeks ago? She'd read two novels, watched six movies and baked two batches of cookies. And on day four she'd thrown Muriel Sterling's stupid book against the wall.

She was all for living the simple life but she didn't want to live it all by herself, for crying out loud. She was ready to get out, see people, oh, and get groceries. At the rate she was going, she'd to starve here. All by herself. Well, okay, after all the cookies she'd consumed she had five new pounds of fat to live on, but still.

She also needed to network, and the sooner, the better. In between the baking and reading and movie-watching, she'd called about both of the help-wanted signs she'd seen in those shop windows only to learn the positions had been filled. Her sister was right (as usual); she should've lined something up before she moved. Jumping and assuming a net would appear had been stupid.

But she was determined not to go splat. Someone in this town *had* to need help. And the only way she was going to find out was to go and meet those someones.

She looked out the window at the falling snow and gnawed her lip. *You don't know how to drive in snow,* she reminded herself. Except she was living in the mountains now. That meant if she wanted fripperies such as groceries, she had to learn to drive in the stuff.

She had snow tires and the ground was level. And she'd gotten here in one piece, hadn't she? It was ridiculous to be such a sissy. She could drive in the snow if she set her mind to it. She just had to take it slow. She could handle that.

Filled with determination, she marched to the little closet where she kept her coat and pulled it out, along with her gloves and scarf. Darn it all, she was going to town.

Once on the front porch she hesitated. More of the white stuff had fallen since Wayne and Jeffrey had shoveled her driveway before leaving, and it was buried under a fresh ten inches. But she was sure the main roads had been cleared. Nonetheless, she took a hike to see. Yep. If she could just get out of her driveway she'd be fine. It was now or never.

She returned home and got the handy-dandy snow shovel she'd found in the shed behind the cottage, then spent forty-five minutes making a path to the road. Then she got in the car and edged it forward.

Holding her breath, she inched out onto the road. The snowplows had come through earlier, but enough snow had accumulated since then to crunch under her tires and make her heart rate increase. She slowly made her way along Juniper Ridge and finally turned onto Icicle Road, one of the main roads into town.

She white-knuckled it for the first five minutes, moving at a sluggish pace, but once she realized she wasn't spinning wildly out of control she began to relax. Okay, driving in the snow wasn't really so hard. She could do this.

By the time she got to town she was exultant. Yes, she was going to be fine living here in the mountains.

Her first stop was the grocery store where she stocked up on essentials—bread, eggs, cheese, rotisserie chicken, hot chocolate mix and eggnog (which was on sale now that the holidays were over). Two older women smiled at her, the guy working in the produce department flirted with her and the checker, after hearing she was new in town, gave her a hearty welcome, along with a quick rundown on some of the town's amenities.

Herman's Hamburgers was the place to go for the best fries in town. Zelda's was the number-one hangout for single women on a Friday night. The Red Barn was where everyone went dancing on Saturdays. Of course, for her chocolate supply she needed to frequent the Sweet Dreams gift shop. If she wanted fabulous baked goodies the top choice was Gingerbread Haus. For gossip and girl time, it was Bavarian Brews and for books either the library or Mountain Escape Books. There was always something happening at the bookstore, and they sponsored several book clubs.

A book club sounded like a great way to keep up with new reads and meet some other Icicle Falls residents. Jen decided to stop at the bookstore on her way out of town.

Mountain Escape Books wasn't the world's largest bookstore, but it sure felt like the homiest. In the children's corner several preschoolers sat on colored carpet squares, spellbound, while an employee read from the latest picture book by George Shannon. A gray-haired man stood visiting with a statuesque redhead behind the counter who looked to be around Jen's mother's age. She saw a retired couple in the nonfiction section, checking out a travel book while nursing lattes, probably from Bavarian Brews, which Jen had heard about earlier. Three women stood chatting in the fiction section. One was blonde and slightly overweight. She seemed to be in her midforties. The woman next to her was tall with long, chestnut-colored hair. She wore jeans, stylish boots and a great red coat. Jen guessed her age to be somewhere in the late thirties. The third woman was Jen's age, maybe younger, with brown hair and big, brown eyes. And a friendly smile.

Jen sidled closer and eavesdropped shamelessly.

"I just finished the book," the well-dressed woman was saying. "I think there's a lot in there. I hope I can figure out how to apply all of Muriel's advice to my crazy life."

Book…Muriel? As in Muriel Sterling? Could they be talking about the book that had inspired Jen to move?

"Well, I sure got a lot out of the chapter on time management," said the woman Jen's age. She saw Jen and offered a friendly smile. "Hi, can I help you?"

So she worked here. "Sorry, I didn't mean to eavesdrop." Well, actually, she had. "I'm new in town."

"A new Icicle!" the fortysomething woman exclaimed. "Welcome."

"Thanks," Jen said "Uh, what's an Icicle?"

"An Icicle Falls resident," said the woman. "My name's Stacy Thomas and this is Charlene Albach."

"Charley to my friends." The well-dressed woman held out a hand for Jen to shake. "I own Zelda's, one of the restaurants here in town."

"The checker at Safeway was telling me about your place. It sounds great."

Charley beamed. "It is."

"And this is Juliet Gerard," Stacy said.

"I work part-time here at the store," Juliet added.

This sparked a conversation about the bookstore and books in general.

"That one you were talking about," Jen said, "is it, by any chance, *Simplicity* by Muriel Sterling?"

Stacy nodded. "It's our book club pick for this month. Have you read it?"

"I have. In fact, that book inspired me to simplify my life and move here."

Stacy blinked. "You just up and moved?"

Okay, did she sound totally wacky? "Well, I only moved here from Seattle. It wasn't that far."

"I'm impressed," Juliet said in awe.

"Where are you staying?"

"I rented a cottage on Juniper Ridge."

"It's nice out there," Stacy said. "I still can't believe you just *moved* here after reading that book."

"You need to come to our book-club meeting," Juliet told her. "We'd love to talk to someone who's putting what's in the book into practice."

"Gosh, I don't want to crash your group." What was she saying? Yes, she did. She wanted her simple life to include more than trees, snow and silence 24/7.

"You won't be," Juliet assured her. "Come check us out. You might like us."

She already did.

The other two women also urged her to come, so, after pretending to consider for a decent amount of time, she agreed and got Stacy's phone number and address. Then Juliet recommended a couple of good reads and she walked out carrying two romance novels and wearing a big grin. She was going to love it here.

The grin faded once she left the quaint downtown area. The snow had been falling aggressively while she ran her errands and visited in the bookstore and she swerved as she turned onto Icicle Road. Oh, this was not good.

It's all flat, she reminded herself. *And you only have one more turn onto Juniper Ridge. You can do this.*

She gripped the steering wheel firmly and took a deep, calming breath. *You can do it, you can do it, you can do it.*

When an SUV zipped up from behind and passed her, she frowned and gripped the steering wheel harder. Of course, she was going to irritate the more experienced drivers, creeping along like this. But better to irritate people than to lose control of her car and hit them, she reasoned.

The car skated down the road with no problem and she let out her breath. Okay, all was well. She'd be home before dark. Boy, that was like something a little old lady would say. She had to stop being such a wimp if she planned to live here. She decided to go a tiny bit faster simply to prove she could. Nothing awful happened. The car kept moving straight ahead. *There. See? Driving in the snow isn't that hard. You knew you could handle it and you were right.*

Anyway, other than that one vehicle, there was no one out here. She had the whole road to herself.

Except…what was this bounding out onto the road? Oh, no! A deer!

She hit the brakes and the car went into a slide.

The deer raced off into the woods and Jen veered toward the other lane going sideways. *Oh, no! Oh, oh, no! Turn into the spin, turn into the spin.* Which way was she spinning?

And what was this coming from the other direction? *Noooo.*

Chapter Eight

Relationships don't have to be complicated.
—Muriel Sterling, author of *Simplicity*

Garrett had joined the Icicle Falls Fire Department for two reasons. First, he'd wanted to help people. Second, he'd wanted a job that provided some excitement. Firefighting met both of those requirements.

His attitude regarding excitement had changed since he'd joined the department, though. Something he'd known on a mental level quickly hit home at a gut level—one man's adventure was another's disaster. The fire that took out Zelda's restaurant had been the final tipping point for him. It was the first one he'd fought in which everything was lost, and seeing the bleak look on Charlene Albach's face as she watched her business go up in flames had been terrible. He still wanted to help people but now he hoped he never had to fight another fire. Still, living in the mountains meant there was always the danger of forest fire, which could be devastating for Icicle Falls. He prayed it never happened. Meanwhile, the favorite parts of his job were school visits and fire-safety inspections. Prevention was everything.

He'd gotten to do both on his latest twenty-four-hour shift, and he'd been in a good mood when he left the station. He'd still been in a good mood when he'd done his shopping, and when he'd picked up his son at kindergarten. But then he'd had to deliver Timmy to Ashley and that had completely eroded it.

Of course, Timmy had been excited. A weekend with Mommy was like a weekend at Pinocchio's Pleasure Island where anything went. No rules, no structure. Just fun, fun, fun. Well, as long as he didn't get into Ashley's makeup. He'd done some decorating with it the last time he stayed (discovering that lipstick was perfect for drawing on a bathroom wall) and she'd yelled at him so much he'd come home traumatized.

Now Garrett was feeling traumatized as he drove down Icicle Road. How he hated dealing with Ashley.

"I'm going to have to bring him back tomorrow morning," she'd said.

"Tomorrow?" Wait a minute. He'd had plans for the next day. He and Tilda were going to play some racquetball and go out for breakfast. And much as he didn't like Ashley's parenting style, she was still the kid's mother and ought to be able to take him for two days.

"I've got plans," she'd said.

"Yeah? Well, so do I."

"Then have your mother watch him." Ashley always had an easy solution that involved someone else doing her work for her.

Meanwhile, there stood Timmy, listening to every word. Garrett wasn't sure how much a five-year-old understood, but he hadn't wanted to take the chance that the kid would feel like a hot potato nobody wanted to keep.

"Okay." He'd tousled Timmy's hair. "We'll go get hamburgers at Herman's. How's that sound, dude?"

Timmy had been fine with that and responded with much jumping around and chanting "Hamburgers, hamburgers!"

Garrett had given his son a friendly guy punch on the arm. "How about you go play and let me talk to your mom for a minute."

Timmy had run cheerfully into the living room, where he'd promptly turned on the TV. God only knew what she let him watch.

Garrett had regarded his irresponsible ex-wife in disgust.

"What?" she'd said defensively.

"Plans? Seriously?"

"Hey, I have a life."

"You also have a son and you only have to take him every other weekend."

"I always take him. When have I not taken him?" she'd demanded.

He'd waved her phony indignation away and moved toward the door.

"Don't you go making me feel guilty," she'd snarled. "It wasn't my idea to have kids, remember?"

Thank God she'd at least lowered her voice. He didn't bother to respond.

If there'd really been a Santa, Garrett would have offered the old guy beer for life if he'd just haul Ashley away. But the new year had arrived and, sadly, she was still here. Garrett shook his head. He was so done with flakes.

"Did you hear that?" he said to the vision of the cute, freckled strawberry blonde who'd been occupying his mind so much lately. But he didn't care how attracted he was to Jen Heath. He wasn't going to pursue any relationship with her beyond that of landlord and tenant.

Watching her in action the day she'd moved into his place had given him a clear idea of what her personality was. All that talk of home-canned food the first day he'd met her had been nothing but a smokescreen. Here was a good-time girl who'd quit her job at the drop of a hat, who'd abandon the work of moving in to play in the snow. Some people would call that being a free spirit. He called it irresponsible. And if she didn't burn his place down it would be a miracle.

He'd seen the car up ahead coming toward him. But now he realized the car was *really* coming toward him, skidding into his lane. What crazy idiot— He turned his truck to the left and skated by the vehicle on the wrong side of the road. Daylight was fading but not so fast that he didn't get a look at the other driver, seeing the expression of terror on her face as she went past him. He also saw that it was his new tenant. He got back in his lane and eased off the road, watching in his rearview as her car skidded into the ditch.

Even though he wasn't going to get involved with her, he sure couldn't leave her there, stranded in the snow.

He climbed out of the truck and trotted over to where her car sat, nose in the ditch, its motor still running. He could hear her sobbing before he got to her door. He tapped on the window and she let out a shriek. Then she recognized him and her expression of panic morphed into one of gratitude.

She lowered the window. "I…I…"

That seemed to be all she could get out. "Turn off your engine," he instructed.

She nodded and cut the engine. She tried to talk again, this time around tears. "I thought I could drive in the snow, but…I almost hit that deer," she finished on a wail.

The deer was long gone. Garrett assessed the situation. There was no point in trying to pull her car out of the ditch. She was still too agitated to drive. "Come on, I'll give you a lift."

"But my car," she protested.

"Is not going anywhere. I'll call Swede and he can send someone to tow it back to your place."

"Swede?"

"He owns the garage in town."

She grabbed her purse and a bag from Mountain Escape Books. "I've got groceries in the trunk."

He nodded and held out his hand for her keys. As she dropped them in his palm he saw that her hand was shaking.

"I could have hit someone." Her eyes suddenly got wide. "I could have hit you!"

"Well, let's be glad you didn't."

"How am I going to live here if I can't drive in the snow?" she fretted.

He figured that was probably a rhetorical question and kept his mouth shut.

He opened the trunk and saw that her grocery bag had tipped, sending stuff every which way. A carton of eggnog lay on its side on top of the eggs. He was willing to bet several of them had broken. A plastic produce bag had spilled its contents and apples had rolled everywhere.

"My apples are going to be bruised."

"Better your apples than your body," he said.

Her lower lip began to tremble.

"It's okay," he said gently. "You're okay." He helped her gather up the food, then they walked to the truck and he called Swede's garage while she dug in her purse, muttering, "I've got my Triple-A card here somewhere."

"Don't worry," Garrett told her as she got inside the truck cab. "We'll sort it out later. Swede's easy."

It only took a couple of minutes to make arrangements for her car to be towed.

"Thanks," she said. "I don't know what I would've done if you hadn't come along."

He shrugged, glad he hadn't come along any sooner. If he had, they would have collided for certain. "No problem," he said.

He swung the truck around and she clutched at the armrest.

"Don't worry, I won't put us in a ditch," he promised. "I've driven in snow and ice all my life."

She still hung on until they'd straightened out. Then she slowly let out her breath.

"See? No worries," he said, and she nodded.

"I don't think I'm ready to drive in snow yet," she said in a small voice.

"You just have to be careful in these shady patches where the road gets slick. You'll get the hang of it."

"I guess you did. Did you grow up here?" she asked.

He shook his head. "Idaho. We moved here when I was a senior in high school."

"That must've been a hard adjustment."

Not if you played football. "I managed."

She rubbed her arms. "So you've lived here ever since?"

"Pretty much," he said, and turned on the heat full blast. "I went away to school."

"But then you came back."

"After a few years." *And got caught by Ashley.*

"I can see why you came back," Jen said. "It's such a cute town, and the people are all so nice."

He had to admit Icicle Falls was a great place to live. And a great place to raise kids. In fact, it would be a perfect place if he could just get rid of Ash. "Yeah, it is."

She looked out the window. "I'm glad I didn't hit the deer."

Garrett was glad she hadn't hit *him*.

"I thought I'd be okay with snow tires. I should have them put chains on."

"You'd be taking them off every time the snowplow came through."

She began to gnaw her lip. He should say something to distract her. *What kind of perfume are you wearing?*

Not that! He cleared his throat. "So, what did you do in Seattle?"

She shrugged. "Worked all the time."

"Corporate mover and shaker?"

"More like office peon. Plus I sold candles at home parties."

So she sold fire hazards in her spare time. "Candles can be dangerous," he warned.

From the way she was looking at him it was obvious he'd just insulted her. "I explain that at all my candle parties. You should never leave lit candles to burn unattended and never burn them near curtains or any flammables."

"I guess you know your stuff," he said, and nodded approvingly.

"I guess I do," she said with an answering smile. "What I don't know about is woodstoves. I never had one. But now I've got the stove figured out, so you won't have to worry that I'll burn your place down."

"Never thought it," he lied.

"Uh-huh."

He pulled up in front of the cottage. Piles of snow marched down the driveway to the road. She'd obviously been busy shoveling. "I've got a plow attachment for my truck. I'll come by when we get snow again and dig out the driveway for you." More exposure to Jen Heath. What was he thinking? He was thinking it would be a nice thing to do, that was all.

"That would be great."

It *would* be—as long as he shoveled the drive and got out of there.

"I thought I was going to keel over shoveling all that snow," she confessed.

Then someone would've had to give her CPR. He shook off the image of his mouth on hers. Damn, where did this stuff keep coming from? "I'll get your groceries for you."

"Thanks."

They climbed out of the cab and she went to unlock the cabin door while he collected the groceries. She had it open and had turned on the lights by the time he reached the porch. It was like walking into a different place with her white leather couch replacing the old sofa. That and the matching chair and fancy coffee table made this dump seem downright stylish. She'd covered the old dining table with a red cloth and a fancy arrangement of candles and greens. The place had gone from looking like the rough-and-tumble little dump it was into something a lot classier.

"Nice," he observed as he set the bag on the counter.

"Thanks," she said. "And thanks again for rescuing me. Can I make you an eggnog latte?"

The place looked good and so did she. Which was why he said, "I appreciate the offer, but I should get going."

"Okay."

He almost breathed a sigh of relief until she added, "Then how about if I cook you dinner? As a thank-you for helping me out."

Oh, no. Dinner would be a disaster. He'd get sucked right in, just like he had with Ash. "No need, really. But, uh, thanks." Now he was edging toward the door like a gauche kid. "Well, take it easy," he mumbled. Then he bolted down the stairs for the safety of his truck.

Jen watched Garrett Armstrong racing for his truck as if his pants were on fire. What was wrong with the man? Surely if he was seeing someone he would have used that as his excuse. *Sorry, I've got to get back to my girlfriend.* Or, *Sorry, I've got to get back to my boyfriend.* He hadn't mentioned anyone. So maybe it was her? He wasn't attracted to her, plain and simple.

She went into the bedroom and checked herself out in the beveled mirror of the antique dresser. She had a cute enough face—oval with hazel eyes. Her nose wasn't bad. Neither was her mouth. Okay, maybe her lips weren't as full as Angelina Jolie's but they were still nice. Her hair was long. Guys liked long hair, didn't they? And so she wasn't a 38D. She wasn't flat-chested, either. The girls were big enough to attract a man's attention. Well, most men's, but obviously not Garrett Armstrong's. What the heck was wrong with her?

"Nothing," she told herself firmly.

So, that left only one alternative. Garrett Armstrong was shy. That flaw could be corrected over time, she decided as she returned to the kitchen to put away her groceries.

That was when she discovered half the eggs in the carton had broken. Which meant scrambled eggs for dinner. Good. A nice simple meal.

She wished she wasn't eating it alone.

Pathetic. He'd run away like a ten-year-old boy.

But it was better to run away than stick around and get sucked in by a pretty face. Garrett wanted his life simple from now on. Well, as simple as it could be considering who his ex-wife was. He suspected Jen Heath was made of stronger moral fiber than Ash, but when it came to crazy and complicated it looked as if she'd be able to give Ash a run for her money.

The incident with the woodstove damper—well, that could have happened to anyone. Except wouldn't someone who'd never had a stove or a fireplace ask how to use the thing before trying to light a fire? As for her skidding off the road, that, too, could happen to anyone. Inexperienced drivers often lost control in the snow.

Only a fool would lose control in his own house,

though, and if Garrett had stayed that was probably what he would've done. If not today, then some other day. She'd have gotten to him eventually. Sooner or later he wouldn't be able to resist the urge to kiss her. And then he'd want more. Smarter to avoid the temptation altogether.

He was going to stick with his plan, find a woman who wasn't ditzy, who had her act together. Like Tilda. In fact, maybe Tilda would be interested in going out tonight, seeing a movie at the Falls Cinema. She was on days at the police station right now. She'd be off by five.

Once back at his place he called her. "Got anything going on?"

"Nope," she said. "What's up?"

"I thought I'd go see a movie tonight. Wanna join me?"

"Sure."

"Good," he said, "'cause racquetball tomorrow isn't gonna happen."

"Oh?"

"Ashley wants me to take Timmy."

"So, her weekend with him is lasting one whole night."

"That about sums it up."

"The woman is a bitch."

Tilda never pulled her punches. "Yeah, she is," Garrett agreed.

"Well, let's do a movie tonight and take Timmy out for breakfast tomorrow," Tilda suggested. "I'll have to wait to beat your ass at racquetball."

Tilda was such a good sport. No complaining that their plans had been ruined, just going with the flow.

Garrett smiled. Yep, Tilda Morrison was exactly what he needed. "Like you beat me last time?" he retorted.

"Hey, I let you win to feed your ego."

"Yeah, sure," Garrett retorted. "Pick you up at seven."

"No need. I'll meet you there."

Every woman should be as easy to be with as Tilda. Yeah, she was perfect—strong and steady. With Tilda there was never any trouble, never any drama.

What would it be like to kiss Jen Heath?

Cass Wilkes from the book club was just leaving Mountain Veterinary with her Saint Bernard, Tiny, when Chita arrived, holding a shivering Hidalgo.

"Oh, no. What's Hidalgo eaten now?" Cass immediately asked.

"Nothing. At least, nothing I know about," Chita amended. "I think he's got an ear infection."

"Oh, poor guy."

"What's wrong with Tiny?"

"Skin infection. But you'll be better in no time, won't you, boy?" Cass patted Tiny on the head and he drooled appreciatively. "I'm just glad Dr. Wolfe was able to fit us in."

"Same here," Chita said. Ken Wolfe was always available for any emergency, and he'd come out after hours more than once to help Hidalgo. "I swear that man is the patron saint of dogs."

"He's a great guy," Cass agreed. "I don't know why nobody's snapped him up. She'd save a fortune in vet bills."

Why had no one put her brand on the man? It sure wasn't because he was bad-looking.

Hidalgo whimpered, reminding Chita that she wasn't here to yak with her friend.

"I should let you guys get inside before Hidalgo freezes," Cass said.

"Or has a nervous breakdown," Chita added, and hurried in.

The clinic's waiting room was cheery, with yellow walls sporting framed pictures of dogs and cats and horses, all patients of Dr. Wolfe's. Many of them were signed. One of a fat, black-and-white cat had "To Dr. Wolfe, love, Spike" written across it in silver ink. Another of a Palomino and its proud owner holding a blue ribbon thanked the doc for keeping Goldie healthy.

Plastic chairs were scattered around the room and a small table held copies of *Cat Fancy* and *Modern Dog*. The waiting room smelled like wet dog.

Hidalgo whimpered.

"It's okay," Chita cooed. "You're going to be fine."

"Hidalgo," the receptionist greeted him. "You're not feeling so good?" To Chita she said, "Dr. Wolfe will have him better in no time."

Chita thanked her and took a seat. She and the unhappy Hidalgo had barely settled in when Dr. Wolfe's assistant appeared to usher them into an exam room.

A moment later they were joined by Ken Wolfe himself. "Well, Hidalgo and Mommy," he said in his gentle voice. "How are we doing?"

"Not good," Chita said.

"Well, let's see. Bring him over to the exam table."

He actually didn't have to tell her. After all the times they'd been here, Chita knew the drill. "Thanks for fitting us in," she said. On such a cold snowy night, surely even a dedicated vet would be anxious to get home.

But Dr. Wolfe didn't seem to be in any hurry. He ran a calming hand along the dachshund's back. "No problem, Chita. We don't want this little guy down for the count."

Chita nodded. She'd already brought Hidalgo in twice during the past month, and she and the doc were now on a first-name basis.

With a man as friendly as Ken Wolfe, that probably would've happened, anyway. Last time she'd been in she'd teased him about his name. "That's why I became a vet," he'd said. "I figured with a name like Wolfe it had to be a sign."

Sometimes Chita wished she'd looked for a few signs on her own life path. She'd been too busy stumbling around. She hadn't worried much about grades in high school, preferring to focus on her social life. Her mother had tried her best to improve Chita's grades by alternately nagging and cajoling, but in the end she'd finally given up and moved on to pushing her other three children, who were more driven to succeed. By the time Chita graduated she didn't have any big-league schools knocking on her door. She had no idea what she wanted to be when she grew up so she'd gotten a job as a waitress at Dot Morrison's Breakfast Haus. There she'd met the man her mother referred to as "that gringo," a truck driver with muscles and a sexy smile. And that had been that.

The marriage had lasted long enough to produce two children and then "that gringo" was out of there. Now he was nothing more than a child support check…and even then, only when she could find him.

She had no regrets when it came to her kids. They were great. But the rest of her life? Was that going to amount to working on an assembly line? Not that she had any complaints about how the people at Sweet Dreams treated her. They were kind and responsible employers. Still, her job wasn't exactly the height of accomplishment.

Were there signs in her life she'd missed along the way? She'd enjoyed crafts and drawing. Could she have become a graphic designer? She'd loved animals. Could she have been a Dr. Wolfe?

Now she studied him as he examined Hidalgo. He was a tall man, fortysomething, with light brown hair and a matching mustache. She was always impressed by how gentle he was with those large hands of his.

A crazy thought flashed into her mind, probably inspired by her conversation with Cass. *Those hands would feel nice on you.*

She pushed it away. Just because she was standing next to a nice, good-looking man was no reason to go into heat.

"You say he's been shaking his head, scratching his ears?" Ken asked.

"Yes," Chita confirmed.

He lifted Hidalgo's ear and the dog yelped. "It's okay, buddy," he said. "We'll get you fixed up, okay?" Another minute and he turned to Chita. "You were right. He's got an ear infection. We'll start him on some oral antibiotics as well as a topical. Then he won't be so irritable," he finished with a grin.

Ear...irritable. Get it? It was hard to be amused while seeing a vision of her budget stretching like a big rubber band until it finally broke. She shook her head at him. "While you're at it, can you prescribe something for me so *I* won't be irritable?"

"A glass of white wine when you get home. How's that?"

"Just what the doctor ordered," she said.

But when she finally got home, she had to give Hidalgo his medicine and make dinner. (And clean up the mess when Enrico dropped a jar of sweet pickles on the kitchen floor.) Then both kids needed help with their homework. After they were finally bathed and tucked in for the night, she tried to read but found she was far too tired.

She gave up and went to bed. As she slipped under the covers she realized she'd never gotten that glass of wine. Ah, well. Just another day in paradise.

"How are you coming with the wedding plans?" Charley's mom asked.

She knew she shouldn't have answered her cell. "Okay," she lied. Actually, she hadn't done much of anything. Between running the restaurant and doing things every other weekend with Dan's kids from his first marriage, her life was busier than it had ever been.

"Have you picked a church?"

"We're not going to have it in a church," Charley explained. "We're getting married at the restaurant."

"I thought you were going to have a simple church wedding."

"I said we were going to have a simple wedding," Charley corrected her. "I did the big church wedding the first time around. Remember?"

"How could I not? It was beautiful. You were beautiful."

"I promise I'll still be beautiful," Charley teased. "Anyway, it's too late to change venues. I already got the invitations printed and they say the wedding's at Zelda's."

"All right, fine," her mother said, annoyed but resigned. "Where are you going to put everyone up? You know you have to find someplace that's wheelchair accessible for Great-aunt Millie."

"I wasn't planning on inviting Great-aunt Millie. We're keeping the guest list small." How many times had she said this?

"I understand, dear, but you can't not invite Great-aunt Millie."

Maybe that was true. She didn't want to hurt her aunt's feelings. Who else was going to be ticked off if they weren't invited? Charley had a vision of her guest list going from one page to a big, long scroll that dropped clear to her feet.

"Oh, and we've got to book someplace affordable for Gerald and Mishmish. He still hasn't found a job and they're on a tight budget. And don't forget your little cousins Josephine and Inga want to be flower girls. By the way, Josephine is allergic to lilies. You did remember that, didn't you?"

"No, I'd forgotten," Charley said as she grabbed her purse.

"Have you picked out your flowers? Valentine's Day will be here before you know it."

"Look, Mom. I've got to get to the restaurant. Can we talk about this later?"

"Of course. But remember, the clock is ticking. And we still have a lot to do."

What was this *we* stuff? She didn't remember asking for help. Not that she didn't appreciate her mother *wanting* to help, but so far all Mom had done was put

together a giant to-do list and then nag her about checking things off. Party favors, bridesmaids dresses (she
hadn't even chosen her bridesmaids yet—and didn't
even know if she wanted to bother with bridesmaids),
flowers, cake (that one would be easy enough—she'd
have Cass make it), the gown, the minister, the photog-
rapher, wheelchair access, flower girls with allergies...
She suddenly wanted to run away. She was marrying a
great guy who came with two great kids. Why wasn't
she having fun? Oh, yeah, because her simple wedding
got less simple every time she talked to her mother.

Mom had a point, though. A wedding was a big deal,
a day to remember. And now that she'd found such a
wonderful man, she wanted to make the day memorable for both of them.

But why was making a memory so darned stressful?

"I'm going to have a nervous breakdown," she announced to Dan when he stopped by the restaurant later
that night to join her in a nightcap.

"Don't tell me, let me guess," he said. "The wedding."

She sighed heavily. "You guessed it."

"You know, this was supposed to be a party. As
in fun."

"I know. I thought it would be so perfect to get
married on Valentine's Day. But I'm not sure I can
pull it off."

He shrugged. "Then we'll get married on a different day. Or we'll elope."

"And deprive my mother of the chance to be at my
wedding? I'd never hear the end of that."

"We'll record it and put it on YouTube."

"Eeew."

He smiled and reached across the table to take her hand. "I don't care when we get married or how. I just want you to be happy. If you're feeling stressed, let's make some changes."

"June weddings are nice," she said.

"They are," he agreed.

"And it's probably stupid to get married on Valentine's Day."

"Probably."

"So we'll do June instead."

"Works for me."

That settled it. Problem solved. The wedding invitations would go in the recycling bin. What the heck— it was only money. Or maybe she could sell them on eBay to some other Daniel and Charlene who actually had time to get married on Valentine's Day.

Oh, yeah. Funny, Charley.

"You okay?" Dan asked.

"Sure. Why?"

"You don't look that happy."

She squeezed his hand. "I'm marrying a great guy. Trust me. I'm happy." Everyone loved a June wedding. June weddings were classic. And she could certainly plan a simple wedding by June.

As long as her mother stopped helping her.

Chapter Nine

There's no better time to make changes in your life than right now.
    —Muriel Sterling, author of *Simplicity*

"Guess what," Juliet said to Stacy. "I talked to Muriel Sterling about meeting with our book club and she's up for it."

Muriel Sterling, the queen of simplicity, was going to be coming to her house? Stacy looked around the room, trying to see it through Muriel's eyes. The Christmas decorations were all stowed away but she'd managed to fill most of the empty spaces in her living and dining rooms. The mantel clock was back on the mantel, along with her hurricane lamps filled with candles, and so were the Hummel figurines her grandma had given her. The pile of books was back on the coffee table, the buffet bloomed with a vase of silk hydrangeas on one side, while the other side was occupied by her great-grandma's chocolate set, a candy dish and a cute little teacup she'd gotten from a favorite aunt. It had a crack so it wasn't good for anything but sitting around looking pretty, which it did quite nicely on the buffet. The pictures had been returned to the walls, as

well as the quilted hanging she'd finished the year before last, and the dining room table had a new centerpiece, a fat candle shaped like a champagne bottle in
an ice bucket, which she always put out for the month
of January.

Was it all too much? What constituted *too much?*
She looked at the pile of junk mail and coupons keeping
her centerpiece company on the dining table, thought
of the bags of post-Christmas bargains she'd already
accumulated that were hidden away in the closet in
Ethan's old room, thought of the drawer full of kitchen
gadgets she never used. The latest had been a small
plastic container with a pump lid, which had promised
to make whipping cream a snap. The only snapping had
been in her shoulder muscles as she worked the stupid
thing up and down in an attempt to get it to do what it
promised. Why had she kept that? Why had she kept
half the stuff in that drawer?

"So, we'll have both Muriel and Jen, who's already
put what Muriel wrote into practice," Juliet was saying. "That should be really inspiring."

Or depressing, Stacy reflected. "It should be," she
said, trying to sound enthusiastic.

"Jon should be waking up from his nap. I'd better
go," Juliet said. "See you tomorrow. This is going to
be one of our best book club meetings yet!"

It was certainly proving to be an interesting meeting, Stacy thought the following evening as the assembled group listened to Muriel Sterling talk about her
life and what had prompted her to write the book. She
was an attractive woman, with a curvy figure, a round
face and chestnut hair cut in a layered bob—the kind
of woman whose age was hard to determine. Judging

by her daughter Cecily's age, Stacy figured she had to be at least sixty. *I hope I look that good at her age,* Stacy thought. Heck, she'd like to look that good now.

All the Sterling women were beautiful, and Muriel's daughter Cecily was the prettiest of all. She had two different men in town interested in her, but so far she hadn't started dating either of them. She sat next to her mother, beaming with pride as Muriel talked.

"After I lost Waldo I wanted to hang on to everything we'd had," Muriel was saying. "But the problem was, I couldn't afford to. I couldn't afford to keep that house, and when I found myself moving to a smaller place I knew I didn't have room for all my stuff. It was hard to decide what to keep and what to let go of. I don't think I was unique in that. I think many of us have trouble parting with things. Madison Avenue has been telling us for years that we need material possessions to make us happy. So we hang on to things even when all they do is weigh us down. We wrap our memories so tightly around our possessions that we start thinking they're one and the same. But I've come to realize they're not."

Stacy squirmed in her seat. Why was Muriel looking at her? Was it warm in here?

"We often have that same problem in other areas of our lives," Muriel continued. "We hang on to unrealistic expectations of what we should be as women and that leaves us overcommitted and stressed. We stay in relationships we shouldn't or try to put together something that's broken beyond repair."

"Guilty," Charley piped up, and everyone smiled.

"We don't always want to move forward," Muriel said. "I didn't. I wanted to stay in the past but my circumstances forced me to make a new life, forced me to get rid of a lot of things I *thought* I needed."

"Like what?" asked Chita.

Muriel shrugged. "Knickknacks, kitchen items I rarely used, videotapes, clothes that no longer fit, books I hadn't enjoyed, gifts I was keeping only because someone gave them to me, extra dishes that wouldn't fit in my smaller house. It was a big step for me and a little traumatic at the time. But I'm glad I did it. My life is so easy now, so simple." She smiled at Jen, whom she'd been introduced to when she first arrived. "And I'm really happy to meet someone else who's taken that step."

"I still can't believe you did that," Juliet said to Jen. "To move someplace where you didn't know anyone." She shook her head in astonishment.

"Yeah, but this is such a friendly town. Look how you've all reached out to me," Jen said. "By the way, thanks for letting me come to your book club. And thanks for giving me a ride," she added, smiling at Juliet.

"I was happy to. Anyway, I think you're a great fit. You're welcome to join us if you want," Juliet told her. "Right, guys?"

"Absolutely," Charley said, and the others echoed her agreement.

"Thanks. I'd like that," Jen said.

"I didn't get a chance to find out when we were talking earlier. What made you drop everything and move?" Chita asked Jen.

"Muriel's book." Jen smiled at their guest author. "My sister gave it to me. I was working two jobs to pay off all my stuff, and I hated my life. I didn't have time for my friends or my family. I had a great condo but I couldn't really afford it and I was never there, anyway. I'm only renting here but I don't mind. I'm not stressed or grumpy anymore. Muriel's right. Having less is more."

"And the more you have, the more you have to take care of," Muriel pointed out. "I can clean my whole house in an hour, and that includes dusting."

It took Stacy an hour just to dust everything. Hmm.

"The less time I spend cleaning, the more I have for my family and friends. I call that a good trade-off," Muriel finished.

"Well, I'm all for simplifying my life," Juliet said. "Anybody else?"

"I could go for that," Cass began. "I think what needs to change most is my schedule. I'm tired of being tired, and I'm ready to give myself a little more time off. Maybe I'll hire someone to come into the bakery a couple days a week so I can stay home."

"I could help you with that," Jen said quickly.

"Yeah? Let's talk later," Cass suggested.

"I wish I could take a few days off," Charley said. "Maybe then I'd actually have time to plan my wedding. By the way, we bagged the idea of getting married on Valentine's Day."

"Seriously? But that was what you really wanted," Cecily said.

"I know, but I can't pull it together. Not with running the restaurant and learning how to be a stepmom. We'll do June instead."

"Well, that'll definitely give you more time," Cecily said.

"I hope so. There's still so much to do, I'll be lucky

if I'm ready by then. My simple wedding keeps getting more complicated. The guest list has doubled and so has my to-do list, thanks to my mom, who keeps thinking up things we just *have* to have. At the rate we're going, this thing is going to put the Kardashians to shame. I guess I'll have to wait until after I'm married to simplify my life."

"With a restaurant, a new husband and stepkids? Good luck with that," Cass said.

Charley gave a dramatic shudder. "Stop, you're scaring me." She turned to Chita. "How about you, Chita? How would you simplify your life?"

"I don't know. I need to think of something because I'm tired all the time. But what can I do? I've got to work. I've got to take care of my kids."

"Are you doing any volunteer work?" Muriel asked.

Chita shook her head. "Leading Anna's Girls of America group. That's all."

"You're the only one leading the group?" Muriel probed.

Chita frowned. "I have to. No one else volunteered."

Muriel nodded thoughtfully but didn't say anything.

"So you're doing it all and none of the other moms help? There's something wrong with that picture," Charley said.

Chita raised her shoulders. "That's how it is."

"That's not how it *should* be. You should quit," Charley told her.

Chita looked shocked. "I can't. The group will fold."

"Do you enjoy leading it?" Muriel asked.

Chita frowned again. "No. It's just one more thing to do. And some of those girls are spoiled brats."

"Hmm," Charley said, "so you're working your butt

off to host a bunch of spoiled brats. Wow, sign me up for that."

"It's a lot of work to keep kids in your daughter's life who may not be the best friends for her," Stacy added. "Sounds like a pretty easy decision to me." Oh, she was good at fixing someone else's life.

"You could have a point there," Chita murmured. "That would free up one evening a week."

"What would you do with one free evening a week?" Muriel asked.

Chita smiled dreamily. "I would sit on my couch and watch all those shows I record but never have a chance to watch." Then she shook her head. "But that's selfish."

"No, that's charging your batteries," Muriel said. "We women take care of everyone else and then forget to take care of ourselves. Perhaps having one evening a week to relax will give you the energy you need to keep going the rest of the week."

"And who knows?" Charley added. "If you turn in your leader badge, maybe someone else will step up and take over."

"That'll never happen." Chita sighed. "But unloading that commitment sure is tempting. *Something's* gotta change."

"It's a new year. Good time to make changes," Cass said.

"Hey, since it's January, what do you guys think about us all coming up with ways to simplify our lives?" Juliet asked. "Then next month we can all share what we decided on."

"I think that's a great idea," Cass said.

"Me, too," Chita seconded.

Cecily shrugged. "I simplified my life when I moved up here from L.A., but I'll be happy to give the rest of you moral support."

"What about you, Stacy?" Cass asked.

"Me?"

"You want to get simple with the rest of us?" Cass was smiling now. It was just a friendly invitation. Why did it feel like a challenge?

"Gosh, I'm not sure what I need to simplify." Was everyone looking around at all her things, judging her, figuring she should lighten her load?

"Maybe nothing," Juliet said diplomatically.

How long does it take you to dust? came the thought. Stacy pushed it away. "Good idea, though," she said for the sake of solidarity.

"Okay, sounds like we're all agreed," Juliet announced cheerfully. "So, next month everybody tell us what you came up with."

And that was that. They took a break to enjoy cheesecake and coffee, then said goodbye to Muriel.

Finally, before everyone left, they picked their read for the next month, *One Day* by David Nicholls, in honor of Valentine's. Thank God it wasn't another nonfiction book, Stacy thought. A little self-help went a long way.

No one's making you do anything, she reminded herself. She was in a book club, not the military. This whole "simple life" thing was only for those who wanted to do it. Her life was simple enough.

The following night she settled in front of the TV to do some hand-stitching on her latest quilt in progress and watch her favorite show, *Weird America*. Every show dealt with strange people doing strange things, including everything from snake handlers to people who believed they were vampires. Tonight's feature, "Hoarders in the Making," made her squirm.

It also made her feel a bit cheated. This was just like another show she'd seen on TV. Really, with all the weird stuff out there, couldn't they do better than this?

She looked in disgust at the shots of one woman's house. The living and dining rooms were crammed with furniture and stacks of magazines and news-papers. Closets bulged with clothes that still had the price tags on them. Linen closets overflowed and bags of extra towels and sheets were piled in every closet (where they could be squeezed in around the clothes). The woman had two refrigerators and two freezers, and both were packed with food, much of which had expired. Same with the cupboards. The place looked more like one gigantic storage unit than a house. The woman herself was probably in her sixties. Unlike her house, she looked put together, slim and well-dressed. No excess jewelry, no strange outfit. If you passed her on the street, you'd never know she lived in a sani-tized dump.

"I'm not like that," Stacy told herself.

The show moved on, and JoJo Burke, the host, began interviewing another woman. This interview was tak-ing place in the woman's motor home, which she'd pur-chased to live in because there was no longer room in her house. From the looks of it, soon there wouldn't be room for her in the motor home, either.

"How do you think this started?" asked JoJo.

"I don't know," the woman said sadly.

"Did you save things as a child?" JoJo probed.

"We didn't have much when I was growing up."

Well, that explained it.

"So, you were making up for what you didn't have," JoJo said.

The woman nodded. "Yes."

"What was the first thing you hoarded?"

"I didn't really *hoard* it. It was part of a collection."

"A lot of us have collections," Stacy muttered.

"What did you collect?"

"Santas."

Stacy gave a start and wound up poking herself with a needle.

"Figurines, ornaments, that sort of thing. And then," the woman said, "I don't know. It grew from there. I began collecting crystal. I was making good money. I could afford to buy things. I didn't want to run out. I bought them on sale."

Dean wandered into the family room. "What's this?"

"Just my show," Stacy said, turning it off.

He sank down on the couch next to her. "Aren't you going to watch it?"

"Maybe later." When he wasn't around to compare her to some hoarder on TV. "Don't you have papers to grade?"

"I just finished. Thought I'd come hang with you. But I don't mind watching your show."

"No, that's okay," she said quickly. "Why don't we watch one of our Netflix movies?"

He shrugged. "Sure, if you'd rather."

She'd definitely rather. All around her lately it seemed as if people were talking about stuff—having too much of it, getting rid of it and, now, hoarding it. What was wrong with having things? Especially if they were nice. Okay, so she had a lot, but so what? That was the American way.

She wasn't like those women she'd been watching. And she didn't care what Muriel Sterling or anyone else said. She didn't have too much stuff and she wasn't getting rid of anything. She'd have to receive a message from heaven, get a visit from the Ghost of Christmas Clutter or…some totally cosmic sign before she started tossing her possessions.

Dean selected a movie featuring a bunch of crooks planning a heist, and she set aside all thoughts of hoarding. (She was so deleting that show without watching another minute of it.) But then one of the crooks said something that brought her mind right back to the subject she kept trying to avoid.

"The old guy has so much he'll never miss those paintings. Hell, it's gonna be days before he even sees they're gone from the walls."

Did she have so much she wouldn't miss some of it? How many scarves did she need? And how many decorations for various seasons and holidays did she have stuffed away that never made it down from the attic? She thought of the kitchen gadgets, the I-have-a-dream dresses hanging in her closet in a size she'd probably never see again.

Still, she might use those decorations. She might lose weight. It was the new year, after all.

The movie played on and the heist continued and Stacy tried to concentrate on what was happening. She hoped those crooks got caught and paid big-time. She didn't care if the person they were robbing had more than he needed. It wasn't nice to separate people from things they valued.

In the end, the crooks got away and she was disappointed. Good thing she'd been multitasking and working on her quilt or she would've been really irritated over wasting two hours of her time.

"There's two hours I'll never get back," she said as the ending credits rolled.

Dean chuckled. "I don't know. I enjoyed that movie."

"Crooks stealing and getting away with it? Yuck."

"Oh, it's not always bad to steal," Dean said.

"What?"

He turned off the TV and kissed her. "Stealing a kiss is always good," he said, and planted another kiss on the sensitive spot behind her ear. "So is stealing someone's heart," he added softly. "You sure stole mine the first time I saw you."

Now he was nuzzling her neck. Okay, she was done quilting. She set aside her work in progress and let her husband steal kisses to his heart's content. Sex on the couch, one of the advantages of being empty-nesters.

She went to bed later wearing a smile.

But she woke up at five in the morning in a state of terror.

It began when her collection of Santas escaped their box and came looking for her. They'd grown to the size of small children and there were so many of them they filled the whole bedroom. Some sat on the window seat. Others piled onto her slipper chair.

"You're going to break that!" she cried.

"There's no room anywhere else," protested the Santa with the glued-on head.

He was right. They covered every inch of floor space. They sat on the bed. One of them sat on her legs, almost crushing them.

"Get off!" she yelled.

The Santa didn't budge. "We're going to smother you," he threatened, and began crawling up her body.

"Let's party," said another, and suddenly they had her Christmas dishes, and plates were flying everywhere. Another Santa had hauled in an entire drawer from her kitchen, the one with all the gadgets she never used. "These could go in my sleigh. I know women who could use them." Meanwhile, the Santa who'd been crawling all over her sat on her chest.

"I can't breathe," she choked.

The Santa leaned over until his face was inches from hers, and now his red nose and his twinkling eyes were gone, replaced by the grimacing face of some dark monster. "That's because you have *too much crap!*" he roared.

She sat up in bed with a gasp, breathing hard. Okay, there was the cosmic sign. She got it. She needed to lighten her load.

Chapter Ten

Less is more. Which is something that goes for the people in our lives as well as the things.
—Muriel Sterling, author of *Simplicity*

Chita had been thinking about clearing her schedule since the book club meeting. Even taking mental inventory of everything that filled her days was exhausting. Saturdays were a blur of errands and cleaning and running kids around. She had Mass on Sundays, followed by Sunday dinner with her siblings at her mother's, and during the week, there was work all day followed by more work once she got home, plus helping the kids with their homework and taking them to their various activities. None of that was negotiable. Then there was book club once a month. She sure didn't want to give that up. It was her sanity break.

That left one thing, one big time-suck. The Girls of America. (Their slogan: Today's Girls Are Tomorrow's Leaders.) Such a worthwhile organization. And they needed volunteers. But sometimes, especially when the girls were being difficult, she wondered if the organization really needed *her*. And if *she* really needed the headaches. She not only had to host the meetings, she also had to prepare for them, organize the activities, make sure she had snacks for the girls.

Why didn't any of the other moms offer to bring snacks or come over to help? Oh, yes, they were busy. That was the excuse she always got when she put out an SOS.

Like she wasn't? Most of these women had husbands to take up the slack. She had…her mother. And Mama had a husband, other children, other responsibilities. She couldn't be around all the time to help her daughter. Considering how much her mother nagged, this was actually a blessing in disguise.

Girls of America night rolled around, and once again Chita had eight girls in her small living room, breaking the sound barrier with shrieks and laughter. She'd lessened the chaos by two. Enrico was at a friend's house and Hidalgo was locked in Anna's room where he wouldn't be tempted to eat the craft supplies.

Tonight was Earth Night, and their craft project was to make jewelry out of recycled items. The two card tables she'd set up were littered with plastic bottle caps, paint, cut-up egg cartons, gum wrappers and glue. She'd learned early on that tomorrow's leaders were also today's slobs and had put plastic dropcloths under the tables to spare her carpet.

Alice Graves, who met all the qualifications for being a handful, was already finished and wearing her necklace. Chita had suggested that she make a second one, but she preferred to toss bottle caps at the other girls.

"When do we eat?" she asked Chita.

"In a few minutes," Chita said. "Would you like to

come into the kitchen and help me get tonight's snack ready?"

"I'm not finished," Alice said, and grabbed a paint-brush.

Right. This was one leader of tomorrow who was probably never going to lead by example, at least not a good example. "Okay. You finish and I'll see about the treats," Chita said. "Five more minutes, girls, then we're going to clean up."

She slipped into the kitchen to cut up the Rice Krisp-ies Treats and pour juice. She was just setting eight plates around the table when her daughter's angry voice drifted in to her. "Am not!" This was followed by giggles.

Madre de Dios, what now? Chita rushed back into the living room. At the sight of her the giggles stopped. Her daughter was looking daggers at both Alice and her sidekick, Zuzu Welling.

Zuzu had an adorable little freckled face to match her adorable little name. Zuzu was a demon child. She kept her gaze down but she couldn't keep the smirk off her face.

"Okay, what happened?" Chita demanded.

Everyone looked at her innocently. No one said any-thing.

Except Anna, who glared at Alice and cried, "I hate you!" Then she ran from the room and up the stairs to her bedroom.

"Alice, what happened?" Chita asked, working hard to keep her voice level. This was taking superhuman effort considering the fact that she could get sued for what she'd like to do to Alice and Zuzu right now.

Whatever they'd done to make her child cry, spanking was too good for them.

"Nothing," Alice said, wide-eyed.

Chita planted her hands on the table and leaned over the child. "I think you'd better tell me, *chica*."

Alice blinked several times and for a moment her lower lip wobbled. But the child had a will of iron. In the end, she narrowed her eyes and stuck out her chin at a pugnacious angle. "I just told the truth."

Chita narrowed her eyes right back. "Oh? And what truth did you tell?"

Anna's friend Emma piped up. "She said you're aliens and you shouldn't even be here and that nobody wants you here."

Chita straightened and backed away, feeling as if she'd been slapped. Alice obviously had heard this at home and now, here she was in Chita's house, spreading the poison. She looked down at the child in disgust. Alice was a spoiled little bully and Chita wanted nothing more than to smack her. And her mother. Or father. Or both. And Zuzu was just as bad. Alice was the more vocal of the two, but Zuzu's wickedness was subtler. For all Chita knew, Zuzu had put those words in Alice's mouth.

"And is this how a Girl of America, a future leader, behaves, spreading things that aren't true?"

"It is true!" Alice insisted. "Zuzu's grandpa said so. He said Anna's probably an anchor."

As in anchor baby, a child born to an illegal alien or undocumented worker, whichever term you used. A parade of choice curses marched through Chita's mind, but she kept them there. "Well, I'm afraid Zuzu's grandpa is wrong. Anna and Enrico and I are all

U.S. citizens, just like you. My grandfather came to this country to work in the orchards and he became an American citizen. Unless you're a Native American—" no one present was "—someone in each of your families also came to this country in search of a better life and had to apply for citizenship. And I would hope they were treated more kindly than you've just treated Anna."

Alice frowned and studied the painted bits of egg carton in front of her and Zuzu's smirk dissolved.

Chita glanced around the table. "Is this how Girls of America behave?" she asked them all. "Do you bully and tease other girls? Do you spread lies?"

A couple of girls hung their heads. Alice scowled. Zuzu tried to look innocent.

"No, Mrs. Arness," Emma said. "They should apologize for being mean to Anna."

"Yes, they should." Chita looked around the table. "Now, I'm going to bring Anna back down here and I want you *all* to apologize."

She went up to her daughter's room with a heavy heart. Prejudice was nothing new. She'd experienced her share growing up, but really, she'd thought people were more enlightened now, especially here in Icicle Falls where everyone was so friendly. Obviously, she'd thought wrong.

She found Anna lying across her bed, sobbing, Hidalgo by her side, whimpering in sympathy.

She sat down next to Anna and stroked her lovely dark hair. "Oh, *bambina*. I'm so sorry those girls were mean to you."

"Make them go away," Anna sobbed.

"They'll be going soon. But first they want to say they're sorry."

"No, they don't. They're only saying sorry 'cause you're making them."

Children were way too perceptive. "I think some of them are sorry."

Anna shook her head violently. "I don't want to go down there."

Chita knew how her daughter felt. She didn't want to deal with those children anymore, either. "You need to hear their apologies and they need to make them."

"They're mean!"

"Yes, they are. But there are mean people everywhere, and the sooner you learn how to deal with them, the better." She gave her daughter's shoulder a supportive rub. "Come on. I'll be right there with you."

The sobs were subsiding into sniffles. Chita went down the hall to the bathroom and grabbed a tissue, then returned to her daughter's room and told her to blow her nose. "There, now let's show them how a true Girl of America behaves."

So back down the stairs they went.

The group was subdued, but little voices floated out to Chita and Anna. "Mrs. Arness is mean…" "My house is way bigger than this house…" "Her dog is stupid. So's Anna…"

Anna balked but Chita gently guided her forward.

They walked into the living room and two of the girls blushed. Had they been contributors to that conversation or were they feeling guilty by association?

"Alice? Zuzu? I think you both have something you need to say to Anna," Chita said sternly.

"Sorry," Alice muttered, her tone anything but repentant.

"Sorry," Zuzu said softly, refusing to look in Anna's direction.

Two more girls added their apologies.

Anna said nothing in return. Instead, she turned and ran back upstairs to her room. Her friend Emma and another little girl went after her, probably to offer comfort.

Chita let them go. "All right, let's get our mess cleaned up."

"Shouldn't Emma and Portia help?" Alice asked.

"They're helping in a different way," Chita replied. *Cleaning up the emotional mess you made.*

The girls were quiet during cleanup, but by the time Chita had squeezed them in around her small kitchen table for treats, they'd forgotten the incident and were talking and giggling again.

One by one the mothers arrived to pick up their daughters. Alice's mother came to pick up Alice and Zuzu, and Chita had a quiet word with her before calling the girls out from the kitchen. "No matter where people stand on the immigration issue, there's no excuse for bullying."

"Oh, my," the woman said weakly. "I'm so sorry."

"So am I," Chita said, "since it was mean and not true. I asked her to apologize and she did, but I thought you should be aware of it."

The woman nodded. "Thanks. I'll...speak to her."

The words held such dread that Chita doubted Alice's mother would ever work up the courage to deal with the problem. Alice obviously ruled that household. What would she be like when she was a teenager?

Chita didn't want to know.

Alice and Zuzu made their exit, followed by the last couple of girls. Enrico returned home, and Chita popped him in the tub. Then she and her daughter had a heart-to-heart about their family history—and about mean girls. By nine, both children were tucked in and Chita was ready for bed, too.

She took a shower and climbed in between the sheets with her book club selection. Prejudice. That was something Muriel hadn't addressed in her book, probably because she'd never experienced it. Chita sighed. Life would be so much simpler if people were nice to one another.

Stacy's observation regarding Chita's involvement as a leader for this little troop of vipers came back to her. *It's a lot of work to keep kids in your daughter's life who may not be the best friends for her.* Maybe it was time to say goodbye to the Girls of America.

The next morning, her daughter confirmed it. They were going through the usual morning rush of breakfast, lunch-making, gathering up homework and feeding Hidalgo. Normally during all this activity Anna was chatty and happy. This morning she was quiet and solemn and it broke Chita's heart. She'd always been able to shrug off her children's minor injuries like skinned knees or elbows. "You'll be fine," she'd say, and, of course, they always were. There was no shrugging off this kind of hurt.

"You need to be brave today," she told Anna, and kissed her forehead. How she wished she could attend school alongside her daughter and loom threateningly over any little bully who tormented her. Or let her stay home. But to keep her away from mean girls they'd have to become hermits. "I know it's hard, but you're a strong girl. And you have your good friends, your true friends, and they'll play with you at recess. You can do this, can't you?"

Anna nodded somberly, then bit her lip. She was on the verge of saying something.

"What is it, *bambina?*" Chita asked.

"I don't want to be a Girl of America anymore," Anna blurted.

So what did she do, tell her daughter to tough it out with kids who didn't like her? The teasing the night before hadn't been the first time her daughter had been unhappy with the Girls of America group. There'd been minor slights and misunderstandings, but Chita had figured it was important for the girls to work out their differences. The situation had gone well beyond that.

Anna's eyes were fearful and pleading. "Please don't make me."

This was supposed to be fun, a wonderful extracurricular activity for her child. It was not turning out to be fun. For either of them. Chita held out her arms and Anna rushed to her side and began to cry.

"Of course I won't make you," Chita said.

Her daughter looked up at her and, with tears still running down her cheeks, smiled. "Thank you, Mama!"

Chita hugged her. *No. Thank* you. *You set us both free.*

That evening Chita called Nancy Norgaard, the district supervisor for Girls of America and tendered her resignation, effective immediately.

"But, Chita, you've been doing such a fabulous job," Nancy protested.

"Thank you," Chita said, "but I'm afraid I just don't have time for it anymore." No time for brats and bullies. "And Anna's ready to move on."

"Oh." Nancy sounded shocked. "Are you sure you won't both reconsider?" she begged. "I don't know who we'll get to take over that group."

Chita felt guilty—for a millisecond. "Well, good luck," she said.

She set her cell phone back on the counter and realized that, for the first time in ages, she didn't feel so tired. She rounded up all her Girls of America leadership material and put it in a box to mail back to Nancy. And now she felt lighter. She should have resigned months ago.

That night her mother called, trying to guilt her into attending a baby shower for her second cousin Juanita on Friday night.

"I can't. I already have plans."

"What plans?" her mother demanded suspiciously.

"Important plans," she said. They involved a bubble bath and a book. Oh, yes, she could get into this simple life stuff.

Stacy had spent the past couple of days going through her house, taking stock of everything she had that she didn't use. Was she a hoarder in the making? That was a creepy idea. She picked up Muriel Sterling's book and went back to the chapter she'd found hardest to finish, the one titled "Less Is More."

It's so easy to let our possessions multiply. And over time that's exactly what they do. I was shocked when I moved at how much I had to pack—dishes, clothes, kitchen appliances and gadgets, linens, bedding, decorations, many of which I hadn't put out in years. I thought of people in poorer countries who are happy with so much less. I thought of how much time and energy it took to maintain all my things. They owned me as much as I owned them. I went through all of them and reassessed their value. Anything I hadn't used in the past three years I got rid of. There was no space for them in my new house and no room in my new life. I got rid of a lot and I can honestly say I never regretted it.

Stacy shut the book and mulled over what she'd just read. Never regretted it. Really? What did she have kicking around that she hadn't used in the past three years?

The drawer full of kitchen gadgets came to mind. She could start there.

She went to the kitchen and opened the drawer. Okay, did she really need that nutcracker? When was the last time she'd purchased nuts that needed to be cracked? Hmm. Ten years ago. The whipped-cream whipper that didn't whip—that could go to some other sucker. The little umbrellas she was going to use to make girlie drinks someday—she'd never gotten around to it, and she'd had them for three years. She'd used that pastry sheet once and didn't like it. She always rolled out cookies and pie crust right on her countertop. And how many latte pitchers did one woman need? How many little glass jiggers? How many kitchen sponge holders? Oh, Lord, she *was* a hoarder.

She spent forty-five minutes in the kitchen, and by the time she was done she had two grocery bags full of goodies for the Kindness Cupboard, the town's local thrift store, which donated proceeds to various worthy causes around town. Okay, on to the bedroom.

Dean came home and discovered her knee-high in a pile of clothes. "Having trouble finding something to wear?" he asked, and kissed her.

"No. I'm purging."

"Purging," he repeated as if it were a foreign word.

"Yes, I'm getting rid of things I don't need."

"Really?" He looked skeptical.

She couldn't blame him. She tended to go through phases. There'd been her cooking-class phase, when she'd taken lessons and then vowed to make something different for dinner every night of the week. That had lasted about a month before she'd decided it was way too much work and had gone back to making her old standards.

Then there'd been her no-sugar diet—no baking, no treats, no ice cream anywhere in the house. Much healthier for them. But then they'd gone out to Zelda's one night and she'd been seduced by the wild huckleberry pie.

"Oh, well, a little sugar won't hurt us," Dean had reasoned.

"Except my hips," she'd said.

"I like your hips just fine," he'd assured her, and that had been the end of that.

Then there'd been her exercise kick, her clog dancing classes, painting class (she was better at quilting). She'd tried numerous different activities with the best of intentions but never stuck with them.

But this was important. She was going to stick with this.

"I'm getting rid of stuff we don't need or use anymore," she informed Dean. "It'll make life so much simpler."

"I'm all for that," he said. "What about the attic?"

"I'll get to it," she promised.

"Wow," he said.

Yeah, wow. By noon the following day she'd gone through all the bedrooms, the linen closet and the hall closet.

"My goodness!" exclaimed Janice Lind, who volunteered at the Kindness Cupboard. "You've been doing some serious cleaning."

"I have," Stacy said. "I'm lightening my load."

"Have you been reading Muriel Sterling-Wittman's new book?"

"I have. How'd you guess?"

Janice nodded sagely. "There's been a lot of load lightening going on around here lately."

"It feels good," Stacy said with a smile.

She said as much to Cass when she went into Gingerbread Haus the next day to reward herself.

"That is seriously impressive," Cass said, handing over a gingerbread boy.

"How are you doing with simplifying your life?" Stacy asked.

"I've hired some new help. I'm going to start taking Fridays off and only coming in mornings on Saturdays. Just the thought of having that extra time is better than a sugar buzz."

"Did you end up hiring our new book club member?"

"I did. She's going to work Thursdays, Fridays and Saturday mornings. I'll get some time off and she'll have a part-time job so it's a win-win."

"I'd say so." Stacy paused for a moment. "You know, I wasn't really in favor of reading that book, but now I'm glad we did. I got rid of all kinds of stuff I didn't need. Even some of my Christmas decorations."

Cass's mouth dropped. "No."

"Well, not a lot," Stacy admitted. "But a bunch of stuff we haven't used in a long time, things I'm not that crazy about anymore. And I unloaded a whole boxful of outside lights."

"That probably made Dean happy," Cass said.

Stacy smiled. "Oh, yeah."

But later the next evening he wasn't quite so happy.

She'd just finished cleaning up after dinner when Dean came into the kitchen. "Hey, babe, have you seen my old army jacket?"

The one he hadn't worn in ages? The one she'd taken to the Kindness Cupboard?

"I can't find it anywhere."

Uh-oh. This was not going to be a good conversation. Like a lawyer she started with a strong opening argument. "You haven't worn that coat in forever."

"Well, I want to wear it tonight to the basketball game. It's not in the coat closet. Did you move it?"

She'd moved it, all right. What to do now? She could feign ignorance, say she had no idea what had happened to his old army jacket, but Dean wasn't stupid. He'd search all the closets and find it in none, and then he'd be back here in the kitchen, demanding to know what she'd done with it.

She switched tactics. She closed the distance between them and put her arms around his neck. "Deano."

His expression turned wary. "Oh, no. Why do I get the feeling I don't want to hear what you're about to say?"

"You know how I've been getting rid of things, lightening our load?"

She didn't have to say any more. He looked at her as if she'd just told him the Seattle Seahawks had been sold. "No."

"I was only doing what Muriel Sterling said to do in her book. If you haven't used something in three years, you should get rid of it."

This was met with incredulity. "You got rid of my *jacket?*"

"You were glad to hear I was getting rid of stuff. Remember?"

"Your stuff, Stace, not mine. Where does Muriel Sterling say you should get rid of your husband's things without asking him? And I don't have that much."

"Well, look at it this way. Now you have even less," she said, trying to ease the moment. Okay, maybe it was more a case of trying to avoid admitting she was wrong.

Her attempt failed. Dean grumbled once in a while, but he rarely got angry. Right now, he was angry. He stood in front of her, hands on his hips (instead of on hers), looking like a thundercloud with legs.

"I don't want less. I want my army jacket," he growled. "Or maybe I should go through *your* closet and start getting rid of *your* clothes without asking. Or better yet, how about I get rid of that box of Santas? I'll bet they didn't go."

"I use them," she protested. And she couldn't remember the last time he'd worn that jacket. Why did he want it now, all of a sudden? Because she'd gotten rid of it, of course.

"Well, I use my jacket," he insisted, "and I want it back."

"But I took it to the Kindness Cupboard."

The thundercloud seemed ready to zap her with lightning. "I guess you'll have to go there tomorrow and get it back."

Take back a donation? That would be tacky. "What do you expect me to say to Janice Lind?"

"Say you made a mistake. Say you gave away something that wasn't yours to give away."

He was looking at her steely-eyed, like a man betrayed. "Okay," she said. "I'll get it back."

"Thank you," he said stiffly.

She kept her hold on him. "Deano, I'm sorry. Am I forgiven?"

The thundercloud vanished, blown away by a long-suffering sigh. "Yes." Now his arms moved around her waist. "And I do appreciate you getting rid of household stuff we don't use. But in the future, can you do me a favor and ask before you decide to dump my personal items?"

She could do that. She nodded and they kissed. Dean wore a different jacket to the Icicle Falls basketball game. Problem solved.

Except the next morning when she went to retrieve the army jacket, she found that her problem hadn't been solved at all. In fact, it had grown.

"Not here?" she repeated weakly.

"We send our clothing donations over to Goodwill

in Seattle to get sold in one of their stores," Janice said. "That way no one in town has to be embarrassed by being seen in something someone else donated. Your things, along with all the others we received over the past few days, got taken to Seattle."

Oh, boy. How was she going to tell Dean about this?

She wasn't. She was going to go over the mountains and scour every Goodwill in Seattle. She grabbed her cell phone and started making calls to her posse.

Chapter Eleven

*Our friendships are one of our greatest trea-
sures.*

> —Muriel Sterling, author of *Simplicity*

"I'll get my mom to watch Jon," Juliet said when
Stacy called her. "How soon do you need to leave?"

Ten hours ago. "The sooner, the better," Stacy said.
Just the thought of someone happily waltzing out of a
Seattle Goodwill with Dean's army coat was tying her
stomach in knots.

"Okay, I'll hurry."

Her next call was to Charley. It was a long shot since
Charley practically lived at her restaurant, but desperate times called for desperate measures.

"I can be ready to go in ten minutes," Charley said.
"But I have to be back here before the dinner rush, so
I'll follow you over to Seattle. Plus, if we have more
than one car, we can spread out."

Spreading out. Good idea. How many Goodwill
stores were there in Seattle? Would they be able to
cover them all in one day?

Chita was working the assembly line at Sweet
Dreams Chocolates, so there was no point in calling

her. There was no point in calling Cass, either, since she couldn't leave the bakery. Maybe Cecily could sneak away from work....

No, Stacy argued. It wouldn't be right to pull her away from her business, any more than it would be to bug Cass. Almost all her friends worked; they had more important things to do than take the day off to help her clean up the mess she'd made of simplifying her life. Fresh panic set in. Who else could she call?

The answer to that was easy. When times got tough, a girl called her mother. Her mother lived in nearby Cashmere and could be at her house in twenty minutes. Of course, calling her mother would also include a healthy dose of unrequested advice. She'd have to endure a minicounseling session. But her mother would come through.

Or not. "I have to take Nana to her doctor's appointment today," her mother said sadly. "Otherwise, I'd love to come to Seattle with you. What's the occasion?"

Stacy decided not to tell her. "Nothing, really. What's wrong with Nana?" At the age of eighty-eight a better question would have been, "What's not wrong with Nana?" Her grandmother had crippling arthritis, a bad heart and cataracts she refused to have operated on.

"Nothing new. This is just a checkup. But you know how much Nana loves going to the doctor. Believe me, I'd much rather be over in Seattle having fun with you."

Fun, yeah. "It's okay," Stacy said. "I'll catch you next time."

Stacy had barely ended the call when her cell phone rang. It was Cecily. "I heard from Charley that you need help. When are you leaving?"

"You have to work," Stacy protested.

"I set my own schedule," Cecily said. "Charley told me it's an emergency and I want to help."

"Thank you," Stacy breathed.

"I'll be over in fifteen minutes," Cecily promised.

Stacy's cell rang one more time. "Hi. Stacy?" said a vaguely familiar voice.

"Yeah, that's me. Who's this?"

"It's Jen, Jen Heath, your new book club member."

"Oh, hi, Jen," Stacy said, donning a friendly I'm-fine-nothing-wrong-with-me voice.

"I heard from Juliet that you need help finding something in Seattle."

Okay, this was embarrassing. She hardly knew Jen. "Well, um, yeah."

"I thought maybe you could use some extra help."

Look at the mess she was causing, dragging her friends over the mountain, pulling in people who were practically strangers.

"Since I lived in Seattle, I could help you find your way around. You know, be a backup in case your GPS fails you."

This was no time to be proud. "Sure. Thanks. I'd love that."

"Great," said Jen. "And I'll call my sister. She lives on the East Side. Maybe she can check out the Goodwill stores there. When are we leaving?"

"As soon as possible," Stacy said. "You remember how to get to my house?"

"I think so. Uh, the roads over there are clear, right?"

They'd had snow the day before, but all the main roads were clear now. Still, Jen was new to Icicle Falls and might not have realized yet how efficient their road crews were. Obviously she wasn't wild about driving in the snow. That was something she'd have to overcome if she was going to live in the mountains.

"You'll be fine," Stacy assured her.

That was more than she could say for herself if she didn't find Dean's army jacket.

Within half an hour, Stacy's team had assembled at her house for Mission Army Coat. They piled into two cars, Juliet and Jen with Charley, and Cecily riding shotgun with Stacy.

"I'm sorry I took you away from work," Stacy said as they traveled over the pass.

"Don't be," Cecily told her. "I needed a break and I hardly ever get to go to Seattle. I just feel bad that this isn't going to be any fun for you."

"Serves me right. I shouldn't have gotten rid of Dean's jacket without asking. I should've known it would have sentimental value." She shook her head. "I wouldn't have been happy if he'd gone through my closet and started purging my clothes, either. It was just that, well, I was on a roll. He never wears that jacket...." She let the sentence trail off.

"I get it," Cecily said. "Sometimes things don't quite work out the way you planned."

Stacy wondered if Cecily was talking about her own life. She'd been in L.A. but had decided to move back to Icicle Falls after helping her family's company, Sweet Dreams Chocolates, sponsor Icicle Falls's first chocolate festival. The second chocolate festival had been an even bigger success, and it was mostly Cecily's baby now.

"But I believe things do have a way of working out," Cecily continued.

Stacy smiled at that. "I suspect you know this from personal experience."

Cecily smiled in return. "I do. I'm glad I closed my business in L.A. It's nice to be home again."

"What was your business?" Stacy asked. Cecily had never talked about it, preferring instead to focus on her family's chocolate company.

"I ran a dating service."

"You mean you were…"

"A matchmaker," Cecily finished for her.

"That sounds like fun," Stacy said. She loved watching *The Millionaire Matchmaker* on TV.

"Not so much. It got old fast."

"But helping people find each other sounds…I don't know, noble."

"That's what I thought," Cecily said. "I had a gift for it. But I got burned out. I'm done matching up people."

"What about yourself?"

"I'm especially done with me. Turns out I'm a lot better at putting other people together with the right person than I am myself. Maybe my life would be simpler if *I* had a matchmaker."

"Even if she found you the perfect man, life would never be simple," Stacy said. What if she didn't find that jacket? Dean would forgive her, of course, but she'd feel terrible.

"It'll work out," Cecily said, reading her mind.

Stacy hoped so.

A little over two and a half hours later, they were in downtown Seattle. Charley checked in via cell phone. "Jen's sister is at the Bellevue Goodwill. She wants to know what the jacket looks like."

"It's light green-and-sand camo and it has a patch

with the name Thomas sewn on the front, above the pocket."

"Okay," Charley said. "Jen tells me the big store is downtown, but there's also a nice one in Ballard. Which store do you want us to take?"

"Take the Ballard one. We'll hit the downtown store," Stacy said. Maybe, if they were lucky, they'd find the coat quickly.

Or maybe they'd be there all day. "It's huge," Stacy muttered as they drove into the parking lot.

"Hopefully, the men's section won't be that big," Cecily said.

It was. "Yikes," Cecily said as they walked in.

Yikes was right. The warehouse full of castoffs seemed to stretch on forever.

Before them were miles and miles of clothes, shoes, books, lamps and small appliances.

"Wow," Stacy breathed, "look at this. Oh, my gosh, there's even a collectibles section." She'd always preferred to buy new items rather than deal with someone's castoffs. But some of these were gorgeous.

She drifted over to the long, glass case stuffed with glassware and knickknacks. A pearlescent orange glass bowl caught her eye. "Carnival glass. And do you believe the price? That's a steal." Her grandmother collected carnival glass. That bowl would make a great birthday present for Nana.

"Maybe we should look at the coats," Cecily suggested.

Oh, yeah. The coats.

They made their way to the men's section, which was packed with everything from shirts to pants. Cecily gestured at one long rack. "There must be a mile of coats here."

"More than that," Stacy said. "But not many of them are army jackets."

It took them less than ten minutes to ascertain that Dean's jacket wasn't there. *Did you really think you'd find it right away?* Stacy asked herself. That would've been too easy, and she suspected fate wasn't going to be so kind to her.

Her cell phone rang. "Nothing in Ballard," Charley reported.

Figured. "Nothing here, either," Stacy said.

"We're going to head farther north. Jen says there's one in West Seattle you might want to try. She's got the address in her phone."

The address was conveyed, and Stacy and Cecily put it in Stacy's GPS. After she'd purchased that carnival glass bowl.

They didn't have any luck in West Seattle, either. And Jen's sister, Toni, struck out in Bellevue and Kirkland. The search party finally met at a Starbucks in the University District. By that time Stacy had consoled herself with more purchases—two vintage Starbucks mugs, a Fitz and Floyd Christmas plate and a Victoria's Secret bra, still new with the tags on and just her size. (Hey, if she didn't come back with the jacket, this was something Dean would appreciate.)

"Who knew you could find so many great things in thrift stores?" she said.

Charley raised an eyebrow. "You've never shopped in a thrift store?"

"Never needed to. I always thought they were kind of grotty."

"They are," Cecily said, wrinkling her nose.

"But they're the best place to shop when you're a broke college student," Charley pointed out. "My roommates and I furnished our whole apartment with stuff from thrift stores."

"I can believe it," Stacy said. "I had no idea what I was missing." Missing. Oh, yeah, Dean's jacket. She frowned and stared morosely into her coffee cup. "Where the heck is that jacket?"

"Someone might already have bought it," Juliet said gently.

Good thing she'd gotten the Victoria's Secret bra. She had an awful feeling she was going to need it.

"We still have a couple of stores left," Jen told them. "Toni's on her way to Bothell to look. And there's the one on Capitol Hill."

"Where's that?" asked Stacy. The most she'd ever seen of Seattle was the downtown and the waterfront.

"It's not far from here," Jen replied.

"Then let's go," Stacy said. Maybe she'd suffered enough. Maybe this time she'd come up with that jacket.

The Capitol Hill Goodwill seemed to have a lot of young customers. "There's a community college nearby," Jen explained as they hurried over to the men's clothes.

A couple of college-age boys stood pawing through the coats. Stacy gasped as one of them pulled out a light green-and-sand-colored camo army jacket. Could it be?

The kid tried it on. It was way too big for him. But it was just the right size for Dean.

She hurried toward them and as she got closer

she was able to see the name stitched on the pocket. *Thomas*. "That's it!" she cried.

The kid was still wearing the jacket. He was about her son's age. Only her son was much nicer looking. This boy had brown hair gelled up into a point—not a good style for someone with a long face—and tattoo art climbing up his neck. He was too skinny and he wore ripped jeans and a T-shirt that had obviously seen better days. He'd probably purchased it here. Now he glanced up at her, surprised.

"That coat you've got, it's my husband's," she told him. "We've been looking all over town for it."

"I guess he didn't want it," said the kid. "Since it's here."

"It shouldn't be. It was all a mistake," Stacy explained. "Could I have it?" He didn't appear to be in any rush to hand it over, so she smiled her lovable, mom-next-door smile and added, "Please?"

He made no move to hand it over.

"It's too big for you, anyway."

He frowned. "Not that big."

Okay, that had been a tactical error. She tried to play on his sympathies. "My husband was really upset that I got rid of it." Anyone with a heart, anyone who'd been raised properly, would give up a coat that didn't fit him in the first place.

This particular anyone had been raised by wolves. He shrugged. "Not my problem."

"It's going to be your problem if you don't give me that coat," Stacy informed him, abandoning her mom-next-door smile.

"Hey, in case you didn't notice, this is a store. People buy things here."

"All right. I'll buy it from you," she said, opening her purse.

"Lady, I haven't even paid for it yet."

"So, I'll pay you not to pay for it." She got a ten-dollar bill from her wallet and held it out to him.

He eyed it, then he eyed her. Speculatively. "You really want this coat, huh?"

Well, duh. "I do." She waggled the bill temptingly.

"If you'd pay ten for it, I bet you'd pay twenty," said the scrawny little brat.

"Twenty?"

"Hey, I've gotta pay my tuition."

"What are you majoring in, robbery?"

"Business."

And he meant business. The kid still wasn't taking off the jacket. "Oh, all right," she said, and pulled out her last ten.

"Or thirty." He slipped off the jacket and dangled it temptingly.

"That's all I have," she said through clenched teeth.

The others had reached her in time to hear this last interchange. "I think I've got ten," Juliet said, catching on. She began to dig in her purse. "Yes!" she crowed, and produced another bill.

"Dude, don't settle for thirty," said the robber's pal, the kind of clean-cut preppy kid you'd expect would offer to change your tire if you had a flat. Looks sure were deceiving.

"I've got five." Jen drew a crumpled bill from her pocket.

The skinny little robber turned to Charley and asked with a leer, "And what have you got?"

With her long legs and shoulder-length chestnut hair,

Charley had plenty. She wasn't as beautiful as Cecily (who was?) but she had style and sex appeal. It probably made Mr. Business Major's day when she sidled up close to him, looking like a hooker about to make a deal.

"I'll tell you what I've got," she said sweetly.

He and his friend exchanged grins, but his died the moment her hand shot out and pinched the back of his neck in what resembled a death grip.

"I've got a real short fuse on my temper."

The kid squinted in pain. "Hey!" he protested, trying to squirm away.

His friend pointed a finger at Charley. "That's assault."

"And this is extortion. Take the thirty-five and give us the jacket or I'll grab you someplace even more painful."

"Okay, okay," he said, his voice surly. He handed over the jacket, took the money and then, with a huff, stomped off, humiliated but thirty-five dollars richer.

The women high-fived one another and chortled.

"That was impressive," Jen said to Charley.

She grinned wickedly as she gave Stacy her prize. "Who says chivalry is dead?"

"You guys, thank you so much," Stacy said. "You saved my life."

"Or at least your marriage," Charley teased. She eyed the coat with a frown. "But I can see why you wanted to get rid of that thing. It's ugly."

"Not to Dean," Stacy said. "I didn't realize this had so much sentimental value. I sure learned my lesson. Never give away a man's things without asking.

And never underestimate what you can find in a thrift store," she added with a smile.

"You know, I haven't poked around one of these places in years." Charley turned to Juliet and Jen. "You guys okay with hanging out for a few minutes before we head back?"

"I've got a babysitter. I'm in no hurry," Juliet said.

"I don't start work until next week," Jen said. "I've got time."

Next Charley turned to Stacy and Cecily. "You guys want to stay for a little longer?"

"I took a vacation day," Cecily said. "I'm good."

And now that the pressure was off, Stacy was ready to enjoy herself, too.

"Okay, I say we check this place out. Meet back here in the men's section in twenty?"

Everyone agreed and they went off in various directions, Charley and Cecily to women's clothes, Juliet toward baby things, Jen to housewares and Stacy to the collectibles.

By the end of the allotted time, everyone came back with something. Stacy had found more Fitz and Floyd, Juliet had scored with a bunch of baby clothes that were nearly new and Jen and Cecily both had coats.

But Charley had scored the biggest of all. "I now have my wedding dress," she announced, holding up a creamy satin gown. It was deceptively simple in design and obviously expensive.

"That's gorgeous," Stacy said.

Charley smiled. "A designer wedding gown for fifty bucks."

"But she looks like a million in it," Cecily said.

"Who knew?" Stacy mused as they paid for their

purchases—including the jacket (another twenty bucks, this time on an old credit card)—and left the store. One woman's junk was another woman's treasure. She'd been missing out all these years. When she got back to Icicle Falls, she had some treasure-hunting to do.

Chapter Twelve

*Even the simplest treat is a feast when shared
with someone.*
> —Muriel Sterling, author of *Simplicity*

"**Y**ou found it," Dean said when Stacy presented him
with his jacket. "Thanks, babe." Grinning, he put it on
and did a Mr. Universe pose. "Still looks good, eh?"

"Still looks good," she agreed.

"Thanks for getting it back," he said, and kissed her.

"My pleasure." No lie there. She'd had a great time
shopping once she'd accomplished her mission.

Dean had coached basketball after school so she'd
beaten him home. Barely. But since she had, she decided not to tell him she'd gone all the way to Seattle
to recover his coat. He'd have been horrified to hear
it had actually left town. He might also, in light of her
recent house-cleansing, have joked about the purchases
she'd brought back. There were so many things men
didn't understand.

He sure wouldn't understand why she returned to
the Kindness Cupboard the next day. Dean wouldn't
see this little thrift shop as unexplored territory, a potential gold mine of goodies. He'd simply see it as a

place for her to find more junk to clutter up their house. But Stacy wasn't looking for junk. She was looking for the good stuff.

"Welcome back," Janice Lind greeted her.

"You're still here?" Stacy teased.

"I'm here a lot."

Janice was an attractive older woman and had been one of the town's movers and shakers for years. Her husband, Swede, owned the garage. Officially he was retired, leaving the running of the business in younger hands, but he still went to work every day. And while he was busy with the garage, his wife was busy with her volunteer work. Her biggest claim to fame was the fact that her cakes always won the annual bake-off that raised funds to maintain historic town buildings.

"We can certainly use more volunteers," Janice added.

"Yeah?"

"One morning or afternoon a week. We especially need people to sort through the donations and arrange the merchandise. And help with boxing up the clothes to send on."

"So you ship the clothes over to Seattle."

"Yes, but we keep everything else. It's fun working here. We get to sift through all kinds of interesting things."

Stacy could imagine. "I'll think about it," she said, and wandered over to a corner display of Christmas decorations, which were marked seventy-five percent off. Wow. This was better than a department store sale.

Within twenty minutes Stacy had amassed a collection of candle holders, swags and figurines (including a new Santa to join her collection).

"Volunteers get twenty percent off," Janice said as she rang up the sale.

Stacy went home with a bag full of goodies and a volunteer application.

Mother Nature decided to decorate Icicle Falls with fresh snow. Jen looked out her window and groaned as the snow continued to fall. Tomorrow was her first day working at Gingerbread Haus. How was she going to get to work if she couldn't get out of her driveway?

You'll just have to wake up early and use your shovel, she told herself. Or...

Garrett Armstrong had promised to come and dig out her driveway when it snowed. This was as good an excuse as any to talk to her woman-shy landlord. She checked the wall clock she'd acquired in Seattle the day before. (Vintage and funky, shaped like a rooster.) Eight o'clock. Was he at work? There was only one way to find out.

"I'm finishing my shift at the station so I can come over later," he said when she called. "There's not much sense in digging you out until this stops."

When would that be? She looked out the window again. Unlike her vintage clock, what she saw there didn't make her smile. The snow seemed to be coming down in buckets.

"It's supposed to ease up this afternoon," he said. "I'll see you then."

"Thanks. I really appreciate it." This time when he came over she'd make sure he gave her a chance to show him just how much.

Meanwhile, she could write. She sat down with her laptop and opened up the document she'd simply labeled "Book." She sat staring at the blank screen, tapping the keyboard, hoping inspiration would come. Her sister made this look so easy. How did she do it?

Jen decided to call her and ask. "I have writer's block," she declared when Toni answered the phone.

"There's no such thing," Toni scoffed.

"Yes, there is 'cause I've got it."

"You haven't figured out what you want to say yet."

"Is that my problem?"

"One of them," Toni joked. "You know, a book's a pretty big project to tackle, Jen-Jen. Why don't you start with something a little more manageable, like a blog?"

A blog? Somehow, that sounded even more challenging than a book. A book you could work on when you felt like it. A blog had to be done on a regular basis. She wasn't sure she could come up with enough material. "What would I blog about?"

"Maybe your new, simple life in Icicle Falls. You might build a following and eventually get a book deal. At least it'll get you started."

"I guess," Jen said dubiously. "This morning all I can think to write is 'I hate snow' about a million times."

Toni chuckled. "I can tell you're loving your new home."

"Actually, I am," Jen said. "I've just got to learn to drive in this stuff. Maybe I should get an SUV."

"Well, don't run out and buy one today," Toni cautioned.

The way it was snowing, *that* wouldn't be happening.

"You can't afford it."

"I bet I could if I traded in my Toyota."

"At least wait until Wayne and I can get up there. Wayne can help you."

Her brother-in-law was a computer geek, not a car mechanic. "Wayne doesn't know anything about cars."

"No, but he's a man, and if you bring a man with you when you're looking for a car, you're not as likely to get taken advantage of."

"Nobody does that anymore," Jen scoffed. Her sister was such a cynic.

"Oh, sure. And I still believe in Santa. If you don't want to wait for Wayne, you could get your landlord to go with you. How is Mr. Hottie, by the way? Have you seen him since he rescued you from the ditch?"

"He's coming over later today to get the snow off my driveway."

"Mmm, interesting," Toni said. "How are you going to thank him?"

"Not the way I'd like to," Jen said, only half-kidding. "I don't think he's into me. Do you think he's gay?"

"No, I've got great gaydar, and I didn't pick up any vibes like that. In fact, just the opposite. I caught him looking at you once and it was very hetero."

"Well, something's off. Why else would he run away when I invited him in?"

"Past his curfew?" Toni cracked. "I don't know. Maybe he's got someone."

It was depressing to hear someone else voice what she'd thought. She said goodbye to her sister and went back to staring at her laptop screen.

A blog, huh? Well, why not? She found a free blog site and played around with the format. Picking a name for her blog kept her occupied for nearly an hour. What

to call it? *This Is What I'm Doing Until I Can Come
Up with a Book.* Lame-o.

She finally decided on *A Mountain View,* hoping
people would get the double meaning of beautiful scenery coupled with her new outlook on life. Then she
added a picture she'd taken of the mountains the first
time she and Toni visited Icicle Falls. Perfect. Now all
she needed was an entry.

She glanced out the window at the blanket of white
in her yard. Thank God the snow had finally stopped,
and the blanket wasn't getting any thicker. She tapped
the keyboard thoughtfully, then began typing....

It all started with a book my sister gave me on
how to simplify your life. I hated the fact that I
didn't have time for anything, so I made some
major changes. I left the city and moved to a
small town in the mountains. For the first time
in months I could breathe.

So true. The stress had melted away since she'd arrived in Icicle Falls and she was loving it up here, in
spite of her scary snow adventures. Hmm. Maybe she
should write about that. She typed on.

But sometimes simplifying your life isn't all that
simple. Take the "simple" fact of snow, for example...

She wished somebody *would* take it. She set aside
the laptop and went to the window to look out again.
She had to admit it was beautiful. But she was way
too social to like the idea of being snowed in by her-

self. She wouldn't mind being snowed in with a certain sexy fireman, though. A fire in the woodstove, some hot, buttered rum…

How did you make hot buttered rum, anyway? Finding a recipe for that sounded like a lot more fun than writing, especially since she wasn't very excited about what she'd written so far.

She found a recipe for the basic batter and smiled. She had all the ingredients and she had rum in the cupboard. She had wood for the stove. Everything she needed for a cozy late-afternoon tête-à-tête. She grinned. Feeling a little like a spider working on a web, she built a fire in the stove (making sure to pull out the damper), then took out butter, brown sugar and spices and got to work. Mixing up a recipe in the kitchen on a wintry afternoon—one of life's simple pleasures. What was better than that? *Sharing it with someone, that's what.* Hee, hee. Who needed an SUV, anyway, when you could lure a handsome man to your house? Not that she was rushing into anything, of course.

As if on cue, Garrett Armstrong's truck made its appearance in her driveway. She threw on her coat and hurried outside, positioning herself where he was bound to see her. She knew he had because he waved. But he didn't stop pushing snow. With his truck and its plow attachment he'd be done in no time and then he'd be gone and she'd have made her buttered rum mix for nothing. She moved closer to the truck and flapped her arms to get his attention.

He stopped the truck and lowered the window, then looked at her questioningly.

"Would you mind coming in for a minute when you're finished?" she asked.

"Sure. What's up?"

"I—I need an opinion on something."

"Uh."

This man sure knew how to make a girl feel wanted. Before he could come up with some pathetic excuse, she turned and went back into the cabin.

A few minutes later he was coming in the door, as wary as a deer entering a forest clearing. A buck. A big, handsome buck.

She was ready for him. She was holding two mugs and handed him one. "Tell me what you think of this."

He regarded it suspiciously. "What is it?"

"Hot buttered rum. I made the mix myself."

He took a sip and looked pleasantly surprised. "It's good. You made this yourself, huh?"

She smiled. "I can make all kinds of things."

He cocked his head and studied her. "I'll bet you can."

"I make a mean veggie wrap. Would you like to stay and try one?"

He took a hasty gulp, then set his drink on the counter. "Uh, no. Thanks. I have to get going."

Okay, he *had* to have someone. *"Got a hot date?"*

"With my kid."

"You're married?" Maybe not. He'd said *kid,* not *wife.* She held her breath.

"Divorced." She was about to ask if his child liked veggie wraps when he added, "I'm seeing someone."

So he did have somebody. *That figures.* A man like Garrett Armstrong wouldn't be unattached. She should have known. "Oh," she said, trying not to sound disappointed. *This is where you let it go,* she told herself. Instead, she asked, "Is it serious?"

He rubbed the back of his neck, a sure sign that she'd made him uncomfortable.

"I'm sorry," she said. "That's none of my business. And there's nothing in the lease that says you have to keep your renters from getting cabin fever."

"Well, we're… It's…complicated."

How was it complicated? Either he was serious about the woman he was seeing or he wasn't.

"You should be good to go now," he said, backing toward the door.

He was always doing that, like a man in a tiger cage, afraid to turn his back. It took all her self-control not to frown. "Thanks for helping me out," she said.

"No problem. Have a good night."

And then he was gone. She sat down on the couch with her hot buttered rum and took another sip, determined to enjoy it. This sip didn't go down as well as the first one and she set it aside.

Who was Garrett Armstrong seeing, anyway?

Chapter Thirteen

*It's only our unrealistic expectations for romance
on special days like Valentine's Day that make it
so disappointing.*
—Muriel Sterling, author of *Simplicity*

It wasn't until the week before the chocolate festival
that Jen learned who Garrett Armstrong was seeing.
She had recently joined Bruisers Fitness Center (New
Year's resolution, of course) and was on her way in
when she encountered him leaving with a tall, fit bru-
nette dressed in workout clothes. The woman's hair
was short and lay flat and damp against her head. She
had the kind of supermodel cheekbones Jen had always dreamed of having but other than that there was
nothing remarkable about her face. It was okay, but
she wasn't a knockout. What was the attraction, then?
The legs, obviously. He liked tall girls. Tall, athletic
girls. Jen wasn't tall and she was about as athletic as
a marshmallow.

She sighed inwardly but forced herself to say a
friendly hello.

That, in turn, forced him to stop and introduce the
other woman. "Jen, this is Tilda Morrison. Jen's my

new renter," he explained to Tilda. No need to explain Tilda to Jen. She wasn't stupid.

Still, Garrett and this woman seemed more like pals than a couple. He never so much as put an arm around her while they stood talking.

"How do you like Icicle Falls?" Tilda asked.

"So far, so good," Jen said. "It helps to have a great landlord," she added, smiling at Garrett.

Now he seemed suddenly uncomfortable. She'd only meant to be nice but the other woman might read more into that remark than she'd meant. *Nothing like failing to think before opening your mouth,* she thought, annoyed with herself. Much as she wanted to start something with Garrett, she didn't want to start trouble for him.

"Well, I should get busy getting in shape," she said, motioning in the direction of the fitness equipment.

Tilda didn't seem the least bit threatened. "Nice to meetcha," she said, then strode out of the building.

"Take care," Garrett said, and followed her out.

Jen watched as Tilda walked over to the patrol car parked near the door. A cop? Garrett was seeing a cop?

They stood next to the car for a moment, chatting. As they did, Tilda's earlier casual expression softened into something Jen easily recognized. That was the look of a woman in love. But they didn't kiss. And there was nothing sexy about their exchange. He stayed another minute, then walked off and she slid behind the wheel and drove away. Why was Garrett hanging out with Tilda if he didn't feel any chemistry? Jen was still trying to puzzle it out when she ran into Cecily Sterling at Bavarian Brews.

"Are you going to the chocolate festival?" Cecily

asked, nodding toward the poster on the wall. It showed a chocolate truffle superimposed over a shot of the town with Sleeping Lady Mountain looming in the background. "It's not to be missed," Cecily said, and told Jen about some of the events.

"Hey, did I move to the right town or what?"

"You did," Cecily said with a smile.

"Maybe I'll see if my sister wants to come up." Toni the chocoholic would love this.

"A whole weekend dedicated to chocolate? Oh, twist my arm," Toni said when Jen called her.

"They've got all kinds of things going on—a chocolate tea, a tour of the Sweet Dreams chocolate factory, free samples, candy-making demos and a Mr. Dreamy pageant. Even a masked ball. You could bring the whole family."

"Or I could come by myself and leave Mr. Non-Dreamy at home," Toni said crisply.

This didn't sound good. "Is everything okay with you guys?" Jen asked.

"Oh, yeah, we're fine. Just dull and boring. Knowing Wayne, he'll have some emergency to deal with. He won't even miss me."

Were Toni and Wayne in more trouble than Toni wanted to admit? They'd seemed fine when they came up to help her move in. But who could tell? Trouble could build under the surface of a marriage and then suddenly erupt. She knew; she'd been there. She sure didn't want to see that happen to her sister, but Toni's discontent was evident, which was too bad because Wayne was a nice guy. It wasn't easy to find a nice guy.

And once you found one…well, it still wasn't easy. Jen wondered if Garrett Armstrong would be hanging around at the chocolate festival. She envisioned him feeding her a truffle and smiled. This was quickly followed by a vision of Tilda Morrison shoving her into a vat of boiling chocolate. She frowned. Why did she have to be attracted to a man who clearly wasn't interested in *her?*

Never mind, she told herself on Saturday as she and her sister immersed themselves in the fun of the chocolate festival. *Your love life will work itself out. That was what Muriel said. Cecily, too. Meanwhile, enjoy the moment.*

There was plenty to enjoy as the sisters strolled among the various booths on Alpine Street in the downtown area. The festival was in full swing and the very air was heavy with the aroma of chocolate.

"This is fantastic!" Toni said, taking in all the booths. "I'm going to spend a fortune. I can feel it."

That wouldn't be difficult. Local artisans were selling everything from paintings and scarves to chocolate tea and soap. It seemed that every eatery and service club in town was represented, and all were offering chocolate of some sort. One of the local church youth groups had a booth selling chocolate doughnuts. Another sold hot chocolate. Of course, the Sweet Dreams Chocolates booth was drawing the biggest crowd, with tourists flocking to have their picture taken with this year's Mr. Dreamy. The Eurythmics' "Sweet Dreams" added a musical backdrop.

Billy Williams, whom everybody called Bill Will, had won the title the night before at the estrogen-driven Mr. Dreamy pageant, where the women came for Sweet Dreams chocolates and a chance to root for their favorite man. The men had paraded around the stage, strutting their stuff while women on a chocolate high cheered and whistled and generally egged them on. Contestants had showed off their talents, some singing (often badly), some dancing and some doing simplistic magic tricks. Bill Will was a shoo-in when he displayed his roping skills, roping a gigantic pink wooden heart bearing the Sweet Dreams logo and then presenting it to Samantha Sterling, who was the president of the company and the moving force behind the town's chocolate festival. A few sore losers had muttered that it was the equivalent of bribing the judges, but most agreed that it was Bill Will's turn to win.

"That was incredibly tacky," Toni had said when it was over. "And fun. We have to find him tomorrow and get our picture taken with him."

"Looks like we found Mr. Dreamy," Jen said now, pointing to the Sweet Dreams booth.

"Let's get over there before his back gives out," Toni said.

They made their way through the crowd to where Bill Will was in the process of sweeping an older woman off her feet. Literally. The woman giggled as her friends gathered around and snapped pictures with their cell phones.

At the sight of Jen and Toni, he unloaded the woman and steered her over to where the Sterling sisters were selling their famous chocolates. "Hey, there," he greeted them. He pointed a finger at Jen. "I've seen you around. You're the new lady in town."

"I am," Jen agreed, and introduced herself.

"Welcome, darlin'," he said, giving her an appreciative once-over. "I'm Billy Williams. Everybody calls me Bill Will."

"I've heard about you," Jen said. Juliet had filled her and Toni in the night before at the Mr. Dreamy pageant. "You're doing a great job representing Sweet Dreams Chocolates."

"I aim to please," he said, grinning. "And who's this you got with you?"

"This is my sister, Toni Carlyon."

"Well, don't pretty run in your family," he said. "You come to get your picture taken with Mr. Dreamy?"

"And to get chocolate," Jen said.

"But first, I need a picture," Toni insisted.

"Of course." Bill Will held out an arm. "Step right up, darlin'."

She handed Jen her phone. "Let's make this a good one," she said to Bill Will.

"All right," he said, and scooped her up in his arms.

Toni grabbed his cowboy hat and put it on her head. "Yee haw."

With her long highlighted hair, pretty face and perfect figure, Toni made a convincing cowgirl. "Oh, that's cute." Jen snapped the picture.

Bill Will set Toni down and she returned his hat. Jen handed back her phone, she looked at the picture and said, "I think I'll send this to my husband. I'll caption it, 'Having a great time. Wish you were here.'"

"That should make him jealous," Jen said.

"I doubt it," Toni said with a frown.

"Okay, Jen, you're next," Bill Will said. Now the music had changed to Big and Rich's "Save a Horse, Ride a Cowboy." "Hey, good idea." Bill Will presented his back to Jen. "Climb on, cowgirl."

Why not? She obliged, hopping onto his back and taking his hat. Bill Will let out a whoop and the crowd around them increased in size. He jumped and Jen yelped, making everyone laugh, including her.

She looked to see if her sister had captured the moment on her phone and caught sight of Juliet from the book club, along with her friend Chelsea. Juliet grinned and gave Jen a thumbs-up.

Then, behind Juliet, she spotted another face, this one frowning in disgust. Garrett Armstrong. Obviously Garrett didn't approve of saving horses and riding cowboys.

Feeling chastised, she slid off Bill Will and returned his hat, thanking him.

"What's the matter?" her sister asked.

"Nothing," Jen lied.

"Right. You're acting like a little kid who lost her balloon."

She felt like that, too. But it was silly to let a disapproving look from her landlord ruin the moment. She'd just been having fun. She was allowed. She glanced over to where he'd been standing and saw he was now moving off in another direction. And he wasn't alone. He had a little boy—probably his—by the hand and his pal Tilda in tow. Shouldn't she be on patrol somewhere?

"Come on," Toni said, "let's get some chocolate."

Jen nodded, determined to forget about her stick-in-the-mud landlord and his stick-in-the-mud opinions. And she wasn't going to indulge in any more fantasies about him, either. So there.

He'd known it the day she moved in. Jen Heath was another Ashley, just out for a good time. She'd moved to Icicle Falls on a whim; no doubt she'd move away on a whim. Or move in with some guy, like Bill

Will. Never mind that she looked like the girl next door with that freckled face and full-lipped smile. It was a facade.

"What's bugging you?" Tilda asked.

"Me? Nothing." He smiled down at Timmy. "Let's go get a hot dog. What do you say to that, buddy?"

Timmy nodded eagerly. "I like hot dogs!" He gazed up at Tilda. "Do you like hot dogs?"

"Sure," she said. "And curly fries. Can't forget curly fries."

Good old Tilda. Another woman would have continued to pester him, insisting something was wrong and wanting to know what. Not Tilda. Being with her was as comfortable as being with another guy.

And that was exactly what Garrett wanted. Yes, sir.

He cast a quick glance over his shoulder. Now Jen was at the booth, sampling chocolate and laughing with Cecily Sterling and a couple of other women. Garrett's eyes strayed to her well-rounded bottom. *Seen one butt, seen 'em all,* he told himself.

Yeah, right. And that was why he had to force his head to turn and his eyes to look straight ahead.

Don't get chummy with her, he reminded himself. *Stay in the truck when you go over to plow snow from the driveway. Collect the rent and scram. Don't stick around to get tempted.*

Why did temptation have to be so…tempting? Damn it all, he wished he'd never met the woman.

You don't have to go out for a fancy dinner to celebrate Valentine's Day. In fact, you don't even need to have a sweetheart. What's important is to make sure you're with people you care about, having fun together. Anyway, sex is overrated.

Jen looked at what she'd written for her blog so far and frowned. Nobody was going to buy that. She deleted the last sentence and continued.

I had fun this past weekend checking out the chocolate festival in Icicle Falls.

No lie. She'd had a great time until she'd seen Garrett. She wrote some more about the festival and posted a couple of pictures, then added her recipe.

CHOCOLATE MADNESS SNACK
(makes 4 cups)

1 cup M&M's
1 cup semisweet chocolate chips
1 cup white chocolate chips
1 cup Hershey's Kisses, whatever kind you like
(my fave is the one with caramel)

Mix everything together and enjoy while watching a great chick movie.

She typed in her last paragraph.

I'll be taking this to my book club tonight. We're celebrating Valentine's Day early and we'll probably overdose on chocolate. What will you be doing for Valentine's Day?

She hit Publish and sighed. What she'd written was fine in theory, but in reality she was bummed that she didn't have any romantic plans for Cupid's big day.

Well, she'd do…something. Maybe she'd treat herself to some Sweet Dreams chocolates and watch a vintage chick flick. That would have to do for this year.

She got to Stacy's house to find the book club was ready to celebrate. Stacy had made chocolate-dipped strawberries in honor of Valentine's Day, which was just a couple of days away, and Cecily had brought treats from Sweet Dreams. Cass had contributed iced gingerbread hearts, and Charley and Chita had provided champagne.

"This is probably as romantic as it's going to get for me this year," Chita confessed as Charley popped the cork on the champagne. "This is also about as much romance as I have energy for," Chita added.

"Romance is overrated," Cecily said.

Jen wasn't so sure about that.

"No way." Stacy held up a glass to be filled. "Not if you have a man who's truly romantic."

"I had a fiancé who was the most romantic guy in L.A.," Cecily said.

"So, how did he get to be your ex, then?" Stacy asked.

"I found out he was being romantic with his former girlfriend whenever I had to work."

Stacy shook her head. "What a bumsicle."

Cecily shrugged. "They're everywhere."

"Not in Icicle Falls," Juliet insisted.

"So, who's the best catch in Icicle Falls?" Jen asked. *Garrett Armstong,* whispered a naughty little voice at the back of her mind. She told it to shut up.

"Luke Goodman," Cecily replied, making Charley

raise an eyebrow at her. "Not for me," she clarified, "but for...someone."

"You're the only someone he wants," Charley pointed out. "Cecily's been collecting men since she moved back," Charley explained to Jen. "Her production manager at Sweet Dreams is crazy for her. So's Todd Black. He owns the Man Cave."

"He's gorgeous." Juliet sighed. "That man should be on the cover of a romance novel."

"There's more to life than gorgeous men," Cecily muttered, and the others laughed at her.

"What about Garrett Armstrong?" Jen asked, trying to sound casual. "Is he with anyone?"

Charley gave a knowing grin. "So, you've been bitten by the Garrett bug."

"No, just wondering," Jen lied.

"He's sort of with Tilda Morrison, the cop," Charley said. "They've come into Zelda's for drinks a few times. But I don't think he's that into her. I don't think he's into anyone. His ex did such a number on him, the man is love shy."

"Is she still around here?" Jen asked.

Charley popped a strawberry in her mouth. "Oh, yeah. That woman is a piece of work. She's always in the bar trying to hook up. Bad enough she broke his heart, but he's got to put up with her being the mother of his kid on top of it. A lizard would be a better mother than that woman."

So, her sexy fireman was nursing a broken heart. That meant he was hanging out with Tilda because...he thought she was safe? Were they just friends? Friends with benefits? She couldn't imagine Tilda *not* wanting to take their relationship beyond that. Would Garrett be interested, though—with Tilda or anyone?

Charley and Stacy had finished filling the champagne glasses and were passing them around.

"Here's to a great Valentine's Day, however we all choose to spend it," said Stacy.

"By myself," Chita said, "doing something I want to do." She grinned. "I took your advice last month," she told Stacy, "I'm no longer a Girls of America leader."

Stacy clinked glasses with her. "Good for you. Hey, maybe now you'll have some time for romance."

"I'll be happy just to find time to watch *Project Runway* once in a while. And get our monthly book club selections read."

"Speaking of books, how are we all doing with making changes in our lives?" Juliet wanted to know.

Silence descended on the room.

"I'm enjoying my simple life," Jen ventured. She smiled at Cass. "And I'm enjoying my new job." Cass was an easygoing boss and Jen was finding that she really enjoyed interacting with the townspeople who came in for a sugar fix.

"It's great having you there," Cass said. She took a sip of champagne. "Once Jen is trained I'll have more time."

Jen felt as if she was pretty much trained already. Still, Cass continued to come into the bakery; she was beginning to suspect that her employer was a workaholic.

"I've delegated some stuff to Neil," Juliet announced. "He's in charge of dinner two nights a week now. And I'm giving myself Saturday afternoons off. I do some shopping in town or take a book to Bavarian Brews and read. Last week I finished the new Vanessa Valentine." She turned to Charley. "How are you doing?"

Charley frowned at her glass of champagne. "I don't think I'll be able to simplify my life until after I'm married. And even though we've put the wedding off until June, I still feel stressed. The other day I was looking at flowers in Lupine Floral with Dan and I burst into tears. All because I couldn't decide between the taupe satin flower bouquet or the blue-and-white bouquet with white roses and hydrangeas." She set aside her glass with a frown. "I'm tired all the time. Dan asked me what I wanted to do for Valentine's Day and you know what I said? Sleep. How's that for sexy?"

"Sounds good to me," Chita said.

"You guys are too young to feel this old. Heck, we all are," Stacy said.

"So, what are *you* going to do?" Charley asked her as they drifted from the kitchen to the living room.

"I'm making us a romantic dinner using the fondue pot and the heart-shaped cake tin I found at the Kindness Cupboard yesterday."

"I thought you were lightening your load. How much stuff have you bought since we went to Seattle?" Charley asked.

"Not that much," Stacy said. Just a few things for the house—plus a coat with a faux-fur collar and some great jeans from a thrift store in Wenatchee.... She glanced around the living room. "Okay, so maybe I was a *little* carried away. But I saved a fortune on everything I got."

"I love how you rationalize everything," Cass said with a smile.

"Heck, everyone rationalizes." Charley shrugged. "Whether it's our overwork or our overstuffed closets." She sighed and slumped down among the sofa cushions. "It shouldn't be that hard to simplify your life. And it shouldn't be so exhausting to plan a simple wedding."

"You know there's no such thing as a simple wedding," Chita told her.

"There's no such thing as a simple anything," Charley muttered. "Even Valentine's Day is going to be ridiculous. The restaurant is booked solid, and I've almost made myself insane planning our Valentine special. Now Dan's arranged some crazy getaway. How am I supposed to leave the restaurant on Valentine's Day?"

"You do have a general manager," Cass reminded her.

"I know. But, well, I like to be there on an important day."

"Your love life is important, too," Cass said gently.

Cass is right, Charley told herself as Dan drove his truck over the mountains toward Seattle. Getting away was a great idea. She just hoped that wherever they were going, it wouldn't take long to get there. And wherever it was, she hoped they had a hot tub. Now, if only she could wheedle their destination out of him. The back of the cab held two overnight bags and a garment bag, and he hadn't let her so much as peek in any of them.

"Where are we going?" she asked, not for the first time.

"I told you, the airport."

"That doesn't tell me anything," Charley complained. "And how can I be sure you packed what I need?"

"Trust me, baby. I've got what you need."

"I know that," she cracked, and smiled at him.

"Anything I forgot you can pick up when we arrive."

He'd had a hard time convincing her to leave the restaurant on one of their busiest days of the year, but now she was glad he'd succeeded. She could already feel the stress falling off her shoulders.

She looked out the window at the snowy landscape slipping by. It was probably just as well that she'd abandoned the idea of getting married at the restaurant. They would've lost a ton of business. Getting married on Valentine's Day was romantic, but it sure wasn't practical. Darn.

"So I guess that means we're not going to the ends of the earth," she deduced.

He sent her a smile. "You don't have time to go to the ends of the earth."

No, she didn't. These days she barely had time to go to the bathroom. So much for simplifying her life.

He'd printed their boarding passes ahead of time and had them hidden in his bag, and their luggage was carry-on, so she didn't find out their destination until they'd gotten to security. "Las Vegas?"

"We're getting married there. At the Chapel of Love," he added, waggling his eyebrows and making the TSA agent smile.

"What?" Was he insane? "We can't just go to Vegas!"

"Sure you can," said the agent and stamped her boarding pass.

"What about my family?" she said once they were through security and on their way to the gate.

"Your parents and sister are meeting us for drinks tonight at the Bellagio, along with my folks and my brother. So is Cass."

"Cass!"

"She left on an earlier flight, along with Samantha and Cecily. Your pal Ella is meeting us for breakfast tomorrow."

He'd planned all this? "No way."

For a moment he looked doubtful. "You were serious about wanting to do this simply, right?"

"Yeah, of course." She'd done the big church wedding with Richard. She didn't want to repeat any of that history. Still…

"When you broke down in the flower shop I got to thinking."

"That you were marrying a crazy person?"

He chuckled. "That you were going to a lot of trouble for something I didn't care that much about. What you said made me think that maybe you didn't, either, that you were just doing all this because you thought it was expected. You said, 'Why does a simple wedding have to be so much work?' So I figured we should go back to what we originally talked about and just have fun with this. Why spend all that money on something that's stressing you when you can have a kick-ass vacation and a no-fuss wedding?"

"You're right." She'd complained her way through every aspect of planning their wedding, from the cake to the dress. But then she'd picked out a great cake. And she'd found that dress… "I just wish I had my dress," she said sadly.

He held up the garment bag. "What do you think this is?"

"You thought of everything." And she still couldn't believe it, couldn't believe all her plans had vanished with a poof. So had the stress.

"I did, as a matter of fact. Tomorrow afternoon you're going to the spa and then shopping. We're getting married at six and then we're doing a progressive dinner, starting with appetizers at Mon Ami Gabi, followed by spicy crab salad at Alain Ducasse's Mix at Mandalay Bay. Then we're hitting Sensi for our main course and finishing up with Bananas Foster at Bradley Ogden." He spread his arms wide. "A simple wedding dinner."

Charley was rarely speechless. She stood there staring at him.

Now he looked worried. "Uh, happy Valentine's Day?"

"Happy everything!" she cried, and threw her arms around him.

Stacy was feeling very pleased with both her thrift-store purchases and herself as she and Dean enjoyed a fondue dinner by candlelight. "This is amazing, babe," he said, scooping out the last bit of fondue with a piece of French bread. He popped it in his mouth. "But we could've gone out, you know."

"I know. I just thought it would be nice to do something simple at home for a change." Not that the raspberry-white chocolate cake had been simple, but when she'd first bitten into it and her taste buds had an orgasm, she'd known it had been worth the effort.

"I didn't realize we even had one of these...what is this again?"

"A fondue pot. I got it at the Kindness Cupboard."

"Is it my imagination or have you been bringing home a lot of stuff from that place lately?" Dean asked.

"It's your imagination," she assured him.

After they'd finished eating, Dean left the table. He returned a moment later with a long, slender jewelry box. "I know you're trying to get rid of stuff, but I figure this won't take up much room."

She opened it to find a bracelet glittering with diamond chips. "Oh, Deano, it's gorgeous."

"Just like my wife," he said.

"This must have cost a fortune," she protested. With two kids in college they couldn't afford this kind of Valentine extravagance.

He grinned. "I learned a thing or two from you. I got it on sale last month."

"In that case, I'll keep it," she said, taking it out of the box.

"How about modeling it for me?" He fastened the bracelet on her wrist, and she stretched out her arm, watching the diamonds wink in the candlelight. "It doesn't show very well with that sweater on," Dean said. He stood behind her and helped her take off the sweater, kissing her neck in the process.

"Now how does it look?" she asked.

He cocked his head, studying her. "I think you should lose the blouse."

The blouse followed the sweater.

"That's more like it," he said, "The jeans are kind of a distraction, though."

She lost the jeans, too. And the bra and panties.

FREE Merchandise is 'in the Cards' for you!

Dear Reader,

We're giving away FREE MERCHANDISE!

Seriously, we'd like to reward you for reading this novel by giving you **FREE MERCHANDISE** worth over $20. And no purchase is necessary!

You see the Jack of Hearts sticker above? Paste that sticker in the box on the Free Merchandise Voucher inside. Return the Voucher promptly...and we'll send you valuable Free Merchandise!

Thanks again for reading one of our novels—and enjoy your Free Merchandise with our compliments!

Pam Powers

Pam Powers

P.S. Look inside to see what Free Merchandise is **"in the cards"** for you!

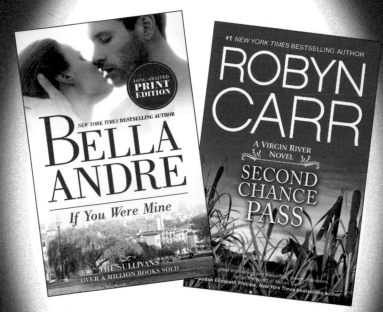

Dean approved, and led her over to the fireplace for the second dessert course.

Ah, yes, there was nothing like a simple, romantic Valentine's celebration.

They'd just gotten out of the shower when the phone rang. Who on earth would be calling? Her mother! But Mom and Dad were going to Zelda's.

Her mother barely gave her time to say hello. "Stacy, your nana's had a stroke."

Chapter Fourteen

*Sometimes it's good to ask yourself, "Do I own
my things or do they own me?"*
                        —Muriel Sterling, author of *Simplicity*

Please, God, don't let Nana die, Stacy prayed as she
and Dean rushed to Mountain Regional Hospital. *At
least not until I've had a chance to say goodbye.* The
thought of losing her sweet grandma made her eyes
prickle with tears.

Dean reached across the seat and laid a comforting
hand on her leg. "It'll be all right."

It probably wouldn't, but she appreciated him for
saying it, anyway.

They got to the hospital to find her family all in
a waiting room. Her uncle Jack sat nursing a cup of
coffee and talking on his cell phone, alerting family
members. Her father was missing, most likely outside,
smoking. Her aunt Vivian was the oldest of Nana's
three children, but she normally worked hard to look
young, keeping up the illusion that she was still a
blonde, maintaining a svelte figure and dressing well.
Tonight she wore sweats and she looked as if she'd aged
ten years, every wrinkle in her face a deep crevice of

pain. She was slumped in a chair, dabbing at her eyes with a tissue. Stacy's mother wasn't in much better shape. She was the youngest of Nana's children, but tonight she looked old and tired. She hadn't bothered with makeup, which made the dark circles under her eyes even more prominent than usual. She was pacing the room as if she could somehow walk her way out of this trouble.

She smiled sadly at Stacy and held out an arm, and Stacy hurried over to hug her.

"How is she?"

Mom shook her head. "Not good."

"Is she going to die?"

"I don't know."

"Can we see her?"

"In a little bit. They're getting her settled in her room."

How long did it take to get an eighty-eight-year-old woman settled? Stacy hugged everyone, helped her mother pace, got some coffee then paced some more. Finally the nurses opened the curtain in Nana's room and allowed everyone to enter.

The woman on the bed looked so small, a fragile outline holding up the bedcovers. They all gathered around her and Stacy's mother took Nana's hand and squeezed it. "How are you feeling, Mama?"

Nana tried to smile. Only half her mouth cooperated.

Blinking back tears, Stacy stood at one end of the bed. *This is where we all end up, sooner or later,* she thought. "Nana, you have to get better. You've still got quilts left in you."

Again, Nana tried to smile. She said something but her voice was so slurred Stacy had no idea what it was.

Stacy lingered until Nana's eyes drifted shut. "You may as well go home, honey," said her mother.

Dean put an arm around her and led her from the room. "I hate this," she said bitterly as they waited in the hall for the elevator.

He squeezed her. "I know. It's hard."

It was just as hard the following day, seeing her grandmother still prone in the bed. "I love you," Stacy told her, and squeezed her hand.

"Oooh, too," Nana slurred.

You, too. It was clearer than the day before, Stacy was sure of it. That had to be a good sign.

"She seems to be getting better," Stacy said to her mother as they went to the cafeteria.

"I don't think she's going to be coming home," Mom said. "Aunt Vivian and Uncle Jack are looking at Cascade Rehab."

"A nursing home?"

"It's a nice one," Mom assured her, "and each room has a lovely view so she can see the mountains."

"She could see the mountains fine from her house, too. Why can't we hire someone to take care of her there?"

Mom didn't say anything.

"You guys don't think she's going to make it, do you?"

"We just don't know." Mom sighed. "But we'll have to put the house on the market."

"Sell Nana's house?"

Her grandmother's Victorian with its small yard in front and large vegetable garden out back was woven into the fabric of Stacy's childhood. She remembered going over there after school for tea parties with her grandmother. She'd admired the Dresden figurines on the knickknack shelf, played with the button collection her grandmother kept in an old woven basket decorated with tassels, had her first quilting lesson on the antique blue velvet settee in the living room. Selling the house seemed wrong.

"Nursing homes are expensive," her mother said.

"But doesn't Nana have money?"

"Not a lot."

"But if she gets well she'll need a house to come back to," Stacy protested.

"If she gets well she'll come and live with me. We've already discussed this with Uncle Jack and Aunt Vivian."

Pared down from a house to a room. How was that going to work? "What about all her things?" Stacy asked.

"We'll have to go through them, decide what to keep, what to get rid of."

Aunt Vivian was a take-charge kind of woman who, on more than one occasion, had said how much she hated clutter. Someone needed to be present to provide some balance. "I'll help," Stacy said.

"It's going to be a big job," her mother warned.

"That's okay. I want to help." *And save as much as possible.*

So the next day Stacy showed up at her grandmother's house, ready to roll up her sleeves. She found her mother and Aunt Vivian in the kitchen with clipboards, taking inventory.

"There's so much," Aunt Vivian said, and her tone implied that this was a bad thing.

"The everyday dishes and good china can go to Christie and Cheron, so that takes care of a lot right there," Mom said. She smiled at Stacy. "I assume you'd like her quilting supplies."

Stacy nodded. But when she went into the spare bedroom she was almost overwhelmed by the bags and bags of material and all the paraphernalia. There was so much. Had it been breeding in here when no one was looking?

Stacy already had every quilting tool ever made, and she sure didn't need Nana's old sewing machine when hers was state-of-the-art. For now, she'd save it in case Nana got better. Same with the iron and ironing board and the pins and notions. She could always take them to the Kindness Cupboard later if…

She bit her lip to keep from crying and turned her attention to the old brass bed. Every square inch of it was covered with dolls and stuffed animals. More of Nana's doll collection occupied a glass-encased cabinet in one corner of the room, as well as the top of the dresser. Who was going to want her doll collection? Nobody collected dolls anymore. At least, nobody Stacy knew.

She wasn't sure anyone collected decorative plates, either, and those marched along the walls in this room. They also occupied space in the kitchen and the little dining room. And Stacy knew her grandmother had more boxes of plates stored in the attic. That was a lot of plates.

Then there were all the Beanie Babies piled up in the closet. Nana had thought they were so cute. For a couple of years everyone in the family had given her Beanie Babies for Christmas, her birthday, Mother's Day.

She could hear her aunt's voice from down the hall. "It's going to take weeks to sort through all this stuff, Lila. We should call an auction house."

Strangers coming in and valuing (or devaluing) Nana's possessions? Ugh, what a sad thought!

"I don't think we could convince even an auction house to take all these plates. No one wants them anymore," her mother said.

"No one wants any of this," said Aunt Vivian. "But we're stuck with it."

"Maybe the teacups. " Mom suggested.

"They're gorgeous. But who uses these old-fashioned teacups? I wish our mother hadn't been such a packrat."

This was the sum of her grandmother's life? Everything she'd treasured was now a nuisance to be gotten rid of? That just wasn't right.

But as Stacy spent the day with her mother and aunt, sorting and saving, she began to feel her sentimental attachment fading. Who cared about American Blue the bear or Allie the alligator? And who needed a Scarlett O'Hara collectible plate. *Frankly, my dear, I don't give a damn.*

"I say we rent a Dumpster and toss all this and be done with it," Aunt Vivian said.

Someone gasped in shock and Stacy realized it was her. What would Nana say?

"Why don't we have a garage sale?" her mother proposed.

"Who do you think is going to buy this?" Aunt Vivian gestured to the boxes of items piled around the living room. "No one will take it even for free. We've tried giving things to everyone in the family. No one wants decorative plates or Beanie Babies. We're lucky someone wants the china."

"I'll take anything you don't want," Stacy heard herself say. Where the heck would she store all this stuff?

"More power to you if you can," said her aunt. "You *might* be able to sell some of those Beanie Babies online, but I'll be surprised if you can."

"Nana wanted the grandkids to have her Beanie Babies," Stacy said sadly.

Vivian shook her head. "No one wants them. Unless you…"

Stacy had never been interested in Beanie Babies. "I'll try to sell them." At least that would provide some extra money for Nana.

"You can probably get something for that Depression glass," her mother said. "And the carnival glass."

"It's so sad to be getting rid of all the things she valued," Stacy murmured. If Nana found out it would put her in her grave for sure.

"I tried to tell her over the years that nobody wants this stuff, but she wouldn't listen," Aunt Vivian said irritably. "And now, here we are dealing with all this… crap on top of everything else." Her voice quavered and Stacy's mom drew her into a hug. Her aunt let out a little sob and Stacy's eyes began to tear up, too.

Her aunt got herself under control quickly enough, but her eyes were red when she pulled away. "We should get back to work. I've only got today and tomorrow and then I have to get back to the office."

"We need to go to the hospital to see Mama later," Stacy's mother said.

"Then let's get cracking," said her aunt.

They went back to sorting and boxing and Aunt Vivian muttered, "By God, I'm going through my place this summer and getting rid of stuff. I don't want to do this to my kids."

It *was* a daunting job, Stacy had to admit. And not at all fun. As she sorted through another herd of Beanie Babies, trying to cull the salable ones from the trash, she couldn't help thinking of all the things she'd been bringing home lately. What would be her equivalent of Beanie Babies?

She'd gotten rid of so much, but ever since discovering the joy of thrift shops she'd brought home a new wave of items to occupy space in her cupboards and closets. Just because something was pretty or a great bargain did she need it? Really?

She was exhausted by the time she got home but she didn't let that stop her from touring her house with a critical eye, a trash bag and a cardboard box. Both were filled within half an hour.

The next day found her at the Kindness Cupboard with donations from both her grandmother's house and hers. Janice Lind pointed at the Old Country Roses china clock perched on one of the boxes and raised an eyebrow. "This looks familiar."

"It should. I bought it last time I was in here."

"And you're tired of it already?"

"I just don't need it," Stacy said. "I don't need any of this. I'm lightening my load," she added. "Again."

Janice nodded.

She'd enjoyed finding the treasures but she didn't need to turn her home into Treasure Island. So, no more thrift stores, no more bargain-hunting. That made her sad and she said as much to Janice as they priced the various things.

"Well, dear, have you ever thought of combining business with pleasure?" Janice asked.

"What do you mean?"

"I mean, perhaps you could start a business selling secondhand items, maybe open an antique store here in town or have a store on eBay. That way you could still treasure hunt to your heart's content, but you'd be matching those special things with people who really want them. Rather like what we do here."

"Gosh, I don't know anything about running a business," Stacy said.

"You're a smart young woman. You could learn. I think an antique store would do well in Icicle Falls. We get a lot of tourists. And tourists like to shop."

"I wouldn't even know where to begin."

"You could begin by talking with Ed York. He's trying to rent out the space next to his wine shop. Not a bad location. Tina's lace and china shop is on the other side. You'd get loads of traffic. You could sell what you found and sell other people's things on consignment."

Stacy thought of Nana's Depression and carnival glass, of the goodies she'd seen when she'd been on her jacket hunt in Seattle. Surely it wouldn't be difficult to stock a small shop. And she had to agree with Dean. She needed to do something. She didn't want to just drift through her empty-nest years.

That night as they worked together in the kitchen, Dean chopping vegetables for a stir-fry and Stacy putting rice on to cook, she mentioned the idea.

"A shop, huh?" he said thoughtfully.

"It's probably a dumb idea. I mean, I really don't have any business experience."

"You worked in retail when we were first married," Dean reminded her.

"Selling china in a department store doesn't qualify me for running a shop."

He shrugged. "It's a beginning. I could help you get started. Between the two of us, we should be able to figure out how to do it. And it's not like there's no one in Icicle Falls to give us pointers."

Dean was right. With all the people in town who owned shops, they wouldn't lack for expert advice. Still, the idea was scary. "I'll think about it," she decided.

But the more she thought about it, the more nervous she became. Shops didn't spring up out of nothing. She'd need money for inventory; she'd have to pay rent. She and Dean had some money in savings but she wasn't willing to risk any of it on a business venture that might be a complete failure.

She said as much to him the following morning.

"It's up to you," he said. "But I think you can do anything you set your mind to, and I'm willing to risk some of our savings to prove it."

She shook her head. "I'm not. Not when we have kids in college."

"You could start out small. Sell things on eBay."

"Janice suggested that."

"Less risk. Of course, you'll have to store your inventory here."

More stuff coming back into the house. "I'd better think about this some more...."

"Up to you," he said. He grabbed his lunch sack

and kissed her on the cheek. "Whatever you decide, I'll support you."

"Thanks, Deano." He was about to rush out the door for work (wearing his rescued army jacket), but she caught his arm and pulled him to her and kissed him appreciatively. "Have I told you recently what a great husband you are?"

"Aw, you're just saying that because it's true," he joked. He gave her one more kiss, then hurried off.

She sat down at the kitchen table with a second cup of coffee. Her mother would be all for this. Mom had been after her for years to get a job. Nana, on the other hand, had always encouraged her in her determination to be a stay-at-home mom. But there were no kids at home anymore. What would Nana say now? Stacy wished she could talk to her, but Nana was too busy trying to stay alive to have the energy to advise her granddaughter.

"I need a sign," Stacy muttered.

The words were barely out of her mouth when the phone rang.

Chapter Fifteen

The best way to ensure things go smoothly is to plan ahead.
                    —Muriel Sterling, author of *Simplicity*

It had seemed like a brilliant idea to go out on Valentine's Day, like a romantic adventure, but Jen had quickly regretted hitting the bar at Zelda's. She'd passed by the dining area on her way in and seen Garrett Armstrong and Tilda the cop eating dinner at a window table. They were just one of many couples enjoying a romantic evening, which had made her achingly aware of the fact that she was alone.

It had taken the shine off her smile, but she'd moved on to the bar, determined to enjoy her evening no matter what. There she'd also found mostly couples. She was about to turn and run when she'd spotted Emily Ward sitting at a table with a group of people. Emily worked at the library. Jen had only been in and talked to her a couple of times, but Emily had seemed friendly. Hoping she'd be open to taking in a Valentine stray, Jen had gone over to say hi and Emily had invited her to join the group, which included two other women and a couple of guys. One had been Bill Will. He'd bought

Jen a drink and flirted with her, but that hardly counted as a romantic adventure since he'd flirted with the other women at the table, too.

Still, it had beaten sitting home alone and she'd enjoyed the drink, something the waitress called a Chocolate Kiss. "I like Chocolate Kisses," she'd announced to the table when Bill Will bought her another.

She'd become instant best friends with Emily and had wound up volunteering to help with the Friends of the Library monthly book sale and to spend one afternoon a week shelving books. This on top of promising Lula Wharton at the Icicle Falls Community Church only the week before that she'd organize the church library. In her tipsy fog her brain pointed out that she'd come to Icicle Falls to simplify her life, not to get overcommitted again. But she'd silenced the warning with a reminder that it was important to make friends. And, boy, was she making friends, flirting with Bill Will and his cowboy buddy, slurping Chocolate Kisses.

Who cared if Garrett Armstrong and his cop girlfriend had now come into the bar? She didn't need Garrett Armstrong to have fun. And to show how little she was interested in him, she'd danced like a madwoman out on the dance floor.

She'd promptly learned that dancing and Chocolate Kisses didn't mix. She'd lost her balance at the edge of the dance floor and managed to fall into Garrett Armstrong's lap. Of course, gentleman that he was, he'd caught her, and held her so she wouldn't continue her downward progress and end up on the floor. He was all solid muscle, and contact with him had been headier than a hundred Chocolate Kisses.

She'd been struggling (halfheartedly) to get to her

feet when she found Tilda Morrison's face right up in hers. "I hope you're not planning to drive in this condition." It wasn't said in concern. In fact, the delivery style pretty much assured her that Tilda would be there to give Jen a ticket even if she wasn't on duty.

Jen had switched to coffee after that. She still wasn't sure which had sobered her more, the caffeine or Tilda's beady-eyed glare.

She wasn't a poacher. She should have assured Tilda that she didn't steal other women's men. But, frankly, that glimpse of the woman's tough side hadn't made her anxious to stick around for girl talk.

But how serious were those two? Because Jen remembered something else about that little Valentine encounter. The look in Garrett Armstrong's eyes when she'd landed on top of him had said, "Sex with you? Absolutely." If Tilda hadn't been there, what would have happened? Who knew?

Now here he was, on Saturday, coming into Gingerbread Haus while she was working. He seemed surprised to see her, and not in a good way. Okay, after hearing about his first wife she got that he was scared of commitment. But, hey, she'd had her heart stomped on, too. That didn't mean you closed up shop and barred the windows, for crying out loud.

This wasn't the time to talk about his love life, though. He had someone with him. At the sight of the little blond-haired boy, her biological clock about had a meltdown.

"Hi," she said to the child. "I'm Jen."

"I'm Timmy. I'm five."

"Do you like gingerbread boys?" Jen asked.

The child shook his head. "I like Snickerdoodles."

"Me, too," she said. "And we happen to have some of those."

The child nodded his head eagerly. "I know."

"We'll take two," Garrett said. "I didn't realize you were working here," he added.

He probably would've avoided coming in if he had. "I just started last week. I thought I should make sure I can pay my rent," she said teasingly.

He obviously didn't get the joke since he didn't smile.

"Cass needed someone part-time," she hurried on, "and this seemed like fun. It's giving me a chance to meet nice little boys," she said, smiling at Timmy. She handed over the cookies and Garrett gave her a five-dollar bill.

"We're going to a movie," Timmy said.

"New Pixar movie," Garrett explained.

"I love those," Jen said.

He raised an eyebrow. "They're kid movies."

"Kids shouldn't have all the fun."

He frowned. "That sounds like something my ex would say."

What to reply to that? All Jen managed was, "Oh." She tried to catch one of the thoughts swirling in her brain. *I'm not like your ex.... You can still have fun and be a responsible adult.... You can even fall in someone's lap.*

"Uh, my change?" he prompted.

"Oh, sure." She counted change out of the cash register and passed it to Garrett. "Well, have a good time."

"Thanks," he said, and shepherded Timmy out the door.

She watched as Garrett pulled a cookie from the bag

and gave it to his son, smiled as the big man took the child's hand and led him down the street, the little boy skipping happily along, eating his cookie. Too late, she knew exactly what she should have said. *I'm not like your ex. Give me a chance and I'll prove it.*

But you don't poach, she reminded herself. Oh, yeah. That.

Toni called her sister, catching Jen just as she was leaving her new job at the bakery. "How's it going up there in chocolate land? Got any hot plans for tonight?"

"I wish," Jen grumbled.

"Yeah, well, me, neither. Valentine's Day was such a bust, I can't seem to work up any enthusiasm."

"How could your Valentine's Day be a bust?" Jen asked. "You and Wayne were going to Canlis. You can't go to one of the nicest restaurants in Seattle and not have a good Valentine's Day."

"You can when your husband's on call and there's a tech emergency at his company."

"You know, I'd understand that on-call thing if he was a doctor and it was a matter of life and death."

"Tell that to Wayne's boss," Toni said. "When thousands of dollars are at stake, it is life and death. At least, that's what Wayne told me."

"I hope you didn't have to leave right in the middle of dinner."

"We got through the main course. But we left before dessert. And when we got home he was on his computer for the next two hours. Talk about a buzz kill."

Toni looked out the kitchen window at the backyard of her suburban mansion. It was all perfectly landscaped. When they lived in their old house, the

smaller one in the modest neighborhood, the yard was
always in a state of wear and tear due to backyard soc-
cer games. She could still picture herself pushing the
kids on the swing. This yard went ignored. Everyone
was too busy with his or her own activities. Even the
deck with its requisite patio table and barbecue grill
rarely got used.

"It's not just Wayne. These days Jordan would rather
be anywhere than home with boring old Mom."

Listen to you, she told herself, *you sound like such
a whiner.* But if a woman couldn't whine to her sister
who could she whine to?

"I feel like my family is breaking apart," she confessed.

"Well, Jordan is thirteen now. She's going to be
more into her friends."

Than with you. Thankfully, her sister didn't finish
that sentence. Toni knew in her head that it was only
natural for her daughter to separate herself, start the
process of becoming her own person, want to be with
her peer group instead of her parents. But Toni's heart
wasn't all that excited about this whole process. And
surely it didn't have to be that way *all* the time. Mothers and daughters didn't need to wage war constantly,
to never do anything together.

"You and I did stuff with Mom when we were teenagers," she argued.

"Yeah, but not very often," Jen reminded her.

Still, when they had it had been fun. Toni smiled
at the memory of baking Christmas cookies together.
And then there was the Sunday afternoon when they
got bored and suckered their mother into playing a

board game with them. "Remember that time we played Life with Mom?"

"How could I forget? She was always a cop."

Toni couldn't help snickering. "She was also the banker and she was terrible at it. She kept mixing up her money with the bank's."

"I still think that was on purpose."

"I want to play Life with my kids," Toni said suddenly. "I want to *see* my kids. The only time I see them these days is when I'm driving them to someone else's house or to meet friends at the mall. I'm tired of them not being here when they're here. They're slipping away, Jen, just like Wayne." She found it hard to finish her sentence. Her throat was tightening. She could feel tears rising in her eyes. Okay, it was that time of month. This was probably her hormones speaking.

"They're growing up," her sister said gently.

No, it was more than hormones. Her children were growing up too fast. Life was so unfair. One minute you were celebrating when the last child finally started kindergarten and you could have a morning of peace and quiet, and the next you were desperately holding on, trying to keep them close to you, wishing you could turn back the clock.

She didn't want to turn back the clock, she told herself. She just wanted to make sure they survived these next few years. She wanted the same kind of closeness with her family that she'd enjoyed growing up. Yes, it was a different world. She understood that. But all the technology in the world couldn't change the fact that family was still family. Darn it all! They were going to stay close even if it killed them.

"I'm going to do something about this," she vowed.

"You guys need to get away someplace where there are no distractions," Jen said. "Like here."

After her weekend at the chocolate festival Toni couldn't agree more. "I wonder what my family would do if I rented us a mountain cabin for our summer vacation," she mused.

"Go through internet withdrawal? Poison your coffee and leave you for dead?"

"Yes, they love me that much."

But Toni couldn't get the idea of a tech-free vacation out of her mind. After she finished talking to her sister she got online and did some poking around.

It didn't take her long to find what she was looking for—a website that offered rustic vacations for people wanting to get away from it all. And lo and behold, one of those places was right in the Cascade Mountains, not far from Icicle Falls. She read the blurb beneath the picture of a quaint log cabin nestled among fir trees.

Cozy cabins allow you to experience nature at its finest while harking back to a simpler time. Go hiking, fishing and picking berries. Cabins come complete with games and puzzles. No TVs, no cable, no Wi-Fi. Enjoy the simple life and connect with those you love.

Perfect. She fished her charge card out of her purse and made a reservation. This summer they were going on vacation and really getting away from it all. She could hardly wait.

"Guess what I booked for our vacation this year," she said at dinner.

"Disneyland!" cried Jeffrey.

"A cruise?" her daughter guessed hopefully.

Her husband said nothing. Instead, he sat at the table, frowning at his pork chop.

Toni pretended not to notice. "No. We're going to have a wilderness adventure."

Jordan's mouth turned down. "Like, in a tent?"

"No, in a rustic log cabin."

Jeffrey was all for it. "Cool!"

"Sounds boring," Jordan said.

"A cabin," Wayne repeated, and he looked about as happy as Jordan

"Not far from Icicle Falls," Toni explained. "Up in the mountains."

"At least let's stay with Aunt Jen," Jordan said. "I don't want to stay in some dirty old cabin."

"I'm sure they're not dirty. Anyway, that would get pretty crowded." Toni smiled. "But we'll see her. And we can go into town and shop," she added, hoping to sweeten the pot.

"I want to go to that bakery where Aunt Jen's working," Jeffrey said.

Her daughter was still looking less than thrilled. "Why can't we stay in a motel in town? With a pool."

Because they have Wi-Fi and cell phone reception. "This will be fun," Toni said brightly.

"I don't want to do it. Let's go to Disneyland," Jordan said.

"Too late. I already booked our cabin."

Jordan stared at her mother as if she'd just sold her into slavery. "This is gonna be dumb."

Her husband's reaction was even stronger. "That was damn high-handed," he said later that night after they'd sent the kids to bed.

Yes, it had been. They always discussed where they wanted to vacation. But this time she didn't want the usual—a nice motel with an internet connection where Wayne could get sucked into his computer. She wanted them all to be together, *really* together, and she said as much.

"So you decided to be benevolent dictator. Is that it? Sorry, Ton. That's not gonna fly. You can go do your mountain thing if you want, but count me out," he said, and went to the kitchen, leaving her sitting on the family room couch.

This was not going according to plan. She followed him and watched while he pulled a bottle of his favorite micro brew from the fridge. "Come on, Wayne. Don't be like that."

He snapped off the cap and took a long draw, then regarded her, stony-faced.

She closed the distance between them. "Please do this. For me? For us?"

He didn't say anything.

"We're drifting apart, Wayne. We're all drifting. We're in the same house but we're not together."

"Oh, for God's sake," he said in disgust. "Don't be so melodramatic."

"I'm not," she insisted. "You spend more time on your laptop and your cell phone than you do talking to me."

"That's an exaggeration. And in case you didn't notice, I'm almost always working on that laptop."

She stepped away and threw up her hands. "That's my point. And it's really pathetic if you can't unfasten yourself from that electronic leash for even a couple of weeks. Where does that put your family?"

"Oh, so now you're going to guilt me into doing this?"

"I'm not trying to guilt you. I'm trying to make a point. Please, Wayne. All I'm asking for is two weeks."

He took another slug of beer. "Okay, I'll make you a deal."

Uh-oh. "What kind of deal?"

"I'll do this back-to-nature thing on two conditions."

"Two!"

"Yeah, two."

Boy, he was pushing it. "Okay, what are they?"

"One, next year I get to pick where we go."

"All right." She could do that. "What's the other?"

"When we get back you stop nagging me about being on my computer."

Nagging, that was rather a strong word. She didn't *nag*.

"I mean it, Ton. That's the deal. Take it or leave it."

If they came home and slipped back into their old routines, the whole vacation would have been for nothing. But if they didn't get away, if she didn't try to break the electronic leash, nothing would change. "Okay. Deal."

"Fine."

He was still looking miffed, so to soften the moment she suggested, "Seal it with a kiss?"

The stone face finally became human again and he smiled. "Good idea."

"I still think this is a dumb idea," he said later as they lay tangled in the bedsheets. "We're city people. What are we going to do cooped up in some cabin for two weeks?"

Weren't men supposed to have a sense of adventure?

Where was her man's? "We can hike and play games. And I signed us up to learn how to fly fish."

Now he seemed interested. "Yeah?"

"It'll be something different," she said.

"You can say that again. You'd better hope we aren't ready to kill one another after the first day."

She suddenly remembered her daughter's teenage wrath at Christmas. And that was over being cut off from her texting for only two days. Other than an occasional visit to town, Toni was about to deprive her for two weeks. And Jeffrey wouldn't have his Wii games. Would he drive his sister nuts? What if they all got cabin fever?

Oh, boy. What had she done?

Chapter Sixteen

*Sharing treasures can be even more rewarding
than holding on to them.*
— Muriel Sterling, author of *Simplicity*

Stacy's grandmother was gone. As her mother and
aunt worked their way through a long to-do list, she
did her best to help. While they made arrangements
with the cemetery and secured the church and minister, she put together the obituary, hired someone to
sing and called friends and relatives to tell them about
the memorial service.

By the time the day arrived she was wrung out. She
walked into the church and was surprised to see so
many flowers. The immediate family had requested
that, instead of flowers, friends and relatives donate to
her grandmother's favorite charity, Samaritan's Purse,
an organization that gave food, medicine and other
kinds of assistance to people in needy countries. They'd
already received many notices of donations to that worthy cause, but Stacy was glad some people had opted
to send flowers. They made her think of Nana's garden in the summer.

The church was rapidly filling up, and it wasn't just

older people. She was happy to see all the members of her book club sitting in the row behind the one reserved for family. There was Juliet and Cecily, Chita, sacrificing a precious day off, and Charley, now married and sporting a wedding ring. Cass had taken time off work. Chelsea and Dot were there, as well, proving that although they weren't coming to the meetings anymore they were still book club members at heart. Even Jen Heath, their newest member, was present.

"Who's minding the store?" Stacy asked Cass as they hugged.

"We're closed for the afternoon," Cass replied.

Stacy was truly touched because she knew a closed bakery meant a loss of business. "You shouldn't have."

"Of course I should have," Cass said. "Who lets friends walk through things like this alone?"

It seemed as if everyone in Icicle Falls (not to mention regions beyond) had felt the same way. During the service, many shared their memories of what her grandmother had done for them.

"She was my Sunday school teacher when I was in third grade," one man said. "She brought cookies every Sunday and that was enough to make me look forward to going to church."

"She was one of my favorite customers," said Pat Wilder, who owned Mountain Escape Books. "She always had a plate of cookies for the staff when she came in."

A woman Stacy's age stood up. Stacy didn't recognize her, but then a lot of names in Nana's address book had been unfamiliar. "We moved away from Icicle Falls twenty years ago, and I'm sorry I didn't get to see Erna," the woman said. "But I'll always remember Wednesday afternoons at her house, learning to quilt."

Stacy felt tears welling up. Nana had taught her to quilt, too. Which reminded her... What were they going to do with all the quilts she'd made?

She had her answer to that question soon enough. Two cousins each took one, and she brought the rest of the quilts home with her, along with the Depression and carnival glass.

The quilts got piled on Autumn's old bed. She stuffed the glassware in any closet or cupboard corner she could find. And even as she piled up possessions she couldn't part with, she thought of her aunt's words. *I don't want to do this to my kids.*

Things could be both a blessing and a burden. If she were to get hit by a truck and die tomorrow, she knew what category everything she'd saved would fall into. *You're not going to be able to keep all this,* she told herself. But then what to do with it? She couldn't just dump it.

The following week her mother phoned. "I got a call from your uncle Jack, who's Nana's executor. He found something she left for you."

"Where? We emptied the house."

"In her safe deposit box. It's an envelope. He says it looks like it's got cash in it."

"But Nana didn't have any money."

"None to speak of," her mother agreed. "She must have been saving this for some time. Apparently she had one for all four of your cousins, too. Anyway, Uncle Jack dropped it by the house, so whenever you want to come pick it up..."

"I'll come by later today," Stacy said.

And when she did and opened the envelope she was shocked to see ten hundred-dollar bills. Along with it was a note.

> This isn't much, my darling girl, but I hope you'll use it for something as special as you are. I'm so proud of you and your creative ability and your sweet family. I wish I could stay around to see what wonderful things you do with the rest of your life, but even as I'm writing this note I know it won't be long before I go to be with the Lord. I love you.
> Nana

Stacy hadn't thought she could cry any more but she'd been wrong. She gave her mother the letter and went to the bathroom for a handful of tissues.

"That's lovely," her mother said when she returned.

Mom had tears in her eyes, too, and Stacy passed her a tissue. "I have no idea what to use that money for, but Nana's right. I should use it for something special."

"Maybe a little trip for you and Dean?" her mother suggested.

"I don't know," Stacy said. Somehow, simply taking a trip didn't seem like the proper use for her tiny windfall.

"Well, you'll think of something."

Two days later, she was driving down Center Street and saw the empty store sitting between D'Vine Wines and Tina's Lace and Lovelies. Suddenly she could see that empty space full of beautiful glassware, homemade quilts, antiques and collectibles. She'd asked for a sign and had wound up with an envelope of money and more than enough inventory to stock a small shop. *What have you got to lose?* she asked herself. She parked her car and went into the wine shop.

Ed York was there, visiting with Pat Hunter, who owned the bookstore. "Stacy, how are you doing?" Pat asked.

"I'm okay," she said. And she was—other than wanting to cry all the time. She turned to Ed. "I understand you're the man to see about renting that retail space next door."

"Did you have something in mind?" he asked, his smile encouraging her to share her idea.

So she did. "What do you think?" she asked when she'd finished.

"I don't know about Ed," Pat told her, "but I think that sounds lovely. And right next door to a shop that sells lace and china? Perfect."

Ed nodded. "I agree."

"Except I've never owned a shop. I have no idea where to begin."

Ed put an arm around her shoulders. "Trust me. It's not that hard. We'll all help you get started."

He gave her a lease agreement to look over and suggested she go home and talk about it with her husband. If she wanted to proceed she could call him. "I've had a couple other people ask about it, but I'll hold it for you for the next twenty-four hours. How's that?"

"That'd be great. I would like to talk to my husband." But she was already pretty darned sure what her decision would be. She practically skipped back to her car. She'd wanted to know what to do next, wanted a sign. Short of skywriting, Nana's gift, along with the available retail space, was about as clear a sign as she was going to get.

"Go for it," Dean said when she told him at dinner.

"Seriously?"

"Seriously."

"But I don't think the money Nana left me is going to be enough to start a business. In fact, I know it's not."

He reached across the table and covered her hand with his. "If you want to do this, we'll come up with what you need."

"Are you sure?"

"Absolutely. I think it's a good idea."

"And will you help me?"

"Of course. Hey, we'll need to build some fancy shelving for that stuff," he said, and she knew he was anticipating all the fun he'd have out in his shop in the garage.

"I was thinking more about the business end, like the bookkeeping."

"That, too," he said. "But you've got to have someplace to put things."

"There's a beautiful, old bookcase at the Kindness Cupboard," she said. "And a vintage drop-leaf table. It's been painted blue but I suspect there's some nice wood under all that paint."

"I'll strip it for you," Dean offered.

The more they talked, the more excited they both got.

"Let's see the lease agreement," he said, moving his plate aside.

She watched impatiently as he read through it.

At last he said, "This looks pretty standard."

"And the location is great."

"Well, then." He raised his wineglass. "Here's to my wife the entrepreneur. And to success."

"To new adventures," she said, and they clinked glasses.

She made her big announcement at the March book club meeting, right after Charley finished showing off pictures from her surprise wedding in Las Vegas.

"That's wonderful," Juliet said.

"A great idea," Cass agreed. "And exactly the right business for you."

"I hope so," Stacy said. "I just hope I don't fall flat on my face."

"You won't," Chita said. "And when you have your grand opening we'll all be there to shop."

"I hope you make a ton," added Jen.

"If I can pay the rent on the shop and have a little left over I'll be fine. I know it's going to sound funny, but I'm not doing this to make a ton of money. I want to match up pretty things with people who'll really appreciate them. I don't need to clutter my house with a lot of stuff my kids won't want. I don't want to clutter my house, period."

She'd already packed up a lot of things to sell at her store and it felt good. The objects she still had actually showed so much better. That wasn't the only benefit. "I feel...lighter. And I have less to dust."

"That sure isn't like my house these days," Juliet said with a smile. "Baby stuff everywhere!"

"That's fun stuff," Charley said.

"It is." Juliet nodded. "Our little guy is certainly keeping us busy. But I still want to have a veggie garden this year." She held out a book with a basket of vegetables on the cover and a catchy title—*Just Beet It*. "This came into the bookstore a few days ago, and I thought it might be fun to read for April. It's a memoir about a woman who decides to live off the land."

"That goes hand in hand with simplifying your life. I'd be up for reading it," Jen said.

Charley made a face. "Gardening. Ugh. I'll read the book, but don't anybody expect me to start growing tomatoes, not with a business to run."

"And a new husband," put in Cass. "You'll have your hands full cultivating that relationship."

"It might be interesting to read, though," Chita said. "I've thought of doing a small garden with the kids. In my spare time," she cracked.

"So, are we good with this book?" Juliet asked.

The others agreed and Juliet promised to order more copies when she went in to work the following day. "Someone can have this one now," she offered.

"I'm not in a hurry for it," Charley said.

"I'll take it," Jen told her. "If no one else wants it."

"It's yours," Juliet said.

She pulled out her wallet and handed over some bills and that was that.

Stacy had to admire her. Jen Heath jumped into new adventures with total abandon. Well, she had her own adventure now and she could hardly wait to open the doors of Timeless Treasures.

The group broke up around nine, the women who had to get up early going home for a good night's sleep and Charley probably going home for a good night of sex. Jen sighed as she got in her car. She loved Icicle Falls and she was glad she'd simplified her life.

But parts of it were *too* simple. Her love life could be summed up in one word—nothing.

She needed to stop fantasizing about Garrett Armstrong and move on.

Still, Jen couldn't resist wanting to visit with him when he came by to pick up the rent. She could envision herself making him lavender tea and giving him home-grown veggies from her garden. That wouldn't be poaching. That would just be...sharing.

She opened the book to the first chapter. "My Love Affair with Dirt." She frowned. She didn't want a love affair with dirt. She wanted a love affair with Garrett Armstrong. But he wasn't cooperating. And then there was Tilda, who'd probably beat Jen with her nightstick if she went anywhere near him.

It looked as if the only bed she was going to see any action in was the flower bed.

Chapter Seventeen

The best new beginnings are often the most terrifying.
                    —Muriel Sterling, author of *Simplicity*

Stacy signed the lease on the space that was going to be her new shop and gave Ed his first month's rent and deposit. Dean met her at the shop after he was done at school; together they measured and talked about where and how she could display her merchandise.

They were halfway through when Ed stopped by. "Thought I'd see how it's going," he said.

"Great," Stacy told him. "I'm excited about this. I still don't know what I'm doing but I guess I'll figure it out."

"You will," he assured her. "And just to make sure you start off on the right foot, maybe you'll let Pat and me take you to lunch tomorrow. You can pick our brains and get some pointers on what all you need to do."

She thanked him, and as promised, the next day Ed and Pat settled her at a quiet corner table in Schwangau and gave her a crash course in business. "Have you got a business plan?" Ed asked.

"A business plan?" she repeated.

"Detailing exactly what you want to do."

She knew what she wanted to do, open a shop and sell pretty household items. And she was doing it. She and Dean had listed their inventory, looked up prices at various online sites, made a budget. Wasn't that plan enough? "I'm not sure I know what you mean."

"He means you need to work out how you're going to run your operation," Pat explained. "Can you afford to hire employees? You'll probably have to hire someone at least part-time. You'll also have to budget for taxes, get a tax ID and have a plan for marketing the shop."

"You'll need a website, of course," Ed told her. "And you'll want to link to the Icicle Falls website and talk to George over at the Chamber of Commerce about getting included in the list of businesses in town."

"Oh, and you'll want to join the Chamber," Pat added. "It's a good way to network."

"You'll need to register your business name," Ed continued. "And, if you haven't done it already, you'd better hop on over to city hall and get a business license."

Stacy nodded, typing on her iPad as fast as she could. "How long is all this going to take?"

"Paperwork can be expedited. You should be good to go by next month," Ed predicted.

She hoped so. She also hoped she wasn't biting off more than she could chew. Was she up to the task?

"It can all be a little overwhelming at first," Pat said as if reading her thoughts. "But when you make your to-do list, put the most important things at the top and then work your way down. You'll get through it."

* * *

The rest of the month flew by as she worked her way through the red tape of opening a business. That part wasn't so much fun but with Dean as her partner in paperwork, she managed. Meanwhile, he refinished the blue drop-leaf table and she started packing boxes of glassware and quilts and knickknacks to take to the shop.

The Saturday before their grand opening, Charley's husband, Dan, helped Dean haul the last of the merchandise and the various shelves and pieces of furniture over to the shop.

Charley and Cecily helped set everything up. Chita stopped by, too, for a couple of hours, claiming her kids were both at friends' houses and she had nothing else to do. What a lie. But Stacy was both touched and grateful.

"Oh, I love this," Charley said, picking up a pink Depression glass candy dish. "How much are you asking for it?"

"For you? Nothing. It's yours."

"No, you can't be doing that," Charley protested. "This is your business."

"Then consider it a wedding present."

"Really?"

"Yes. I want you to have it. Same goes for you," she said to Chita. "If you see anything you want, tell me. My big goal is to match these things up with people who are going to love and appreciate them."

"And to make money," Chita reminded her.

"That, too, but like I said before, I'm not out to get rich. I only need to make enough to keep the nice things circulating."

"You won't have any trouble doing that," Chita said. "Look at this. You've got a whole set of these pink glass plates."

"Hopefully, someone will want them."

"For sure." Chita nodded. "I could just see those in a cute little tearoom."

"I wish we had a tearoom here in Icicle Falls," Cecily said wistfully. "Too bad my sister lives in L.A. I could see her doing something like that."

"Is she still catering?" Chita asked.

"Caterer to the stars," Cecily said with a smile. "She'll never come back. She loves it in L.A."

Chita made a face. "I'll take Icicle Falls over some big city any day."

"Me, too," Cecily agreed.

"Me, three," Stacy said. As far as she was concerned, Icicle Falls was the perfect place to live. Here people really cared about you.

Her friends all proved it. As her grand-opening day approached, everyone helped, both with setup and various contributions. Cass had connected her to a customer who had an old kitchen queen cupboard to sell, giving Stacy her first consignment piece, one she knew would walk out the door in no time. Charley was busy combining two households and had donated an oak bookcase for displaying items. Jen had brought over several ornate candle stands. Charley's husband had helped Dean install shelves in her backroom and the two men had fixed up an old desk scrounged from Juliet's mom so Stacy would have a place to do her paperwork.

In the days before the grand opening, Stacy's moods alternated between excitement and trepidation. This

was such a good idea. This was such a lame idea. The
business would do well. The business would flop. Everything was ready. She'd forgotten something. What
if her window display didn't attract any customers?

Maybe no one would be interested in handmade
quilts, antiques and vintage decorations.

The night before the big day, she lay in bed staring
at the ceiling. Finally, when the clock hit 2:00 a.m.
she got up and went to the kitchen to heat some milk.

She was just pouring some flavored syrup into it
when Dean joined her. "Can't sleep?" he asked, coming
up behind her and slipping his arms around her waist.

After nearly twenty-four years of marriage he could
read her mind. Not that it was hard to do tonight. "I
keep wondering if this was a dumb thing to do."

"You had the money. God knows you had the merchandise."

She turned around to face him. "But what if nobody buys it?"

"In that case we'll pull the plug and take the stuff to
the Kindness Cupboard. Or sell everything on eBay."

Then she'd be a failure and would have wasted
Nana's money. She could feel the sting of encroaching tears.

"But it's going to be okay," he insisted as if sensing
he'd said the wrong thing.

"I just hope we get a lot of people tomorrow."

"Don't worry. We will," he said, and kissed her.
"Come on back to bed."

"I can't sleep," she reminded him.

"Me, neither, and since we're both awake…" He
waggled his eyebrows.

"You are such a horn toad."

"And you love it," he retorted. "I promise by the time I'm done with you, you'll sleep like a baby."

And he was right. She was still sleeping soundly when the alarm went off at eight.

"Come on, Sleeping Beauty," Dean said, giving her shoulder a rub. "Time to wake up and carpe diem."

This was it. She was ready. She hoped.

Before Stacy had even opened the store, family, friends and neighbors were gathering outside Timeless Treasures.

"Better let them in before they break down the door," Dean said, pointing to where her mother stood in front of the window, waving.

She turned from Nana's old china hutch where she'd been rearranging her Depression glass display yet again. Suddenly, her heart was thumping like a blender on high speed.

Okay, time to introduce Icicle Falls to its newest shop.

She unlocked the door and threw it open. "Welcome, everyone!"

"Oh, darling, it all looks so lovely," her mother said, taking in the walls Stacy and Dean had painted a pale rose color.

Vintage lamps and two crystal chandeliers bathed glassware and knickknacks in a romantic glow. *The shop is lovely,* Stacy thought with a satisfied smile.

"Thanks," she said. *And thanks, Nana, for making this possible.*

"Surprise!" cried her daughter, poking her head around the door.

"Autumn!"

Sheila Roberts

And there was Ethan right behind her.

"What are you two doing here?" Stacy demanded. "Don't you have tests to study for or parties to go to?"

"We can study anytime," said her son, whose less-than-stellar grades showed how well that philosophy was working.

"We didn't want to miss your big opening," Autumn said, coming up to hug her. She gazed around. "Was some of this stuff Nana's?"

Stacy nodded. "I'm finding good homes for all of it."

"Looks like it's all girl stuff," Ethan said.

"It pretty much is," Stacy admitted. "Go see if you can find something for your girlfriend."

"Yeah, great idea," he said. "Will you give me a deal?"

"Maybe," Stacy answered with a smile.

Pat Wilder and Ed York were the next in line to say hi. Pat handed Stacy a huge flower arrangement. "This is from everyone at the Chamber."

Those weren't the only flowers to arrive. Lupine Floral delivered another arrangement of spring flowers, this one from her book club.

"They're gorgeous," she said later to Juliet when she and her husband, Neil, came in with baby Jon.

"I wish I could take credit for it," Juliet said. "It was actually Jen's idea. She'll be over later, by the way, as soon as she's done with her morning shift at the bakery. Cass is coming in after she closes up and everyone else should be here pretty soon."

"You guys are the best," Stacy said.

"Hey, girlfriends support one another. Oh, and I think I found just what I want," she said, looking past Stacy, her eyes getting big. "That cat clock with the

moving tail and eyes will be perfect for Jon's room. I'm
going to snag it before anyone else does." And with that
she was gone and another well-wisher took her place.

"This is so nice," Olivia Wallace gushed. "I know
I'll find something here I can use in the lodge."

Stacy couldn't imagine the Icicle Creek Lodge need-
ing anything. The place had a fully functioning kitchen
and was decorated beautifully, but she encouraged Olivia to look to her heart's content.

She smiled as she watched people moving from display to display, admiring things. Nana would be so
proud.

Dot Morrison stood at the counter where Stacy and
Dean had set up their cash register, getting out her
credit card while Dean rang up a tin sign advertising
Yakima apples. The counter's glass display case held
costume and fine jewelry, which Stacy had figured
would make tempting impulse buys.

Right now two people were being tempted. Darla
Stone, Mayor Stone's sister, and Hildy Johnson, who
owned Johnson's Drugs with her husband, Nils, stood
peering in, pointing to their favorite bits of bling. Both
women had a reputation for being shopping buzzards,
always trying to get something for a steal.

She went over to them, figuring Dean would need
help withstanding their collective bargaining power.
"Hi, ladies. I see you found the best stuff in the place."

"You have some lovely things here," Darla said.

"A little pricey," added Hildy.

"Oh, not really," Stacy told her. "We researched everything online and these are all reasonably priced."

"Well, you can ask whatever you want for something
online. That doesn't mean you'll get it," Hildy said.

"Is there anything in particular that interests you?" Stacy asked.

Darla pointed to a designer sterling estate ring with amethyst-and-marcasite accents that Stacy had purchased online. "I'd love to see that."

Seeing was about all she'd be able to do. That ring would never fit on Darla's pudgy finger. Stacy reached into the case and brought it out, anyway.

Sure enough, it didn't fit, although Darla did her best to force it over her knuckle.

"Let me try," said Hildy, whose fingers weren't any smaller.

Stacy watched and thought of Cinderella's stepsisters. "You know, rings can be a challenge," she said diplomatically. "Have you seen this?" She pulled out an antique art deco filigree necklace with a pink glass stone.

"Oh, that's so pretty," Darla raved.

Stacy walked around the corner. "Here, try it on."

Darla took the necklace and her bargain buddy helped her clasp it around her neck. Darla's neck wasn't exactly swanlike and the pendant instantly became a choker.

"I don't think it flatters you," Hildy said, sparing Stacy from having to choose between being truthful and making a sale. "Let me try it."

Darla pouted but removed the necklace and handed it over. It hung better on Hildy but somehow it didn't seem like a fit. Once more, Stacy felt torn. "Gosh, I don't know," she said dubiously.

"Let me see the mirror," Hildy demanded, and Stacy gave her the vintage sterling silver mirror.

Hildy frowned at her reflection, and Stacy glanced

around the display case for another piece. She found it in a large necklace with silver-and-copper bangles. "Now, this would look great."

Hildy exchanged the delicate necklace for the larger piece and slipped it on.

"Oh, yes," Darla approved, "that's you."

Hildy regarded herself in the mirror. With her thin lips, beaky nose and practically nonexistent chin she was something to regard. "Yes, this is lovely." She took it off and examined the price tag. And frowned again. "It's overpriced."

Just like half the items in Johnson's Drugs. Stacy would have actually given the necklace to someone who loved it and couldn't afford it. But no way was she letting Hildy go skipping off with it for a song.

"Gosh, I guess it's not for you, then," Stacy said regretfully. "Too bad, because it really does look great." No lie there. Hildy might not have been the most gorgeous jewelry model, but the piece was beautiful.

Hildy studied the necklace. "Well."

"For heaven's sake, buy the thing," said Dot, who'd returned with yet another bargain.

Hildy scowled at her. "Mind your own business, Dot."

"I am minding my own business. If you don't want it, I do."

"I'll take it," Hildy told Stacy.

"I know you're going to enjoy it," Stacy said as Hildy gave it to her to ring up.

"Yes, I will," Hildy agreed.

The transaction completed, she and Darla made their way through the throng of shoppers toward the door.

"Sorry you didn't get a chance at the necklace," Stacy said to Dot.

"I'm so broken up," Dot said with a wink.

Well, duh. Of course, Dot had simply been goading Hildy into that purchase. "Thanks," Stacy said.

"Paying full price isn't always a sin. Here." She handed over a vintage Log Cabin Syrup tin. "Thought this might look cute on my counter at Breakfast Haus."

"It would," Stacy said, and handed it back. "On the house."

Dot shook her head and shoved it back at Stacy. "Oh, no. You're a business, not a charity."

"But, like I keep saying, the whole purpose of this business is matching things up with people who'll appreciate them."

"And paying the bills. Don't you have kids in college? Ring it up, kiddo."

Stacy opened her mouth to protest but Dean took the tin out of her hands, saying, "The customer is always right, babe."

With people like Dot for customers, how could she lose?

Her daughter had wandered over to the jewelry counter now. "That's pretty," Autumn said, pointing to the filigree necklace Darla had tried on earlier.

It would look beautiful on her daughter. "Try it on," Stacy said.

Autumn did and the necklace lay perfectly on her chest. It was stunning with her fair skin and blond hair. She picked up the antique mirror to check out her reflection, and smiled.

"Happy birthday early," Stacy said.

Autumn's eyes lit up. "Really?"

"Really."

"Oh, Mom, thanks!" She leaned across the counter and hugged her mother.

"You know, someone else almost bought that," Stacy said.

Autumn touched her fingers to it. "I'm glad she changed her mind."

"Obviously, it was just waiting for you," Stacy said.

She said the same thing to several other customers as they brought their treasures up to the cash register. It was so thrilling to see objects she'd saved from Nana's place or had picked up at thrift stores finding new homes.

"At this rate you're going to have to go look for more merchandise," Dean said.

More trips to thrift stores. Gee, what a shame.

By the end of the day, Stacy was exhausted and if feet could cry hers would have been howling. She said goodbye to Cass and Chita and turned the sign on the door to Closed. "I'm pooped," she told Dean.

"Me, too. And I thought teaching was hard work."

"All I want to do is go home, take a bubble bath and then flop on the couch and read," she said.

"Except we've got the kids staying overnight," Dean reminded her. "And *they* want to go to Bavarian Alps for pizza and then come home and play Hearts till all hours."

Spending time with her kids? She'd rally.

Their family evening was the perfect ending to a perfect day, and Stacy was smiling when she went to bed. Her shop was a success. This had been a great idea.

* * *

This had been a dumb idea. On Monday only half a dozen people had come into Timeless Treasures.

One of them had been Tina Swift, who owned the lace shop next door. Tina had oohed and ahhed over everything and had purchased Nana's chocolate set. Stacy had been delighted that the antique Limoges china had gone to someone who would appreciate it—until she saw it on display in Tina's shop window, marked up to three times what Stacy had charged. Horrified, she'd marched right in and bought it back. So much for that day's profits.

The next day she'd had three customers, all lookie-loos who didn't buy anything. And on Wednesday it was just her and her timeless treasures. She closed up early, went to the Sweet Dreams gift shop and bought a pound of salted caramels.

At least she wasn't buying stuff, she told herself. Consumables, that was the way to go. Nothing you could keep.

The problem was, she would end up keeping this candy—on her hips. She ate it all and by the time Dean got home from work she felt sick.

"How'd it go at the shop?" he asked, and that made her feel even sicker.

She should have bought two pounds of chocolate.

Chapter Eighteen

We all make missteps. Even those can lead to something good, although we don't always see it at first.

—Muriel Sterling, author of *Simplicity*

"**D**idn't you write an article at Thanksgiving about baking bread?" Jen asked her sister.

Toni abandoned her computer to go search for more coffee. "Yeah. Don't tell me, now you're baking bread."

"Well, I *was* baking bread. But it didn't rise very much. Why do you think that was?"

"Hey, I'm no expert," Toni protested.

"You've got to know more than me. Come on, take a guess."

"I really don't know. Maybe you killed your yeast. How hot was the water you dissolved it in?"

"Hot enough to dissolve it. I boiled it."

"Good Lord. There's your problem. It should've been lukewarm. Otherwise, you'll kill the yeast."

There was a moment of silence while her sister took in this information, followed by, "I guess that explains it. I'll have to try again."

"So, other than failed bread experiments, how's the idyllic simple life?"

"Great. It's been a little cold, though."

"In the mountains? Gosh, what a surprise."

"Ha-ha. Anyway, it's supposed to warm up over the weekend and on Saturday after I'm done at the bakery I'm renting a Rototiller and tilling my garden plot."

"All by yourself?" Weren't those things heavy to lug around?

"Not exactly. I've got help coming."

"So you're finally making progress with Mr. Hot Britches?" Toni asked.

"No," Jen said, some of the happiness slipping out of her voice.

"Oh. Then, who?"

"One of the local boys."

"As in teenager?"

"No."

"Okay, so a possible boyfriend?"

"Not really."

"This is harder than trying to pull teeth out of a goldfish. Are you going to spill or what?"

"There's really nothing to spill. It's just Billy Williams, the cowboy you met at the chocolate festival."

"Mr. Dreamy? Oh, rough life." How she'd love to be in her sister's shoes right now, living in a romantic little mountain town, baking bread, working part-time in a bakery and hanging out with sexy cowboys. The grass was sure looking greener up there in Icicle Falls. "Sometimes I think you had the right idea," she said with a sigh. "I wish I could transplant my family to a new location. And a different time," she added grumpily. "Before computers and cell phones." She was willing to bet Wayne would've had more energy working on a farm every day than he did working on computer software programs.

"But think what a pain *your* job would be without a computer," Jen said.

Her job would be more of a pain, but her life would be a heck of a lot easier.

"Anyway, feel free to transplant yourself up here for a visit anytime. When *are* you coming up to see me again, by the way?"

Their summer vacation seemed aeons away. "Next week," Toni decided.

Why not? She was almost done with her article for *Family Circle,* then she just had to finish the research for one she was proposing to *Parents* magazine on the newest teen party drugs to watch out for. After that she could take a break.

Her family wouldn't miss her if she was gone for a couple of days. They probably wouldn't miss her if she was gone for a couple of weeks. Well, except as a chauffeur and cook. But they could manage on their own. In fact, it would do them good to have to manage on their own.

"I can't wait! You can come to my book club with me. And we can shop and eat chocolate and hike."

"Since when do you hike?" Toni scoffed.

"Since I moved up here. I want to, anyway. I hear there are Indian petroglyphs on a trail by Icicle Creek. That would be good to blog about."

"How's the blog coming? I read your last post about waiting for spring in the mountains. Very cute."

"I saw that you left a comment."

"And I wasn't the only one."

"Yeah, I'm up to a whopping thirty-four followers," Jen said. "And five of them are in my book club."

"You'll get more," Toni assured her.

"I hope so. Meanwhile, I'm enjoying it. I still haven't come up with an idea for a book, though."

Toni couldn't help smiling. This book would prove to be yet another harebrained plan of her sister's that would come to nothing.

Of course, she'd thought the same thing when Jen announced her determination to move, and that was turning out fine. Everything seemed to be going smoothly for her sister up in Icicle Falls. Toni was glad that after all the emotional upheaval Jen had endured, the road was finally leveling out for her and she was happy. And having fun.

Fun sounded like an excellent idea to Toni. She decided she was going to hang out with someone who wanted to do something other than text or play video games or work long hours. She was going to get sister time and Sweet Dreams chocolates and home-baked bread. She was going back for a second helping of life in Icicle Falls.

Saturday brought blue sky and sunshine, a perfect day for Jen to put in a garden. Life was good.

Pat at the bookstore had cautioned her not to plant until the end of the month, but she figured since it was now April she could at least get the ground ready. The book she'd been reading stressed the importance of having rich soil, primed with fertilizer, so she'd start by getting everything dug up and fertilized.

She'd just arrived home from her morning shift at Gingerbread Haus and had the coffee on when a big red truck driven by a man in a cowboy hat pulled up in the driveway. Bill Will had his window down and she could hear the country music blasting all the way into the house. He opened the door and hopped out, a vision in boots, jeans and a tight T-shirt with a denim jacket thrown over it, his Stetson low over his face.

He looked as if he belonged on a romance novel, but Bill Will was proof that you couldn't always judge a book by its cover. It hadn't taken Jen long to realize that the man was more of a lovable doof than a romance hero.

Of course, look who she was measuring him against. How could he compete with a man who raced into burning buildings to save people?

Bill Will saw her as he trotted over to the front porch and gave her a big smile and a wave. True, he was no Garrett Armstrong, but he was a nice guy, and they'd have fun putting in this garden.

She swung the door wide and he greeted her with a half tip of his Stetson. "The gardener's here, ma'am."

"Would the gardener like a cup of coffee before we get to work?"

"Sure. Why not?" He sauntered inside and glanced around. "Hey, this place isn't half bad."

"I like it," she said. "Take anything in your coffee?"

"Nope. I'm tough."

"I guess so," she said, pouring him a cup. "It's really sweet of you to help me do this."

She'd run into Bill Will in the grocery store earlier in the week and had flirted with him in the frozen food aisle. When she'd told him about her garden project, he'd been quick to offer his help, and she'd been happy to accept.

At one point she'd entertained the idea of asking her landlord for assistance, but then decided against it. Tilling part of a yard probably wasn't on the list of required landlord duties. Anyway, between having to show her how to work a woodstove, rescuing her from a ditch and shoveling snow, he'd undoubtedly had enough of helping her. She suspected that was why he collected his rent and scrammed as fast as he could. (Well, that and Tilda, the so-called girlfriend.) Jen was coming across as too high-maintenance. This—her garden—would shatter that misconception. Yes, the woman bakes her own bread *and* tills her own soil. Nothing to it.

She and Bill Will chatted for a few minutes, mostly about him and how he was saving up to buy a place of his own. "'Cept I only got about a thousand in the bank," he said. "I need to find me a rich woman. Got any money, Jen?" he asked with a smile.

"Yeah. Tons. Can't you tell?"

"Aw. Well, there's more to life than money, right?" He set down his mug. "Let's get moving. I'm itchin' to try out that machinery."

She'd already marked the area where she wanted the garden. "I thought I'd put it over there," she said, pointing to a sunny corner of the yard she'd set off with string and some small yard stakes.

"Okay," he said with a nod.

She watched, feeling a tingle of excitement, as he let down the tailgate of his truck and dragged out the tiller. Home-grown lettuce and spinach and peas and carrots. This was going to be great.

Bill Will took the tiller over to the future home of

Veggie Central, started it and began to churn up the earth. She should plant sunflowers, too, she decided.

She was so immersed in her garden daydream that it took her a minute to realize the tilling had stopped. "I think we got a problem," Bill Will called.

Had he hit a rock? She hurried over to where he was squatting in front of clumps of grass and sandy soil, examining a network of pipes. "What's that?" she asked. Whatever it was, something was wrong with it, she thought, looking at the water gurgling from several that had been severed.

He pushed back his hat and scratched his head. "Well, I'm no expert on stuff like this, but if I had to guess I'd say that's your drain field."

"Drain field?"

"You know, your septic system. I think we just tore something up."

A sick feeling landed in the pit of her stomach. "Can you fix it?"

He frowned at the mess in front of him and shook his head. "If you need a horse broke or a fence mended I'm your man. This...well, you better call your landlord."

The sick feeling swelled. "Oh," Jen said weakly.

Bill Will straightened up. "Sorry to ruin your day, Jen, but we better not till any more until you know where all your drain field is. You don't want to do any more damage."

She'd just done more damage—to her tenant-landlord relationship. "Call Armstrong right away," Bill Will advised.

She could hardly wait.

Her trepidation must have shown on her face because Bill Will threw an arm around her shoulders and gave her a hug. "It'll be okay. He's a good guy. He'll understand."

Jen wasn't so sure.

After finishing his shift at the fire station, Garrett had gotten his groceries, stopped by his folks' place and called his sister in Yakima. That checked off everything on his to-do list. Timmy was with his mother—so far, so good there—and the rest of the day was all his.

How to spend it? He could do some work on his house, go for a hike, camp out for a while at Bavarian Brews with his laptop and surf the Net. The possibilities were endless.

His cell phone rang. *Oh, God, please don't let it be Ashley.*

It wasn't. But seeing who was calling left him just as rattled as if it had been. An image of a short little strawberry blonde with freckles danced before his eyes. Jen Heath, aka Lucy Ricardo II. What did she want?

"Hello," he answered warily. Every time Jen called it meant trouble for him. Heck, just looking at her was trouble. Because he liked what he saw. And he couldn't afford to, not if he wanted to stay sane.

"Um, Garrett?"

Something in her voice told him he was going to be sorry he'd taken the call. "Hi, Jen. What's up?"

"Well, I have a small problem...."

Chapter Nineteen

Life runs so much more smoothly when we don't delay saying, "I'm sorry."
— Muriel Sterling, author of *Simplicity*

Garrett arrived at his rental just as Billy Williams was driving away. Jen Heath stood in a corner of the yard by a section of torn-up earth, looking like a mourner at a graveside. *Oh, no. The drain field.*

Garrett clenched his jaw. Damn it all, he'd known his day was going to get turned upside down the minute he saw her name on his phone. "It's hard to explain," she'd said when he'd asked what was wrong. "I think you'd better just come over." And that had left his imagination free to run rampant. She'd run into a ditch again. She'd caught the kitchen on fire. She'd... Who knew? With Jen Heath it was always a surprise.

Bill Will stopped his truck, which had the instrument of destruction sitting in the bed, and Garrett pulled up alongside it. "What happened?"

Bill Will reached under his hat and scratched his head. "Well, Garrett, she wanted to put in a garden."

Garrett swore under his breath.

"I thought she'd checked it out with you. Didn't realize she had me digging up your drain field. I quit as soon as I figured it out."

Garrett supposed he could thank God for small favors. "I appreciate that," he managed.

"Don't be too hard on her. She didn't know."

Don't be too hard on her? He wanted to throttle her. Bend her over his knee and spank her. A vision of his hand on that cute, curvy little butt sent his thoughts skittering in a whole other direction, and that did nothing to improve his temper. The last thing he needed was to be attracted to another Ashley, which, of course, was exactly what Jen Heath was turning out to be.

He nodded and said a curt thank-you to Bill Will, who skedaddled. Then he parked his truck and got out.

"I'm so sorry," she greeted him as he made his way across what had once been a perfectly good drain field. "Can it be fixed?"

"It can." He took in the cracked pipes and the gurgling water, the clumps of grass and soil, and clawed his hand through his hair.

"Don't worry, I'll pay for it," she said.

An ache was starting behind his right eye. A muscle twitched in his jaw.

"Are you mad?" she ventured.

"Mad? You just tried to take out my drain field. Why would I be mad?"

A moment ago she'd looked ready to cry. Now she looked ready to smack him. "I didn't do it on purpose."

"If you'd checked with me," he began.

"I didn't think I needed permission to put in a garden."

"I could have told you where the drain field was and saved us both a lot of trouble," he said, finishing

his sentence. In his aggravated state, he couldn't help
adding, "But then I'm beginning to think that trouble
is your middle name." Suddenly he was on a roll and it
felt so good he kept on rolling. "Is this a gift you share
with everyone or are you just out to get me? First you
try to burn my place down, then you're sliding around
on the road like a guided missile, trying to take me
out. Now this. You're like the twelve plagues of Egypt.
What's next, locusts?"

"Well, that was rude," she said in a shaky voice.

Yeah, it was. But she was driving him nuts. So was
the fact that the idiot part of him somehow felt the need
to give her a hug.

No! No hugs. He clawed through his hair again, took
a couple of steps away and let out his breath in a hiss.
"You tried to destroy my drain field and you're getting
on *me* about being rude?"

"It was only a few pipes."

"Well, I'll be sure to tell the septic guy that when
he gives me the bill for this mess."

"I said I'd pay to fix it."

Oh, no. Here came the tears. He held up a hand.
"Okay, okay." He pulled his cell phone out of his jeans
pocket and started for the truck.

"Where are you going?" she called.

"Away." *Far away.*

She trotted after him. "Are you calling someone to
come and fix this?"

"Yes."

"Thank you," she said stiffly.

"You're welcome," he said, equally stiff. And now
they were done talking. He hoped.

"Um, Garrett."

Or not. He forced himself to stop, to turn and look at her.

"Obviously, that wasn't the place to put a vegetable garden. Is there any place I can—"

He knew exactly where she was going and he cut her off. "No." The word almost exploded from his mouth. "No more digging. Anywhere. Understand?"

She took a step back, bit her lip and nodded.

"Good," he said curtly. "I'll get someone out here as soon as possible. Meanwhile, try not to use any water. Don't wash any dishes, don't do any laundry, don't flush the toilet."

She frowned. "How long will it take to fix?"

"A lot longer than it took you to wreck it," he snapped, and started for his truck again. But not before he saw her face flush fire-engine red.

"Okay, that was so uncalled for," she muttered.

The ache behind his eye wasn't an ache anymore. Now it felt as if his eyeball had been pierced with a flaming arrow, and the flame was spreading across his forehead. "You're right. Sorry."

That obviously wasn't enough. (Big surprise, since he'd said it grudgingly.) She put her hands on her hips. "I can't believe I thought you were so nice when I met you. Boy, was I wrong."

This made him mad all over again. He was the nicest guy he knew. The fact that he hadn't murdered his ex was proof of that.

"Yeah, well, first impressions are deceiving, aren't they?" he retorted. He completed his trip to the truck and yanked open the cab door. "I thought you had your act together."

"I do!" she cried. "I pay my rent on time, and I'm paying you a lot more than this dump is worth."

If she figured she was going to skip out and leave him high and dry, she could think again. "Well, you signed a lease on this 'dump' for a year," he reminded her.

"And it's going to be the longest year of my life," she retorted, her voice quavering.

"Mine, too, babycakes." Now her eyes were flooded with tears. It was definitely time for him to go.

He climbed into the cab and yanked the door shut with enough force to rattle the windows. He got his friend Dan Masters, who owned Masters Construction, on the phone and Dan referred him to someone who could fix the mess. "Can you do it today?" Garrett asked the man after explaining his problem.

"Yeah. It'll cost you, though, being a weekend and all."

"Just so it gets done," Garrett said. He ended the call and roared off down the road, shooting gravel in all directions. The sooner the job was finished, the better. Who knew what further damage Jen Heath was liable to do if he waited?

That was all it took to turn his mind back to their conversation at the cottage. What a jerk he'd been. His reaction had been completely inappropriate. He'd not only been rude, he'd been downright mean. Maybe he wasn't such a nice guy.

He was going to have to apologize.

Best not to go empty-handed, he told himself, and drove to Lupine Floral.

At the flower shop Heinrich, one of the owners, helped him pick out an arrangement of pink-and-white roses with a small box of Sweet Dreams chocolates tucked in the bouquet. Chocolate and flowers—Garrett knew enough about women to know that was a good combination. He carefully set the box on the seat next to him and then headed…for home. No sense going over there until the pipes were fixed.

You're stalling.

Okay, he was, but he needed time to figure out what he was going to say to Jen. He went back to his place. The house was pretty much bare bones. The living room was furnished with a sofa and armchair that he'd bought to replace the furniture Ashley had made off with, an old coffee table his folks had given him and his big-screen TV (another thing he'd had to replace after Ashley left). Timmy had a nice bed and dresser, but Garrett was using an old brass bed similar to the one in the cabin; he'd scrounged it from his grandma. He went into the kitchen and made himself a ham sandwich, then sat down at the vintage red Formica kitchen table, which had also been his grandma's. (Ashley had wanted that, too, but he'd managed to pry her greedy fingers off it.)

His belated lunch tasted like ashes. *You are such a jerk,* he told himself, shoving away the plate. *Get over there and admit it.* Instead, he stalled for another couple of hours.

Finally, his cell phone rang and he saw that it was his drain field expert. He answered with, "Are we good to go?"

"Good as gold."

And he'd probably need a fortune in gold to pay the guy, Garrett thought as he ended the call. Jen had offered, but after the way he'd treated her, well, he knew who needed to foot the bill. Anyway, he was willing to bet she couldn't really afford to pay for the repairs.

Now he had no excuse to delay. He climbed back in his truck and drove to the cottage, all the while trying different word and sentence combinations like working the pieces of a puzzle, hoping to form the perfect apology. The pieces still hadn't come together when he pulled the flowers from the truck and walked up to the front door of the cabin.

He didn't have to knock because the door opened. "I saw you coming," she said.

He held out the flowers. "I was a jerk." Impressive, he thought in disgust. Hey, he was a firefighter, not a poet. Anyway, that about said it all.

She took his offering and buried her face in the flowers, inhaling. "They're lovely. Thank you."

"There's chocolate in there, too," he said, pointing to the little gold box.

Speaking of chocolate, what was that he smelled? Cookies? His nose directed his gaze to the kitchen where he spied a plate of cookies covered in plastic wrap and tied with a red ribbon.

"I love chocolate." She stepped aside. "Come in." He was about to say he had to get going when she added, "Please?"

He nodded and walked in.

"I have something for you, too," she said, and hurried over to the kitchen counter. She picked up the plate of cookies and returned, holding it out to him. "This can't make up for...for the accident, but I wanted you to know I was sorry."

He sighed. He'd been a shit and here she was, baking him cookies and apologizing. That never would have happened with Ashley. "You have nothing to be sorry about. I was way out of line."

She smiled and wrinkled her nose, making the freckles on it dance. "Yeah, you were. How about some milk to go with those cookies?"

He should leave. But it would be rude to take her cookies and run, especially after their earlier confrontation. "Sure," he said, and settled on her white couch.

She beamed at him. Just the way Ashley used to when she'd talked him into doing something he hadn't wanted to do.

Except he realized he wanted to sit on Jen Heath's couch and drink hot chocolate and eat those cookies she'd made him. Ashley had never made him cookies.

She set two glasses of milk on the coffee table, as well as a second plate of cookies. "Those others are for you to take home," she explained.

"You didn't have to do that." Not that he was objecting to home-baked cookies, but he knew he didn't deserve them.

"I wanted to. Anyway, I like to bake."

Tilda's idea of baking cookies was to pick up a bag of Oreos. Not that it mattered. He liked Oreos fine, and Tilda was perfect.

Jen joined him on the couch and she picked up her glass and raised it. "Let's toast."

"Okay," he said, and picked his up, too. "What should we toast to?"

"New beginnings."

"I'll drink to that," he said, and they clinked glasses. He took a cookie and bit into it. Just like the kind his mom made. He nodded. "Good."

"Cookies are my specialty," she said. "I'm trying to master bread."

Cookies and bread...and home-grown vegetables. He'd been unreasonable earlier. "About the garden," he began.

"Oh, let's not talk about that," she said quickly. "I want to forget the whole thing."

"Me, too," he admitted. "I'm not usually like that." At least he hadn't been since he and Ash got divorced.

She studied the contents of her glass. "I can't blame you for being mad."

"I want you to have your garden," he said.

Now she brightened. "Really?"

"Yeah. Let me come over and till it for you, though. Okay?"

She nodded. "Okay."

They had just started talking about what she wanted to plant when his cell phone played the theme music for the old TV show *Law & Order.* Tilda. *Crap!*

"Dude, where are you?" she asked.

They were supposed to be playing racquetball at Bruisers about now. "Oh, man. I forgot. I'll be there in fifteen minutes."

"Hey, if you've got something going..."

He did, but he already knew he shouldn't go any further with it. "No, that's okay. I'll be there." He ended the call. "Sorry," he said to Jen. "I forgot I'd promised to be somewhere." He set down his glass and stood.

"Oh. Of course," she said, sounding disappointed. She fetched his plate of cookies and handed them to him.

"Thanks for these."

She smiled. Jen Heath had a great smile. "Thanks again for the flowers. I'm glad we're friends now."

He smiled back. "Me, too." Friends. Was that a good idea?

Probably not, he thought as he drove away. Friendship could easily morph into something else if his hormones had anything to say about it. He was beginning to suspect there was more to Jen Heath than met the eye. For one thing, she had a heart, which was more than he could say for his ex. But she was still impetuous and flaky. And trouble.

He was done with trouble. Now he wanted stable. He wanted emotional peace and some measure of calm in his life to balance out the storm that was his ex-wife. *Stick to the plan,* he told himself even as he pulled a cookie out from under the plastic wrap. *Stick to the plan.*

Chapter Twenty

Love is never as complicated as we make it.
            Muriel Sterling, author of *Simplicity*

Well, there went Saturday night, Jen thought as she watched Garrett's truck hit the road. For a few minutes she'd actually entertained visions of stretching milk and cookies into dinner. Those had disappeared with an almost audible poof when his cell phone rang. Where did he have to be? And with whom?

She remembered the ring tone. *Law & Order*. Tilda the cop. Tilda the buff. Tilda, who probably didn't tear up drain fields.

You have to stop being so fixated on this man, Jen scolded herself. *He's seeing someone else.* There were other men in Icicle Falls and she needed to start checking them out. That was how a smart woman moved on with her life.

She put in a call to Cecily Sterling to see if she'd like to get together. "Hi, what are you doing tonight?"

"I'm meeting Juliet and her husband for dinner at Zelda's. Want to come?"

It was one thing to see if a girlfriend wanted to go

out, but another thing altogether to insert herself into someone else's plans. "Oh, I don't think—" she began.

Cecily broke in before Jen could finish. "We're going dancing at the Red Barn after," Cecily added. "A great chance to learn how to two-step."

Dancing did sound like fun, but… "I don't want to crash the party."

"There's no such thing here in Icicle Falls. We always have room for one more. And you haven't been to the Red Barn yet. You've got to experience that."

Yes, she did. "Okay," she said. "Do I need a cowgirl hat?"

"I'm sure there'll be at least half a dozen cowboys who'll be happy to lend you theirs."

Jen ended the call with a smile. All right. Dinner and dancing. And so what if she wasn't doing it with Garrett Armstrong? There were other fish in the sea, other Icicles in Icicle Falls.

She went to her closet to see what she had that would be suitable for dancing. There was a short, black denim skirt. That would work. And a sleeveless flowered blouse with ruffles. That would work, too. No cowgirl boots, darn it all. She'd have to make do with flats.

Or she could spend some of her paycheck from Gingerbread Haus on boots. And eat beans for the rest of the week. Between boots and dinner out, she'd be making a big dent in her budget. She stood for a moment, gnawing on her lip. Oh, what the heck. She'd get the boots. She was halfway to the door when she remembered she had an unexpected bill for repairing a drain field looming on the horizon. Okay, flats would be fine.

Zelda's was packed, but Cecily and Juliet and her husband had scored a table by the window, which gave them a lovely view of Sleeping Lady Mountain. Juliet had barely introduced Jen to her husband, Neil, when their waitress, Maria Gomez, arrived to take their drink orders.

"I need a huckleberry martini," said Juliet. "Have you tried those yet, Jen?"

"No." And she wasn't going to anytime soon, not until she'd saved enough money for repairs to the drain field.

"Oh, you have to," Juliet urged.

"Or a Chocolate Kiss," Cecily chimed in.

"Oh, no. Those are deadly," Jen said. The last time she'd indulged in Chocolate Kisses she'd fallen in Garrett Armstrong's lap.

Never mind him. You're moving on.

"I'll have a Chocolate Kiss," Cecily told Maria.

"Beer for me," Neil said. "Diet Coke for you, babe?"

Juliet nodded. "Drinking takes away a dancer's edge."

"Or makes a man brave enough to dance," cracked her husband. "And a huckleberry martini for our friend here," he said, pointing to Jen. "Put it on my tab."

"Oh, I couldn't," Jen protested.

"Sure, you can," Juliet said. "We're rolling in money. He just got a raise," she added with a grin.

"All right, Neil," Cecily said, and they bumped knuckles.

Okay, that took care of drinks. Jen searched the menu for the cheapest item. Soup. She liked soup.

"So, Juliet tells me you're new in town," Neil said to Jen. "How are you liking Icicle Falls?"

"I love it here," Jen replied.

"She's in Garrett Armstrong's rental," Juliet said.

Neil made a face. "That place is kind of a dump, isn't it?"

"I've got it fixed up," Jen told him. "Actually, it's perfect for me. I don't need a lot."

"Not when you're simplifying your life," Juliet said.

"Speaking of, did you get the spot for your garden tilled?" Cecily asked.

"Well, no."

Juliet frowned. "Did Bill Will flake out on you?"

"No. He was wonderful. We just, uh, had a slight setback."

"Like what?" Juliet asked.

"Um." Jen looked around the restaurant, hoping for something to distract them. Thank God, Maria was walking toward them. "Oh, here come our drinks."

They placed their orders (main course items for everyone but Jen, who ordered smoked salmon chowder), then Maria gathered the menus and left.

"So what happened with the garden?" Juliet was like a bloodhound. She never lost the scent of a good story.

"We encountered a little problem."

"Like what?" Cecily asked.

"Like the drain field."

Neil's eyebrows went up. "You hit the drain field?"

Jen gave a quick nod and took a fortifying sip of her huckleberry martini.

Neil let out a guffaw. "Oh, that's rich."

Jen shook her head sadly. "Sometimes simplifying your life isn't that simple."

"No kidding," Neil said with a frown. "Every time Juliet does something to make her life simpler, mine gets more complicated. I have to make dinner two days a week now."

"Poor baby," Juliet teased.

"And I've still got to till our garden," he said.

"Just look out for the drain field," Jen cautioned. "I can tell you, it's not a good thing if you hit those pipes."

Now Charley was showing two new customers to their table, Garrett and Tilda the cop. Jealousy took a bite out of Jen's good mood.

"Hey, there, Garrett," Neil said, forcing the couple to stop. "How's it going?"

The two men shook hands. Garrett nodded to the other women and said hi to Jen.

"Jen was just telling us what happened today," Neil said.

Why had he brought that up? Jen could feel the flame of embarrassment engulfing her cheeks. "They were asking about my garden," she muttered.

"It could happen to anyone," Garrett said with a shrug.

If only it *had* happened to anyone—anyone but her. At least they'd restored friendly landlord-tenant relations.

Tilda raised a curious eyebrow but didn't say anything. She didn't appear to be a big talker...unless she was threatening the competition with a ticket.

Charley had realized that her parade had come to a halt and she joined the party. "Hey, guys, how are your drinks?"

"Great as always," Neil said. Then to Garrett and Tilda, "You want to join us?"

"I'm sure Charley can find a couple more chairs," Juliet put in.

"Another time," Tilda said, making the decision for

both of them. "Take care," she added, and started moving away; Charley took the hint and went with her.

Garrett nodded goodbye and followed them.

"I can see who's wearing the pants in that couple," Neil said. "But hey, when you've got a hot woman, who cares?" He grinned at Juliet.

"You're so full of it," she told him.

Jen downed the rest of her martini, stuck on the whole hot-woman thing. Tilda was attractive in a Lara Croft, Tomb Raider, way. She wasn't cover-model beautiful, but in that leather jacket, the tight-fitting red top and butt-hugging jeans, she was the embodiment of all those sexy lady cops who populated TV cop shows. Everything about her, from the way she walked—*look at my ass but touch it and I'll break your arm*—to the expression on her face—*I am so tough that once you've had sex with me you'll know you're a hard-ass dude*—seemed geared to appeal to the kind of man who liked adventure. Nobody wanted a marshmallow these days.

"So, what garden?" Tilda asked as soon as she and Garrett had ordered a couple of beers.

"Huh?" Garrett pulled his mind away from the image of Jen in that flowered top.

Tilda leaned back in the booth and studied him in a way that made him feel like a criminal in a lineup. "The garden?"

Now that he had a little distance from the event, it was sort of funny. "Well, Jen decided she wanted to put in a garden, so she got Bill Will out to till a spot for her."

Tilda rolled her eyes. "Bill Will. I can see it now."

Garrett shook his head and smiled. "Of course, she

managed to pick the part of the yard where the drain field is."

"No way," Tilda scoffed.

"Oh, yeah. I swear that woman has a gift for taking the simplest thing and turning it into a sitcom."

"I bet you weren't laughing."

"No," he admitted. "I wasn't. But we made up." Made up. Did that sound too personal, like he had something going with Jen? Yes, judging from the odd look Tilda was giving him. "We fixed the problem," he amended. "Got Grover's Septic to come out."

"That had to cost a pretty penny."

It wasn't going to be cheap, but even though it was Jen's fault, Garrett wasn't going to charge her.

"You're gonna make her pay for it, aren't you?" Tilda asked.

"We'll work it out." Tilda didn't need to know how.

"This chick is a pain in the butt," she observed.

"Yeah, she can be." Garrett thought of the cookies she'd made. "But she's a nice pain."

"Yeah?" Tilda didn't sound happy to hear it.

Garrett grabbed his menu. "I'm starving. What looks good to you?"

After dinner Jen and company were off to the Red Barn. Cecily had been right; Jen met plenty of men who were more than willing to lend her their cowboy hats. Bill Will and two of his buddies taught her how to do the country two-step, and Cecily and Juliet dragged her out on the floor every time there was a line dance. When they finally left the noisy little honkytonk, her ears were ringing and her feet were throbbing. She'd given her phone number to a cowboy and a local wine grower, and her social life was looking up.

What were Garrett and Tilda doing right now?

"I really liked that movie," Tilda said as Garrett drove her back to her house. "Bruce Willis still kicks ass."

"Yeah, he does," Garrett agreed. He and Tilda had enjoyed a pleasant evening—a good dinner followed by a good movie.

Well, when he'd been paying attention the movie was good. His mind had wandered, straying to thoughts of Jen Heath. What was she up to? He'd been willing to bet she hadn't gone straight home after dinner. He'd played on Neil's fast pitch team the year before, and he knew the guy and his wife went dancing at the Red Barn on a regular basis. They'd probably all headed over there after dinner. So who was Jen dancing with now?

None of your business, he reminded himself. *She's your tenant, nothing more. You have a woman. Right here.*

They pulled up in front of Tilda's place. She didn't wait for him to come around and open the door. Tilda wasn't that kind of woman. She did wait for him to join her once they were out of the truck, and they fell into step, strolling up her walk.

"Thanks for the movie," she said. "And dinner."

When they'd first started doing things together, they'd shared the tab, but Garrett always felt awkward doing that and he was slowly edging them toward something a little more...traditional. Of course, when a man picked up the tab, it meant he was interested—

but now Garrett found himself suddenly ambivalent about the message he was sending.

They reached her door. She turned and leaned against it. "You wanna come in?"

Garrett knew what that meant. He could tell by the look in her eyes. Tilda was ready for more than friendship. Hell, so was he. He'd been celibate for way too long. Still, he hesitated.

She raised an eyebrow.

"We don't want to rush things."

"Rush? Dude, I know you got burned and you want to take it slow, but I've seen slugs move faster than you."

"Hey, I don't want to take advantage of you."

She rolled her eyes. "Great. I had to pick a gentleman."

"Yeah, I'm afraid you did."

She smiled and shook her head. "And I shaved my damn legs and everything."

That made him chuckle. He leaned over and gave her a kiss good-night, just a friendly kiss.

She slipped her arms around him and changed it into a friends-with-benefits kiss. Whoa. It would be so easy to keep that going, to let the fire she'd lit turn into a blaze. Every ounce of testosterone in him wanted it.

But it didn't feel right. Not yet. He took her hands and gently unlocked them from around his neck. "Hey, you do that too much and I might just forget I'm a gentleman."

"That's what I'm hoping," she said.

"How did such a good cop get to be such a bad girl?" he teased.

She grinned. "Remember who my mother is."

Yeah, Tilda had her mother's edgy humor. Dot Morrison was probably something else in her day. Tilda would probably be something else in bed if Garrett would let her. Well, he would. Soon.

And as he went back to his truck he told himself that his reluctance to log in some sack time with Tilda had nothing to do with a certain strawberry blonde with freckles and a tendency to wreak havoc wherever she went.

It wasn't only Jen Heath who had a gift for that. When he picked Timmy up from his ex on Sunday, the kid was on a sugar high, racing around the apartment like the Road Runner on speed.

"Timmy, stop it!" Ashley yelled.

She was wearing a tight black top that was cut low enough to give a man an eyeful and skintight jeans. A few years ago that would have turned Garrett's burner to high. Today he just looked at her and frowned.

"What did you feed him?" he asked. Wasn't the mom supposed to ask the dad stuff like this?

She shrugged.

"Hey, buddy, what did you have for breakfast this morning?"

"We had doughnuts!" Timmy leaped onto the couch and began jumping up and down.

Garrett scooped him up. "How many doughnuts did you have?"

"I had three!" Timmy said, still going at it like a Mexican jumping bean.

Ashley acted surprised. "Three?" she repeated.

"What, you didn't give him three doughnuts?"

"No. You think I like it when he gets like this?"

Garrett stared at her, mystified. "Then how is it he came to have three doughnuts?"

"I had a jelly doughnut and a chocolate doughnut and a really long doughnut," Timmy bragged.

"A maple bar?" Garrett guessed.

Timmy nodded enthusiastically. "It was really good."

"I bet it was. And where was Mommy when you were having the really long doughnut?"

Timmy shrugged.

"I was busy doing something," Ashley said.

Probably her nails.

"Not that it's any of your business," she added.

"It is if you aren't paying attention to what our kid is eating," Garrett snapped, and headed for the door.

"Oh, yeah, and you're so perfect."

He knew he wasn't a perfect parent, but at least he paid attention. He decided not to respond to her taunt. Instead, he said to Timmy, "Let's go see Grandma."

"Grandma!" squealed Timmy. He wriggled to get down and Garrett released him. The child bolted for the door, yanked it open and was out of the apartment like a shot and running down the hallway.

"See you in a couple of weeks," Garrett said, wishing he didn't have to.

"No, you won't. I'm going out of town."

"Timmy, wait!" Garrett called. Then, to Ashley, "Where are you going?"

"That's none of your business, either."

Timmy had apparently developed deafness and was already at the stairs. In another minute he'd be in the parking lot. Garrett didn't have time to stand around and argue. "Fine," he said through gritted teeth, and hurried off after his son. Whatever loser his ex was hooking up with, it was just as well that Timmy wouldn't be exposed to him.

Maybe he already had been. Once they were in the truck Garrett learned that Timmy had a new toy, a jackknife.

"Look what Mommy's friend gave me," Timmy said, pulling it out of his pocket.

Great. Give a five-year-old a knife. Was his ex-wife really this stupid? And how stupid did that make him, since he'd fallen for her in the first place? "That's pretty cool." He held out his hand. "Can I see it?"

Timmy passed it to him. "He's gonna teach me to…" Timmy screwed up his face. "Whit…whit—"

"Whittle?"

"Yeah."

"That's real nice of him." Was the goon also going to sew up his son's finger when he cut himself? Garrett still remembered his first jackknife. He'd begged and begged until his parents finally caved and gave him one for his eleventh birthday. And, of course, he'd proceeded to cut himself the first time he tried to use it. Every boy wanted one and every boy usually managed to slice himself. Timmy was way too young for this.

Timmy put out his hand, but instead of returning the thing, Garrett slipped it in his shirt pocket. "Tell you what, let me hang on to this for you. Okay?"

Timmy's smile vanished and he shook his head. "I want to show Grandma."

"I'll show it to Grandma," Garrett assured him.

Now Timmy's sunny disposition began to do a disappearing act. "I want my knife," he whined. "I want to show Grandma."

"Don't worry. She'll see it," Garrett said. "Hey, what do you think Grandma's making for Sunday dinner?"

Timmy wasn't going to be distracted. "I want my knife," he insisted.

"I'll give it back to you a little later. When you're old enough to learn how to use it and not hurt yourself."

That turned on the tear spigot. "I want my knife!"

Garrett clenched the steering wheel. "Let's see what Grandma says," he suggested, hoping to bring in someone else to share his bad-guy status.

Timmy wasn't having any of it. Now the crying began in earnest. "I want my knife!"

"Well, you're not getting it," Garrett said, losing his patience. "You'll hurt yourself."

Was this going to be how it was for the rest of his life, him being the bad guy, always having to do damage control? It was a depressing thought.

They arrived at his parents' house with Timmy still sobbing.

"What's wrong with our little man?" his mother asked, holding her arms out to Timmy.

The child ran into them and upped the drama level with even louder sobs. "Daddy took my knife."

Garrett's mother looked at him questioningly.

"One of Ashley's new 'friends' gave him a jack-knife."

His mother nodded. "Well, Timmy, I bet your daddy's just keeping it safe for you until you're older. Don't you think?"

Timmy shook his head violently. "I want my knife."

"You know what? I made some peanut butter cookies. Would you like one?"

"He already had three doughnuts for breakfast," Garrett told her.

She frowned in disapproval. "All right, then, how about some string cheese? And then you can help Grandpa fill the bird feeders," she said to Timmy.

At this the sobs began to subside. Timmy got his string cheese and was then handed over to Garrett's dad to help with the important job of feeding the birds, and Garrett's blood pressure returned to normal.

"That woman is a disaster. What you ever saw in her I can't imagine," Garrett's mother said as he settled down at the kitchen table with a cup of coffee.

That was because his mother wasn't a man. "You've told me that before, Mom," he said irritably.

"Well, I'm telling you again," she said as she checked on the pot roast. "You'd better make sure the next woman you pick has her act together."

And Jen Heath didn't qualify, Garrett reminded himself when he went over later in the week to till a plot for her garden. His mother had to help a friend with an emergency so he brought Timmy with him after he got out of kindergarten. Jen had played hide-and-seek with Timmy while Garrett worked, and he'd just given her brownie points for being good with kids when she ruined the good impression she'd made.

"I got some strawberries at the store yesterday. How about some strawberry sundaes?" she offered.

Timmy nodded eagerly. "I like sundaes. My grandma makes sundaes."

"Well, let's see if I can make one as yummy as your grandma's," Jen said. She looked at Garrett.

"I'll pass," he said, wiping his sweaty brow.

"How about a Coke instead?"

"That'd be great," he said. "I'll load up the tiller."

"Okay, then. You want to help me?" Jen asked Timmy.

"Okay," he said, and followed her into the house.

By the time Garrett came in, she and Timmy were hard at work, Timmy pulling stems off the berries and Jen slicing them.

"Okay, now we need ice cream," she said as Garrett came back from washing up. She took ice cream from the freezer and handed it to Timmy. "And whipped cream." She got a can of whipped cream from the fridge and gave Timmy a playful squirt on the nose.

He giggled and wiped it off, licking the cream from his fingers. Back at the counter, she dished up ice cream, topped it with the berries and whipped cream and then squirted Timmy again. And then she was chasing his son all over the cottage with the can. Next she'd be feeding him doughnuts.

"Okay," he said, "let's eat those sundaes." He got up and went to take the can from her.

"Oh, no. You can't have my whipped cream," she said, hiding it behind her.

"Oh, yes, I can," he insisted, backing her toward the kitchen counter.

Now he had her pinned and he was suddenly aware of every curve of her body.

"What will you give me for it?" she teased. The words were barely out of her mouth when she seemed to catch the sexual overtones. Her expression grew more serious and she licked her lips.

He pressed closer, feeling her softness against him.

Go ahead, urged some little devil on his shoulder, *kiss her.*

Except his son was present. Still, he was tempted…

"Squirt Daddy!" Timmy yelled.

She obliged, bringing the can around and shooting him square in the face. Whipped cream went up his nose and down his chin and he stepped back, blinking.

"Oh, I'm sorry," she said, and set the can on the counter. "I didn't mean for so much to shoot out." And then she was giggling.

Timmy was laughing uproariously. "You look funny, Daddy!" He grabbed the can and aimed it at his father.

"Timmy, no," Garrett protested, but it was too late. Next thing he knew, his T-shirt was covered in whipped cream. Nice.

"Okay, enough," he said with a frown. He got a kitchen towel and started wiping off his shirt. "You're a bad influence," he informed her.

She smiled, displaying two dimples. "It's good to have fun."

Ah, yes, that was her mission in life, to have fun. Just like Ashley.

They sat down to eat their sundaes while Garrett nursed his Coke. "So, there's no guy in Seattle wishing you hadn't moved up here?"

She shook her head and studied her sundae. "No."

"That's hard to believe. There has to be someone."

"There was. It didn't work out."

"Was it serious?"

She stabbed at her ice cream. "Until we got divorced."

"Oh. Sorry."

She managed a little shrug. "It's been almost two years. I'm moving on."

But moving with baggage in tow. Nobody escaped without some. He knew. He had his own share of post-divorce luggage.

Here was another reason he couldn't allow himself to get interested in this woman. Timmy needed stability. *He* needed stability.

Timmy was now licking his bowl. Garrett removed it from his son's hands. "I think you're done, buddy."

And they were done here. No more friendly landlord-tenant relations.

"We'd better get going," he said.

She looked at his half-finished drink and blinked in surprise. "Oh. Well, thanks for tilling my garden plot."

"No problem," he said, pulling Timmy's chair out from the table. "Come on, buddy, time to go." Before he and Jen got any chummier. "Call me if you need anything," he said in parting, then gave himself a mental kick. The last thing he needed was Jen Heath calling him.

He said his goodbyes, took his son and got out of there. Once they were home, he called Tilda. "So, what are you doing tonight? Want to come over for pizza and a movie?"

"Yeah. I'm up for that."

So was Garrett. He was going to be smart about women from now on.

Jen cleaned up the kitchen and then went outside to prep her garden. She found a shovel in the shed and her bag of fertilizer and got busy fertilizing her soil. As she worked she tried to analyze what had happened.

One minute Garrett Armstrong was sending out signals that he was interested and the next he'd shut down.

It had to be because she'd said she was divorced. But so was he. What was his problem?

Not what, who. As long as he was with Tilda, he was off-limits.

What do you care? You just met two nice men at the Red Barn.

And they liked to dance. They probably liked whipped cream fights, too. They probably wouldn't hold it against her that she'd made a poor selection in the love department the first time around. And she'd probably have the same physical reaction if one of them backed her up against her kitchen counter.

Okay, that was hoo-ha. She'd gotten more of a charge in that one moment with Garret than she'd gotten from a whole evening of dancing with her two new admirers. Her love life stank worse than the stuff she was spreading in the garden.

She frowned at a clump of fertilizer and beat it to death with her rake.

Chapter Twenty-One

Sometimes all that stops us from having a better life is...us.

—Muriel Sterling, author of *Simplicity*

"Yay, you're finally here!" Jen greeted her sister as Toni climbed out of her SUV. She'd expected Toni earlier in the day and now the afternoon shadows were lengthening.

"Thank God," Toni said as the sisters hugged. "Interesting, isn't it, how once I'm about to leave suddenly everyone needs me? Between getting Jordan's history day project up to the school, and delivering the homework Jeffrey forgot, and *then* having to email Wayne a list of who needs to be where when, I thought I'd never get out the door." She shook her head. "You should have heard him this morning. You'd think I was abandoning him to life in prison instead of a few days in charge of his own kids." Her smile turned wicked. "What a shame. He'll have to see firsthand how much I do."

"So, are you coming up here to see me or to teach your husband a lesson?"

"Yes," Toni said with a smile. "I hope you've got the cards out. I'm ready for some Hands and Buns."

"You bet. And I've got homemade limoncello and bruschetta. I just have to toast the bread."

"I'm famished."

Once inside the cottage, Toni sniffed. "Do I smell chocolate?"

"Yup. I'm trying a new recipe for brownies."

"Homemade limoncello, bruschetta, brownies… Who are you?"

Jen smiled. "I'm a woman who has time to enjoy life now. That's who I am. Of course, I'm not exactly swimming in money these days, but with my new lifestyle I don't need that much."

"No shopping sprees?" Toni teased.

"Who needs to shop when you can garden?"

"Garden?" Toni echoed.

"Here, put your stuff in the guest room, then I want to show you something," Jen said, leading the way down the hall.

Toni stowed her overnight bag and joined Jen out on the back deck.

Jen pointed to a patch of dirt. "Behold my future garden."

"You, the black thumb queen?"

Toni was a master gardener. Jen suddenly felt foolish showing off her little veggie patch. "Well, it's not much."

"I think it's great! You'll have to weed it, you know."

"Ha-ha. I know."

"So, what have you got in there?"

"Carrots, beets, lettuce, spinach and onions. Everything I need for a perfect salad."

"And I saw lavender in your flower beds."

"Great for everything from cooking to making bath

salts and sachets. You're all getting homemade presents for Christmas this year," Jen said proudly.

"Good for you, sis." Toni smiled. "Tell me again why I thought moving up here was a bad idea."

For once, one of her impulses had paid off and she loved hearing her big sister admit it. "I can't remember."

"Me, neither," Toni said with another grin. "Pour the limoncello and let's play cards."

Once they were settled with their drinks and snacks, Toni returned to the subject of the garden. "So, what happened to your front yard?" she asked as she put together a canasta of tens.

Jen had conveniently neglected to tell her about the first tilling fiasco. That had been too embarrassing, and she'd known Toni would have plenty to say about it. Her sister had never come right out and said it, but Jen was well aware that Toni considered her a screwup. Hardly surprising in light of her failed first marriage and the bad decision to buy a condo and leave herself financially strapped. Toni didn't do things like that, even if she did like to complain about her family. At least Toni *had* a family.

"That didn't turn out to be a good spot for the garden," she said.

Thankfully, Toni nodded and let the subject drop. Then she picked up a new one. "Are things heating up between you and the fireman?"

Jen frowned and reached for her drink. "Not really."

Toni shook her head. "I don't get that man. You said he's got someone but that he doesn't seem too interested in her."

"That about sums it up," Jen said. She sighed and played a card.

"Well, he's an idiot," Toni decided. "Find somebody else."

"I'm working on it," Jen said, "but so far there isn't anybody else who interests me."

Toni drew her cards and considered them. "You do get a bug up your nose sometimes, you know."

She sure had one up her nose now. She was hopelessly, ridiculously fixated on Garrett Armstrong. She sighed. "Let's talk about something else."

"Okay, how's the blog coming? I'm liking your posts."

Her sister the writer liked her blog. That made Jen happy. "I'm enjoying it. But like I said, I still don't have an idea for a book."

Not that she had to write one in order to fill her time. Between her job, volunteering at both the Icicle Falls library and organizing the one at church, she was getting busy all over again. It was so easy to say yes whenever someone asked her to do something. And everything sounded interesting or worthwhile, so she just jumped right in.

Instead of sharing this, she said, "Are you going to help me brainstorm?"

"Sure," Toni said.

But there was no chance to brainstorm that night, not when they were busy drinking, eating and playing cards. The following day was equally full with shopping, lunch at Zelda's, dinner with Cecily and then book club.

Everyone was delighted to meet Toni and welcomed her as if she were an old friend. Juliet was especially excited when she learned that Toni was a master gardener. "Have you read this book?" she asked, holding up their selection for the month.

Toni shook her head.

"I found it really inspiring," Juliet went on.

"Not me," Chita told her. "I'm too busy simplifying my life."

"It didn't do much for me, either," Charley said. "But I'll happily eat all those extra zucchinis you übergardeners bring in."

"I'll share," Juliet said. "If I can spare any. I'm already making plans for chocolate zucchini cake, zucchini muffins and zucchini bread. Oh, and zuccini pizza."

Stacy cocked an eyebrow. "Zucchini pizza?"

"Oh, yeah," Juliet said. "I got the recipe online."

"I'd better add some zucchini to my garden," Jen decided.

"So are Jen and I the only ones doing a garden?" Juliet asked.

"I guess so," Cecily replied.

Juliet rolled her eyes in mock disgust. "You're all a bunch of lightweights."

"No, we're just simplifying," Charley said. "And growing a garden on top of keeping up with a family and running a business does not make for a simple life."

"Speaking of business, how's the shop doing?" Chita asked Stacy.

Stacy bit her lip and stared at her glass of lemonade. "It could be better."

"You have to give it time," Charley told her. "It takes a while to build a customer base."

Stacy nodded, but she looked as if she wanted to cry. "I thought this was such a good idea."

"Hey, it is," Cass assured her. "This is our slow season, but business will pick up starting at Maifest, and then we'll have lots of people coming up for the summer, and things will be good clear through December. You just have to hang in there for a few more weeks."

"Or until tomorrow," Toni said. "I want to check out your shop. And I brought my credit card."

That made Stacy smile. "You can bring your sister to book group any time," she told Jen.

"Since when are you into antiques?" Jen asked later as she and Toni drove back to the cabin.

"Since tonight. I bet I can find something in that shop."

And, sure enough, she did. By the time Toni was done checking out Timeless Treasures the next day, she'd amassed quite a collection of goodies—a china cup and saucer to give their mother for her birthday, a vintage necklace she knew Jordan would like, a carved Jim Shore Easter creation and a set of Fiesta ware mugs.

"Now, all I need is about twenty more customers just like you," Stacy said as she rang up the sale. "Although I'd settle for one or two."

So far they were the only ones in the shop. Poor Stacy. She'd worked so hard at this. Jen hoped Cass was right and business would pick up. Otherwise, Stacy was going to be back to having a houseful of stuff. Nope, there was nothing simple about simplifying your life.

It was a typical Saturday. Chita had piles of laundry to do, a son to drive to baseball practice, a house to clean. She looked around and decided the dusting and vacuuming could wait. She put the kids to work cleaning their bathroom, and while they did that, she threw in a load of laundry. Quesadillas and canned chili would take care of dinner. And now she had time to breathe.

She also had time to stop by Stacy's shop after dropping Enrico off at the baseball field.

There were no other customers and Stacy sat at the counter by her cash register, doing something on her computer. She raised her head when the shop bell jingled and her face lit up at the sight of Chita and her daughter.

"Hi, guys," she greeted them.

"Thought we'd come see what new things you've gotten in since your grand opening," Chita said.

Anna was drawn instantly to a display of a little-girl-size china tea set. "Don't touch anything," Chita cautioned. "Just look."

"That's new," Stacy said. "I took it in on consignment."

Anna was gazing at the tea set as if it were the Holy Grail. "It's so pretty."

"How much?" Chita asked Stacy in a low voice.

"I'll make you a deal."

Her daughter would soon be too old for tea parties. Now was the time to indulge her. She and Stacy did some quick negotiating and then the tea set was Anna's.

"Thank you, Mama!" she cried, and about hugged the life out of her mother.

Okay, that had been worth every penny.

The bell over the shop door jingled again, and a man entered. A tall, slender, fortysomething man with light brown hair and a mustache. Ken Wolfe, the veterinarian.

Stacy greeted the newcomer. "How's everything in animal land?"

"No big trauma this week, no casualties." Now he smiled at Chita. He had a darned nice smile. "We haven't seen Hidalgo in a while. Has he been behaving himself?"

"Yes. It's a miracle."

"Is there anything I can help you find?" Stacy asked.

He scratched his head. "I'm looking for a gift for my sister. She's got a birthday coming up."

"I'm sure I've got something she'll love," Stacy said. "Does she like china, decorations? Is she interested in quilts?"

He scratched his head again. "I'm not sure. I'll just browse for a while."

"Of course," Stacy said.

He turned to Chita. "Maybe you can help me."

The tone of his voice, the way he was looking at her…was Ken Wolfe interested in her? Chita caught Stacy's smile out of the corner of her eye and found herself blushing.

"What would you pick out?" he asked.

"Something for the kitchen," Chita said.

"Food for thought," he punned. "My sister's a foodie. She'd probably like something for the kitchen."

Chita led him to the section where Stacy had arranged a number of kitschy kitchen items. "This is adorable," she said, pointing at the small pedestal glass dome with three teacups stacked inside.

"What would you do with it?" he asked with a rather confused expression on his face.

"Use it as a centerpiece for a tea party." She could see herself using it the next time it was her turn to host a shower. And with so many women in her large extended family either getting married or getting pregnant, she was bound to have the opportunity.

"I don't know," he said.

She picked it up. "Then I'll have to get it for myself." And that was the absolute last thing she was buying. Her bank account wouldn't accommodate any more spending. Still, it was good to splurge once in a while and she hadn't done any splurging in a long, long time. "I think I'll throw a tea party one of these days." Maybe for Mother's Day. She could have her mother and her two sisters and their daughters over. She smiled at the thought.

"You know, you have a lovely smile," Ken said. "I rarely see it when you come into the clinic."

"That's because I'm always worried about Hidalgo." *And how I'm going to pay the latest vet bill.*

"Well, it's nice to see." He pointed to an empire-waist blue apron with a swirling black floral print. "Hey, what about this?"

"That's nice," Chita said.

He folded it over his arm. Decision made. "I'll give it to her early. She's having a dinner party tonight, French theme. This looks French, doesn't it?"

"Oui," Chita agreed.

Now he tilted his head and turned to her, considering. "I don't suppose you'd be interested in French food, would you? Beef bourguignon."

Ken Wolfe was asking her out? Was that what was happening? She blinked in surprise. Had he been sending signals all along and she hadn't picked up on them?

Maybe they'd been too subtle. She'd certainly known when Jose Fuentes, who worked in the Sweet Dreams warehouse, had been interested. Nothing ambiguous about what he'd said, especially when he added a bump and grind to demonstrate. *Go out with me tonight and you could get lucky, Chita.* Ick.

"And Julia Child's raspberry Bavarian cream for dessert," Ken added.

"What do you know about Julia Child?" Chita teased.

His cheeks took on a reddish tint. "I'm kind of a foodie myself. I'm actually bringing the dessert."

A dinner with grown-ups. That sounded wonderful. But… "My children," she began.

"I'll babysit," offered Stacy, who'd been shamelessly eavesdropping.

"There you go. Now all you need is a string of pearls."

"We have those here," Stacy said.

"So, what do you say?" he asked.

"Oui."

Later that evening, Chita found herself wearing a sundress and the cultured pearls Stacy had insisted on giving her, seated at a dinner table with five other people and discussing everything from food and books (her favorite subjects) to politics (not her favorite subject). And all the while, Ken had kept her wineglass filled and made sure she felt included. His sister and her friends had been equally welcoming. It had been an evening of quiet sophistication, like something out of one of her book club novels, she thought as he drove her home.

There'd been one tense moment when Ken's sister

had asked what she did for a living. Not for the first time, she wished she'd had more ambition when she was younger, that she hadn't settled so quickly for the life she had.

"I work for Sweet Dreams Chocolates," she'd said, and then had steered the conversation toward chocolate preferences. It was a bit of sleight of hand she'd mastered over the years to focus attention away from the specifics of her job.

Working at a chocolate factory probably sounded like fun to most people, but standing on her feet in front of a giant conveyor belt doing quality control wasn't all that much fun. It sure didn't require much in the brain department. A waste of a good brain, she thought now, and remembered her high school English teacher saying the very same thing when she'd earned a D in class for not bothering to turn in her homework.

"Your sister is lovely," she said. "And the dinner was great." This was a lifestyle she could get used to.

"She's not bad," he murmured, like a typical brother.

"And I never get tired of talking about books," Chita said. "Sometimes it seems like a long wait till my next book club meeting."

"You mentioned your book club at dinner. What do you read?"

"Anything and everything. Fiction, memoirs, even some nonfiction."

"Oh, yeah? What was the last nonfiction book you read?"

"A book on gardening. Not something I'm interested in."

"Me, neither," he said. "When it comes to gardening I don't carrot all."

"That was bad," she said with a smile.

"Well, then, lettuce move on to a new subject," he said, making her groan. "Sorry. Sometimes I can't help myself. What else have you read?"

"We read Muriel Sterling's new book on simplifying your life, which I've been trying to do. Between the kids and work, it gets a little crazy."

"Working at Sweet Dreams has to be a fun job, though," he said. "What exactly do you do?"

She could feel her cheeks heating. *It's good, honest labor,* she reminded herself. But it was far from satisfying. "I work in the factory."

"You say that like you're ashamed of it."

She shrugged. "Maybe I am. Sometimes I think I could have done more with my life."

"Your life's not over yet," he said.

They were at her house now. He shut off the engine and turned to look at her. "So is your life too crazy to add a man to it?" He slid his arm across the top of the seat and his fingers found her hair.

Just that little touch was enough to start a slow melting deep inside her. "I don't know." She hadn't wanted to get involved with another man. Hadn't wanted to risk her heart. Or her children's hearts. But Ken Wolfe was tempting. Now he was playing with her hair. She was going to turn into a puddle here in the front seat of his fancy 'stang. "Maybe for the right man."

He smiled. "Want to go out again?"

"First, tell me how it is that such a handsome man is single."

"I'm looking for the right woman."

She cocked her eyebrows. "That was a sly answer."

"But true." He leaned across the seat and urged her

toward him. The look on his face made her mouth go suddenly dry. He kissed her. It was a slow, sexy kiss. Oh, boy. He'd have to pour her out of the car now. By the time he was done, her lips were vibrating, and so was the rest of her.

"Would you like to go out with me next week?" she asked.

He smiled. *"Oui."*

The minute she was inside the house Stacy wanted to know all about her date.

"It was fantastic," Chita said. "And it got me thinking."

"About sex?" Stacy teased.

"What's that?" Chita joked, and flopped on the couch.

"Something you're about to experience in the near future, I'm betting."

"Well, that would be nice." There was an understatement. "But I'm thinking my life could be...more."

"How so?"

Chita picked up a large bowl that held a few half-popped kernels of popcorn. Stacy and the kids had obviously been partying. She took one and chewed on it. "These people I was with were all smart. They had degrees, interesting jobs. His sister and brother-in-law are brewmasters. The other couple owns an orchard." She frowned. "And me? I work on an assembly line."

"Not just any assembly line, though. Your company makes chocolate."

Chita sighed heavily and set the bowl aside. "Yeah, well, if I owned the company..." She sighed again. "I haven't done anything with my life."

"You *are* doing something with your life. You're

raising two great kids, and you're doing it single-handed."

"It's just that, well, I don't know," Chita finished lamely. "It sure would be nice to do something new."

"You still can. Your life's not over yet."

Chita smiled. "That's exactly what Ken said."

"Ken sounds like a smart man. I hope you're going out with him again."

"I am."

Stacy smiled. "Then that makes you a smart woman."

She just hoped she was smart enough for Ken Wolfe.

Chapter Twenty-Two

Simplifying your life can be as challenging as it is rewarding.

— Muriel Sterling, author of *Simplicity*

I'm really loving my simple life. My garden is coming along well, and today I'm trying something new. I'm going to make candles. In simpler times people always made their own candles. Although I think in simpler times it didn't cost as much. Wax, wicks, coloring, fragrance, a pouring pot, double boiler. My goodness! I did read online that you can use birthday candles for your wicks, and you can recycle wax and use old jelly jars. So that's what I'm doing. I went to the Kindness Cupboard, our local thrift store, and found just about everything I need. Well, except the coloring and fragrance. That I ordered online. Now I'm set. This is going to be fun!

The day Jen picked to make her candles happened to fall on the first of the month, when Garrett always stopped by to collect the rent. That had nothing to do with why she was picking this particular day, she told herself. But she knew she was lying.

"So I want to impress the man," she muttered, placing the fire extinguisher on the counter. (Purchased after the woodstove fiasco.)

Her sister was right. She needed to find someone else. The manager of the produce department at the Safeway was nice enough. She'd actually had a date with him. They'd gone to the Falls Cinema to see a movie. And had run into Garrett and Tilda. Jen had found it impossible to concentrate on the movie after that, and next time her friendly produce man had called she'd come up with an excuse to ditch him. She'd also dated one of the local Realtors, but with his fancy car and fine-art collection, he'd been more into himself than her. As for her admirers from the Red Barn, they were nice but there was no spark.

Still, there were plenty of other men in Icicle Falls. Plenty of men! She didn't need to hang around waiting for Garrett Armstrong to get a clue. Except here she was, with her makeup on and wearing her cutest top and her shortest shorts.

She was in the middle of melting wax, using her makeshift double boiler, when he tapped on the cottage door.

He was earlier than usual. She'd hoped to have her candles poured by the time he arrived. She ran to the door and threw it open. "You're early."

Both his eyebrows went up. "Is that a problem?"

"No, no. It's just that I'm in the middle of making candles."

"They don't have any at the store?"

"Of course they do, but I thought this would be interesting to try. Come on in," she said, then hurried back to the stove. "I don't want to leave this wax un-attended for too long."

"You're melting wax?" His tone of voice betrayed a certain lack of confidence.

"Hey, I know what I'm doing," she assured him. "I'm not a complete idiot."

"I believe you," he said, and sauntered into the kitchen. He eyed the fire extinguisher. "Baking soda will work, too."

Okay, so she'd overcompensated "Just making sure," she said.

"Would you like any help?"

He was only offering because he thought she'd burn the place down but she decided not to quibble over his motives. Instead, she gave him her sweetest smile and said, "That's really nice of you."

"That's me, Mr. Nice. What do you want me to do?" he asked, looking around at the collection of jam jars lined up on the counter.

"You can be in charge of the baking soda," she said, and took the box out of the cupboard. "Do you always provide this kind of service to your tenants?"

"Never had a tenant before."

"So I'm your first."

"Yep. And you've been a memorable one."

She frowned. "I don't think you meant that in a good way. Oh, here, it looks like my wax is ready to pour." She pointed to the box of birthday candles sitting next to the jars. "Would you mind helping me with my wicks?"

"Birthday candles?"

"I read that they make great candlewicks. Get one out and hold it in the jar while I pour the wax."

He seemed less than excited about this idea, but gamely took a candle from the box and held it in the middle of a jar. "Don't burn me."

"I'm not an idiot," she said again. Although now she was nervous. She took her pouring pan to the counter. She was standing so close to him she could almost feel the current zipping between them, and that made it hard to concentrate. She bit her lip and focused on her job, pouring very slowly. Nothing bad happened and she smiled. "There. See? No problem. Let's do another."

So they went on to the next candle. And, once more, Garrett's hand survived the experience.

Maybe after two successes she was getting cocky. Or maybe he'd moved his hand just a little. She wasn't actually sure. But the third time didn't prove to be the charm. She managed to splash him with hot wax, making him flinch. Which meant that his hand jerked and she really got him.

"Yow!" He pulled his hand away and the wick fell sideways.

"Oh, no. I'm so sorry," she said, setting aside the pan. "Let me get some ointment."

"Cold water," he said, turning to the faucet. "Got some ice?"

She nodded and took ice out of the freezer, putting some in a quart-size plastic bag. "I'm sorry," she said again. "I don't know how that happened."

"No worries," he said.

"Your poor hand," she fretted, giving him the bag.

"It's okay," he said as he applied the ice to his wound.

Why was it that every time she encountered this man something went wrong? "Things like this don't happen when you're not around," she tried to explain.

"Yeah?" He looked dubious.

"Does it hurt?"

"Not much. I'm tough."

She bit her lip. "Maybe I should just buy my candles."

"Maybe," he agreed.

"You know, I really am not incompetent."

"I never said you were."

"But that's what you were thinking."

He shrugged. "Not everyone's cut out for candle-making."

"Or assisting in candle-making," she teased.

He smiled. "Or assisting in candle-making. We can't be good at everything."

"Hold that thought," she said, and hurried down the hall to the bathroom. She snatched some ointment from the medicine cabinet, along with a box of bandages.

When he saw what she was holding, he shook his head. "I don't need that."

"Yes, you do," she insisted. "I took first aid. You need to protect the skin."

She took the top off the ointment tube and, obviously resigned to his fate, he put down the bag of ice and let her play Nancy Nurse.

As she took his hand, she couldn't help observing how big it was, just like the rest of him. Big and solid.

Once more she was aware of that current flowing between them. She peeked up at his face and saw him giving her *that look,* the one a man wore when he wanted to kiss a woman.

Her lips were suddenly dry and she had to lick them. It was getting warm in here.

"You've got a nice touch," he said as she applied the ointment.

His voice had gotten softer. Was it her imagination or was he leaning closer to her? She could feel her pulse rate picking up. It was *definitely* getting warm in here.

"I can smell those candles."

She swallowed. "They aren't scented. Must be my perfume." Or his aftershave. He smelled…delicious.

"It's nice." He sounded like a man who'd been hypnotized. *You're falling for this woman. Falling, falling.*

That would be okay with Jen. She so badly wanted a stable man, a good man, she could build her new life with. *This man,* her heart kept insisting. Stupid, don't-take-no-for-an-answer heart.

Garrett suddenly came out of his trance. He cleared his throat and she could feel him pulling away. "That'll probably do it."

Oh. As in stop fondling his hand? She took out a bandage and carefully stuck it on. "See? There's something I'm good at. Actually, I'm good at a lot of things," she added. "Words with Friends—I always beat my sister and that kills her, since she's the real writer in the family. Playing cards, organizing stuff." Okay, she had to stop. She sounded as if she were applying for a position. She supposed, in a way, she was. "What are *you* good at?"

She could think of one thing he was probably great at. Ooh, it was *so* hot in here.

"Hitting a baseball, I guess. Swinging a hammer. And I've been known to win my share of card games."

"Bet you couldn't beat me."

Instead of rising to the bait and suggesting they play a game, he said, "I'm not even going to try. I'm sure you're a force to be reckoned with." His cell phone dinged to tell him he had a message. He glanced at it, then said, "I should get going."

"Then I'd better get you a check. I hope you don't have to spend any of it on a doctor's visit."

"I'll be fine," he said.

She wrote him a check and handed it over.

"Thanks," he said.

She nodded. "See you around town." Probably with someone. Who'd just messaged him? As if she couldn't guess.

She walked him to the door, then watched as he climbed into his truck and drove away. So much for impressing her landlord.

That was a moment of temporary weakness, a sneaky hormone attack, a chemical reaction. No matter how cute and sweet Jen Heath was, Garrett wasn't interested.

But he had to admit *she* was interesting. He was fascinated by the way she was always up for trying something new. But every new thing she tried seemed to go slightly wrong, whether it was driving in the snow, planting a garden or making candles.

And that's why you're with Tilda, he told himself. Thank God.

So that vision of Jen in her little pink top and her

butt-hugging shorts could go find some other sucker
to annoy.

She sure looked good in pink.

With a growl of disgust, he pressed harder on the
gas pedal and turned off Juniper Ridge.

"What's with the bandage on your hand?" Tilda
asked when she stopped by the fire station the next day.

Garrett had meant to take it off but he'd been too
busy and forgotten. He focused his attention on washing down the fire engine. "No big deal."

"What happened?"

"I burned it."

"I thought you could cook," she teased.

"Didn't do it cooking." Okay, that was dumb. He
should've just let her think he'd burned his hand on
the stove.

"Yeah? What happened?" she repeated.

Better to be straight up, he decided. Anyway, it was
kind of a funny story. "I went to pick up the rent the
other day, and my tenant was making candles." He
shook his head at the humor of it all.

"What, and she threw hot wax on you?"

"No, I was helping her."

"Hmm. Cozy."

"Well, it was that or let her burn the house down.
Although she did have a fire extinguisher handy."

"Considering her history, good idea."

"Anyway, she spilled some wax on me. No big deal,
but she wanted to bandage it, so I let her."

"Wasn't that nice of you?" Tilda had a smart mouth
to begin with, and that was okay with him, but today

her comments had a razor-sharp edge to them. And she wasn't smiling.

Time to change the subject. "You want to do something later this week?" Tilda was on swing shift but he figured she'd be up for some racquetball or getting breakfast at her mom's place.

"I don't think so."

"Oh. You got plans?"

"Not with you." She spun around and started for her car.

He turned off the hose and followed her. "Hey, what's going on?"

She stopped, crossing her arms and glaring at him. "You tell me." If her tone of voice hadn't been a big enough clue that he'd stepped in it, the expression on her face sure was.

"What do you mean?"

She pointed a finger at him. "I don't play games." Then she started walking to her car again.

He hurried after her. "I don't, either."

"Good. Because I don't want to waste time on someone who isn't interested in me."

"I'm interested," he protested.

She stopped at the car door. "Yeah? Well, let me make this clear since you're not getting the picture. We've been hanging out long enough that I'm ready for this to go somewhere. If you want to chase after your tenant, that's fine. We'll call it quits right now."

"I don't want to chase after my tenant." Well, maybe part of him did, but he wasn't about to give in to it. "I want someone who's got her shit together. You know that."

"Yeah, well, you talk a lot."

"Come on, Tilda, give me a break."

She opened the car door.

"I've got tickets to the Mariners game."

"Yeah?"

"Yeah. How does a day in Seattle sound? We can go to the game and then check out that big Ferris wheel down on the waterfront."

She looked at him, considering. "You'd better not be yanking my chain."

He held up both hands. "Wouldn't dream of it."

She smiled. "Good. 'Cause I'd hate to have to pistol-whip you."

He smiled back. "I'll call you."

She nodded and got in her car and drove off, while Garrett returned to his fire truck. Okay. That did it. No more helping his tenant make candles, no more helping her with her garden, no more cozy friendly chats. Jen Heath was cute and she was fun. But she was the kind of woman who would turn a man's life upside down with her crazy antics. He already had one woman doing that. Tilda, on the other hand, would never tear up his septic system or spill hot wax on him. She'd be good to his kid and she'd keep Ashley in line. Yep, Tilda was the way to go.

Had Jen ever been on that Ferris wheel in Seattle?

The first week in May had been so dead, Stacy had considered buying a gravestone for her shop door. Rest in Peace, Timeless Treasures. We Tried.

But come Maifest weekend, lo and behold, the tourists arrived in town. They came in every variety and combination—sisters, girlfriends, mothers and daughters, families. And they all came into the shop. Or so it seemed. At one point it was so crowded she thought she'd need a traffic cop. And almost everyone who wandered in wandered back out with a quilt or a vintage knickknack or antique.

"Where'd everything go?" Dean asked when he showed up later to take her out to dinner.

She beamed. "It's gone. Isn't that great?"

He smiled and nodded. "You did it, babe. You're a success."

And now I need to restock. Which meant more shopping. Oh, what a shame. "My feet are killing me," she said, "and I'm so ready for pizza."

"The heck with pizza. We're going to celebrate." Dean hugged her. "I'm taking my baby to Schwangau."

Linen tablecloths, crystal and fine china, candlelight—the simple life. Stacy was so glad she'd figured out how to link downsizing with finding her own unique career path. She was sure Nana would be proud.

Fortunately, they were early enough that they managed to snag a table for two.

"Now that you're a successful businesswoman we can eat here all the time," Dean joked as they settled in with their menus.

She wouldn't mind that. Schwangau was the most expensive restaurant in town. The food was excellent, but mostly what people came for was the atmosphere. If you wanted to impress someone or celebrate a special occasion, Schwangau was the place to go.

And someone was out to do some impressing, she noted when she ran into Chita and Ken Wolfe, who were coming in as she and Dean were leaving. They said their hellos and then left them to enjoy their dinner.

"Looks like something's starting there," she murmured as she and Dean walked to the car.

"Spring, when a young man's fancy lightly turns to thoughts of love," Dean said.

"Did you just make that up?"

"Nope. Stole it from Lord Tennyson."

She shook her head. "Give it back to him."

Chita took in her elegant surroundings. Wood paneled walls, tables decked to the nines in linen tablecloths and fine crystal, waiters in white jackets bearing trays laden with food that looked as if it belonged on a page in *Bon Appétit*.

"This is lovely," she said.

He seemed surprised. "You've never been here?"

She'd lived in Icicle Falls for seven years and she'd never eaten at Schwangau. Pretty pathetic. But she'd moved to town from Yakima, newly divorced and broke. Eating at fancy restaurants had to take a backseat to other things, like paying for groceries.

"This isn't exactly the kind of restaurant you take small children to." Unless you were rich.

He nodded. "I remember when my son was little. I wouldn't have brought him here, either."

"You have a son?"

"He lives in Seattle with his mother. He's in middle school now. He comes over to stay with me in the summer when he can go tubing on the river and hang out at the pool."

"He's lucky he has you in his life," Chita said, thinking of her children's deadbeat dad.

"I wish I saw him more." Ken's face clouded.

"So, who moved away, you or her?"

"She did. She got a job offer from Microsoft. I told her to take it. We'd make it work. And we have."

"You ever consider moving to Seattle?"

He frowned. "I'm not a big-city guy. Icicle Falls is my home now. It always will be."

"This is a special place," she agreed.

"Full of special people," he added, smiling at her.

She sighed. "I'd like to be special."

"You already are. You're a beautiful woman with a beautiful heart."

"I'm thinking of going to school," she blurted. "Only online classes, but..." Her voice trailed off.

"That's great," he said. "What kind of classes? What do you want to do?"

She'd been thinking a lot about what she'd like to do with the rest of her life, but now she felt foolish telling him. "Would you laugh if I said I want to be a vet? Or at least a veterinary assistant?"

"Not at all."

"I've always loved animals. I thought it might be a good direction to go. I could start small, take some on-line college courses." She shrugged. "At least I'd feel like I was *doing* something for myself. I wasted my life when I was young. Now I want to do...more. Be more."

The waiter appeared with their wine just then and poured it for Ken's approval. He sniffed and swirled and tasted and nodded. Once the wine was poured and the waiter had faded back into the shadows, Ken lifted his glass. "Here's to being more. Hard to imagine because you're already so much, but I say go for it."

This man was wonderful. When would the bubble burst?

Maybe it wouldn't, she thought later that night after

he'd kissed her good-night. "I hope you'll go out with me again," he whispered, his breath tickling her ear.

For another kiss like that? Definitely.

I don't have any big vacation plans for the summer and I'm not going to make any. That's because I'm happy living my new simple lifestyle. My garden is off to a great start and I've harvested rhubarb from my front flower bed.

Later today I'm going to make strawberry-rhubarb upside down cake. My friend Stacy served it at our book club meeting last night and gave me permission to share it with you. I hope you enjoy it. (By the way, we're reading John Steinbeck's *Travels with Charley* now. You might enjoy that, too.)

Strawberry-Rhubarb Upside Down Cake

Ingredients for filling:

2 cups rhubarb
2 cups strawberries
2 tbsp cornstarch (you may need to use a little more if your berries are really juicy or if you're using frozen fruit)
½-¾ cups sugar (I used half a cup but you might want to make your filling sweeter)

Ingredients for batter:

1¼ cup flour
¾ cup sugar

1¼ tsp baking powder
½ tsp salt
¼ cup butter
½ cup milk
1 egg
1 tsp vanilla

Directions:

Combine strawberries and rhubarb in a large pot
with sugar and cornstarch and cook over low
heat until the mixture thickens, then pour into a
lightly greased 9-inch pie pan. Mix your batter
ingredients and then spoon over the fruit. Bake
at 350°F for 25 minutes or until the cake part is
done. Serve warm with whipped cream.

Okay, that's all for now. My garden is calling me!

Jen was up to her elbows in dirt, sweating under a
late-afternoon sun, when Garrett stopped by to collect the June rent. She'd seen him around town a few
times, always from a distance, usually with the cop.
Don't waste any more energy on that man, she'd lec-
tured herself. But just like when she was in college,
she hadn't paid much attention to the lecture.

She'd been singing her rendition of the latest Adele
song at the top of her lungs and hadn't heard him come
around the corner. His casual hello just about gave her
a heart attack.

And she was in no shape to get taken to the hospital.
Here she was, looking about as sexy as a burlap sack.
Her baggy T-shirt and shorts didn't exactly show off

the merchandise. Her hair was dirty (she'd planned on washing it later) and she was sweaty. Lovely. Oh, well. She was done with Garrett Armstrong.

"Is it the first already?" she greeted him. Where had the time gone?

Silly question. She'd gobbled it up being busy working, volunteering, hanging out with the girls, gardening, dancing at the Red Barn (trying to find a man who turned up her thermostat the way Garrett did, which was beginning to seem impossible).

"How's the garden?"

"Come see for yourself," she said as she stood up. Her lettuce was starting to curl into balls, and next to it, the spinach was also in the middle of a growth spurt. So were the carrots and beets.

He nodded. "I'm impressed."

She bent to pluck out a shotweed she'd missed. "I think I might have a green thumb." She turned to smile at him. He wasn't looking at her thumb, though.

Realizing he'd been caught, he quickly yanked his gaze from her behind. But it was too late. He knew that she knew he'd been looking.

"Would you like some iced tea?"

He shook himself, like a man coming out of a dream. "Uh, no. No, thanks. I...have to be somewhere."

It took all her willpower not to frown. He might have been with Tilda the cop, but he wasn't really *with* her. If he was, she wouldn't feel this electricity between them.

"Well, then, I'll just write a check. Come on in," she said. She pulled up some lettuce and went into the house with Garrett behind her. Was he looking at her butt again?

She wrote his check and gave it to him, along with the lettuce. "A little something extra."

"Thanks," he said.

"You're welcome."

Now they were standing there, him saying nothing, just looking at her, and her looking right back. "Are you sure you wouldn't like some iced tea?"

"No. I'd better get going."

"Big date?"

"Something like that."

She was tired of beating around the bush. "So, you and the lady cop, are you…friends?"

"We're more than friends," he said, not quite meeting her eyes. "Tilda's a good egg. And she's…stable."

"Stable," Jen repeated. This was all he could come up with for someone he was seeing? "Well, that sounds romantic."

He frowned. "I don't want to be romantic, Jen. I've been there, done that. It didn't work out. I've got a son. He needs stability. Hell, I need stability. I'm not interested in being with a…" He aborted the sentence but it was too late.

"A what?"

"Never mind."

"A flake?"

He let out his breath in a frustrated hiss. "That's not what I was going to say."

"You were looking for a nicer way to put it?"

"Jen, you're a really nice woman," he began.

"But a flake," she finished for him. "Well, you can think what you want, but I'm not. Not in the things that count, like kindness and loyalty. And that's more than I can say for…some men." She thought of Serge, giving up on them so quickly, and the tears slipped from her eyes and onto her cheeks. She turned her back, ashamed to let Garrett see them.

She suddenly felt his hands on her arms. "Jen, I'm sorry. I didn't mean to make you feel bad."

She shook her head. "It's okay. It's just that, well, you've never really gotten to know me, and yet you've already made up your mind about me." She turned back, scowling at him. "But guess what? I've made up my mind about you, too. Now, if you'll excuse me, I need to get back to my weeds," she said, and hurried down the hallway to the back door.

"Jen," he called after her, but she kept going.

"Write your address down on that pad of paper," she said over her shoulder. "From now on I'll mail you my rent check. And don't worry, I'll pay on time. Because I'm *not* a flake!"

She slammed the back door. There, that would show him. She was never going to worry again about finding a man who measured up to Garrett Armstrong. Anyone was better than him!

Garrett scrawled his address on her stupid pad of paper. Damn it all, how had a pleasant conversation, a check and some lettuce deteriorated into this? Oh, yeah, the flake thing. He hadn't said she was flake. She'd jumped to conclusions.

But she *was* a flake. Not the selfish, mean-spirited kind his ex was but a flake nonetheless. So it was just as well that this had all come to a head, just as well she'd told him off. Now she'd stop sending out those signals women sent when they wanted a man. Now he could really concentrate on his relationship with Tilda.

Now thoughts of Jen Heath would stop sneaking into his mind at the most inopportune times, like when he was kissing Tilda.

Yes, this was all for the best.

The pencil snapped and he threw it on the counter and stormed out of the cottage. When her lease was up, she was gone. He'd boot her out and sell the place. He was through with being a landlord.

Too bad she wasn't gone from his dreams. That night she found him. He was in her vegetable garden, pulling carrots, and she sneaked up on him. She was wearing those same ratty clothes she'd had on when he was at her place earlier, and she looked every bit as sexy to him in his dream as she had in real life.

She picked a tomato off one of her tomato plants and rubbed it in his face, saying, "Get out of my garden."

"I'll come into your garden any time I want," he retorted. Then he grabbed her and kissed her.

Suddenly Tilda was there in her cop uniform. She had a garden hose and she turned it on them full force. "I'm not wasting any more time on you."

Next Ashley arrived, wearing a bikini and an evil smile and carrying a shovel. With a cackle she lifted it up and swung at him.

"No!" He woke up, breathing hard. He ran a hand through his hair, then he fell back on his pillow and waited for his heart to slow down. A man's life shouldn't be this complicated.

Chapter Twenty-Three

There's nothing quite as satisfying as getting back to nature.
—Muriel Sterling, author of *Simplicity*

The last week in June found Toni and her family winding up the narrow mountain road to what would be their home for the next two weeks.

"When are we gonna get there?" Jordan whined from the backseat. "I'm gonna puke."

They'd been doing a lot of twisting and turning on this narrow, potholed road, and Toni felt a little queasy herself. "Do we need to stop the car?" she asked.

"No," Jordan replied grumpily.

"We've got a quarter mile left to go," Wayne said.

Toni passed back her water bottle. "Here, sweetie, have a sip of this. We're almost there."

"This is stupid," Jordan muttered.

And she didn't change her opinion once they saw the cabin. It was a small log affair snugged in among fir trees and huckleberry bushes with a front porch and two wooden rockers, which Toni thought were quaint.

The inside smelled musty and Jordan wrinkled her nose. "This is gross."

"It'll smell okay once it's aired out," Toni assured her, and hoped she knew what she was talking about. The living area wasn't large and the Early American–style furniture had seen better days. But the braided rugs on the floor and the red checked curtains at the windows gave the room a homey touch. The woodstove would take the chill off in the mornings. In fact, they'd have to start a fire to take the chill off now and it was early afternoon.

Jeffrey had run down the hall and ducked into one of the bedrooms. His voice echoed out to them. "Cool. Bunk beds! I get the top one."

Jordan turned to look accusingly at her mother. "I have to share a bedroom?"

"It's only for two weeks," Toni said.

"I don't want to sleep in the same room as Jeffrey. He farts."

"That's what windows are for," Wayne said as he lugged a suitcase toward the other bedroom.

"Or you can sleep out here on the couch," Toni suggested.

Jordan eyed the couch and made a face. "Eeew."

"Well, then, go check out your bunk."

Her daughter picked up her backpack and trudged down the hall, looking as if she'd just been sent to a jail cell. A year earlier she'd have seen this as a great adventure, Toni thought sadly. It was a good thing she hadn't committed them to staying any longer than the two weeks.

She took the bag with the extra towels and bedding and went to investigate her bedroom. Oh.

Wayne was standing at the foot of the bed, frowning. "I see a backache in the making."

She took in the sagging mattress. "It looked better in the picture online."

"There's a surprise."

"Oh, not you, too," she said. She felt ready to cry.

He hugged her. "I said I'd be a good sport and do this and I will. It's no California king, but we can manage."

Sleeping on a crummy bed was probably above and beyond the call of being a good sport. "I'm sorry about the bed."

"Don't worry about it."

"I love you," she whispered, and kissed him just as their son bounded into the room.

"Hey, Mom, can I go find the creek?"

"As soon as the car's unloaded," Toni said.

Jeffrey was off in a flash.

"Well, at least someone's happy to be here," she said.

"Hey, I'm happy," Wayne told her.

But he wasn't happy about being cut off from the world. The kids had come in from exploring the woods and she was about to start dinner when he said, "I think I'll run into town and see if I can get reception for my phone."

"I want to go," Jordan piped up.

"Can we go to that pizza place?" asked Jeffrey.

Had no one noticed the presence of chicken on the counter and the pan on the stove? "Hey, guys, we're here to get away from it all, remember?" Toni tried to keep her voice light and her smile in place. "Anyway, I'm making dinner. We're having old-fashioned fried chicken."

"Fried chicken. All right!" whooped Jeffrey.

"We haven't had that since last Fourth of July,"

Wayne said. He rubbed his hands together. "Bring it on."

"Are we ever going to town?" Jordan demanded.

"Of course we are," Toni assured her. "We'll go down to see your aunt Jen and hit the swimming pool. But tonight, let's enjoy our new digs."

Her daughter rolled her eyes and slumped back against the couch cushions to play a game on her phone. That was all she could do since she had no reception up here. Oh, too bad.

Jeffrey went to the bookcase, which was stocked with some ratty paperbacks and a bunch of games. "Hey, this looks cool." He handed one of the boxes to his father.

"Battleship. I haven't played that since I was a kid," Wayne said.

"They had this when you were a kid, Dad?" Jeffrey sounded amazed.

"Yeah, back in the Stone Age. Come on, I'll show you how to play it."

Toni smiled as she assembled her ingredients. Maybe this would work out, after all.

Later that night, after dinner, they played a board game called Settlers of Catan and her daughter got so involved in the game she forgot that she was miserable. She was even laughing. This was the Jordan they all knew and loved. *Welcome back,* Toni thought.

"Longest road. I just won!" Jordan finally exclaimed.

"Okay, who wants hot chocolate and s'mores?" Toni asked.

"Me!" cried Jeffrey.

"Go out to the fire pit and help your father build a fire, and Jordan and I will get the makings."

For the next half hour they sat around the fire pit, drinking hot chocolate and waiting for the fire to die down so they could roast their marshmallows. While they waited, Wayne dredged up every scary story he could remember, including the woman with the golden arm. Both kids shivered in delight as their father loomed over them, chanting, "Who's got my golden arm?" And when he grabbed Jordan and moaned, "You do!" she let out a screech loud enough to frighten away the wildlife for miles around, making Jeffrey double over with laughter.

Once the marshmallows had been roasted and the s'mores eaten, the kids were getting quiet and Jeffrey was yawning. At last they were both drooping and Toni said, "Okay, guys, time to get ready for bed."

Neither one protested. After an afternoon of running around in the woods, they were so tired, even a sugar buzz couldn't revive them. They trudged off to brush teeth and change, and Toni took the leftover food inside, while Wayne dealt with putting out the fire.

Jeffrey was already asleep when Toni and Wayne went into the room to kiss the kids good-night and Jordan was halfway there.

"They'll sleep like logs," he said as they tiptoed back down the hall.

"I will, too," Toni said. "All this fresh air makes me sleepy."

"You that tired?" Wayne asked as she flopped on the couch and picked up her novel.

She looked up to see a familiar glint in his eye, one

she hadn't seen in a while. She put down her book. "Maybe not."

Now he was on the couch next to her.

"So you finally have time for me?" she couldn't help teasing.

"Nothing else to do up here."

"Oh, ha-ha."

"Reminds me of our honeymoon," he said, drawing her against him.

"Except we were in a luxury condo in Hawaii."

"This isn't so bad."

She studied his face. "Really?"

"Really. It also reminds me of being at camp when I was a kid. Except we didn't get to have sex."

"I bet you fantasized about one of the counselors, though."

"You bet I did. Mitzi Ballantine. Come here, Mitzi," he joked, and bent his head to kiss her.

She pulled away. "Isn't it past your bedtime, camper?"

"Way past. Better tuck me in," he said, and this time she let him kiss her. And do other things...

Oh, yes, it had been a great idea to come up here.

And it still seemed like a great idea for the next couple of days. One morning they took fly-fishing lessons. Everyone had a fun...until Jordan lost her balance and fell in the icy water, and that was the end of that. Later that day, Jeffrey managed to make contact with stinging nettles and came running into the cabin howling.

"We're having fun now," Wayne teased that evening when they'd finally sent two grumpy kids to bed.

"Tomorrow they'll have forgotten all about this," Toni predicted.

Sure enough, the following morning, after a breakfast of eggs and blueberry pancakes, the kids were ready for fresh adventure. For Jordan that meant going into town and hanging out at the pool. And, of course, texting her friends.

"We'll get around to that," Toni promised, "but today I thought you might like to go look for the lost bride."

Jordan was intrigued. "Who's that?"

"A real live ghost," Toni said. She took out the brochure she'd picked up at the Icicle Falls tourist center on her last visit to Jen. "Her name was Rebecca, and way back, more than a hundred and fifty years ago, she came to Icicle Falls as a mail-order bride."

"A what?" Jordan asked.

"In the pioneer days, there were women who promised to come west and marry men they'd never met."

"Eeew," Jordan said in disgust.

"For some women it was an opportunity. Maybe she hadn't met the right man back home, or no one had asked her to marry him."

"Because she was ugly," Jordan surmised.

"Not this woman. She was beautiful, and Joshua Cane, the man she married, had a brother named Gideon, who fell in love with her. The two brothers fought over her."

"Did they kill each other?" Jeffrey asked eagerly.

"Not exactly," Toni said, and began reading from the brochure. "Legend has it that one day Rebecca and Gideon both disappeared. Some people thought they ran away. Others thought her husband killed them."

"What happened to the husband?" Jordan asked.

"Nobody seems to know," Toni said. She continued

reading. "People began to see Rebecca's ghost up by the falls. Soon everyone was looking for the ghost of the lost bride. And people still see her today."

"I don't want to go," Jeffrey said suddenly.

"She's not like the woman with the golden arm," Toni assured him. "In fact, this is a ghost people look for. Seeing the lost bride is good luck, like spotting a leprechaun. If you see her, it means you're going to get married soon."

Jeffrey stuck out his tongue. "I'd rather see a leprechaun. I'm too young to get married."

"So, where can we find her?" Jordan asked.

"We have to go up Lost Bride Trail," Toni replied.

Wayne shook his head. "You guys can leave me at the river. I'll do some fishing."

"So much for family togetherness," Toni muttered.

"You created this monster," he reminded her. "I want to get in some more fishing before we go home."

"I wish we never had to go home," Jeffrey said.

Now, *that* was gratifying.

"All right, everyone, let's get our water and our trail mix and hit the trail. We'll see who can spot the lost bride first."

"Mom, you don't want me to see the lost bride yet," Jordan cautioned her.

"But if you do, maybe it means there's a cute boy in your future," Toni teased. "Or a cute girl in yours," she added to her son.

"Yuck," he said, and went to put on his shoes.

Ten minutes later they were out the door, cell phones and electronic toys forgotten. They left Wayne at Icicle Creek with his fly-fishing equipment, then made their way to the trailhead.

Toni was feeling very pleased with herself as they started up the trail. Fresh mountain air, good exercise— Yes, this had been a great idea. The hike was supposed to be a fairly easy one, and that was fine with Toni. Hiking wasn't something she ever did. The only place she walked other than the treadmill in her office was on the golf course. And if that was eighteen holes instead of nine, she always opted for a cart.

The sun hung in a blue, cloudless sky, and she hadn't gone far before its warm rays coaxed her into taking off her sweatshirt. A butterfly flitted past her and landed on a lady slipper. It was so lovely up here, so peaceful.

"My feet hurt," Jordan complained.

Well, almost peaceful. Toni swung her backpack off her shoulder and got out a chocolate-covered granola bar. "Here. This should make them feel better."

"I want one, too," Jeffrey said.

So did Toni. They paused for a break, sitting on some boulders that ran along the creek. Toni took in the scene and smiled. "Isn't it pretty?"

"It's kind of creepy." Jordan looked around. "I mean, there's nobody else here but us."

"Lots of people hike this trail," Toni said.

"Well, I don't see anybody. When will we get to the waterfall?"

"Soon." Toni hoped her daughter didn't ask her to be more specific. They still had a mile to go.

Jeffrey had finished his granola bar. He handed the wrapper to Toni and then bounded off. "I wanna follow the stream," he called over his shoulder.

"You be careful," Toni warned. Part of her wanted to insist he come back and stay on the trail with her. But to a little boy that wasn't any fun. She decided she'd let him enjoy himself…as long as she could keep him in sight.

They started walking again, and after five minutes of hearing her brother's whoops as he hopped from rock to rock in the creek, Jordan, too, veered off the trail.

A few minutes later Toni could see her down there with Jeffrey. They were laughing and skipping stones. It was a picture-perfect moment. Darn. Why hadn't she brought her camera?

They walked on another quarter of a mile, her on the trail, the kids below. Now Toni could hear the rumble of the falls. The trail was taking a turn away from the creek and soon she wouldn't be able to see them anymore. "Okay, you two. Come back up here," she called.

Like all children, they developed sudden deafness, hopping their way along the creek from rock to rock.

Of course, it was hard to hear over the noise of the water. Toni raised her voice. "Come on back. Right now, you two!"

Jordan started back. Jeffrey kept hopping.

Jordan's voice carried up to Toni. "Come on, Jeffrey. Mom's gonna get mad."

She reached over to grab him and he danced away.

A bad decision because in an effort to dodge his sister he slipped on a wet rock and went down. Part of him went down. But one foot had somehow gotten caught between two rocks.

Toni was on her way down the bank even as her son cried out in pain. "I'm coming!" she yelled.

She arrived to find him in torrential tears as Jordan tried to dislodge his foot. "It's okay," she told him, her voice reassuring. "Here, sweetie, help me move the rock."

Between the two of them, they got his foot freed. Toni inspected it, feeling for broken bones. She was pretty sure they'd dodged that bullet, but it was going to be a nasty sprain.

She bent in front of him. "Here, climb on. I'll piggy-back you up to the trail."

She hadn't given her son a piggyback ride since he was five. He was twice that age now and weighed as much as a small horse. She found herself panting as she struggled up the bank and her heart was pounding so hard she thought it might break through her chest. Once they reached the trail, she set him down on a nearby boulder and took another look at his ankle. It was already starting to swell. This was not good. How was she going to get this child down the mountain?

Chapter Twenty-Four

*Even when your life doesn't go according to plan,
take time to appreciate it.*
—Muriel Sterling, author of *Simplicity*

Today I'm going to hike up Lost Bride Trail, a
popular local landmark near Icicle Falls. I can
hardly wait to see the waterfall. Maybe I'll even
catch a glimpse of the ghost of the lost bride, a
woman who disappeared back in pioneer times.
They say if you see her it means there's a wedding in your future. I'll post pictures later so you
can try and spot her.

"This is beautiful," Jen said, gazing at the cataract
before her. "Right, Tiny?" she said to the Saint Bernard
who was Jen and Cecily's hiking companion. She gave
the dog's head a pat and Tiny wagged his tail.

Jen had taken to borrowing Cass's dog whenever
she went for a walk or a short hike. Cass was happy
for Tiny to get the exercise and Jen was glad to get
her dog fix. She'd always wanted a dog, but, for once,
she'd reminded herself that she was trying to simplify
her life and refrained from impulsively running out

and getting one. Better to wait. Meanwhile, she could always borrow Tiny.

She took out her cell phone and snapped a picture of Lost Bride Falls. She wished she'd invited her sister along. Toni had talked about bringing the kids up here.

"I'm glad you're finally getting a chance to see it," Cecily said. "Want me to take a picture of you with the falls in the background?"

Jen nodded. "Here, Tiny, let's get your handsome doggy self in the picture, too." She pulled the dog close and he cuddled up to her, drooling on her shoe.

Cecily snapped the photo and they checked it out. "Good picture of Tiny's drool," Cecily observed.

Jen laughed. "And a great one of the falls. It was nice of you to play hooky from work today and show me." She gave Tiny a moment off his leash so he could go down to the creek for a drink, then turned to admire the falls again.

"I'm not feeling too guilty about that," Cecily said. "I put in enough time working on the fall catalog last week to burn out half my brain cells. This week I'm taking it easy." She plucked a wildflower and put it in her hair.

"Do you ever have trouble finding the balance in your life?" Jen asked.

"Not since I moved back home. And I always make time for friends." Cecily picked another flower and handed it to Jen.

"How about romance?" Jen asked shyly. She'd heard that Cecily had two men dangling after her. It was probably rude to be so nosy, but she couldn't resist asking.

"A woman should always make time for romance,

too," Cecily replied in a thoughtful voice. "But making time and meeting the right person are two different things." She pointed in the direction of the falls. "See anything?"

Jen had hoped to catch a glimpse of the town's famous ghost, but all she saw was tons of water plummeting over rocky crags. She shook her head. "No wedding in my future, I guess."

"You don't *have* to see the ghost to have a wedding in your future," Cecily said. "Somehow, I've got a feeling you're going to find someone special here in Icicle Falls."

Jen had also heard about Cecily's famous intuition. She had a gift for steering people toward their perfect match. "Anyone in particular come to mind?"

Cecily just smiled. "I think you'll figure it out," she said, and started off down the trail.

Well, that was a disappointing early morning hike. No sign of the lost bride and Cecily Sterling and her impeccable intuition had been no help at all.

"Jordan, do you have your phone?" Toni asked. She'd never thought she'd hear herself say that.

Jordan stared at her as if she'd gone nuts. "You haven't let me bring it anywhere."

"My foot hurts," Jeffrey whimpered.

"I know, sweetie," Toni said, wiping the tears from his cheeks. "We're going to get you to a doctor as soon as we can." And it looked as if the only way that was going to happen was if she carried him. How she wished Wayne had come with them. How she wished she had a cell phone so she could call him! Was there reception up here? Who knew? She would've welcomed the chance to find out.

She got her son onto her back again and they set off down the trail. How long would she be able to do this before she collapsed?

Don't think like that, she scolded herself. A mother could do anything.

Except carry an eighty-pound boy down a mountain trail. After twenty minutes, she stopped. "Okay," she huffed. "We need to take a break for a minute."

Jeffrey was still crying and his ankle looked like a cantaloupe. What circle of hell was this?

"Here, Mom," Jordan said, handing Toni her water bottle.

The only good thing about this awful experience was that it was bringing out the sweet girl Jordan had always been—until recently. "Thanks," she said, and gulped down half its contents. She was sweating like a pig and even half a bottle of water barely quenched her thirst.

"How much longer?" Jeffrey asked.

"I'm not sure," Toni said. "I hope not too much."

He began to cry again and she wanted to join him.

"I can help carry him," Jordan offered.

"No, you'll hurt yourself." Toni already knew this from personal experience. The muscles in her back were shrieking.

"Mom! I hear something," Jordan said.

Toni strained to hear. Yes! Voices! Other hikers were coming down the trail. Maybe they had a cell phone. "They should catch up to us in a couple of minutes."

"My foot hurts," Jeffrey reminded her.

"You're being very brave. Just a little longer now," Toni promised.

He nodded and rubbed his eyes.

A few more minutes brought the hikers into sight, two women and a large dog. One of the women was Cecily Sterling, whom Toni had met when she'd attended the Icicle Falls book club meeting with Jen. The other was... Toni blinked, sure she was hallucinating. Her sister never hiked. "Jen?"

Jen broke into a smile. "Hey, sis! You should've said you were going to hike this trail today. We could all have come up together." The words were hardly out of her mouth when she took in the scene. "What happened?"

"Jeffrey fell and sprained his ankle," Toni said.

"Mom's been carrying him down the mountain," Jordan added.

"Seriously?" Jen gaped at her sister. "You should have called for help!"

"We didn't have our cell phones with us," Toni said. "Anyway, I figured there probably wasn't any reception."

"Actually, there is here," Cecily told her. "You lose it higher up the mountain, though."

Great. If they'd had their darned cell phones, they could have called someone.

"My foot hurts." Jeffrey's voice was plaintive.

Cecily immediately took out her cell. "I can call 9-1-1."

"We'd just lose time waiting for someone to come," Jen said. "I've got a better idea. Jordan, help me find two long sticks." And with that she plunged off the trail into the brush, Jordan following her.

"What are you doing?" Toni called after her.

"We're going to put Tiny to work and haul Jeffrey down the mountain," her sister called back.

"Good idea," Cecily approved. "I'll have someone meet us at the trailhead."

Within ten minutes they'd cobbled together a make-shift dogsled with branches and sweatshirts and Tiny's extendable leash. "Okay, Tiny, mush," Jen said.

Tiny fell into step beside her and the little parade started down the trail. "You're going to have some adventure to tell your friends about when you go back to school this fall," Cecily said to Jeffrey, who was trying hard not to cry.

They were almost at the trailhead when they saw two medics coming their way. *Saved,* Toni thought, and breathed a sigh of relief.

One of them, a burly twentysomething guy, knelt in front of Jeffrey. "How you doing there?"

"I'm okay," Jeffrey said, wiping the tears from his cheeks.

"Hurts a lot, doesn't it?" the medic said as he examined the foot. To Toni he murmured, "It looks like a sprain, but you'll want to get it X-rayed to make sure it's not broken."

Toni had been brave all the way down the trail, but now she was done. She burst into tears.

"It's okay, Mom," Jordan said, putting an arm around her.

She hugged her daughter fiercely and vowed never to complain about her family's obsession with technology again.

The rest of the day was spent first at the emergency room in the little Icicle Falls hospital and then back at the cabin, getting Jeffrey set up with ice packs, ibuprofen and ice cream. Fortunately, the medic had been correct; he only had a sprain. That evening Jen arrived with root beer, popcorn and a board game. And once the kids were settled, she brought out the other goodies she had in her trunk—wine and chocolate.

"After the day I had, this is exactly what I need," Toni said as she took a sip of wine.

"I figured as much," Jen said.

Toni looked over her wineglass at her husband. "Remind me never to complain about our technology again."

He smiled and raised his own glass to her. "But there's such a thing as balance. It's been good for all of us to have a little less technology and a little more time together."

"I'll drink to that," Toni said. She took another sip and then sighed. "I just hope I haven't scarred our kids for life."

Or ruined the Fourth of July, which was right around the corner.

Meanwhile, though, Jeffrey was happy to spend the following day playing Battleship with his dad, while Toni kept Jordan busy baking cookies. Once the cookies had been delivered to the invalid on the couch, Jordan took some for herself and flopped in a chair on the porch to paint her toenails.

She hadn't been out there more than five minutes when Toni heard a bloodcurdling scream. Her daughter ran inside the house and slammed the door shut behind her. "There's a *bear* out there!"

"A bear?" Toni rushed to the window and looked

out just in time to see something big and black disappearing into the woods.

"A bear? Cool," Jeffrey said, scrambling up from the couch, his ice pack falling forgotten on the floor.

"Whoa there, don't be walking on that foot," Wayne cautioned.

"It's gone now, anyway," Toni said. *Thank God.* But would it come back?

"I'm not going outside here anymore," Jordan said, glaring at Toni as if it were all her fault they'd been invaded by the local wildlife.

"There was nothing mentioned in the website about bears," Toni said in her own defense. If there had been, she would never have brought them here.

Later that afternoon, her daughter tossed aside the ratty book she'd been reading and said, "This is boring."

Okay, maybe they should've gone to Disneyland. At least the wild animals there were fake.

"How's Jeffrey's ankle?" Jen asked when she and Toni met for coffee at Bavarian Brews a couple of days later.

"I think he'll be good to go by the Fourth, thank God," Toni said. "No bounce house or climbing wall for him, but as long as there's food he'll be happy."

"And what about Jordan?"

"She's totally over rustic living. She saw a bear and hasn't so much as gone out on the porch since then. I could barely get her to go out to the car to come here."

"So that's why you're in town today."

"The natives were getting restless. It was either

bring her in or risk getting stabbed in my sleep with a fork."

"So nobody's having fun?"

"Oh, they're okay today, now that they're at the pool. And Wayne's back at the river fly-fishing. I haven't seen him this relaxed in ages. In fact, I haven't *seen* him this *much* in ages."

"That's good, right?" Jen said, sipping at her latte.

"Absolutely," Toni replied. "So what if our children hate us? That whole parent-child thing is overrated."

"Don't worry. You'll be a hero after the Fourth. I've heard they do a great job up here."

The door to the coffee shop opened and in walked Garrett Armstrong. He gave the sisters an uneasy nod as he passed by on his way to the counter.

"Jerk," Jen muttered.

"Hey, he's still not engaged, is he? Otherwise, you'd have heard."

"He's as good as engaged," Jen said with a scowl.

"I don't care what he told you. He wants you. He just needs to realize it."

"Well, I don't want him. The cop can have him. I told you that."

"Yeah, you did. But you were lying and we both know it. Come on, it ain't over till it's over."

"Trust me." Jen sighed. "It's over. Not that it ever really started."

"Well, if he doesn't see how fabulous you are, he deserves to be with a second-rate woman."

"I'm not sure a cop falls in that category," Jen said, and frowned at her latte.

"Yeah, it's hard to compete with someone who'll

give you a ride in the squad car. She probably lets him turn on the siren."

That made Jen smirk.

"Anyway, there are plenty of other men up here."

"Absolutely," Jen said, but her gaze drifted across the coffee shop to where the handsome fireman was picking up his drink.

Poor Jen. She really had it bad. She'd managed to simplify her life beautifully, but what good was that if her love life stank? Toni wished she could help, but when it came to connecting with the right man, a woman was on her own.

As Jen had predicted, Icicle Falls did go all out for the Fourth of July. The night of the third, Toni and her family came down for the street dance, which featured a local band. The kids pigged out on nachos and hot dogs and corn on the cob, and Jordan found two boys to flirt with. They both wore braces, but they were cute and cocky, and surely the stuff a thirteen-year-old girl's dreams were made of. Ah, how Toni remembered those days.

She enjoyed watching the dancers later as she and her family sat at a picnic table and devoured ice cream bars. One dark-haired man with glasses was really something to watch.

"That's Juliet's brother, Jonathan," Jen explained. "He lives in Portland now, but he and his wife come back here for all the festivals and holidays. I hear he's still the best dancer in Icicle Falls."

"He doesn't have anything on me," Wayne said.

"Uh-huh." Toni rolled her eyes.

He stood up and held out his hand to her. "Come on, babe."

Wayne had never been much of a dancer, but she appreciated his willingness to get out there and try. And since the band was playing a slow song, she figured he wouldn't have to try too hard.

Sure enough, about all he did was sway them back and forth. But it was sweet and romantic. "I've still got the moves," he joked.

"That you do," she said, playing along, "and not just on the dance floor."

He grinned and kissed her right there in the middle of the crowd. Oh, yes, coming up here and getting away from it all had been absolutely inspired. It might not have been a perfect vacation, but it had been a perfect chance for her and Wayne to rekindle the romance in their marriage. Maybe, just maybe, they'd be able to keep the flame alive when they got back to the real world of overwork and distractions.

Jen was getting dizzier by the minute. Her buddy Bill Will had found her and insisted they have a dance and now he was tossing her around like a Frisbee. Still, she was having a great time. She'd seen everyone she knew—her book club, some of the women from her new church, her library pals. She loved it here!

The needle on her fun meter dipped shortly after her dance with Bill Will. They were getting corn dogs when she caught sight of a little boy wandering through the crowd. It was Timmy, Garrett's son. Where was his father?

"Well, hi there," she said. "I'm the lady from the bakery. Remember me?"

He nodded. "I'm looking for my daddy."

"I bet he's looking for you, too," she said. "Want me to help you?"

The little boy nodded again. Then he eyed her corn dog. "I like corn dogs."

She smiled. "Would you like this one?"

Timmy grinned eagerly.

"Guess I'd better buy you another," Bill Will said.

"Guess so," she agreed.

Once they all had corn dogs, she took Timmy's hand. "Let's go find your daddy."

"Uh, I'll catch up with you later, then," Bill Will told her. "I think I'm on his shit list."

Poor Bill Will. The septic fiasco hadn't been his fault. "I'm on his shit list, too," she said. But she didn't care because he was on hers, as well.

"Save me a slow dance," Bill Will said, and melted into the crowd.

She decided her best bet was to take the child over to the bandstand and ask the bandleader to make an announcement. They had just started in that direction when a slender blonde wearing white shorts and a tight red top stopped in front of them. She glared at Jen and demanded, "Who the hell are you and what are you doing with my kid?"

So this was the man-scarring ex.

"Mommy!" Timmy was all smiles now.

"Oh, you're Timmy's mom. You have a sweet little boy," Jen said, opting for diplomacy.

"Timmy, do you know this woman? Why aren't you with Daddy?" she barked before he could answer, making the child burst into tears.

So much for the Miss Congeniality approach. "I'm afraid he got separated from his dad," said Jen.

The other woman narrowed her eyes. "Are you here with Garrett?"

Before Jen could answer Garrett arrived on the scene. "Thank God," he said, and scooped up the little boy.

"Nice job you're doing keeping track of our son," the woman greeted him. "And you give *me* a hard time for letting him eat doughnuts. At least I've never lost him in a crowd."

"I was getting him something to drink and he wandered off," Garrett said irritably.

"Yeah? Where's the drink?"

"I left it behind to look for Timmy. It's okay now, buddy," Garrett told the crying child.

"Timmy, do you want to come with Mommy?" asked the woman.

The little boy buried his head in his father's shoulder and shook it back and forth.

Hurt flashed across the woman's face, followed quickly by anger. "You'd better spend less time chasing women and more time watching our son," she snarled, stabbing a finger at Garrett. Then she turned and marched off, leaving Jen blinking in shock over the exchange she'd just witnessed.

"Oh, my," Jen said weakly.

"Welcome to my world." Garrett's face was stony. To the child he said, "Remember, buddy, you've got to stay right with me."

"I did," the child protested. "But you got lost and I couldn't find you."

Garrett hugged him. "Well, never mind. What's this you've got?"

Timmy held out his corn dog for Garrett to sample.

Garrett shook his head. "It's all yours." He looked directly at Jen. "Thanks for taking care of him."

"No problem," she said. His heartfelt gratitude, the sudden friendly feeling between them—it was enough to make her forget that he thought she was a flake and that she was mad at him.

"Sorry you had to witness that," he said. He glanced past Jen and frowned.

She turned and saw the blonde melting into the milling crowd on the arm of a heavily tattooed man in an unbuttoned Hawaiian shirt.

"I can't blame her for being upset, I guess," Jen said. "She's never met me. For all she knew, I could have been kidnapping your son."

"Oh, yeah, I could tell she was all upset about it."

"I think she was at first. I think it was a real shock to see her son with a stranger."

Garrett gave a snort of disgust. Obviously he wasn't convinced. "Right. Anyway, I'm glad you found him. How are you liking the dance?"

"It's great," she said. Even if she wasn't dancing with him.

"I thought I saw you out there," he said, nodding to the boogying throng.

"I was. Have you been showing your street dance moves?"

"I save my moves for more private dances."

"Oh, so in other words, you really can't dance," she teased.

"I've got a few moves. You here with someone?"

Saying she was there with her sister didn't exactly make her sound like primo love real estate. "I'm with friends."

He nodded, taking that in. "Girlfriends?"

"And guys." She hadn't come with Bill Will, but they'd already hung out enough that she figured it counted.

"You with Bill Will?" he asked.

She cocked her head. "Not everyone thinks I'm a flake."

His face took on a guilty flush. "Jen, I'm sorry, but—"

She cut him off. "You should be. I sure don't appreciate being lumped in the same category as your ex-wife." Especially now that she'd met the woman.

"That was a mistake," he said humbly.

"Well, we all make mistakes," she said, determined to be gracious.

Timmy was done with his corn dog. "Come on, Daddy, let's get something to drink," he urged.

"Okay, buddy. Just a minute." Now Garrett was looking as if he had something important to say. "Jen, do you think we could...start over?"

"Again?"

"Yeah, again."

Tilda chose that moment to show up. "Good," she said. "You found him." She acknowledged Jen's presence with a nod and managed a smile. It didn't reach her eyes, though.

"Daddy was lost," Timmy explained.

"Come here, you," Tilda said, taking him from Garrett's arms. She tickled him, making him squirm and laugh. Tilda, the perfect stepmother.

"Well, I'd better…" Jen pointed in the general direction of the dancing throng.

He nodded. "Nice running into you. I'm glad we had a chance to talk."

"Me, too." She wished they could have a chance to do more than talk. The band was starting another slow song. She'd love to find out what kind of moves Garrett Armstrong had.

"Well, uh, see you around," he added.

"I'll be around." Hmm, that sounded…predatory. Tilda thought so, too, judging by her expression.

"I'm looking forward to the fireworks. I hear that's not to be missed."

"It's crazy," he said.

Now Tilda inserted herself into the conversation. "It's enough to make us crazy, isn't it?" She looked to Garrett for confirmation. Team Tilda-Garrett. How chummy!

"So, you'll both be working tomorrow?" Jen asked, politely including Tilda in the conversation.

"Oh, yeah." Tilda rolled her eyes. "Some fool is bound to shoot off a finger with a firecracker. And we'll get a ton of calls about drunken neighbors trying to burn down the forest."

"That's a very real danger," Garrett said. "We'll be down by the river with the truck."

"Maybe I'll see you then," Jen murmured.

"He'll be busy," Tilda said. *So there.* To Timmy she said, "Hey, kid, you ready for some shaved ice?"

Timmy nodded eagerly.

"Let's go, then." Tilda started walking off with Timmy, obviously expecting Garrett to follow.

"Well, uh, thanks again," Garrett said. "See you tomorrow."

"Dude, come on. We're starving," Tilda called, and he trailed after her. Like a dog whose owner had just given the leash a firm yank.

Jen reminded herself that she didn't poach other women's men.

But what if the other woman was losing her grip on the man? What if the man was beginning to see his flaky tenant in a new light?

You still don't poach, Jen told herself sternly.

It was hard to remember that when she saw him the next night. She was with Toni and her family, and they walked right by the fire truck carrying their snacks and blankets and fireworks.

He actually called out to her.

"Go say hi," Toni said with a grin. "You've got to keep up good tenant-landlord relations."

"Cool," Jeffrey said, all ready to join her.

"Not you." Toni grabbed him by the shirttail. "You're staying with us."

"Aw, Mom. I want to check out the fire truck," Jeffrey protested. "Anyway, I'll be with Aunt Jen."

"Who doesn't need your company right now," Toni said, and steered him away.

Jen headed over to where Garrett stood. Gee, what a shame that Tilda had to work.

"How's it going?" he greeted her. "Did you guys do the parade today?"

"Oh, yes. The parade and the arts and crafts booths." She looked around. "This crowd is huge."

"You add the tourists to all the locals and you get a crowd."

"That could be a lot of fires to put out."

"We're up for it," he said.

"No Timmy tonight?"

"Not while I'm working. My mom has him."

"Nice to have your mom nearby," she said.

"Yeah, considering..."

"Who you married?" Jen supplied.

"Something like that."

"She really screwed up your life, didn't she?"

He shrugged. "I got a great kid out of the deal, but she does make my life crazy. I sure don't need it to get any crazier."

There it was again, just in case she still hadn't gotten the message. Even though they were now officially pals, even though he was attracted to her, he'd never make a move on her. So, why was she wasting her time talking to him?

"I'd better catch up with my family," she said.

For a moment she thought maybe he was going to say something else, something like "Don't leave." But instead he nodded. "Have fun."

"I intend to. Life's too short to settle for less." There, that oughta give him something to think about.

Garrett watched Jen make her way through the crowd. She had her strawberry-blond hair in a ponytail and it swung jauntily as she walked—the girl next door out to enjoy the fireworks. He'd bet they could make some real fireworks together.

If he hadn't gone down the crazy road with Ashley, he'd have been willing to do just that. But he couldn't afford to take any more chances on love. No more jumping in and hoping it paid off. He wanted—no needed—a sure thing. Jen was too big a gamble.

He leaned against the fire truck and frowned at the passersby. *Damn it all, Jen Heath, why did you have to come to Icicle Falls?*

"I've never met someone who could sleep through a fireworks display," Ken teased Chita as he and her little family followed the crowd of departing revelers down the path in Riverfront Park to the parking lot.

"I'm so tired," she said. "Studying on top of work and keeping up with the kids..." She shook her head. "I don't know what made me think I could do this."

"You can," he insisted as he picked up a drooping Enrico. "You just need a little help."

"I have a lot of help," she said, smiling up at him.

Ken Wolfe had slid easily into her family's life, coming over and cooking dinner on Friday nights so she could study, attending Enrico's Little League games, showing her what family life could be like with the right man.

"You could have more," he said. "All you have to do is ask."

She didn't respond. She'd carried the load on her own for so many years. Asking for more, as he'd suggested, wasn't that simple.

But later, once the kids were in bed and the two of them sat cuddled on the couch, he brought up the subject again. "What if you didn't have to work?"

Chita sighed. "That's not my life, Ken. You know that. I have to work."

"We could fix it so you didn't have to."

"What? Are you offering to be my sugar daddy?"

she joked. Then the expression on his face registered. "What are you saying?"

"I'm saying I want to be a bigger part of your life. Marry me?"

"M-marry?" she stammered.

"I love you, Chita, and I want to be there for you on a permanent basis. I'm hoping you feel the same way about me."

Was she dreaming? Good things like this didn't happen to Chita Arness. She blinked. Okay, she hadn't imagined what had just happened. He was still here, sitting beside her, looking at her hopefully.

"I wish you'd say something," he said. "You're killing me."

"Yes! I say yes," she said, and kissed him.

"I'm the luckiest man alive," he said. Then he kissed her again. And that was when the real fireworks started.

Ken had said her life wasn't over yet. He'd been right. In fact, it was just beginning.

Chapter Twenty-Five

Facing challenges head on is the best way to meet them.
—Muriel Sterling, author of *Simplicity*

The end of the week found Toni and her family packing up to go home. "I hate to leave this place," she said as she stuffed the last of her clothes in a suitcase.

"Yeah, it's been great." Wayne eyed the overflowing suitcase. "You're not going to get that closed."

"Sure, I am."

He shook his head. "How is it that women can wind up with more clothes at the end of a vacation than they had at the beginning?"

"You know the answer to that," she teased.

"Yeah, it was a rhetorical question. I did figure since we were in a mountain cabin you wouldn't have much exposure to the shops in town, though."

"Silly you. Here, come and help me."

With her sitting on the suitcase and Wayne zipping it shut they finally managed, and he hauled that, along with a tote bag full of toiletries, out to the car.

With their personal items packed, Toni went to

work on the kitchen. In half an hour that, too, was dismantled.

"You can take this box out to the car while I clean the sink," she said to Jordan.

"Mom," Jordan protested, looking nervously toward the great outdoors.

"I promise you no bear is going to eat you between here and the car," Toni said.

"I'll clean the sink," Jordan offered.

"All right." Toni scooped up the box of leftover groceries to take out to Wayne, who was in charge of packing everything into the back of the SUV.

Jeffrey, who'd never succumbed to bear phobia, had been helping his dad load up. "Here's one more," she said, handing the box to Wayne.

"That's all we've got room for. No buying anything else when we go through town."

Toni shook her head solemnly. "Wouldn't dream of it."

Ten minutes later, they were winding down the mountain road. Half an hour after that, they were at Gingerbread Haus, getting cookies for the trip home and saying goodbye to Jen. Then it would be back to the real world, Toni thought, feeling mildly depressed. *Back to our busy, tech-obsessed, disconnected life.*

"I wish we weren't leaving," she confessed to her sister.

"But we're not that far away. You guys should come back for Oktoberfest."

"We'd better see you before then," Toni said.

"You will," Jen promised.

"Meanwhile, be careful on your hikes," Toni advised. "And always take your cell phone with you," she added with a grin.

"Yes, Mother," Jen said with a laugh. "You sure you don't want to stay for a few extra days and hike up to the Enchantments with Cecily and me?"

Toni had heard that the collection of lakes high in the mountains was gorgeous, an extraordinary experience. People actually had to make reservations far ahead of time to go there. Still... "No, thanks. I've had enough of hiking. I'm going to stick to tennis and golf."

"I want to go," Jeffrey piped up.

Wayne steered him toward the door. "Next year, pal."

Jen came around the counter and gave her sister a hug. "I'm glad you guys had such a good visit."

"Come on, Toni," Wayne called. "Let's hit the road."

She and Jen exchanged one last hug, then Toni hurried out the door after her family. Everyone settled back in the SUV with their treats and they were on their way back home. Toni looked wistfully at the quaint downtown with flowers spilling from the flower boxes on the Bavarian-style buildings. Shoppers were strolling along the sidewalk, enjoying lattes and the morning sunshine. The sound of a child's laughter drifted in through her open window.

"You love it here, don't you?" Wayne said.

"I do. There's something magical about this place."

"Gonna write an article about it?"

"For sure—how our family of four bonded in six hundred square feet."

"Write about seeing the bear, Mom," Jeffrey said excitedly.

"Ugh." Jordan shuddered. "I think we should stay in town for our next vacation."

"Would you like to come here again?" Toni asked, surprised.

"Yeah!" Jeffrey replied.

"Definitely," Jordan agreed. "But not way up in the mountains. No more bears."

"I wonder how much a condo is here," Wayne said thoughtfully. Even though the one fish he'd caught had barely been big enough to fill a small frying pan, he was now hooked on fly-fishing.

"I doubt we could swing it," Toni said. They had braces to pay for and college to save for and…if she sold a few more articles a month, could they put aside enough for a down payment? "Want to come back up for Oktoberfest and look? Just for the fun of it?"

He grinned. "Why not? A guy can dream."

So could a woman.

As soon as Jen finished her shift at Gingerbread Haus, she hurried back to the cabin to meet Cecily, who was going to be her hiking companion and trail guide to the Enchantments. Cecily had planned to go with another friend who'd backed out at the last minute and had asked Jen if she wanted to step in and take the friend's place.

She'd readily agreed.

And then wondered what she'd agreed to. It would take the whole afternoon just to get to their first stop, Snow Lake.

"I hope I'm up for this," Jen said as they made their way along Snow Creek Trail. "I've never done much hiking."

"You did fine on Lost Bride Trail," Cecily assured her. "And you can't live in Icicle Falls and not hike, not with all this gorgeous scenery."

She was right about that. The mountains, the greenery, the wildflowers—this was Mother Nature at her most beautiful.

"Just don't sprain your ankle," Cecily teased. "We don't have Tiny with us."

"But we have cell phones," Jen said, holding hers up.

"It won't work once we get higher. We're on our own. Hope you brought enough ramen in your backpack."

"I've got instant noodles, jerky, trail mix and dried fruit. Oh, and water."

"And I brought some chocolate," Cecily said.

Ah, the advantages of being friends with someone whose family owned a chocolate company.

The hike had started out easy, with lots of switchbacks. But as they continued, the terrain became steeper, and pine trees and brush replaced the fir and wildflowers they'd seen at the lower elevations. By the time they reached their camping spot for the night, Jen was sweaty and exhausted. And they still had to set up the small tent Cecily had brought.

"I don't think I'm cut out for this mountain woman stuff," Jen groaned.

"You'll feel better after a swim in the lake and some chocolate," Cecily told her.

Cecily knew what she was talking about, Jen decided later as she sat in front of their little campfire and enjoyed herb tea and chocolate-covered almonds while listening to Cecily's stories about some of the horrible clients she'd had when she owned her match-making service. This was fun.

The next day, after several hours of hiking, she revised her opinion again. This was *work*. The muscles in her legs were screaming and she had a blister forming on one of her little toes.

But then they arrived at Lake Vivian. "Oh, my," she said, taking in the serene lake glittering with diamonds of sunlight. Majestic mountains cradled it. She caught sight of an eagle swooping across the cloudless sky. The air was so fresh she felt as if she were inhaling ice cubes. She whipped out her cell phone and took a picture, but the picture didn't do justice to what she was seeing. "This was worth every blister."

"It is incredible, isn't it?" Cecily said. "The first time I ever hiked up here was with my dad. I was in middle school." She gestured toward the trees. "My sisters managed to get lost. They'd wandered off when Dad was setting up the tent, even though he'd told them to stay near the campsite. My poor dad was so scared. I, wonderful sister that I am, was just mad because we had to waste time looking for them." She grinned at Jen. "I hope you're not planning to wander off."

"No way," Jen said fervently. "My blisters wouldn't let me," she added, grinning back. "Anyway, I wouldn't dare. I couldn't call for help. No cell phone reception up here, right?"

"That's right."

"So what do we do if we have an emergency?" Jen asked. She suddenly remembered that bear her sister had seen at the cabin. Maybe this hadn't been such a good idea, after all. They'd met very few hikers on their way here. Who would help them if they encountered a hungry bear?

"Don't worry. I've got my brother-in-law's hand-held ham radio."

Yet another thing Cecily the superhiker had managed to stuff in her backpack. But Jen was relieved that she had, especially after the bear incident. "At least they'll know where to look for our remains if we get eaten."

Cecily snickered. "You city girls are such weenies."

They set up their tent, and then cooled off in the lake. By the time they returned, other campers had appeared—a fortysomething couple who looked fit enough to scale Mount Rainier without even getting winded. It turned out they were newlyweds.

"Which accounts for the fact that they don't want to stick around and yak with us," Cecily said with a grin.

"It's really beautiful up here, but I don't know if this would be my idea of a romantic honeymoon," Jen said, watching them move to their campsite farther down the lake.

"Different strokes," Cecily said.

As the afternoon wore on, more campers showed up, fanning out to secluded spots around the lake— a family of four, two middle-aged men, three college boys and another couple.

"This is a popular area. That's why they make you get reservations," Cecily explained. "I'm glad you could go at the last minute. I'd have hated to lose mine."

"I'm glad I came," Jen said.

Cecily indicated the blister Jen was covering with a bandage. "In spite of the blisters?"

"In spite of the blisters. No pain, no gain."

"More like no pain with better-fitting hiking shoes," Cecily said.

They had just polished off some chocolate when Jen noticed a growing haze in the distance. "Is that… smoke?"

Cecily shaded her eyes and peered over to where she was pointing. "Oh, gosh, it sure looks like it."

Jen had a sudden uneasy feeling. "A forest fire?"

Cecily shook her head in disgust. "Probably caused by some careless campers who didn't put out their fire properly. Or a cigarette."

Jen stared at the angry sky. "How close are we to that?"

"Not at all. That's Round Mountain. It's three mountains away."

"I hope no one's over there camping," Jen said.

"If there are, I hope the forest rangers got them out."

Three mountains away, Jen told herself as they settled in for the evening. Still, it was hard to enjoy her instant noodles and jerky. That distant smoke robbed her of appetite. She thought that when she crawled into the tent she wouldn't sleep a wink, but she was dead to the world almost the minute she got inside her sleeping bag.

When she came out in the morning, she found Cecily already awake and watching the sky with a frown on her face. And it wasn't hard to see why. The distant smoke had grown into something more ominous, a huge, end-of-the-world mushroom cloud of gray accented with bright red.

"What happened to the three mountains in between us?" she asked.

"Good question," Cecily said, and went to fetch her radio.

Jen sat on a log, listening nervously as her friend talked.

"The fire's at Rat Creek?"

Jen had no idea where Rat Creek was, but she realized the fire was closer to them than they'd originally assumed. She gnawed on her lip as she listened to snatches of conversation, trying to distract herself from the sick feeling in her stomach.

"Helicopters?...There's more than just the two of us....I don't know how many campers are here. At least twenty....The top of Aasgard Pass? Yes, we can find it."

A helicopter? Aasgard Pass? Jen's stomach really began to roil. "What's going on?" she asked as soon as Cecily finished talking on her radio.

"I just talked to the fire department."

"And they're sending in helicopters?" The sooner, the better. Cecily shook her head and Jen's heart dove straight into her roiling stomach. "They can't help us?" she asked weakly.

"There's too many of us to airlift. They're going to helicopter in two park rangers to escort us out."

"Okay." That could work.

"Meanwhile, we've got to round up everyone who's up here camping and get them to Aasgard Pass."

"Where's that?"

Cecily hesitated for one uncomfortable moment.

"It's not close by, is it?" Jen guessed. She was going to puke. Or pass out. Maybe both.

"Let's just say that your blister might have company by the time we get there." Cecily began to take down the tent. "Come on, we've got to hurry. We have a lot of people to find and a lot of distance to cover."

Jen kept her own fear at bay while she scoured the area for campers to alert, but once everyone was assembled and making their way to the meeting spot, she had plenty of time to think. What if the fire trapped them on the trail? She'd die. She'd never see her family again. Or her little mountain cottage. Or Garrett Armstrong. And death by fire, what a horrible way to go! When they finally reached their destination—a large meadow near the trail they'd use the following morning—she did, indeed, have more blisters. She was also sweaty and miserable. And, oh, so scared.

But she did her best to hide it, trying to distract the two grade-school boys in the family of hikers who'd had set their tents up near her and Cecily, playing memory games with them. They were in the middle of playing My Grandfather Has a Library when four more people joined their group.

They were young, athletic and as grimy as everyone else. And one of them was Tilda Morrison. Tilda! What was she doing out here? Like the three men she was with, Tilda was out of breath. In between gasps, she managed to tell Cecily that she and her friends had been rock climbing.

"We had to leave everything and run," Tilda said, and collapsed on the ground.

"We've got people coming to escort us out tomorrow," Cecily told her.

Tilda shook her head. "The fire, it's everywhere."

"We'll make it out," Jen said, conscious of the two wild-eyed boys standing next to her. She offered Tilda her water bottle.

"Save it. You'll need it," Tilda said.

"So will you. At least take a drink."

Tilda murmured her thanks and took a quick swig.

The newcomers finally settled in, and everyone sat in a circle, watching the pluming, angry red smoke that had taken over the sky.

"Man, this sucks," said one of the teenage boys. "My mom's gonna be so worried."

"Hell, *I'm* worried," one of his friends muttered.

"Haven't had a fire this bad in years," one of the older men said, rubbing his gray stubbled chin.

That's encouraging, Jen thought.

She heard crying and turned to see that it was the younger of the two boys. His mother hugged him, promising that they'd all be fine, but it wasn't helping.

"Your mom's right, you know," Jen said. "The firemen and the forest rangers will meet us tomorrow and get us out. Just like in the movies. You've seen how firemen save people in the movies, haven't you?"

The boy's sobs began to subside.

"Who knows? Maybe someday they'll make a movie about us," she added. "Do you like movies?"

He sniffed and nodded.

"What one is your favorite?"

He named the latest Disney offering.

"I haven't seen that one. Can you tell me what happens in it?"

The child launched into a detailed description of the plot, and his mother smiled gratefully at Jen. The tears were gone by the time the boy finally concluded his narrative and Jen shared some of her dried apricots with him.

"Not bad," said Tilda, who was seated a few feet away. "You're good with kids."

Jen shrugged. "That was for me as much as it was for him."

The parents tucked in their children, and a couple of hours after that the older people crawled into their tents. The rest of the stranded party stayed up, keeping vigil, watching the flames in the distance.

Tomorrow they'd be walking through that, Jen thought, shuddering. She prayed they'd come out alive.

Chapter Twenty-Six

A crisis often shines the light on our true priorities.

—Muriel Sterling, author of *Simplicity*

Garrett's first reaction when the fire was called in had been fury. He'd bet a whole year's salary that this forest fire had been caused by some careless camper. Now acres and acres of forest would be destroyed and human lives might be lost. The police would be busy evacuating everyone in town.

Police? *Shit!* Tilda was off rock climbing with some of the guys on the force. They were bound to be caught up in this. Battling a fire was hard enough, but battling it knowing someone you cared about could be killed took superhuman emotional control.

There was no time to worry about Tilda. He had to concentrate on doing his job, and right now his job meant working this section of trail, helping other fire-fighters make sure the fire didn't engulf it. Their job was to keep it clear so the forest rangers who'd been sent to bring down stranded hikers from Aasgard Pass could get everyone to safety. The blaze was monstrous and it was like fighting a fire-breathing dragon.

Fortunately, strike teams had been brought in from other areas to help, so they had more resources than normal. They'd taken the fire trucks up as far as they could; back in town, other firefighters did structure protection.

Now Garrett and Paul Meadows, a fellow fire-fighter, were partway up the trail, trying to beat back the flames so a large group of stranded hikers could get out safely.

It was hotter than hell inside his gear. In addition to his Nomex, he wore a hard hat, goggles and a ban-danna, and his hands were sweating inside leather gloves.

A retardant plane swooped over the blaze to the east, dumping a load of dirt on the flames and send-ing smoke in all directions. A flaming log came roll-ing down the trail, and Garrett and Paul jumped out of the way just in time. It stopped thirty feet away and they attacked it with their pulaskis. Where was the forest ranger with those hikers? They needed to get them out of here.

After what seemed like an eternity, he caught sight of a ranger herding a very scared-looking collection of people down the trail. He scanned the crowd for Tilda. There she was, thank God, looking none the worse for wear. And walking between her and Cecily Sterling was Jen Heath. *Jen?* Garrett's heart did a sick flop. Jen Heath had been up in the Enchantments? There was no opportunity to say anything. He had a job to do. But he wished that job included personally escorting this party down the mountain to safety. Right now, though, the best way he could protect them was to battle this fire with all his might. *Oh, God, keep them safe!*

* * *

Jen's trip down the trail had been terrifying. Her throat was parched and she was so hot it was all she could do not to scream from the misery of it. The crackling of flames devouring wood and the crash of falling trees assailed her ears. She was too terrified to cry. She probably didn't have any tears left in her, anyway. They must have all dried up in the heat.

She saw firemen on the side of the trail dealing with a burning log. It was hard to tell under all that equipment, but one of them was tall like Garrett and had broad shoulders. She almost hoped it wasn't him. Would he be okay? Would any of them?

What felt like hours later, they finally made it out. A fire truck was parked up the road; firefighters were everywhere with their shovels and hoses. She felt as if she were in a disaster movie. If only they could fast forward to The End.

The forest service had a bus waiting at the trailhead to take them to the ranger station. There they were greeted by a female ranger who gave them all bottled water. Water had never tasted so good.

One of the little boys began crying from sheer nervous tension. "It's okay, we're safe now," his mother said, holding him close. "Aren't we?" she asked the ranger.

"You're safer than where you were."

"I want to go home," the boy said, and began to cry.

"I know, honey," his mother said. "So do I."

"Can you get us back to Icicle Falls?" Cecily asked.

The ranger shook her head. "The town's been evacuated. All except the restaurant where they're feeding some of the firefighters."

"Oh, no. Has any of the town burned?" Jen asked.

"No, but it's not safe to go back yet. We'll get you to your homes as soon as possible. Meanwhile, we have sandwiches and coffee."

"Food, yeah. I'm starving," said the skinniest of the teenage boys.

They all gathered in a small conference room where a platter of sandwiches had been set out on a table surrounded by chairs.

"I hope Sweet Dreams will be okay," Cecily worried.

"I hope my mom's okay," Tilda said.

"She should be," Cecily told her, "since they evacuated the town."

"She'd better have gone," Tilda growled. "It would be just like her to stay in town and... Shit."

"What?" Cecily asked.

"I'm laying odds that Breakfast Haus is the restaurant that's feeding everyone." She left the table and strode out of the room.

A few minutes later she was back, and she didn't look happy.

"She's the one feeding the firefighters?" Cecily guessed.

Tilda nodded and blinked furiously in an obvious attempt not to cry. "I don't care if she is my mom. When I get back, I swear I'm going to kill her." She bit her lip and looked away.

Too late. Jen had seen the tears. "I'm sorry," she said.

Tilda just nodded.

Several hours later, they were still at the ranger station. Jen had read every brochure there and had played countless games of tic-tac-toe with the little boy.

She was studying a poster showing the different hiking trails in the national forest when the door opened and in walked two firefighters, fresh from the battle. Their fireproof jackets were grimy and the acrid smell of smoke preceded them into the building.

One took off his head gear and gaped at her. "Jen, thank God." She barely managed to stutter his name before Garrett crossed the room and pulled her to him. "Thank God you're safe," he said, hugging her.

Safe, and in Garrett Armstrong's arms. She wrapped her arms around him and pressed her face against his smoky, grimy chest. He was still alive! Even as she hugged him harder, she felt his lips brush the top of her head, her hair. Okay, next stop the lips.

She had just lifted her face so he could kiss her where it counted when a voice from behind them said, "We're *all* safe."

He gave a guilty start and dropped his hands like she was a hot cinder. Jen stepped away, her face burning with guilt. *You do poach other women's men, after all. You've been doing it all along.*

"Tilda," he said stupidly. And then he went over to her and hugged her and told her he was glad she was safe. But it was forced; Jen could clearly see that.

It was obvious that these two weren't a match. And if they ever got out of this alive, she'd tell Garrett that.

Meanwhile, Tilda was in no mood to share. She led Garrett to the room where the sandwiches were and kept him company while he ate. Next thing Jen knew, Tilda was talking with the ranger and then she was out of there.

"Hey, how come she gets to leave?" protested one of the teenagers.

"She's police. She's needed."

Where? There was no one left in town.

Oh, except at Breakfast Haus. "I hope Dot's okay," Cecily said to Jen as they watched Tilda leave in the wake of Garrett and the other firefighter.

"I hope Tilda gets to her okay," Jen said. Much as she wished Tilda would drop out of the picture, she had no desire to see her turned into a crispy critter.

The fire raged for two more days and the stranded hikers found themselves stuck at the ranger station. But at least there were bathrooms with soap and water. And there was food.

Jen didn't see Garrett again, but other firefighters and park rangers came and went, keeping them abreast of how the situation was progressing. She learned that the ranger station was one of two base camps, the other being a fish hatchery a couple of miles outside of town in the other direction. Some of the men actually went home to sleep, although they were getting very little. She hoped Garrett was all right.

At last the fire was contained and the hikers were bused back to Icicle Falls. The whole town smelled of smoke, but the buildings were intact.

"Thank God," Cecily breathed when they got back into town. "It's still here. We can borrow my mom's car. I know where she keeps her spare key. Then we'll go pick up my car at the trailhead and I'll run you home."

Jen hoped she had a home to go to. Juniper Ridge was outside of town, and the fire had crept awfully close.

Hardly anyone had returned yet, and Icicle Falls felt like a ghost town. "This creeps me out," Cecily muttered as they walked past the deserted shops on Center Street.

"It doesn't feel like Icicle Falls without the people," Jen said. "Or the flowers."

The lovely blooms that had filled the window boxes and hanging baskets on the buildings were now dry and lifeless.

"The shop owners will plant more," Cecily said. "Everyone will work as hard as they can to get our town back to normal."

It would take a lot longer to get the surrounding forest back to normal, Jen thought sadly.

A couple of men in fireproof attire were going into Breakfast Haus on the corner as two others came out. "Dot deserves a medal," Cecily said.

"I'd vote for that," Jen agreed. "Hopefully, her daughter wouldn't kill her before the mayor could pin it on her."

Cecily smiled. "Dot does make Tilda a little crazy sometimes." She stole a glance at Jen. "Not that it's any of my business, but I got the impression that you were making Tilda a little crazy, too, back at the ranger station."

Jen felt her cheeks flush. "I don't think Tilda and I are ever going to be BFFs."

"Could that have anything to do with Garrett Armstrong?"

Oh, Lord, was she *that* obvious? "Why do you ask?" Jen hedged.

"No reason, other than the way he grabbed you when he first saw you."

"He was just glad I was safe," Jen said.

"Mmm-hmm," Cecily said knowingly.

"He and Tilda are together."

"He and Tilda aren't a match, trust me."

And Cecily, with her famous love instincts, would know. "But they're still together." And the day they got engaged would be the day Jen moved back to Seattle. Much as she loved it here in Icicle Falls, she couldn't bear the idea of having to watch Garrett live happily ever after with another woman.

After some car juggling, Cecily dropped Jen off at her cottage. She was relieved to see it still standing, but smoke hung heavily on the air like a deathly perfume, and she didn't have to look far to see the devastation the fire had caused. Part of Snow Mountain was now a forest of charred stumps.

"That is so sad," she said, taking in the ugly scene.

"Yeah, it is," Cecily said. "Of course, it'll grow back, but that will take years."

So much beautiful forest ruined. The person responsible probably had no idea he or she had caused all this. Maybe, for that person, it was just as well. The guilt would be unbearable.

"Well, it's been an adventure," Jen said to Cecily as she got out.

"I hope this hasn't turned you off hiking. Or living in the mountains."

"I must admit Seattle is looking pretty good right now," Jen said. But that had more to do with a certain firefighter than it did with the forest fire.

"You'd miss this place and come back."

Jen sighed. "Thanks again for being my guide."

"As they say, we'll have something to tell our children."

If she ever had children. She was thoroughly depressed when she entered her cottage. She'd left her stressful two-job life in Seattle, found a wonderful new community and new friends who could be the lifelong kind, and yet she was depressed.

She made a cup of mint tea from the wild mint she'd picked and dried, then sat on her couch and stared at the woodland scene outside her window. "I hate my life," she muttered. Hadn't she said those very words only a few months ago? This was a bad pattern she was falling into. New beginnings followed by failure.

You haven't failed, she told herself. Just because she wasn't with the man of her dreams, that didn't make her a failure. And so what if she hadn't started the book she'd talked about writing? She was happy with her blog.

Boy, did she have a lot to blog about now. Surviving a fire was no small thing, for her or the town of Icicle Falls.

She got her laptop from the coffee table and opened a new document. Almost of their own volition, her fingers began to move over the keyboard.

I don't know if I'll ever be able to enjoy a bonfire again. Or casually light a fire in my woodstove. Not after what happened to me on *the mountain.*

She typed on, the words flowing and the tears falling as she thought of how close she'd come to losing her life. She thought of all the firefighters who'd fought that blaze and the forest ranger who'd risked his life to get her and the other stranded hikers to safety, of the rangers who'd fed them and operated the base camp. Then she thought of people like Dot Morrison who'd stuck around to lend support. Icicle Falls wasn't the kind of town to curl up and die in the face of danger.

There were a lot of stories to tell here, not just hers but the town's. She had more than a blog here. She had her book.

Her cell phone rang when she was in the middle of a sentence. But seeing who was calling she knew she had to take it.

"Are you okay?" Toni demanded.

"Yes, I'm fine."

"Thank God. Where are you?"

"I'm back home."

"Don't you ever check your messages? Mom and I have been calling. We've been going crazy over here."

"Tell her I'm fine."

"You should tell her yourself."

"I will. But right now I'm in the middle of a sentence. I've got my book idea!"

"I'm just glad you've still got your life," Toni said.

Several hours later Jen had the first chapter of her book done and a good sense of where she'd like to go with the rest of it. It would be a combination memoir and a history of Icicle Falls. A special town like this deserved a book.

That meant she had to stick around to finish it. No running away. She was going to make her life great, and she'd do it right here in this great town.

Over the next couple of days as she worked on fleshing out her book, she realized that she couldn't give up on any part of that life. Which meant she wasn't giving up on Garrett Armstrong. Tilda would have to find some other man because Jen the Poacher was here to stay.

The past two weeks had been hell, fourteen days of fourteen-hour shifts. But Garrett was proud to have been part of the team that had fought that nightmare fire and won, and he was thankful there'd been no loss of life.

He checked in on his son, who was staying at his folks' place, and then went home to sleep for a million years, leaving his mom to hand Timmy off to Ashley for the weekend.

He fell into bed Friday afternoon and didn't wake up for almost twenty-four hours. After a shower and some bacon and eggs, he almost felt ready to face the day, or what was left of it.

First he went through his messages. Of course, his mom and grandma had called. His mom knew he was safe now and had probably told his grandmother, but he'd call Gram, anyway, because she'd want to hear from him personally.

He'd been pleasantly surprised when his mom told him Ashley had actually offered to take Timmy for a few extra days if she needed a break. He was even more surprised by the tearful message Ash had left on his voice mail, ordering him to stay safe.

There was another one from her, too. "I hope you're doing okay. Timmy's fine with me for the weekend. Get as much sleep as you need. I promise I won't ask you to take him back early."

He stared at his cell. "Who are you and what have you done with my ex?"

His final message was from Jen. "I just wanted to say that I hope you're all right. The town is safe now, thanks to you. Well, and all the other men and women who risked their lives. Um, I'm writing a book about the fire and how everyone came through it. If you'd be willing, I'd love to interview you."

An interview. He could do…an interview.

He phoned his grandmother and then started to punch in Jen's number. Wait. Maybe it would be better if he ran over to the cottage instead. He wanted to see how much damage had been done to the surrounding area, anyway.

When he drove up, he was glad to see that the place had escaped, but it was unnerving how close the fire had come. Trees only a couple of miles away were singed stakes poking at the sky. Such a damn waste. And they'd probably never find out who started it.

Jen met him at the front door dressed in shorts and a T-shirt, her hair swept up in a ponytail. The way she smiled at him made his heart turn over. *You're just glad she's safe,* he told himself.

"You must have gotten my message," she said. "You didn't need to come over, though. I could've interviewed you on the phone."

"That's okay. I wanted to make sure everything out here was all right." He walked inside and sniffed. It always smelled good in here. "What's that I smell?"

"I'm trying to master the art of pie making."

Pie. He loved pie. "What kind?"

"Blackberry." She frowned. "It didn't turn out very well. It's too runny and I didn't put enough sugar in it."

"I think you need a second opinion," he said.

"Okay, but you have to give me your *honest* opinion."

He crossed his heart. "Promise."

She sat him down at the table, then cut him a good-size piece and put it in front of him. It was definitely juicy. And whoa, a little tart. He tried not to make a face. "Not bad."

"You're lying," she said with a laugh.

"Okay, good effort," he amended.

"This should help," she said, and shoved a yellow sugar bowl in his direction.

While he sprinkled sugar on his pie she fetched her laptop from the couch and set it up opposite him at the table. "Are you sure you don't mind talking about this? It must've been scary."

"It was when I was worried about...people I know." He'd almost said "you" but that would've been misleading.

She spent the next twenty minutes asking him about what he'd experienced. Then they strayed from the fire to his life in general and why he'd become a firefighter. And after that, they moved from the subject of saving lives to life in general, and starting over.

"I think starting over is a good thing," she said, "but it's really important to start over with the right person."

The way she was looking at him made him edgy. "Uh, yeah, it is," he said, and checked the time on his cell phone. "You know, I should——"

"Get going," she finished for him.

He nodded. "I have to—"

"Be somewhere," she said with an irritated smirk. "But that's okay. I have to be somewhere, too."

Who with?

The words were on the tip of his tongue when she stood and said, "Thanks for the interview."

He got up, too, and trailed her to the front door. "Thanks for the pie."

"The next one will be better."

But he'd make sure he wasn't around to eat it. He wasn't having any more of these cozy chats with his tenant. And when the lease was up, he was still selling this dump.

How many times had he said that or something like it? Well, never mind. This time he meant it. He got in the truck and returned to his house.

But once there he felt restless.

He should call Tilda, see if she wanted to do something. The danger was over, people were back in town. He knew she'd be around. He should have heard from her by now. Hell, even Ashley had checked in. What was with Tilda?

Maybe she was waiting for him to call her. Or maybe she was in no mood to talk to him after she'd caught him hugging Jen at the ranger station. But that hadn't meant anything. He'd just been glad she was safe.

Okay, that was bullshit. He knew it and Tilda probably knew it. How had he gotten into this mess, anyway? What was the matter with him? He didn't want any more chaos in his life. He wanted to be with a woman who would help smooth out the rough spots, not create more.

Well, then, he'd better prove it, both to Tilda and himself.

"Yeah?" she answered when he called her.

"Hey, you want to hang out tonight?"

"Why?"

"Don't be pissy. Come on over and let's order a pizza and watch a movie."

"That sounds like a thrill a minute."

He'd had enough thrills to last him for a long, long time. All he wanted was a nice, quiet evening. And maybe a chance to get lucky. "Come on, Til."

There was a moment's silence. "Fine," she said at last. "I'll be there in about an hour."

Good, he thought as he tossed the phone on the kitchen counter. Tonight he was taking his relationship with Tilda to the next level. He was going to get serious, and they were going to settle down and have a nice, calm life. And he felt good about that. Yeah, he did.

And every time a seed of doubt tried to plant itself in his mind, he reminded himself of that.

Tilda arrived promptly at six. She wore her black leather jacket and under it she had on a tight black top. And she was wearing a skirt. He had no idea she even owned one. He let his gaze travel down her legs and that was when he saw she was wearing a pair of red high heels. Heels? Tilda never wore heels. She looked like an Amazon. Or a dominatrix. An Amazon dom. Yeah, he'd made the right choice.

"You look good," he said.

"You're finally noticing?" She held up the bottle of champagne she'd been carrying. "Wanna celebrate?"

"Celebrate?" Was this some sort of dating anniversary?

"You know, the fact that we're still alive."

Oh, that. "Great idea."

She set the bottle on his coffee table. "And you know what people often do when they've faced death."

"Pray?" he guessed.

"Yeah, that, too. But I was thinking of something else." She pulled a set of handcuffs out of her pocket. "I still haven't seen your bedroom."

He stood rooted to the living room floor. "Uh." *This is it, the elevator to the next level. Come on, get moving.*

She dangled the handcuffs. "Am I gonna have to search the place without a warrant?"

"Don't you want some pizza?" What kind of inane thing was that to say?

"I need to work up an appetite," she said, and started down the hall.

He followed after. *This is a bad idea,* whispered a little voice at the back of his mind.

Are you nuts? argued his hormones. *Speed it up. What are you dragging your feet for?*

It was more a case of *who* he was dragging his feet for. He knew. He had to break it off with Tilda. Tonight. No matter what he'd told himself, this wasn't going to work. And it wasn't fair to her. Why try to turn friendship into something more when there was really only one woman he wanted?

He walked into the bedroom.

"I'm glad you have the right kind of bed," she said. "I should've known you'd have an old-fashioned one. You're a romantic at heart, aren't you?"

"It was my grandma's." Ashley had gotten the other bed. This girlie one wasn't to his liking at all. "I'm gonna replace it."

"Too bad," she said. "Guess you'd better enjoy it while you can."

He had to say something now, before this got completely out of hand.

"No more playing hard to get," she teased.

Was that what he'd been doing? He thought he'd been taking it slow. "Til," he said, walking up to her.

She smiled wickedly and snapped the cuff on his wrist.

"I can't do this."

"I know, you bastard," she said sweetly.

"What do you mean?"

She gave his arm a yank and cuffed him to the bed. Then she started for the door.

"Hey," he protested. "What are you doing?"

She didn't answer.

"Tilda! Where the hell are you going?"

She turned at the doorway. "How stupid do you think I am?" She didn't wait for an answer. Instead, she walked down the hall, her high heels clacking on the hardwood floor.

What the hell? "Tilda!" he hollered. "Tilda!"

A moment later he heard a car drive off.

She was leaving him here, chained to his bed?

He gave the handcuffs a vicious tug, succeeding only in trashing his wrist. Roaring in frustration, he kicked the nightstand, tipping the lamp off it and sending it to the floor with a crash. "Tilda!"

Damn it all. Was every woman in Icicle Falls a whack job?

Chapter Twenty-Seven

How wonderful life is when you have your priorities straight!
—Muriel Sterling, author of *Simplicity*

Everyone was back in town and ready to celebrate. And that included the Icicle Falls book club. The women were meeting at Zelda's for dinner, and Jen could hardly wait to tell them about her book. Maybe Cecily's mom would be willing to look at it, maybe even advise her on what to do next.

The restaurant was packed when she walked in at seven and she'd bet that every other eatery in town was equally full. Charley greeted her with a hug. "I saved us a table at the back, and I'll join you when I can."

"Join them now," said her husband, who'd come in right behind Jen. "I can handle seating people."

Charley looked at him dubiously.

"Don't worry. I've managed to figure out how to read a seating chart," he told her. "Go on, celebrate."

"Okay," she said. "Thanks. If you need help, you know where I am." She linked her arm through Jen's. "We are so glad you made it back to us in one piece."

Cecily was already at their table, nursing a drink.

She raised the martini glass in salute. "Hey there, fellow survivor."

"Is that a wild huckleberry martini you're drinking?" Jen asked.

"Yep. And for dessert I'm having a Chocolate Kiss and to heck with the calories."

"Amen to that." Jen slid into her seat. "Life is too short."

"And yours was almost really short," Charley said, sitting next to her. "We were so worried about you guys."

"Well, we dodged the bullet," Cecily said. "Except it looks like somebody's in trouble," she added, nodding at the entrance.

Jen turned to see Tilda in her cop uniform, walking toward them, frowning.

"Uh-oh," Charley muttered. "What did you guys do?"

"I didn't do anything," Cecily said.

"Me, neither," insisted Jen. Unless it was a crime to want another woman's man.

Tilda stopped beside Jen's chair. "Jen Heath, I'm going to have to ask you to come with me."

Too shocked to speak, Jen merely blinked.

"What did she do?" Charley demanded.

Tilda held up a hand. "This is none of your business."

"It sure is. She's my friend."

"Come with me, please," Tilda said in her no-nonsense cop voice.

Jen obediently got up.

"You can't just haul her off without telling her why," Charley protested. "You've got to read Jen her rights."

Tilda grabbed Jen by the arm. "You have the right to remain silent." She pointed a finger at Charley. "You, too, Albach."

"It's Masters now," Charley snapped. "And don't be expecting a drink on the house next time you come in."

Tilda ignored her and marched Jen through the crowd. People were gawking, and Jen's face flamed.

"I don't know what I've done," she wailed as they walked out the door.

"Nothing, you bitch. Now shut up."

"What?"

Tight-lipped, Tilda marched her to the patrol car. "I've been looking all over town for you," she growled. "Watch your head." She put her hand on Jen's head and shoved her into the backseat. Then off they went. At least she hadn't turned on the siren, Jen thought miserably.

Five minutes later, they were parked on a quiet side street in front of a run-down old Craftsman-style home. What on earth was going on here?

Tilda opened the car door. "Get out."

"I don't understand!"

"I don't, either." Tilda shook her head. "We were going strong. I was perfect for him."

Garrett. Jen's heart plummeted to her toes. Had Tilda snapped? Was she about to march Jen into that house and hack her to pieces? Was she going to pull out her gun and use Jen's head for target practice?

"But then you came along."

"Tilda, please," Jen begged. Surely she couldn't have survived a forest fire only to get whacked by a jealous woman.

"I knew he was in love with you practically from the first time he saw you, the fool."

"I..." Jen stopped. She had no idea what to say to this woman.

"I know," Tilda said. "Shit happens. So does love. He's waiting for you." She reached into her shirt pocket and took out a key. "And I want my damned handcuffs back when you're done," she said, forcing the key into Jen's hand. Then she returned to her patrol car and drove off.

Handcuffs? Jen smiled and went into the house.

Garrett was pissed. No, he was more than pissed. He was in a rage. He'd kicked the fallen lamp across the room, given the bed an angry shove (hurting his wrist again) and sworn a blue streak. Now he was sitting on the edge of the bed, thinking of what he was going to do to Tilda once he got his hands on her.

He felt as if he'd been here forever. When the hell was she going to send someone to get him out of these things?

He heard the sound of a car door shutting outside and frowned. He'd heard several cars go by since he'd been stuck in here. And dogs barking. Even heard some kids laughing. Probably the kids down the street, riding by on their bikes. He'd called for help, hollered until he was hoarse, but no one had heard him. This was worse than prison. At least in prison you got water and something to eat. And had a place to piss.

He heard the front door open. Help was here at last. "In here!" he called. Which of her cop buddies had she sent to set him free? Jimmy Durango? Jamal Lincoln? Oh, they were all going to have a good laugh about this. And, of course, they'd trot on over to the fire station and tell his buddies. Paul would never let him live it down. He ground his teeth.

"Hello?" called a soft voice.

Wait a minute. He recognized that voice.

Once again, he heard the sound of high heels on hardwood. A few seconds later, Jen Heath stood in the doorway. She was wearing a tight little pink dress and pink heels with flowers on them. She was gorgeous and he wanted her. Not just now but for a lifetime. He was probably going to spend the rest of his life like Ricky Ricardo, bouncing from one crazy domestic adventure to another, but he didn't care.

"You look amazing," he told her.

"You look…" She faltered. "Good."

He frowned. "Tilda did this to me."

"I know," she said. "She brought me here." She came and sat next to him on the bed. "Would you like to get loose? I've got the key."

Suddenly he wasn't in such a hurry to leave. He slipped an arm around her waist. "You've got the key to something else, too."

She raised her eyebrows.

"But then you knew that all along, didn't you?"

"What have I got the key to?" she purred. "Come on, say it."

"My heart, damn it." He pulled her to him and kissed her.

"But I'm a flake," she reminded him.

"You're the sweetest flake I ever met. Aw, Jen, I've been a fool."

She smiled. "Yes, you have."

"Give me another chance?"

She took a moment to consider. "Well…"

He didn't wait for the rest of the answer. He kissed her again, this time more thoroughly. She smelled delicious and her lips were so soft. But…

"I sure could use my other hand," he said.

She grinned, showing off dimples, and took the key out of her bra. "Promise?"

"Sorry I'm late," Juliet said, slipping into her seat. She glanced around at the others. "Where's Jen?"

Cecily picked up her martini glass and regarded it with a sly grin. "I have a feeling she's busy."

Summer ended and the days fell away like autumn leaves. And Jen *was* busy…but not with a long list of activities. She'd scaled back and dedicated herself to finishing her book. There was one activity she didn't cut, though. Book club.

In September the women read *The Apple Orchard* by Susan Wiggs. The apple streusel Jen made and brought to the meeting was a big hit.

The women picked a Stephen King novel for October. Jen brought her sister, Toni, who'd come up with her family for Oktoberfest and to check out condos. They decided to wait before they bought but Jen was convinced that before the year was over, her sister and brother-in-law would buy something. Everyone came in costume, and Jen was the first to guess the significance of Charley's vintage maternity top.

Sure enough, Charley and Dan were expecting, and her big announcement prompted a flood of hugs and congratulations. Jen had come dressed as the lost bride of Icicle Falls. She wasn't positive but she thought she'd seen the famous ghost when she and Garrett hiked Lost Bride Trail in September. If she had, everyone knew what *that* meant.

In November the women read Bunyan's *The Pilgrim's Progress* and shared things for which they were thankful. Stacy was not only thankful that her shop was doing well but that her son's college grades were improving.

When it was Jen's turn to share, she looked around the room with tears in her eyes and said, "I'm thankful I got to move to my little cottage on Juniper Ridge and meet all of you."

"Not to mention a certain fireman," Charley added with a wink.

"That, too."

I can't believe it's December already. I've been in my new home for almost a year and I love it. Let me tell you, losing my stressful, go-nowhere life was the smartest move I ever made. So if you're not happy with your life, don't wait any longer to change it. The best thing you can do for yourself is to figure out what's important and then let everything else fall away. I did it and so can you!

Jen reread what she'd just written for her blog. Yep, that about said it all. Now it was time to get over to Stacy's house for this month's book club meeting.

Stacy's house was decked out for the holidays, not quite as much as the year before, but tastefully, she decided, surveying her living room. A few pieces of her Victorian village graced the fireplace mantel, and the nativity set now occupied the buffet, which meant there was room for plates and cups on the coffee table.

When the women had finished their discussion of Dickens's *A Christmas Carol,* Juliet set down her cup of eggnog and said, "Before we exchange our Secret Santa gifts, how about assessing the year of simplifying our lives? I'd say we did a pretty good job."

"I think so." Stacy smiled, admiring her simply decorated living room. Less really was more.

"I'm certainly glad I simplified mine," Jen said. "I learned that it's easy to get too busy no matter where you live, and I had to cut out a couple of commitments so I could meet other goals."

"Emily Ward over at the library still misses you, by the way," Stacy told her.

"You can't do everything," said Chita.

"Look who's talking," Charley teased.

"At least now I'm busy with things I *want* to do. And I have help."

"Where are you and Dr. Wolfe going to live once you're married?" Juliet asked her.

"He's selling his condo and moving in with us. We need the room," she replied, "now that we've got a blended family. And three dogs," she added, rolling her eyes. "And I thought I had my hands full with Hidalgo. Now I've got a golden lab and a basset hound to deal with."

"But you'll have a live-in vet to take care of them," Juliet said.

"Hey, and if you end up working for him after you finish your veterinary assistant program, he'll have free help," Charley joked.

"Just part-time help," Chita corrected her. She

smiled. "I'm so looking forward to finally being at home more often."

Juliet turned to Jen's sister, Toni, who had joined them for this special meeting. "And how about you, Toni?"

"My family is as tied in to their technology as ever. But we've made some changes," Toni said. "Friday nights are now family nights. And I'm the queen of Wii bowling."

Then she grinned at her sister, who was sitting beside her on the couch. "I think Jen probably has the best news to report."

"Thanks to Cecily's mom, I sold my book," Jen announced. "Muriel not only helped me whip it into shape, she also introduced me to her editor."

"That is so cool!" Juliet exclaimed, and the others chimed in with their congratulations.

"You're going to be a famous author," Chita predicted.

"I don't know about that, but I'm excited," Jen said.

"That's *all* you have to tell us?" Cecily asked with a frown. "I was sure you'd have some other news."

Jen unzipped a side pocket on her purse and pulled out a diamond ring. "Oh, like this?" she asked, and slid it on her finger.

The room erupted in squeals.

"I thought so," Cecily said smugly.

Cass laughed. "The famous Cecily Sterling intuition strikes again."

"Well, that and the fact that I told her back in September that I saw the lost bride when Garrett and I were hiking up by the falls," Jen said with a smile.

"This calls for a toast," Juliet said, and raised her glass of eggnog. "To simplifying our lives."

"Which isn't always that simple," Charley pointed out, and they all drank.

"You know, I've done some thinking about that," Toni said, "and I've come to the conclusion that it's not so much about simplifying our lives as making them right for us."

"I'll drink to that." Charley raised her glass. "Here's to life. Whether it's simple or complicated, the important thing is to make it good."

And as far as Stacy could tell, they all had.

And they all would.

* * * * *

Acknowledgments

I thoroughly enjoyed my adventures in Icicle Falls this time around, and I had good company. Thanks to Lily-Ann Wilder for sharing her scary adventure in the Enchantments with me. Also thanks to Todd Cook, forest ranger, and Kelly O'Brien from Station #3, who generously shared their expertise. I have my brain trust to thank for watching over the process of writing this book: Susan Wiggs, Anjali Banerjee, Lois Dyer, Elsa Watson and Kate Breslin. You guys rock. And finally, big thanks to my editor, Paula Eykelhof, who is amazing, and Paige Wheeler, the guardian of my career and sanity, who is equally amazing. I also want to say a big thanks to the wonderful people at Harlequin who work so hard to make each book special. With so many great people helping along the way it's impossible not to love what I do for a living. And to you, the reader, a special thanks for taking time out of your busy schedule to visit with my characters. Thanks one and all!

From _New York Times_ bestselling author

SUSAN MALLERY

**comes a poignant new story in her
Blackberry Island series, about love, family and
finding the courage to reach for your dreams.**

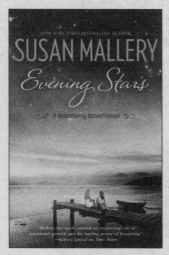

Small-town nurse Nina Wentworth is more "Mom" than her own mother ever was. She sacrificed medical school—and her first love—so her sister could break free. Which is why she isn't exactly thrilled to see Averil back on Blackberry Island, especially when Nina's life has suddenly become…complicated.

Nina unexpectedly finds herself juggling two amazing men, but as fun as all this romance is, she has real life to deal with. Averil doesn't seem to want the great guy she's married to; their mom is living life just as recklessly as she always has; and Nina's starting to realize that the control she once had is slipping out of her fingers. Her hopes of getting off the island seem to be stretching further away…until her mother makes a discovery that could change everything forever.

Available now, wherever books are sold!

Be sure to connect with us at:

Harlequin.com/Newsletters

Facebook.com/HarlequinBooks

Twitter.com/HarlequinBooks

www.Harlequin.com

Cedar Cove

The #1 *New York Times* bestselling series from

DEBBIE MACOMBER

is now a Hallmark Channel Original Series

Available now!   Available now!   On sale March 25.

Wherever books are sold.

New York Times Bestselling Author
DEANNA RAYBOURN

Pursued by their adversaries. Chased by their feelings for one another.

Famed aviatrix Evangeline Starke never expected to see her husband, adventurer Gabriel Starke, ever again. They had been a golden couple, enjoying a whirlwind courtship amid the backdrop of a glittering social set in prewar London until his sudden death with the sinking of the *Lusitania*.

Five years later, beginning to embrace life again, Evie embarks upon a flight around the world. In the midst of her triumphant tour, she is shocked to receive a mysterious—and recent— photograph of Gabriel, which brings her ambitious stunt to a screeching halt.

With her eccentric aunt Dove in tow, Evie tracks the source of the photo to the ancient City of Jasmine, Damascus, where nothing is as it seems. Leaving the jewelled city behind, Evie sets off across the punishing sands of the desert to unearth the truth of Gabriel's disappearance....

Available wherever books are sold.

Be sure to connect with us at:
Harlequin.com/Newsletters
Facebook.com/HarlequinBooks
Twitter.com/HarlequinBooks